The Library of
Light and Shadow

Also by M. J. Rose

FICTION

The Secret Language of Stones

The Witch of Painted Sorrows

The Collector of Dying Breaths

The Seduction of Victor H.

The Book of Lost Fragrances

The Hypnotist

The Memoirist

The Reincarnationist

Lip Service

In Fidelity

Flesh Tones

Sheet Music

The Halo Effect

The Delilah Complex

The Venus Fix

Lying in Bed

NONFICTION

Buzz Your Book (with Douglas Clegg)

What to Do Before Your Book Launch (with Randy Susan Meyers)

The Library of Light and Shadow

A Novel

M. J. ROSE

ATRIA BOOKS

New York   London   Toronto   Sydney   New Delhi

ATRIA BOOKS

An Imprint of Simon & Schuster, Inc.
1230 Avenue of the Americas
New York, NY 10020

First Atria Books hardcover edition July 2017

ATRIA BOOKS and colophon are trademarks of Simon & Schuster, Inc.

For information about special discounts for bulk purchases, please contact Simon & Schuster Special Sales at 1-866-506-1949 or business@simonandschuster.com.

The Simon & Schuster Speakers Bureau can bring authors to your live event. For more information or to book an event, contact the Simon & Schuster Speakers Bureau at 1-866-248-3049 or visit our website at www.simonspeakers.com.

Manufactured in the United States of America

10 9 8 7 6 5 4 3 2 1

Library of Congress Cataloging-in-Publication Data

Names: Rose, M. J.
Title: The library of light and shadow : a novel / M. J. Rose.
Description: First Atria Books hardcover edition. | New York : Atria Books, 2017. | Series: The Daughters of La Lune
Identifiers: LCCN 2016042004 (print) | LCCN 2016051669 (ebook) | ISBN 9781476778129 (hardcover : acid-free paper) | ISBN 9781476778143 (ebook)
Subjects: LCSH: Women artists—Fiction. | Nineteen twenties—Fiction. | BISAC: FICTION / Historical. | FICTION / Romance / Gothic. | GSAFD: Historical fiction. | Gothic fiction. | Occult fiction.
Classification: LCC PS3568.O76386 L53 2017 (print) | LCC PS3568.O76386 (ebook) | DDC 813/.54—dc23
LC record available at https://lccn.loc.gov/2016042004

ISBN 978-1-4767-7812-9
ISBN 978-1-4767-7814-3 (ebook)

This book is dedicated to my friend Randy Susan Myers because as Elbert Hubbard said: "A friend is someone who knows all about you and still loves you."

To draw you must close your eyes and sing.

—PABLO PICASSO

The Library of
Light and Shadow

Dear Mademoiselle Duplessi,

When I visited your studio in May to sit for my portrait, I found you most agreeable, so I do hope you will consider my request seriously. According to the process your brother had described to me, I expected to receive a painting depicting my innermost emotions. I wanted to share my deepest feelings with the man I cared about. To share my dreams with him in a special, private way.

Days later, when your brother delivered the portrait to my home, I was appalled. Yes, you depicted what was in my heart but not the adoration that fills it. Instead, you painted a secret not to be shared. Especially with the man I hope to wed. It was to be kept between me and his dear former wife. Whom I loved and cared for. Whom I helped in the end—even if your horrible painting shows me in the one moment when my help looks like anything but.

I refused the portrait, and I paid your brother whatever I could and begged him to destroy the painting.

I'd assumed he did.

Until I had a visit from a friend who saw that same portrait in the Duplessi Gallery in Cannes. So yesterday, I traveled south from Paris to see for myself.

I have just come back from the viewing and am distraught that this scene of the darkest day of my soul is hanging on the wall where hundreds of people can gawk over it and gossip about me.

You portrayed me as a murderess. You turned me into a killer. You exposed only a small part of the story and left out proof of my innocence. My dearest friend was in pain. She wanted to die. To end her suffering and that of her husband, who experienced so much pain watching her.

I helped her, yes, but out of compassion.

Not because I wanted her to pass out of this world.

But you illustrated the scene with a wholly sinister aspect.

And now, because of your brother's callous greed, how many have already been exposed to this lie? And what can I do? Retract their vision of it? I can tell people it's your fantasy. Not my truth. Some might believe me. Others won't.

The man to whom I am betrothed won't.

The damage has been done. My ruination has been set in motion. I fear the authorities will come after me now.

I sit here in my hotel room at a loss. And before I take more drastic steps, I am appealing to your kind nature, begging you to remove the painting from the gallery and keep it from further viewing.

I am afraid I will not be able to withstand the judgment of those I love if they see the painting . . . if they see this half story before I can tell them its entirety.

I beg you to help me,
Thérèse Bruis

Chapter 1

Silk lined the blindfold. Deep maroon in color, so dark, like dried blood. Magenta mixed with black if I were to create it on my palette. As I slipped it over my face, I felt the smooth fabric caress my cheeks, cool and delicious.

I recognized a familiar and particular combination of feelings well up in me: expectation, excitement, and the thrill of fear. Guilt that I was peeking in on what was not my right to see and bliss at giving in to the irresistible temptation to look deeper despite a potentially dangerous outcome.

With the blindfold on, I felt more at home in the world than at any other time. Except when Mathieu held me in his arms. But those days were long past, and my life was so different now that I often wondered if my brief time with him was real or imagined.

Adjusting the elastic wrapped around my head, positioning the blindfold just the right way, I saw only darkness. Not a sliver of light invaded its black.

Around me the sounds of the party faded. In the silver and black living room high above Central Park, the guests were still laughing and talking, drinking champagne, admiring their reflections shimmering in the huge round mirror over the fireplace.

But I had left the pleasures and attractions of the party and slipped inside a shell. Cocooned, I focused on sounds of rolling waves. Memories dredged from the beach in Cannes where I grew up. The sea echoes relaxed me, lulled me . . . I let go of the tensions of the actual world, opened to the magic. I became receptive.

"Delphine, aren't you ever going to draw me?" The impatient whine from the slightly drunk partygoer splashed into my thoughts like a rock thrown into that blue-green water.

I reacted to her entreaty more slowly than usual. I never drank when I was drawing, but that night, for some reason, I'd felt nervous and had a bit of champagne. The good French stuff, smuggled into America so that all these bright young things could drink it out of wide-mouthed glasses imported—just like the wine—from my home country. Fine Baccarat or Lalique you could crush by holding too tightly. Crystal picking up the lights and sending rainbow flickers onto the walls and the men's starched white shirts and the women's beaded gowns. With my blindfold on, all was possible, and if I listened hard enough, I could even hear the effervescence in that champagne bubbling to the surface.

Breaking the law was never as much fun as it was in 1925, in this other city of lights, New York. Everyone who had lived through the Great War was still running away from its horrors. Trying to forget. Skyscrapers rose overnight, changing the landscape, dreamed up from the minds of architects determined to prove that tomorrow held promise. Painters, sculptors, furniture designers embraced the rounded lines and geometric cleanliness of Art Deco in their effort to give the world order. Lovers threw out all rules of propriety. Having affairs became as acceptable as indulging in bonbons. Seduced by the allure of motoring trips, we all took off in sleek, elegant cars that shone in the sun like jewels as we tried to outrace the past. Everyone, it seemed, smoked opium or marijuana at soirees that never really ended. All of us were desperate to believe that the future could be as bright as the moon, which we watched fade in the sky while we kept partying—gay and delighted and sad and lost.

Between the fingers of my right hand, I held the silver pencil that my father had given me on my sixteenth birthday, warming the precious metal. I could feel my name, Delphine Duplessi, engraved in script on the barrel.

Reaching out with my left hand, my fingers felt for the edge of the smooth paper. I had my boundary and began to draw. The air around me grew cooler and swirled like a vortex, as if I were caught in an unrelenting current, the way it sometimes did. A harbinger of disaster. I wanted to stop, but once I'd begun a session, I wasn't capable of ending it prematurely.

Sittings for full shadow portraits, as I called them, took place over several days at the Tenth Street studios where William Merritt Chase had once had his own studio and I now had mine. This sketch was merely a party favor. An amuse-bouche of what I could do. A live advertisement for more work. I took every commission my brother Sebastian arranged for me, but it was difficult for him to manage my career from across the ocean in France. I needed to supplement my income.

The new year promised to be my best ever. I was becoming wildly popular. When I worked, I wore a uniform of a simple white smock over a dark skirt, but at parties I had the appearance of a chic guest—dressed in the fashionable slim shift that hit just above the knees with feathers and fringe, bejeweled in the bespoke pieces my sister Opaline created for me. I spoke with a French accent and provided just the kind of entertainment the city's avant-garde hostesses craved. It was only February, and I was booked through May.

That cold night, with the guests partying on around me, my hand moved quickly as I filled the page with the image developing in the deepest recesses of my mind. The process, a mystery even to me, involved only two steps.

First, for a period of about three minutes, I studied the sitter's face, noticing its planes and curves, lines and contours. I didn't search. Didn't question. Didn't engage in conversation. I just observed. Usually, my sitter squirmed a little after the first ten or twenty seconds. Most people are unaccustomed to being specimens. My staring was often uncomfortable for them. Only Tommy Prout, the man I was engaged to, had enjoyed it, but he'd been flirting. And he—unlike anyone I'd ever met—had no shadow secrets. Not one. Probably what attracted me to him. That and his love of art. His parents were collectors, and he treated me like one of the masterpieces that graced the walls of their Beekman Place mansion. I, foolishly, thought that would be enough.

During a session, once I burned the sitter's face into my mind, I would slip on my blindfold, shut out the noise of the party, and concentrate on hearing the sounds of the sea stored in my memory. And then, listening to the waves pound the shore, I would start to draw, letting my imagination take over. It is easier to describe it thus, but in fact it was my second sight that took over.

Because, you see, I was not just an artist. I was a woman who had been blinded as a child and whose sight had been brought back by magick. And in the process, I had been given a gift—or, depending on your point of view, a curse. I had the ability not just to see people for who they were but also to see the secrets they harbored. The darkest, most hidden desires of their souls.

And like a thief, I plucked those images from their hearts and turned them into a parlor game. Surrealistic caricatures they could take home and frame. Or burn. And therein lay the source of my compassion, my sorrow, and my own ruination.

Chapter 2

I had already sketched a dozen guests by midnight on that cold February 5, 1925, in Betsy and Fred Steward's penthouse. I'd delighted and surprised my sitters with silly secrets and made them ask over and over again how I knew this or that about them.

"I hadn't even told my wife I was planning that!"

"I only found out yesterday. How did you know?"

"Yes, yes, I had forgotten all about that little escapade, it was so long ago!"

Clara Schiff was the last portrait of the evening. Twelve was my limit, but my employer for the night had begged me to do just one more, for it was Clara's birthday that week.

I agreed. But I shouldn't have. I was a little tipsy and very tired. Is that an excuse? If I'd been more alert, would I have realized that the image I was committing to paper was so incendiary?

I'll never know, but I don't think so. I've never been adept at censoring the scenes that come out of the shadows. A little more than four years before, I'd done a painting that changed the entire trajectory of my future. It haunted me still. If only I were able to understand more about the images that came to me. Not just for poor Clara's sake. But for my own.

She sat in the black velvet armchair Betsy Steward had set up next to my easel and stool, in the corner of the living room adjacent to the terrace doors. For ten minutes, I drew her portrait. Quite a long time when you are wearing a blindfold. Even longer for the person sitting and watching the artist draw and not being able to see the sketch.

The graphite in my silver pencil, number 5B, glided over the eighteen-by-twenty-four-inch cream-colored, smooth-grain stock as smoothly as swimming in a currentless sea. The movement of my hand, the pressure of the stylus, all part of the sensuous nature of the act. The paper took the line and held it in a lover's gesture. The sensation never ceased to thrill me.

For that reason and more, I am particular about my supplies. In a pinch, I went to Sam Flax, where the quality and variety were the best I could find in New York. But I preferred the shipments my brother sent from Sennelier, on the Left Bank. My mother had bought her very first paints there in 1894 with money she made by pawning a jeweled jade frog she had stolen from my great-grandmother. It was a story I loved to hear her tell when I was a little girl. I'd picture her pocketing the bibelot, frightened that she was going to be caught but desperate to get money for her supplies. Then I'd see her standing on the line at the pawnbroker's with my father, whom she'd only met a week before. As she described it all, I would experience the wonder of her walking into Sennelier's marvelous shop for the first time. Looking around at the shelves and shelves of paper, paints, crayons, pastels, easels, canvases—an Ali Baba's cave of treasures for any artist.

My mother and I are descended from a long line of artists going back to the sixteenth century, when my ancestor, a famous courtesan named La Lune, seduced an even more famous painter, Cherubino, into teaching her how to paint in exchange for being his muse.

For a while, the arrangement worked. Then La Lune made the mistake of falling in love with him. Cherubino returned her emotions, but then he cast her aside for Emperor Rudolf of Prague, no less.

Distraught but determined to win Cherubino back, La Lune traded her most valuable jewels for an old crone's lessons in witchery. The plan was to cast a spell to make her irresistible to her lover once again.

But the spell failed.

In the story my mother repeated to me, my sisters, and my brother, Cherubino became ill from the potion and died. And La Lune's ability to fall in love with anyone else died with him.

Refusing to accept her loveless fate, La Lune, using the crone's magick, extended her life while she searched for an antidote to the curse. Even after her body failed, she kept her soul earthbound as she continued her quest. La Lune spent the next three hundred years trying to merge with one of her descendants so she could feel love once more. But her spirit was too powerful. Those she chose to incubate died, often by their own hands, driven mad by the succubus inside them.

Only one was strong enough to incorporate La Lune's spirit and not be broken, and that was my mother, Sandrine Salome Duplessi. After the merging, she even took on her ancestor's name and became the first woman to attend L'École des Beaux-Arts, the most prestigious art school in France—if not the world—and became one of the finest artists of her generation.

By the time I left Paris for New York in 1920, my mother's paintings in the gallery on the famed rue Botie were selling for twenty thousand francs. Just one rung below those of the world-famous Pablo Picasso.

Of all her children, I was the only one to inherit my mother's ability or desire to spend life inhaling turpentine and smearing dabs of oil-infused pigment on a canvas. My professional ambitions, as I considered them back then, were even greater than hers, because in addition to her art, she had a life that she cherished. She married the man she fell in love with and had four children. She was capable of casting spells and saving people's lives, changing their luck, curing their sadness, or punishing them for their misdeeds. My mother was satisfied to be one of the best at what she did, but I wanted to be *the* best, because it was all I would ever have.

Like my ancestor and all the daughters of La Lune who came after her, we are cursed to have only one chance at love in our lives. When I met Mathieu, I knew immediately he was that chance. And then I lost him only four months later. All because of my hubris in believing I was powerful enough to chase away his demons.

For the rest of my life, I would have to live with the knowledge that I'd never bear his children. Never grow old with him. Never feel passion for anyone else. I would live out my days haunted by Mathieu's shadow portrait and the memories of our affair that ended too soon.

My sitter's high-pitched voice interrupted my reverie. "You've stopped drawing. Does that mean you're done, Delphine? My neck is aching, and I need more champagne!"

The moment when I sense I've finished a portrait doesn't arrive like the closing notes of a symphony, with a crescendo and fanfare. There's no ceremony. Rather, it's a stillness. My right hand simply stops moving.

As I became aware of holding the pencil once again, the jarring sounds of the party and the comingled scents of sweat and perfume, champagne and cheese assaulted me. Reluctantly, I returned to the present from that alternative plane where there was nothing but me and my interpretation of a dream.

I took off my blindfold and inspected my work.

"Can I see?" Clara asked pathetically, in the same high whine she'd used to entreat me to get started, then stop.

When I finally looked at it, what I had drawn always came as a shock to me. Technically, I had seen the images in my mind, on one level was aware of them but not in a visceral way. If you'd stopped me in the midst of the exercise and asked what I was putting down on the paper, I would be able to tell you, because it existed behind my eyes in a kind of cinematic tableau. As if I had stumbled on a movie set in Nice at the Victorine studios, where my mother occasionally painted elaborate sets. And yet the finished product always shocked me. Splashed my sensibilities like the first dip in the icy Mediterranean in early May.

Had I done this? Dragged this scene out of the ether and put it down on paper?

Clara rose, ran over, and stood behind me. For a few seconds, she was silent.

"Oh, no, Delphine. Oh, no. You have to hide it." Her voice was past whining now, edged with real fear. The color of the air around her was turning icy blue.

As part of the second sight that I'd developed during the year when I was blind, I occasionally saw the air around someone turn color when they were in a highly emotional state.

To me, it looked like a halo glow, a shimmer of phosphorescent shine. Certain shades denoted different states. Blue the color of robin's egg shells was a deep calm. A gray sea blue was depression. Anger was a sunset orange. Love was dawn's rose. Denial was the purple gray of a storm cloud. Pale, pale icy blue, the color of the air around Clara, was panic.

I didn't understand. What had I done? I inspected my surrealistic illustration of Clara's secret. The drawing was a step away from reality but rendered with utter clarity. Nothing impressionistic. I was a draftsman first, having taken years of drawing lessons before going to L'École in Paris in 1919 to study painting.

The man in this drawing was on his knees. Well, his body was that of a man. His head was a stag's but with a very human expression nothing short of idolatry. This half-man, half-beast was worshipping—naked and quite erect—at a shrine. The shrine was the equally naked body of Mrs. Clara Schiff. She sat upon a velvet cushion on an elaborate throne that would not have been out of place in the court of Louis XV.

On her head was a crown of cavorting putti, sexy little naked angels, making lewd gestures. Under the headdress was a feline face with large almond-shaped eyes. Like her lover, she was half-woman, half-beast.

Suddenly, I understood.

If the man on his knees had been Clara's husband, Ari Schiff, who was at that very moment making his way across the white and black marble floor, the evening would have ended with curious glances, oohs and aahs, and probably some praise for my ability to render these creatures so lifelike and familiar.

The evening might have gone equally well if the man in my drawing wasn't recognizable.

But the man-stag was neither Ari nor unidentifiable. The man lusting after Ari's wife was clearly his brother, Monty, whose reputation for seducing women, making outlandish deals, and taking grave risks always made for breathless gossip.

Despite their father, Reuben Schiff, owning a prestigious brokerage house, both brothers were in the importing business. Which we all knew was code for their real occupation. The brothers were bootleggers, defying Prohibition to supply New York and New Jersey with the best wine and liquor they could bring in through Canada. They'd started out working together, but after a personal rift involving Ari's first wife, they split up the business.

Ari was in charge of the importing, Monty the distribution. They had separate offices and intermediaries and as little as possible to do with each other. Monty also owned one of the most popular nightclubs in Manhattan, which gilded his wealth and reputation. And he was, at that moment, also making his way over to where I sat. Monty and Ari crossed the floor from opposite directions, both alerted by Clara's too-loud protestations.

Ari reached her first. Before he could even see the drawing, she burst out with "It's only a parlor trick, Ari. It's all Delphine's fantasy."

I wanted to tell her to shut up. That her nervous reaction was the very worst way to handle the situation. That with every single excuse she blurted out, she was hurting her case. But it was too late.

Ari pushed her aside to inspect my drawing of his naked wife, who, even as a cat, had Clara's face. Her lovely bow lips were pursed, her wide eyes half-closed, her high level of animation subdued into an expression of lust about to be satiated. Leaning backward, her legs spread, she awaited the encounter.

Her paramour's expression was every bit as telling. The bold look in his eyes, the way his lips parted, how his right hand reached for her breast, and, of course, his erection all made any other interpretation of the scenario impossible.

I had captured the lovers in the throes of an anticipated passionate and completely adulterous embrace.

"My brother?" Ari turned away from my drawing and to his wife. "What am I looking at, Clara?"

"It's Delphine's twisted mind. Not one iota of the truth. It's her imagination. Her portraits are always weird and strange. Tell him, Delphine," she pleaded.

Ari didn't give me a chance. "Don't lie to me, Clara. Everyone knows exactly what these drawings are. And even if she is a charlatan, she didn't come up with this scenario on her own out of thin air."

"Maybe she did. You did, didn't you?" Clara turned back to me, desperation in her voice. All signs of inebriation gone, chased by the panic that surged through her.

"Yes, yes, I did. I made it up," I said. I would have agreed to anything to defuse the situation, because I could see the danger in a colored haze of orange around Ari's form.

Monty reached our sorry group. He stood on Clara's other side. Taller and darker than Ari, with a wicked smile he wasn't wearing just then, he was the more charming and popular of the brothers.

Both were invited to all the best parties, but it was Monty the women flirted with and invited into their beds. It was Monty the men invited to play golf and to whom they offered cigars.

"What is all this fuss?" Monty asked. "Certainly, there can't be anything that—"

He walked around so he could see the drawing. After he took it in, he looked to me, to Clara, and finally to his brother.

"You are not going to take some silly drawing seriously, are you?" Monty asked.

"So you are going to claim this is just the artist's wild fantasy, too?" Ari responded.

"Calm down, Ari," Monty said, in a soothing voice that belied his concern. As he spoke, I noticed he'd positioned himself between Ari and Clara, protecting her from her husband's rage.

"Calm down? While I stand by and watch my brother try to destroy my life? Again?"

The Schiff scandal that had turned the brothers against each other was well known among New York's social set. After returning home from the war, Ari had married a woman named Mabel Taub. Within six months of the wedding, Monty had seduced his brother's wife. Ari divorced Mabel, and shortly thereafter Monty married her. A year later, she died in a tragic train accident.

And now the two brothers stood face-to-face. History, if my drawing was to be believed, repeating itself.

Chapter 3

"Delphine didn't make this up. The two of you are having an affair!" Ari shouted.

"You're imagining things," Monty said, also raising his voice.

"Oh, really?" Ari asked in a nasty snarl.

"Both of you have to stop," Clara cried.

Accusations continued to fly back and forth above the din of partygoers who had no idea what was transpiring in our corner.

From halfway across the room, Tommy looked over in our direction. A friend of Ari's, he'd recognized his voice and was concerned. I motioned to him, and he broke away from his conversation and pushed through the crowd.

Monty was now trying to soothe his brother. "This isn't the place to discuss it, Ari. You have to calm down."

Ignoring his brother, Ari grabbed the drawing off my easel. Pushing past Monty, he shoved the offending illustration under his wife's face. "Tell me what is going on!"

"It's nothing, Ari." Clara's voice trembled. "It's Delphine's fantasy."

"Tell me the truth!" Ari stepped even closer to her.

"Please, Ari," she begged, tears filling her eyes.

"Tell me!" He rubbed my drawing across her face in an ugly, violent motion. Graphite smeared her pale peach skin.

Tommy had reached us, and together he and Monty pulled Ari away from his wife.

"That's enough for now, Ari. You are terrifying Clara," Monty said, as he fought off his brother's efforts to keep from being restrained.

"Enough for now? Are you insane? You seduce her and turn her into a whore and then tell me it's enough?"

With a great surge, Ari pulled free of Tommy's and his brother's grip.

The scene that ensued belonged in a horror film, not a Fifth Avenue penthouse filled with millionaires and flappers.

Ari fumbled into his suit pocket and pulled out a gun with a mother-of-pearl handle. Absurdly, it gleamed in the party's soft lights, for a moment just another jewel among the diamonds, emeralds, and rubies adorning the guests. Then, like a snake, it slithered into the spotlight, threatening an end to the gaiety. A poisonous reminder that evil is never far from laughter.

I sucked in my breath and watched as Tommy sidled up to Ari and tried to cajole him into letting go of the gun. "Now, now, Ari, there's no need for that."

"No," Clara whispered, and then kept whispering that one word over and over. Even to this day, it is always in my mind when I picture the scene. "No no no no no no no no no no no no no no no no no no no no no . . ."

With the gun pointed at him, Monty, almost too calmly, glanced around. He seemed to be measuring the size of the gathering. Assessing the danger of a gun in such a crowded room. Looking back at Clara, he smiled at her. A moment of tenderness passed between them in the midst of the madness.

Our little group was in the corner beside the terrace that wrapped around the penthouse and hung high over the avenue. Even though it was a cold night, with so many guests packed into one place and with so many different perfumes mixing and so many people smoking, our hostess had left the door cracked open to let in fresh air.

Smoothly, despite having a gun pointed at him, Monty began backing up, stepping through the door and going outside onto the terrace. He was mitigating the damage his brother could do in the congested apartment. Quickly, Ari followed Monty outside. So did Tommy. Clara tried, but I stopped her, putting my arm around her trembling body and holding her back.

"Stay here," I said. "There's nothing you can do, and it's too dangerous for you to be out there."

She turned to face me, terror contorting her features. The lovely creature who had been sitting for me just minutes ago was gone. She was Eve now, a temptress, in pain—no, in agony—confronting her sin and panicked by what she had wrought.

"It just happened one day," she whispered urgently, as if telling me would make it right. "I just couldn't seem to help myself. Every time I turned around, Monty was always there, charming and exciting, while Ari was so taciturn and grumpy all the time, and then—"

Pop.

Clara and I froze, staring out at the scene on the terrace, both of us certain that Ari had fired the gun at his brother. But they were both still standing, flinging accusations at each other.

I turned around. Over at the bar, Fred Steward, the party's host, not realizing the drama unfolding across the room, had opened a new bottle of champagne. The noise we'd heard was a cork popping.

Clara clutched my arm, her nails digging into my skin. "What is going to happen? What are they going to do to each other?"

I held on to her as she struggled to go out to the terrace.

"I don't know."

Locked in some primeval battle, the brothers created a horrifying tableau with the marvelous nighttime skyline of New York behind them. A surrealistic canvas of forefront juxtaposed against backdrop, two unmatched scenes.

As Ari, gun pointed, advanced on his brother, Monty backed up, talking to him without pause. We couldn't make out the words, but clearly they weren't effective, as the gun remained pointed at Monty.

"Is Ari going to pull the trigger? Or is he just trying to frighten Monty? What is Monty saying?" Beside me, Clara kept up a stream of questions, not one of which I could answer.

Suddenly, Monty's face twisted into a pained smile. He must have said something that enraged Ari, who raised his arm and aimed the gun more squarely at the center of his brother's chest.

Monty took a step backward to get farther away from the gun and his brother and the nightmare he'd put himself in the middle of. And then he took another step. And another. And then one step too many.

"Oh, God, no!" Clara cried.

She saw what was happening before I did. My eyes were frozen on the gun itself. At how the mother-of-pearl gleamed in the moonlight, opalescent and resplendent. But Clara had been watching Monty. The man she loved. The man who, in that very moment, she lost.

The iron railings on the terrace must have been old or rusted or just not strong enough to withstand the pressure of Monty backing up against them. It didn't matter why. It happened. The railing gave way, and Monty fell into the darkness as, at exactly that moment, we heard another sound.

Pop.

Not more champagne being opened. Not that time. Ari had fired. The flare lit up the terrace.

What was he thinking? That he had to be the one to destroy Monty? Not to allow fate to take a hand? Had Ari forgotten for the moment that we were twenty-six stories above the pavement? Had he thought Monty was getting away?

Either the sound of the gunshot or the realization that Monty had fallen roused Ari out of his rage-induced state. Understanding what had happened, he rushed toward the gaping hole and leaned over so far it looked as if he might be about to follow his brother.

Just then, Tommy darted over, grabbed him around the waist, and pulled him back.

Clara and I stayed where we were huddled, holding on to each other, staring at the men, her husband and my fiancé, as they stood side by side at the edge of the abyss.

Chapter 4

The morning newspapers all carried the story. The Champagne Suicide, they called it. Despite Tommy's efforts to shield me from being questioned, the police had asked me for a statement, and every article included my name and my involvement in the tragedy.

The incident began when French artist Delphine Duplessi, who is something of a regular at blue blood parties, drew a cartoon of the deceased with his sister-in-law in a compromising position. According to Mimi Palmer, a party guest, Duplessi's drawing left nothing to the imagination, and as soon as he saw it, Ari Schiff went after his brother, accusing him of seducing his wife. Monty Schiff either fell or jumped off the twenty-sixth-floor terrace. Currently, his death is being reported as a either suicide or an accident, pending further investigation. One source in the police department said there is a possibility that Ari Schiff will be accused of second-degree murder, since he was threatening his brother with a loaded pistol when the accident occurred.

As is the custom in the Jewish religion, the funeral was held within twenty-four hours. Given the scandalous way Monty had died, his family was anxious to have him put to rest as quickly as possible, in the hopes of curtailing the attention focused on them. Not only did they have to endure the tragedy and the farewell, but as soon as Monty was buried, they would need to attend to the business of hiring lawyers and helping their other son avoid a prison sentence.

Despite the family's wishes, and as I had expected, the scene at Temple Emanuel on Forty-third Street and Fifth Avenue was anything but private. The press crowded the sidewalk, shouting questions, cameras at the ready to snap pictures of the society mourners.

Tommy's parents, friends of the Schiffs, preceded us out of the car. As Tommy escorted me from the curb, one of the reporters recognized me and pointed me out to his photographer.

Click. Click. Click.

I shielded my face and walked with my head down.

"I told you it wasn't wise for you to come," Tommy whispered harshly, as he hurried me toward the front door to the temple.

"Given my involvement, how could I stay away?"

"This will do nothing but stir up even more gossip about you."

I turned to look at him. "Gossip would only improve my popularity. You're upset about how it will affect you because of your association with me. That's what you mean, isn't it?"

His reaction didn't surprise me. Since we'd become engaged the month before, Tommy's attitude toward my work had changed, albeit subtly. What he'd thought was fascinating before suddenly worried him. How would the patrons of one of Manhattan's largest banks, which his father owned and where he was a junior partner, take to a wife who was not only French but also something of a psychic? If only he knew the whole truth. That I was, in fact, a witch.

Secrets bind families together. While many in occult circles knew that the Duplessis were the descendants of La Lune, we didn't discuss our abilities outside of a very tight and trustworthy circle. They were not something to boast of or to brag about. In New York, I had made light of my ability to paint people's secrets and never alluded to myself as a witch. I never even used the word *clairvoyant*. *Psychic* or *mind reader* were benign, acceptable, and all the rage.

Now, seeing this new side to Tommy made me wary, but I put aside my concerns. He'd grow used to it, I thought.

Tommy's marriage proposal had come as a surprise. And I'd surprised myself even more by accepting. It was time to put the past behind me, I'd determined. To acknowledge that I could never be with Mathieu and that the kind of love I'd had with him and longed for still was lost to me forever. With Tommy, I could have a life in New York City that would be creatively fulfilling and different from what I knew in France. Without familiar landmarks and triggers, there would be nothing to send me into a tailspin of memories of my time in Paris. I could avoid the past as I made a future with Tommy, who doted on me and appreciated me. I found him funny and smart and more than handsome enough to enjoy being in his arms. If the deep passion that I'd felt with Mathieu was absent, if the sense of souls connecting was missing, that was fine. A love like the one I'd left behind was as much pain as it was pleasure. Even if it had been possible, I never wanted to live on that plane again.

"Yes, that's what I mean," he said. "I don't want people to think I'm marrying a female Harry Houdini. Or worse, one of those Lower East Side charlatans and fake fortune-tellers reporters love to write about."

As we stepped through the door, out of the afternoon sunlight and into the temple's dark foyer, I glanced at my fiancé. Shadows hid the expression in his eyes.

Even though he'd voiced concern about my reputation before, he'd never been so vulgar about what I did. Perhaps it was just the stress of the situation, I thought, as we followed the crowd inside. Tommy's parents had already taken seats in a pew by the rear of the temple, where we joined them.

"I don't understand," Tommy's mother, Florence Prout, asked her husband. "Why this rush to bury the dead? And why is there no viewing?"

"I don't know," Whitley Prout said.

Mrs. Prout looked at Tommy.

"I don't know, either," he said.

Since they were Protestant, that didn't surprise me. But I knew the answer, so I offered it. "Our religion is all about respect," I explained. "For the living and the dead. It's more respectful to bury the body as soon as possible, before it can alter. And more respectful to the mourners, so they can begin the healing process. The lack of a viewing is also a form of respect. Tradition teaches that it's not respectful to look at someone who cannot look back."

The expression on Mrs. Prout's face went from disturbed to horrified. The air around her began to color. It was turning the pale green of disgust. What had I said? There was no time to find out, because at that moment, my attention was riveted on Clara Schiff, who was walking down the aisle with Ari by her side.

Never had I seen two such lost souls. The aura of misery around them was its own deep purple shade of black. Shrouding them and casting them in gloom.

Yes, Ari had been furious with his brother and in that moment on the terrace had certainly wanted to kill Monty. Ari's pride had been profoundly wounded. He'd been humiliated. For the second time, his brother had cuckolded him.

But the fact was, Ari had not killed Monty. No, Monty wouldn't have fallen if he hadn't been backing away from his brother's pointed weapon. But he had fallen, not been pushed or shot. It didn't matter, though. Parsing the facts wouldn't change that forever; even after the stain of Monty's blood on the pavement was washed away, there would still be a stain on Ari's heart. His brother had died looking down the barrel of Ari's gun. Yes, Monty had done a despicable thing in cuckolding him. But they were brothers. And there were bonds between siblings that ran deeper and darker than could be explained. I was a twin, and I understood.

What I didn't understand yet, because I was still in shock, was that the stain of the death was also on me. And it would, in time, threaten my sanity and alter the course of my career.

As people continued to file into the shul and take their seats, I became aware of Tommy and his mother whispering. I couldn't catch enough words to make out what they said, but their facial expressions told me that she was still upset and Tommy was trying to calm her. When Mr. Prout, who was the farthest away from me but had the loudest whisper, joined in the conversation, I heard him say the word *Jewish* twice, as if it was a question.

My attention was drawn to the front of the temple, where the rabbi appeared from behind one of the high stone archways flanking the altar. Behind him, the ornate bronze gate where the Torah was kept glowed in the candlelight. Growing up, I'd had no formal religious training. My father was an atheist. And although my mother's family was Jewish, the only religion she believed in was the worship of art.

When I'd lived in Paris, my great-grandmother exposed me to Judaism, teaching me about my heritage and taking me to Friday-night services. A practicing Jew, she was disturbed by my mother's lack of respect for our religion.

But then, so much about my mother bothered Grand-mère, as I called her. That Sandrine had allowed the sixteenth-century spirit of La Lune to invade her and use her body as a host was the most deeply disturbing of my mother's transgressions. Although my great-grandmother's feelings about Sandrine had softened over the years, given the opportunity, she always warned my sisters and my brother and me that my mother had made a grave mistake by letting La Lune in and that generations of our family would suffer the consequences, just as generations before her had. The world was not kind to those involved in the dark arts. People fear what they do not understand.

We had ancestors who had been ostracized, driven from their homes, misunderstood, and even killed for their abilities. And others who were so overburdened by their power that they killed themselves.

The rabbi took his place behind Monty's simple coffin. Tradition dictated that the box be made of the plainest wood and put together with wooden pegs. No metal at all was used. Also in keeping with custom, there were no flowers. Everyone was equal in death, both the rich and the poor. Dating back to the days when Jews lived in ghettos and few had money, these traditions freed the bereaved from spending more than they could afford.

"Welcome," the rabbi said, "to the family and friends of Montgomery Schiff on this sad and solemn occasion. We will begin by reciting the El Malei Rachamim on page thirty-nine of your prayer book."

The rabbi led the congregation in the recitation of the Hebrew memorial prayer. I didn't hear Tommy or my future in-laws making any effort to read along, even though on the opposite page from the Hebrew was an English transcription they could have easily followed.

I knew that living in New York and being part of the financial community, Tommy's parents were friendly and did business with many Jews. Surely they had attended other funerals of their peers who were of the Hebraic persuasion. So why were they so obviously disturbed and silent?

More than once, I saw Mrs. Prout watching me. We'd met quite a few times, and both she and her husband had been lovely and welcoming. He'd even spoken to me in French. Both of them were art lovers, and they owned a small but quality collection that included two Renoirs, a Morisot, and an Utrillo, all purchased during their trips to Europe. We'd enjoyed very pleasant conversations about the state of the art world and my own ambitions. But Mrs. Prout's expression when I caught her eye now belied those past pleasantries.

Was I surprised? Not really. I'd been in the news. Connected to a scandal. And that wasn't what was done by members of the upper crust. The only times it was proper for your name to appear in the paper was when you married and when you died. Certainly not when a lewd drawing you had created led to a murder attempt and a tragic accident.

After the ceremony, Tommy's parents said their good-byes, as chilly as the February afternoon. They weren't going to the burial with us. We joined the cortege to Mount Zion Cemetery in Queens. In the car with us were two of Ari's friends who had been at the Steward party, and the conversation revolved around the incident.

Tommy and I weren't alone until the end of that long terrible day when he saw me home. We stood in the hallway while I fumbled in my purse for my key. Opening the door, I was greeted by the familiar brew of commingled scents: the turpentine and oils that were the smells of my trade, a hint of coffee, which was all I drank while I painted, and my own scent, from the House of L'Etoile, the only perfume I wore. It had been one of the gifts Mathieu had given me, and our short-lived love affair was over before I'd finished that first bottle. Each year since, I had ordered a refill. Wearing it was a way to stay connected to a dream that, for a moment in time, had come true.

Although the studio I rented was only one very large room with a tiny kitchen and a bathroom tucked into corners, it was perfect for me. The working area took up two-thirds of the space. The twelve-foot ceilings and the large north-facing skylight gave the impression of spaciousness even amid the clutter. A full wall of shelves overflowed with art supplies, art books, and my "searching" books. These were esoteric volumes I found in out-of-the-way bookstores about mysterious realms, magical talents, biographies of mystics and seers, treatises on the occult and spiritualist movements, histories of witchcraft and alchemy, and tales of the Cathars and Templars in the Languedoc area of France, close to where I had grown up in Cannes.

With all the books, the supplies, and my pencil studies, there was no visible wall left. Over the years, I'd tacked up drawing after drawing, so that in places the artwork was as thick as a sketch pad. Portraits of my parents and siblings, my great-grandmother, and friends I'd left in Paris hung over the white marble fireplace. The three easels set up under the skylight held paintings in various states of finish.

A comfortable couch covered in rust velvet separated the living area from the work area. An emerald-green silk shawl with salmon-colored fringe and embroidered red roses hid the badly stained wooden top of a rickety side table. Behind it was my bed, a bentwood Art Nouveau wonder my father had designed and shipped over from France. A lavender satin comforter my great-grandmother had given me lay atop it. I'd added pillows in all shades of purple, blue, and green and had placed beside the bed a large celadon and grass-green opalescent vase—cracked, of course—that I'd found in a secondhand shop and had filled with iridescent peacock feathers.

"Do you want to come in?" I asked Tommy. I knew he often felt claustrophobic in my overcrowded living quarters and preferred his sleek uptown apartment, but that afternoon he followed me inside.

"Yes, I suppose so. We need to talk."

I anticipated a lecture about curtailing the party-favor work and was about to ask him to postpone the harangue, but then I decided it would be preferable to get it over with.

"Do you want some wine?" I asked, before he could start.

"I certainly do. The last three days have been the worst I've had since the war. But not wine. I think there's some of that scotch left that I brought here?"

I poured his drink and my wine and brought them over to the couch. Tommy was sitting with his elbows on his knees, his head in his hands.

"Do you have a headache?"

He looked up. His eyes were bloodshot, and his face was twisted into an anguished expression.

"No. Nothing that simple," he said, as he reached for the glass and took a long sip of the amber liquid.

Clearly, he was bereft and upset, but so was I, and I had no solace to offer. I was too raw. What I really wanted was for him to take me in his arms and soothe me. But he didn't.

We both sat in silence and sipped our drinks.

"Everything was my fault," I finally said, breaking the silence.

"Not everything. You didn't make Clara sleep with her husband's brother." Even though his words were solicitous, his tone was angry, exasperated.

"But I exposed them."

"They committed the deed, Delphine."

"Which would have remained their secret if not for me."

"For God's sake." He stood up quickly, jostling the table. "No one cares what you did. No one gives a rat's ass about you."

My wineglass shook in my hand, and a splash of red liquid spilled onto the couch. One more stain to cover with a shawl.

Tommy didn't notice. His back was to me as he stood in front of the windows, looking four flights down into the snow-covered courtyard.

"You were just the party favor that exploded in everyone's face. Didn't I ask you to stop this work when we became engaged? I told you that I would help pay your rent here until we were married. Why didn't you? Is your independence that important to you? This will be the legacy and demise of my generation—a war that gave women a taste of their capabilities and freedom. The jack let out of the box."

"That's not fair—" I started to argue.

"It doesn't matter," he interrupted. "It's too late." He turned and looked at me, the anger in his eyes replaced with sadness.

"What is too late?" I asked.

"I can't marry you, Delphine."

"Because of what I drew?"

"No, because of what my parents found out about you."

I'd expected this to happen. Was prepared for it. My mother had discussed it with my sisters and me since we were little. How to defend ourselves and explain our gifts. How to diffuse the misconceptions. I'd even collected a list of luminaries, from Arthur Conan Doyle to Thomas Alva Edison, who visited psychics.

"My mother and father are quite horrified," Tommy said.

"Of course they are. Monty died a horrible death. And the way the news stories described it all . . . my blindfold and the lewd drawings. Of course they are, but—"

"Not about that, darling," Tommy said, with a hitch in his voice that confused me.

For the last two years, we'd been an item that had raised quite a few eyebrows in the Prouts' world. Their son was a golden child, who'd excelled at tennis and mathematics, who'd left Harvard in his junior year to enlist, who'd come home a war hero and immediately joined his father at the family bank. As far from an artistic soul as anyone could be, Tommy was a swimming pool. I could see all the way to the bottom without spying any surprises, unlike in the sea's depths, where all was hidden even in the brightest sunshine.

The relationship had been exactly the kind I'd craved after my mysterious and painful foray into passion with Mathieu.

My mother told me that the moment she met my father, she knew she would love him forever. That didn't happen to me. But the first time I saw Mathieu, I did think I already knew him. I recognized his face from dreams that I'd put down in my journal. In some of those early surrealistic exercises, he was a lion. Golden and strong. Powerful and sleek.

For weeks, I had tried to convince myself it was a coincidence— that I must have seen him on the street before visiting the bookshop where I actually saw him in the flesh for the first time. But as hard as I tried to convince myself, I knew I didn't believe it. How, then, was it possible that I'd drawn him before ever seeing him? What did it mean? Those questions were the leitmotif of my life. How was any of what I did possible? What did any of it mean? And what was the purpose?

By the time I was five years old, I had been drawing with a talent that my mother told me she hadn't developed until she was in her twenties. When I was eight, I was blinded when a child threw lye at me and destroyed the soft tissue of my eyes. For fourteen months, my life was in shadows, without light or color or shape or form. Then my mother's magick restored my sight. But with it, I had second sight. How? Why did my mother have an ability that others in our lineage didn't? And why were only the women in our family affected? All my sisters had gifts but not my twin, Sebastian. And why did I have to paint Mathieu's portrait and see that nightmare in the shadows? I'd run away from him, from Paris, and saved his life, but I couldn't save our life together. I had fled to New York, only to wind up in the midst of this scandal.

"Delphine, we have to call this off for a while," Tommy said now.

"But you said it yourself. I just drew the picture. I'm simply a line in today's tabloid story. Forgotten as soon as another scandal breaks. You said it yourself. I wasn't the one caught in my brother-in-law's bed. I didn't hold the gun on Monty. I know your family has a certain standing. Haven't you explained to them that it's not sorcery that helps me draw, just simple thought reading?"

He took my hand. "They didn't take any of that seriously. What they found out today is worse."

"What did they find out today?"

"It makes us . . . it makes it all impossible."

"What does? What are you talking about, Tommy?"

"Delphine, why didn't you ever tell me you were Jewish?"

Chapter 5

My studio on Tenth Street was haunted. Not by ghosts. That was my older sister Opaline's special gift, communicating with those who have passed over. No, my studio was haunted by the frustrations of all the artists who had come to New York to try to make their mark. Who worked tirelessly at the ethereal task of taking brush in hand to create a statement worthy of attracting a gallery owner's attention. Of tempting a stranger to part with his lucre in exchange for a piece of the artist's soul on his wall. Of capturing the interest of a critic to write favorably of just one painting. Of getting noticed by a museum director who could move him or her out of the masses of artists in the shadows and into the spotlight's glow.

The artist who had inhabited my studio before me had failed at all those efforts and hanged himself. Which was the reason my rent was so much lower than that of others in the building. Robert Stanislaw's sad end didn't discourage or frighten me, as it had several other prospective tenants, but it did bother me enough to write my mother and ask her what I could do to cleanse any lasting negative influences he'd left behind.

Dear Delphine,

Gather one pure beeswax candle for each area of the studio. A crystal goblet—use something lovely. A small dish of sea salt. A vial of sandalwood oil. And five branches of dried sage.

First, open all the windows. Then dissolve the sea salt in hot water and put it in the glass. Sprinkle the floor with the water. Next, anoint each candle with sandalwood oil and light them. While they are burning, put the sage in the sink and set it on fire. Once it's burned down but still smoking, walk through the studio with it, making sure you smoke out any place where shadows can gather. All the while, whisper an invitation to the energy, telling it that it's free to go, that you are releasing it.

Finally, spray some of your lovely House of L'Etoile perfume to help put your energy into the air and because you might not like the scent of all that sage.

All my love,
Your Maman

There wasn't much Stanislaw had left behind that I'd kept. The High Victorian wallpaper and furniture in the studio had been depressing to live with. Brown not being one of my colors, I'd had the place painted a soft, light peach color to go with the hardwood floors I had discovered under the carpets. I decorated in autumnal colors. Rugs and fabrics in rusts, ambers, topazes, and forest greens.

Once I'd lit the candles and filled the room with the scents of sandalwood and sage and then my own fragrance, the energy did feel clean and positive, and it remained so for years. But all that changed after Monty's funeral. Even the winter sun coming in from the skylight felt too bright for my eyes. Any hint of hope or joy seemed blasphemous.

My grief over Monty's death, mixed with my anger at Tommy

and my self-loathing, overwhelmed me. Because of a secret I had sketched out, someone had died, and my life was forever altered. Although the signs had been there all along, alerting me to the possible dangers involved in revealing the secret lives of others, this marked the first time my work had truly betrayed me. Never had it caused such tragedy. Could I even go on? What other damage would I create by continuing?

I'd known that the potential for disaster existed. I'd had two warnings. First when I drew Mathieu's portrait and then when I received a letter from a woman named Thérèse Bruis, who had sat for me weeks before. I'd already decided to leave Paris by then—to save Mathieu's life—when her plea to remove her painting from Sebastian's gallery arrived. I had never received such a missive before and was ashamed and appalled that I'd contributed to this poor, lovely woman's sorrow. But it was her unhappiness that gave me the excuse I needed to explain my departure to Sebastian, who assured me that he would take care of the situation. He was my beloved twin, my savior, and as shocked and disappointed as he was at my leaving, I knew he would follow through on his promise.

Once I arrived in New York, why hadn't I stuck to my resolution to give up drawing secrets? Why couldn't I instead just paint what I saw with my eyes, not my mind, as my contemporaries did? Didn't I have proof that my ability was not always a source of good and light but could be a dark and dangerous thing?

Why had I allowed Sebastian to cajole me, via his letters and visits, into taking on more shadow commissions? Mathieu had disapproved of Sebastian selling my gift. But even the thought of his disappointment wasn't enough to dissuade me.

Had I succumbed because I desired success and notoriety and knew it would be easier to attain through magick? Had I agreed to please my twin? Sebastian basked in being my manager. He was so proud of my success. Had I continued to paint for his gratification and squelched my own concerns?

Or was it that while I had fled to New York in anguish, the move gave me a surprising dose of freedom? As much as I missed my family and the ease with which I had entrusted all aspects of my career to Sebastian back in Paris, I experienced an independence in New York that I'd never thought possible, especially for a woman. While our roles had evolved during the war, once it ended and men returned to the head of the table, women all over the world were soon enough sent back to the kitchen, literally and figuratively.

While Sebastian visited twice a year, an ocean's distance kept him from insinuating too much. I was getting more and more of my own commissions, and I destroyed any paintings that my clients didn't want made public—not that this happened very often. I thought I was becoming liberated from Sebastian's protection—and I reveled in it—until the Monty and Clara incident.

For the next three days, I kept the curtains drawn. I draped a black chenille throw over my beautiful couch, stripped the coral silk off the rickety table, and hid all the pillows under the bed. I shrouded the studio in darkness and sat in front of my easels staring at the work I'd done before the accident.

A month earlier, the owner of the Saperstein Gallery had expressed interest in a surrealistic shadow portrait I'd done of a woman turned into a flower—or a flower turned into a woman. He'd said that if I could bring in a series, he'd consider including me in a group show. For years, my work had been shown in my brother's gallery in Cannes, but I'd never had a New York or Paris exhibition. Since January, the dream of the show had kept me up night after night working on the Petal Mystique paintings, as I had named them.

But after the accident and Tommy's departure, I couldn't pick up where I'd left off with the series. I didn't know if I could paint at all or if I should even be allowed to paint. I had done irreparable damage with my talent. Didn't I have to pay a penance? Serve my time?

Whenever I reached for the blindfold, it burned my fingers as if it were on fire. I worried that if I put it on, the heat might hurt my eyesight. My worst fear was returning to a sightless state. I still had a recurring and troubling nightmare of swimming in the sea, alone, no longer tethered to my brother, not knowing if I was swimming out farther or toward shore. I'd wake up in a sweat, filled with panic.

It wasn't just a bad dream. During the year when I was blind, Sebastian was my eyes. Because we both loved to swim and spent our summers by the shore, he'd devised a way that I could still enjoy the water. He'd tie a rope around his waist and then around mine. Long enough to give me the freedom to swim, it also gave me security.

One afternoon, in seas that were a little rougher than usual, the rope broke. At first, I didn't realize that I was no longer tethered to Sebastian. When I did, I panicked. Just as I screamed for my twin, a large wave crashed over me. I took in a huge mouthful of water. Twisting and turning in the surf, I didn't know what to do. Terrorized, I struggled, fought the waves. Feared they were winning.

"Sebastian!" I shouted over and over, but every time, the crashing waves swallowed his name.

And then, finally, I felt his arms pulling me to him. Holding me. He was only eight years old, but his little-boy arms were strong enough to save me that day. Seconds later, there was sand underfoot. I hadn't drifted far out at all but had been caught up in a rough current close to shore, where it was just deep enough that my feet hadn't reached bottom.

That was the last time I went swimming. The last time I stepped into any body of water other than a bath. Even after my sight returned.

Lonely, melancholy, unable to work, I still hadn't gone out on the fourth day after Monty Schiff's funeral. Barely hungry, I was managing on what I had in the studio: black coffee, a few eggs, a half dozen apples, a wedge of cheese, and bread that became more stale with each passing day. I drank what was left of the red wine my brother had brought over from his last visit. And then started on the white.

Sleep was my only escape from the nightmares I lived during the

day, as I replayed the scene at the party as if it were a film reel. Another *Society Scandal* but starring Clara instead of Gloria Swanson.
The drawing of Clara and Monty refused to fade out of my mind; it
became even more lurid and frightening.

On my fifth afternoon of isolation, I finally picked up a brush and
tried to paint the scene but with changes, as if I could reverse what
had happened by altering it.

After an hour, I dropped my brushes into a jar of turpentine to
clean them and then stared at the hideous mess I'd made. This was
nothing like my style. The quality was subpar. I couldn't bear the sight
of the blood-red, muddy brown, and gray chaos.

Running into my kitchenette, I grabbed the sharpest knife I had.
Returning, I passed by the mirror and saw my image. And I froze.

Scrying is an ancient art that witches use to receive hidden information about the past, the present, or the future. Some extremely
adept scryers see spirits that move as if in a film. They can speak to
them and hear their responses.

The earliest scryers used bowls of water, gazing into the reflective surface until they saw images. Early mirrors, made of polished
copper, silver, brass, or mercury behind glass, were more stable and
became the scryer's preference.

In ancient Rome, the young men who gazed into mirrors at an
angle, avoiding their own reflections, seeing both the unknowable
and the future, were known as blindfold boys.

My mother had studied scrying for years but had limited ability.
She was able to see her children in the reflections but only our present, never our futures. Once, during the war, she saw such trouble-
some visions of my sister Opaline that she left Cannes to go to her
in Paris despite the dangers of wartime travel. Opaline told me later
that the night my mother arrived, Opaline had been contemplating
suicide. I wondered if my mother could see me in New York, wishing
she could sail across the ocean and save me.

After I lost my sight, part of the treatment required that I keep my eyes closed. For an eight-year-old, that was hard to do. So my mother made me a blindfold. Once I started wearing it, my version of scrying began. And my mother took to calling me a "blindfold girl."

After my sight returned, we realized that my scrying powers were not limited to the blindfold. I could also see in mirrors and other reflective objects in the right light. Often without trying, I saw secrets in the shadows, lurking in the reflective depths. Usually, they were better left unseen.

The day I'd moved into the Tenth Street studio, I'd covered the old tin-mercury mirror in the entranceway with a chiffon scarf to avoid any unintended visions. But sometimes a breeze from an open window blew the scarf off. As it must have done that fifth day after Monty's death.

In the silvery mottled surface, I saw my own ghostly figure, knife in hand. A reflection of lamplight danced on the blade's edge, mocking me with its sparkle. I'd drawn a scene like that once before and then destroyed it. As if tearing it to shreds would obliterate the prophecy.

I hacked the painting of Clara and Monty, too. I plunged the knife into the canvas and pulled it down. The tear sounded like a scream. I attacked it again. Plunge. Pull. Scream. Plunge. Pull. Scream. Ribbons of blood red, black, and gray fell to the rug.

Knock. Knock.

In a daze, I heard the thuds. Looked around. Found myself sitting on the floor, surrounded by the shredded painting. The empty frame, sans canvas, had fallen off the easel and lay crookedly beside me.

Knock. Knock.

"Delphine? Delphine? What is going on in there?"

Disoriented, I was too confused to get up.

"Delphine? I swear, if you don't answer, I'm going to get the police."

"I'm coming!" I called out, no idea if my voice even carried.

"Delphine?"

I stood, staggered to the front door, and opened it.

Clifford B. Clayton, my neighbor and "American uncle," as my family called him, caught me before I collapsed.

"There, there, darling. What's gotten into you? It sounded like someone was being murdered in here." He surveyed the scene as he held me up.

"Yes, yes. I was just painting, and . . ." I didn't know how to explain.

"It looks like you were painting but something went very wrong." He guided me to the couch. "You just sit down. I'm making us tea laced with something strong. You'll drink it and feel better, and then we'll talk this out."

We'd spent so much time together over the years that we knew where everything was in each other's studio. Obediently, I sat and waited, trying to answer his questions as he boiled the water and fixed a tray.

At fifty-five, Clifford was a colorful character on New York's art scene. His Art Deco paintings of stylish interiors and the people who inhabited them were highly sought after, and he was enjoying one of the most productive periods of his career. His charming manner endeared him to many hostesses, and as a result, he'd been divorced twice and claimed he'd never marry again.

When he was in his twenties, he'd fled his Midwestern hometown to study in Paris, where he and my mother met while attending L'École des Beaux-Arts. They had remained friends ever since. Whenever he visited France, he would stay with us for a few weeks in Cannes. When I told my parents I wanted to move to New York, they asked Clifford to help me get settled. He did more than that. He took me under his wing.

The timing had been perfect. Robert Stanislaw's studio, situated down the hall from Clifford's, had been empty for more than a month, and Clifford secured it for me immediately. With him nearby, I was less nervous about New York and being on my own for the first time, and he soon introduced me to other artists, writers, and intellectuals living in the neighborhood.

Often, we popped out to get lunch together to break up the hours of painting. In the evenings, we'd taken to sharing some wine before we went our separate ways. On Sunday nights, which he said was family night, I joined him at a neighborhood restaurant on Minetta Lane for spaghetti.

"Here we go." Now Clifford brought over the tray. "Tea without anything stronger. I saw the empty bottle of wine on the counter and am guessing you've had enough." He handed me a cup. "Now, tell me. What is this mess, child? What have you done?"

He'd been away for more than a week, painting the home of a wealthy Hudson Valley society matron, and had only returned that afternoon, so he'd missed the stories about the Steward party.

"But you were no more responsible for that poor man dying than I am," he said, after I'd explained. "Don't you dare let yourself believe that. They were lovers, sweetheart. They were tempting fate every time they were together."

"But lovers get found out. They don't die."

"You know, sometimes they do."

"And *you* know, most of the time they don't."

"So that's what all this is about?" he asked, gesturing to the shredded canvas on the floor. "And this?" He pointed to the curtains and the mess on my bed. "It looks like you haven't stepped out of this place in days."

"Five days," I said, and told him the rest. About the funeral and Tommy and holing myself up in the studio and trying to repaint the past to change it.

When I was done, he took my hands and held them in his. "You have been through hell, haven't you?"

There was nothing to say. I nodded.

"I'm just going to my studio to get something. I'll be right back in a jiffy. You stay put, all right?"

Less than a minute later, he returned with an amber bottle in hand. He went into the kitchen and returned with a glass of cloudy water.

"I want you to drink this down, and then I'm going to put you to bed and come back later after you've gotten some sleep and then take you out for dinner. No more crying. No more slashing paintings, all right?"

It felt good to have someone tell me what to do. I took the glass from him. Whatever he'd put in it tasted bitter, but I drank it. And then I let him tuck me into bed. Before he had even left the room, I was asleep.

Chapter 6

During the walk to John's on East Twelfth Street, Clifford said he was forbidding any serious conversation over dinner. "You need to stop thinking for a while, darling."

And I did. We drank bootleg wine—but he stopped me after two glasses—and ate plates of spaghetti with red sauce and big, fat meatballs, while Clifford told me all the latest gossip, including a salacious story about a seduction scene he'd witnessed between his Hudson Valley hostess's husband and one of their dinner guests.

The wine, scandalous tales, rumors of outrageous sales, and stories about critics who'd gone too far preoccupied me, and my mood lifted.

Back outside on the sidewalk after dinner, we found it had started to snow. There's a special kind of quiet on city streets during a snowfall. A lonely but lovely silence, as if everyone has stopped—stopped loving, hating, walking, talking, cleaning, working—just to watch the crystal flakes fly out of the sky and shroud the world in pure, exquisite white.

We walked back in the peaceful cold. Snow fell in my hair and caught in my eyelashes and settled on top of Clifford's ever-present homburg.

When we reached the studio, my self-appointed parent in absentia announced that he was coming in with me.

"We'll clean up a little and have some more tea."

"Brandy? And I don't need a minder."

"Tea. And actually, I think you do."

Once inside, he went to the kitchenette and made us both tea. Handing me a cup, he asked, "Where's the broom? You're going to sit and drink your tea, and I'm going to clean up some of this mess."

I tried to argue, but he wouldn't have it, so I finally pointed out the broom and dustbin and settled myself back on the couch.

"I think you should come and paint in my studio for the next few days," Clifford said as he swept. "I'm having models in for a mural. I don't think it's wise for you to be alone here, brooding."

"I won't brood."

"No? Then what will you do? Do you have any commissions this week?"

"I don't."

"And you said you canceled all the parties you were engaged to attend?"

"Yes. I can't go back to that. Not when I can't trust myself to censor the images."

"Any appointments to see friends?"

"There were, but they were with Tommy." I took a sip of the tea. The burn felt good after saying my ex-fiancé's name out loud.

"How about going without him?"

"I don't want to have to explain anything."

"You're not embarrassed, are you?" Clifford looked at me. "That's not like you."

"I am—but not about being Jewish. No. And not about us no longer being an item."

"Then what is it?"

"I'm embarrassed that I ever let it get as far as it did with Tommy. That I thought I could actually have a future with someone like him. That I introduced him to all my friends and got chummy with his."

"When you say 'someone like him,' what do you mean, exactly?"

"He's not very soulful, is he?"

Clifford stopped sweeping and raised his brows. "No, darling. *Soulful* is not a word anyone has ever uttered about him."

I laughed. It sounded strange to me after so many days of crying.

"But don't worry. None of us, the artists who are your real friends, ever thought for a moment that you'd wind up marrying Mr. Moneybags."

"Clifford!"

"I know, I know. One should never speak ill of the dead . . . and so on. But Delphine, I know his type. I'm a fixture inside their homes. I've been painting the social set for years, darling, and they are just not like us. He was an aberration. You were flirting with New York's blue bloods and trying them on for size. You'd never have made it to the altar with Tommy Prout."

"You don't know that."

"Oh, but I do." He started sweeping again. "You belong with someone who notices the beauty in what is strange and wonderful in this world. Who sees the magic in you and doesn't want to tamp it down but rather fan its flames."

I went to the window and looked out. The snow was heavier. There was already at least an inch, and it looked as if someone had dressed the trees in lace.

"I knew someone like that once," I whispered against the glass, telling the snow, not Clifford. When Mathieu had kissed me, I hadn't just felt passion but something deeper. When he held my face in his hands and our lips were pressed together, it seemed as if the world locked into place. As if everything made sense and fit. As if our being together was ordained and sacred. I felt bound to Mathieu in the most profound way. But it was an impossible pairing. The only way to protect him was to leave him.

I tried to hold in my sob but failed.

"What did I say?" Clifford had come up behind me. "I didn't mean to upset you."

I shook my head. "You didn't say anything wrong." I sighed. Then tried to smile. "I'm getting so very tired of crying."

Chapter 7

My mother was my painting teacher until I turned nineteen, when we both decided I'd do well to get a broader education. I was already too influenced by her, and she wanted me to find my own style as much as I did. Paris and L'École des Beaux-Arts were the obvious solution. L'École was the Notre Dame of schools. Every great painter from Jacques-Louis David to Delacroix, from Fragonard to Matisse and Rouault, and my mother's mentor Gustave Moreau, had attended. In 1894, my mother had been its first female student. But by the time I began my studies there in 1919, there were quite a few women attending.

Since my great-grandmother, my older sister, and my brother were all in Paris, I had family to live with, which made the whole plan feasible. The City of Lights was far too sophisticated, my parents said, for me to live there on my own. I'd grown up in the south of France, which was calmer and more genteel, and I wasn't as urbane as most city dwellers, they reminded me. Focusing so much on my art, I hadn't yet learned the ways of the world.

I enjoyed living with my great-grandmother in our family home in the sixth arrondissement. Maison de la Lune, as it was called, was one of a half dozen four-story mid-eighteenth-century stone houses that shared a common courtyard backing up onto rue du Dragon.

Decorated and designed to please her gentlemen friends, her salons and "fantasy bedrooms," as Grand-mère called them, were the stuff of legend. In the old days, only rich men had been able to afford the many pleasures found inside. But Grand-mère had a soft spot for soldiers, too, and they could enjoy offerings for far less.

Grand-mère had given me my mother's bedroom on the second floor and her studio in the bell tower. The oldest part of the house, that ancient wing dated back to the fifteenth century and had been imbued with magick by my ancestor, the original La Lune.

For all my parents' concerns, Grand-mère was quite liberal. One of France's great courtesans, she believed in women's equality and freedom and wanted me to explore all the opportunities her great city offered. She gave me a generous allowance on top of what my father provided and set few rules. The one she stressed was that if I chose to take a lover, I would promise to be careful and follow all the steps she outlined to prevent pregnancy.

Nothing, she insisted, could ruin a woman's life more than an unwanted child. Just as nothing was as rewarding as having a wanted one. Her son, my grandfather, had died before I was born, and Grand-mère could never speak of him without a smile accented by tears.

The war had ended in late 1918, and by 1919, there was a certain fierceness to Paris. As if people had been holding their breath and were finally letting it go and couldn't get enough fresh air. My brother was attending the Sorbonne and studying business administration, since his ambition was to open an art gallery and sell both my work and my mother's. He was also living at Grand-mère's house. As a man, he could come and go as he liked, but when it came to me, he was even more overprotective than our great-grandmother. Sebastian checked up on my whereabouts all the time. Mostly, he was worried that a young man would try to seduce me.

"You're vulnerable," he'd remind me. "You're not a city girl. These Parisians, especially those back from the war, are wily and know how to turn a girl's head."

"I'm not interested in romance, Sebastian. I only care about paint-ing," I always told him.

"You say that now, but there'll be a man who comes along, and you'll feel differently. He'll sweep you off your feet, and you'll forget you ever picked up a paintbrush."

I'd laugh at him, and as soon as he went out or retired to his bed-room, I'd sneak out and meet my friends in the bars in Montmartre, or in their studios, where, unlike me, they lived in squalor and artistic glory.

I'd meant what I'd told him. I really wasn't romantically interested in the young men I met. I was in love with painting. With seeing. Losing my sight for that long year and then regaining it had given me an appreciation that ruled my world. I yearned to learn all the tricks and hone my ability, so that one day, I could put down on can-vas the strange dream world that I saw all around me, with all of its shine and gloss.

Despite my freedom, I didn't take a lover the first few months I lived in Paris. I fraternized with the other students, joining them after class around the corner for coffee or wine at La Palette, visiting museum exhibits, going to nightclubs.

The war was over, but everyone was still learning how to live without a threat hanging over them. Paris was trying to heal, but she was wounded. And there seemed an endless flow of young disfigured or wounded men. Most of the men and the boys who'd been to war still had a glazed look in their eyes. What they had seen at the front couldn't be unseen. What they had endured couldn't be unlived.

During those first months at L'École, in addition to studying painting, I began learning more about my esoteric heritage at the feet of one of my mother's mentors, the publisher and mystical leader Pierre Dujols, who owned the Librairie du Merveilleux at 76 rue de Rennes, only a few blocks from Grand-mère's *maison*.

The bookshop also functioned as a salon frequented by all sorts of occultists, magicians, kabalists, hermeticists, and alchemists. France had been home to mystics since the Middle Ages. Spiritualism had been popular since the nineteenth century, and even the most respected dignitaries dabbled in the dark arts. In 1853, Victor Hugo began conducting a series of more than one hundred séances to contact his drowned daughter. The painters Eugène Delacroix and Gustave Moreau, the writers Honoré de Balzac and Gustave Flaubert, and the astronomer Camille Flammarion, just to name a few, were all fascinated with alternative beliefs.

Aside from the serious occultists and magicians, the bookshop also catered to people who were simply curious, like the Manhattan partygoers at the Stewards' penthouse who were fascinated by the idea of psychics, séances, and so on but would never have gone so far as to step into witchcraft.

Dujols had spent his whole life studying various disciplines and searching for the philosopher's stone. Often in the evening, his wife, Marie-Louise, offered card readings, palmistry, and séances. Although she was only in her early fifties, she had long white hair. With her very black eyes and strong bone structure, she looked like a Pre-Raphaelite painting I'd once seen of a Delphic oracle.

After the war erupted, the police began to reinforce an ancient law against fortune-telling in order to protect the country's desperate citizens who were trying to make contact with deceased loved ones. So many had been duped by charlatans. Madame Dujols had a true gift and the deepest respect for those who came to see her. Even so, she was forced to conduct readings in a hidden room of the bookshop in order to avoid arrest.

Immediately after meeting me, she asked if she could study my palm. Hesitant at first, I relented when she told me how she'd read my mother's palm when she was only a little older than I was and how she'd seen me in my mother's life line.

"I told her she would have four children," Madame Dujols said. "And Sandrine pulled back her hand as quickly as if I had burned it."

I laughed.

"I saw you and your brother, twins, caught in the currents. I told her that one day, you would save him from drowning."

"Very close," I said, impressed. The stories I'd heard about her and her remarkable clairvoyance were true. "He saved me. Not the other way around."

During the evenings and afternoons I spent with Marie-Louise, we talked about my second sight, and she shared stories of her own abilities and how she had come to integrate them into her life and not be afraid of them. Her advice came too early for me. I wasn't yet scared of my powers. They hadn't been exposed to the world yet. They remained untested. By the time I discovered how destructive my gifts could be, she was in Paris and I in New York, and I could only remember some of what she'd imparted.

Madame Dujols read my palm several times. She said she saw a break in my life line, a brush with death. And we both decided it was the afternoon that Sebastian and I had been swimming, when the rope had come loose and I'd almost drowned.

"And there will be two men in love with you."

"Only two?" I was twenty, and it didn't seem like enough.

She laughed and then said, "To have one man truly love you is a gift. Two is a miracle."

"Which will I marry?" I asked.

She shook her head. "I'm not sure."

"Do you see something wrong?"

I knew that unlike some clairvoyants, Madame Dujols didn't hold back when she saw danger or disaster or death.

"Does he die?" I asked.

"It's possible, Delphine. I'm just not sure. Let's look again in a few months. The lines change. Did you know that? Destiny is not fixed. It's a probable path, but life alters it. Otherwise, how boring life would be, *non?*"

All that fall and winter, I attended gatherings at the Librairie du Merveilleux and met many fascinating people, some of whom were working on the most arcane projects.

Pierre Dujols was writing and publishing several books. Two of his protégés, Eugène Canseliet and the much older illustrator Jean-Julien Champagne, were often found at a table poring over the rare manuscripts that filled the shop's shelves. There was talk that the two of them were working on a groundbreaking book, *Le mystère des cathédrales*. Their thesis suggested that alchemical secrets were encoded in the stone carvings and structures of Gothic cathedrals.

By May 1920, Paris was awash with flowers and leaves bursting forth on all the trees. Often after school, I walked through the Luxembourg Gardens to find scenes to sketch, honing my skill at capturing a scene quickly.

On May 16, in the late afternoon, I was walking around the pond, attracted by the young children with their toy sailboats.

The sun was in my eyes, and there was a curious shimmering around the white sails, making each of them look like a passage to dreams.

I'd just taken out my journal, turquoise leather with unlined sheets, and was sketching when I saw Mathieu Roubine, a man I recognized from the bookshop. He was Pierre Dujols's nephew, and he was helping a little boy who was fretting over a sail that wouldn't unfurl.

I watched with curiosity. I'd never been introduced to Mathieu, but from the first time I'd seen him, he'd looked oddly familiar. His interactions with the child made a charming tableau, but I didn't start sketching them because I was a sentimentalist. I was there to practice, and the composition of the tall man and the small boy had a symmetry to it that made a good design.

I'd thought it would be challenging to capture the sweetness and the details. To get the right expression of worry on the boy's face, the concentration on Mathieu's, and the movement of their hands and bodies bent toward each other.

Mathieu's reflection swam on the surface of the pond. The simulacrum seemed ripped. Light was pouring out through the center of Mathieu's back, as if he were made of paper and had been torn in half.

Mesmerized, I continued watching the watery image as a shadow crept up behind him. A man with the face of an insect—a metallic head, ovoid dark eyes, a hose where his nose and mouth should have been. Only when I saw the bayonet he held, pointed at Mathieu, did I realize the man was wearing a gas mask.

"Mathieu, watch out! On your right!" I shouted, as I ran toward him.

Startled, Mathieu looked up.

I continued running, prepared to—what? Push the attacker out of the way? I was hardly tall enough or strong enough to have done much good. But I wasn't thinking. I just knew he was in danger. Terrible danger.

I was in such a hurry that I didn't see the young girl on the bicycle. Afterward, between her sobs, she claimed I had run in front of her. Her wheel hit my right leg. I fell forward toward the pavement.

Mathieu was by my side in seconds. "Are you all right?"

Ignoring the throbbing pain in my leg, I looked around behind him for the assassin. No one was even close except the child. Where had the attacker run? Impossibly, he'd been there one moment and was gone the next.

"Are you all right?" Mathieu asked again.

The boy was watching us, seemingly delighted by all the excitement.

"Me? No. Yes. It doesn't matter. There was a man . . ." I turned and looked around again in confusion. "There was a man behind you."

"There was no one here."

"Yes, he was right behind you. Wearing a helmet—it was gleaming in the sun."

"A soldier?" the boy asked, even more excited. "With a helmet? Like a Hun?"

Mathieu's gaze shifted away from me, off to the distance. "But that's impossible." He reached up and brushed his golden hair off his forehead. His gaze returned to me as he peered into my eyes. "Who are you? How do you know what happened to me? How do you know my name?"

"I don't know what you mean about what happened to you, but I know who you are from the bookshop. I'm there quite often."

Mathieu cocked his head. "I haven't seen you." He seemed bothered. Then he looked over at the boy, at his boat, and back at me. "Can you wait a moment? I have things I need to ask you, but I was just in the midst of salvaging my nephew Charles's sailboat."

I nodded and prepared to stand, but I was a bit wobbly.

"Let me help you up."

He held out his hand, and I took it. His fingers were rough. His grip strong. Almost too strong. Once he'd pulled me up, I tested standing on my leg. There was only a little pain. I reached down and touched it. My stocking had ripped, but there was no blood. By that night, though, I'd probably be black and blue.

"You'll wait?" he asked again, anxiously.

"Of course," I said. "I need to get my supplies and my notebook anyway."

I walked back to the bench where I had been sitting, barely limping. My pencils and case were there but not the journal. Then I remembered. I'd been holding it. When the girl on the bicycle hit me, had my notebook gone flying?

I searched around but didn't see it anywhere. There was only one other possibility. I walked up to the edge of the pond. There was my lovely turquoise sketchbook, lying on the bottom of the shallow concrete pool.

"You dropped it because of me." Mathieu had come up beside me.

"No, because the cyclist hit me."

"But she hit you because you were running to me. Let me get it for you." He rolled up his sleeve and reached down into the water.

I was glad his back was to me, because I was sure I winced. His arm was a mass of ugly scar tissue, ropes of twisted, bubbled, white skin, stretched tight and shiny. I didn't have to ask. We'd all seen far too many war wounds. But compared with most, he was one of the lucky ones. He still had that arm, and from watching him fish my journal out of the pond, I could see that it functioned properly.

I tried to look away before he turned back, but he caught me staring. He handed me the journal. His fingers, I noticed, were unharmed and unscarred.

"I'm afraid it's ruined," he said, as he rolled his sleeve back down. For a moment, I thought he was talking about his injury, but then he continued. "And it looks like it was once quite a lovely sketchbook."

I didn't know what to do with the waterlogged and swollen mess dripping onto my shoes, so I put it down on one of the green metal chairs that ringed the pond.

"Will you allow me to buy you a café crème or a glass of wine?" he asked.

"So you can ask me questions, you mean, about what I saw?"

He smiled. It seemed an effort and a bit restrained. Almost as if he were giving away a secret. "That, too. Aren't you direct?"

"I suppose I am. I've never understood people who talk around things. My great-grandmother says it's not a very feminine or socially acceptable trait."

"Well, I don't understand people like that, either. There's enough in the world not to understand without them mucking it up even worse by being coy or obtuse," he said. "So your great-grandmother would find me socially unacceptable as well. But you won't, will you? So please accept my poor apology and a libation."

Before I could answer, the little boy Mathieu had been helping came running up, tugged on his jacket, and asked Mathieu if he could finish fixing the boat. He looked at me.

"It will only take a few minutes."

"Go ahead."

In the shop, I'd only seen Mathieu from a distance and not often.

But now I had time to study him. He looked to be a little older than I. Perhaps twenty-four or twenty-five. As he bent over the boat, the wind blew his hair onto his face. Light brown shot through with strands of gold that he wore parted down the middle, waving to his shoulders. It wasn't in style at all. Short, polished haircuts were all the rage. Were Mathieu's Bohemian looks a statement of individuality or a defiant stance against the establishment? I imagined him in a painting done by Jean-Auguste-Dominique Ingres, the famous eighteenth-century artist and one of my favorites. He'd paint him dramatically, at the bow of a boat or atop a steed, battling a foe.

Mathieu's face was a study in contrasts, from his wide forehead and aristocratic sharp nose to his almost too gentle mouth. There were secrets in his blue-gray eyes, unreadable to me, and an invitation.

I wasn't sure if I'd ever seen a man quite as beautiful.

He finished his repair of the toy sailboat and returned.

"The wine?" he asked.

I nodded.

"Wonderful. Let me just tell my sister-in-law I'm leaving. That's her, there."

When he returned once more, he offered me his arm, and we left the pond, Mathieu leading us toward the north exit of the gardens.

Looking back on it now, I don't remember feeling that those first steps were portentous. I did not know then that I'd met the man whose soul could speak to mine. Who would change the trajectory of my life. Who would tear my heart open.

As we walked, the twilight deepened, and the temperature dropped. Crushed grass and sweet wisteria scented our progress to the pavilion, where he secured us a table inside.

The Art Nouveau decorations were tasteful despite being ornate. The grapevine theme carried through the intricate carvings at the bar, the wrought-iron light fixtures, and the stained-glass shades and window panels. I hadn't been in every home, store, restaurant, or café that my father had built, but it only took me a few moments to know this was his work.

Mathieu ordered a carafe of red wine. As soon as the waiter departed, I asked him if he'd known that my father designed the restaurant.

"Is that why you brought me here?"

Mathieu looked at me quizzically. "Wait. Your father is Julien Duplessi? I've admired his work for years and have sought out all his buildings."

I nodded.

"I couldn't have known. I don't even know your name." He gave me half of one of his hard-won smiles. "Even though you know mine."

I introduced myself.

"Now I understand. My uncle and aunt have spoken about you— and your mother, of course. She's quite well known in their circle."

I nodded. "She met your uncle when she first came to Paris. They've been friends for twenty-five years."

The waiter brought the wine and poured us each a glass.

Mathieu held his glass out to me. I raised mine. He kissed the rim of my glass with his. He seemed about to say something, then changed his mind and finally said, "To an auspicious meeting. Thank you for coming to my aid."

I took a sip, as did he. And then his glance rested on my notebook. I'd put it on the corner of the table beside me. Picking it up, he examined the soggy mess.

"If you'll allow me, I can take it to my shop and try to salvage it. I'm a bookbinder, and I might have more luck than if you just set it on a radiator. You deserve at least that for coming to my rescue."

"Well, it looked like you needed saving."

He was silent for a moment. And I could almost hear him running through different responses in his mind. "I did." His voice dropped. "I still do, I think." His words sounded the way his burnt-vanilla, honey, and amber cologne smelled. He had a rich, gold-toned voice.

"Now, please, will you tell me again what you saw?" He hesitated. "I just hope I can bear hearing it."

I held off, a bit afraid. He was leaning forward intently. His eyes bored into mine. Worry lines creased his brow. His whole body appeared tensed, alert, as if about to be dealt a blow.

"It's all right. Go ahead," he urged.

"It's going to seem strange, and you probably won't believe me."

"I'm not sure why, but I think I'll believe anything you tell me."

His words sent sparks running across my shoulders and down my arms. My cheeks felt warm. I wasn't sure what to say. Sebastian had recently started getting me paid commissions for shadow portraits based on my peculiar expertise, but we never revealed my process. We simply said that I was good at reading minds and made it sound playful. But I knew I could trust Mathieu with knowledge of my special gifts. He was part of Dujols's world and associated with people who claimed to have far more bizarre talents than scrying.

"When someone sits for a portrait, if I put on a blindfold and keep my eyes closed, I can sketch shadows of things that have happened to them."

"Scenes from their life?"

"Yes. Usually secrets. Almost always secrets."

"But you weren't drawing me," he said.

Now came the embarrassing part. "Actually, I had been sketching the scene of you helping your nephew."

"And you closed your eyes?" he asked.

"The sun was shining right in my eyes. For a few moments, I couldn't quite see the real scene. When I opened my eyes, I saw the reflection of a man approaching you in the water. Or so I thought. Sometimes images also appear to me in a mirrored or reflective surface."

"So you're a scryer?" he said, with a mixture of awe and curiosity. "It's an ancient art. And you do it while you are drawing? That's quite astonishing. Does my uncle know?"

"He does, but I asked him not to tell anyone. I'm still learning about it."

"You can trust me. Now, tell me as exactly as you can. What did you see?"

"A man in uniform. Wearing a gas mask. And a helmet gleaming in the sun."

Mathieu's eyes clouded over. The odd blue-gray transformed into indigo.

"He was creeping up behind you, pointing a rifle . . . a bayonet and—"

"Stop."

"You don't believe me," I said.

He remained silent. The only movement on his face was a throbbing vein on the right side of his forehead. And then he stood up and walked away without a word. At first, I thought he must be headed to the WC, but no, he walked right out of the café.

Astonished, I didn't know what to do. I'd never been abandoned in a restaurant before, or anywhere else, for that matter. I didn't have enough money with me to pay the bill. I was furious. So what if what I'd said seemed unbelievable? He'd asked. He'd wanted to hear. Except it was my fault for telling him, wasn't it? My mother and I had talked about this before I'd left for Paris. We kept our abilities to ourselves. We didn't share them with people unless we knew them well and had developed a sense of trust. As I had just experienced with Mathieu, even the most open minds sometimes had trouble grasping what sounded impossible.

I picked up my glass to get the waiter's attention. If I was going to have to hand over my necklace for the owner to hold until I retrieved money from home and came back to pay, I thought I might as well enjoy more wine. I was certainly upset enough to want it.

It wasn't unusual for a woman to sit in a café alone, but I was uncomfortable nonetheless. People around us had seen Mathieu get up and leave. But that wasn't really the cause of my upset. I was disquieted because while Mathieu had sat across from me, looking at me and listening to me, when he'd reached out to take my sketchbook, I'd experienced an awareness of him unlike anything I'd ever felt before.

I'd liked boys in school well enough and had a few crushes for short periods of time. But they never amounted to anything more than girlish fantasies. My sister Opaline had a boyfriend long before she was my age, and I used to spy on them, even sneaking down to the beach to watch them. I was twenty years old, and I'd never gone to the beach with a boy at night. As I'd told my brother, I was satiated with my love of painting. With learning.

But Mathieu, with his golden hair and his eyes full of encroaching evening colors and his reticent smile, had touched something in me.

"I apologize." He was standing behind me.

I turned. More glad than I should have been that he'd returned and at the same time angry that I'd opened up to him and he'd walked out in the middle of my tale. I felt like a fool.

He pulled out his chair, sat back down, and drank half his glass of wine before he said another word. "I shouldn't have run out like that. But I couldn't listen to what you were telling me."

"No, it was my fault," I said, as I pushed back my chair, the legs scraping harshly on the tile floor. Now that he had returned to take care of the bill, I could leave. "I shouldn't have told you. I know you think I was making it up and trying to take advantage of you somehow. But I'm not. It's too complicated. That's why I don't talk about it." I made a move to get up out of my seat, feeling a tear slide down my cheek. I needed to leave before I embarrassed myself further.

But Mathieu grabbed my hand. "Don't go. I do believe you. It's complicated for me, too." He took a breath. "I don't talk about it, either. What you saw is what happened. We were ambushed. I can only remember parts of it." He closed his eyes for a moment and then opened them and began again. "A German soldier attacked me. What happened afterward . . . it's all blank." He began to rub his right arm. "But I have the evidence that he ripped my arm and my back to shreds. I almost died, but I didn't. So many in our unit died that day. My brother died. The worst day of my life. So please stay . . . Maybe you can see the rest of it."

My tears were flowing more freely by then. Not out of anger or embarrassment but empathy. Mathieu stopped talking, took his handkerchief, and wiped my eyes. As he did, he opened my heart and stepped inside.

The following week, there was a package by my place at the breakfast table. I opened it and found a sketchbook bound in Persian green-blue turquoise leather that was much more vivid and luxurious than the journal I'd accidentally hurled into the pond at the Luxembourg Gardens. This one shimmered like a piece of jewelry, all the more special because of the decorative silver tooling. Concentric circles in a modern design floated like bubbles coming up through water, and in the center, where two of them met, were my initials in block letters.

Opening the fine leather cover to the frontispiece, I read the words Mathieu had inscribed:

> *"To love beauty is to see light."—Victor Hugo*
> *I couldn't save your book, but please accept this one in exchange.*
> *From a very grateful believer,*
> *MR*

I sucked in my breath, remembering that long year when I had seen no light and had no beauty to look at. When in that darkness I had started to see secrets . . . secrets I was afraid of still.

In time, Mathieu's gift became more than a sketchbook. In addition to my drawings and notes about the art I saw and the art I wanted to make, I wrote everything that Mathieu and I did into my Book of Hours, as I came to call it. I created a log of every day we were together, where we went, what we saw, what we said.

Even then, at our very beginning, I had a premonition that my time with him was limited. That I had to preserve each memory like an insect in amber, for the days when I would be alone and bereft, missing him, mourning him, wishing for a different ending from the one I wound up forcing.

And so it was that four years later, in New York City, after Monty died, after Tommy and I parted ways, after I stopped wearing the blindfold and stopped painting, it was to my Book of Hours that I returned again and again. Reading each precious day over and over. If I could imagine no future, at least I could remember the oh-so-glorious past.

Chapter 8

I've decided only to share Mathieu here, in the journal he
made me, my special Book of Hours. I don't want to speak of
our romance out loud or try to fit it into mere conversation.
Normal words can't describe the magic of us. They will dilute
what is exceptional and wonderful and make it sound like
something ordinary.

I almost didn't see Mathieu today. We'd planned to meet
outside the florist shop two blocks from Grand-mère's house.
She was otherwise entertained, and I thought it would be easy
to slip out, saying I was going to an extra drawing class. She
usually didn't require any more detail than that, and I wasn't
usually any more forthcoming.

But as I was walking out the door, Sebastian arrived
home and urged me back in. Full of excitement, he grabbed
my hand and pulled me into the parlor to tell me about the
Russian noblewoman he'd met at the art gallery that handled
our mother's paintings, where Sebastian sometimes worked

*learning his trade. And that now Madame Botolosky wanted
to have her portrait done by me.*

*I was pleased, of course, but these commissions matter more
to Sebastian than to me. My concentration is on my classes.
Maman's training was excellent, but she focused mostly on
my style and substance. I agree with my professors, who have
pointed out that my composition and perspective sometimes
show room for improvement.*

*My goal—a lofty one indeed—is to have a painting in the
prestigious 1920 Salon d'Automne. An extreme effort because
I'll be competing with the Montparnasse painters—Marc
Chagall, Amedeo Modigliani, Georges Braque, and Georges
Gimel. All older, more famous, and far more experienced than I.*

*While I measure myself against these well-established
artists, my brother measures himself not just by how many
commissions he obtains for me but also by how high up in
society the sitters are. I want him to succeed. I need to know he
is happy. But today, despite my efforts to please him, I didn't
want to stay and discuss his newest conquest.*

*I wanted to see Mathieu and was afraid that if I was late,
he'd leave.*

*Torn, I longed to run off but felt that I'd be abandoning
Sebastian. As if anything I don't share with him is a betrayal.*

*Finally, I told my twin I was going to be late for a class
and, adding guilt to the other emotions coursing through me,
rushed out of the house.*

*I ran down the block and turned the corner, hoping Mathieu
would still be there, fearing he wouldn't be. But he was. Standing
still, the sun glinting in his golden hair, he was leaning against a
lamppost, reading a small book that, when I got closer, I saw was
a leather-bound volume of poems by Musset.*

*When I approached, he smiled and proceeded to read a
stanza out loud to me:*

Again I see you, ah my queen,
Of all my old loves that have been,
The first love, and the tenderest;
Do you remember or forget—
Ah me, for I remember yet—
How the last summer days were blest?

And then he took my hand, tenderly, carefully, as if it were fragile instead of a painter's well-exercised hand, and together we walked to a café on rue Jacob.

Inside, he got a table and ordered us two coffees. After the exuberance of his reading, we were a bit shy with each other and quiet. But the silence was comfortable in an unusual way. At least for me. I couldn't stop staring at him, no matter how hard I tried not to. But he was staring at me, too. We laughed, and after that, it was easier to talk.

When he realized I'd only been living in Paris since I'd started at L'École in September and had spent so much time at school that I hadn't really explored the city, he declared that he was taking it upon himself to be my guide.

"But I'm not going to show you the Paris of tourists . . . not even the Paris of the bourgeois. I'm going to show you my secret city."

Just the words thrilled me. The promise felt like an embrace.

Chapter 9

The morning after my dinner with Clifford, in that first week after Monty Schiff's death, New York City was immobile. More than five inches of snow had fallen overnight and was still coming down. I made a pot of coffee and was sitting by the window watching the flakes, lost in the same mindlessness I'd been wallowing in for a week.

At ten, Clifford knocked at my door, insisting that I come over and bring my sketchbook and pencils and work with him.

"I'd really rather not, I'm feeling—"

"I told you last night," he interrupted. "I'm not leaving you alone." And he gathered up my supplies.

Against the wintry scene outside his window, Clifford had set up an ersatz garden. Two men in summer suits and three women in flimsy chiffon dresses lounged on a picnic blanket. Paper flowers grew out of paper grass. Paper trees were taped to the window.

An uptown restaurant had commissioned the mural, paying handsomely to have a Clifford Clayton original grace their walls. Diners would enjoy his charming, slightly salacious, always beautiful scene and never guess that the flora and fauna and blue skies had begun in a snowstorm.

I didn't want to be there. But Clifford was stubborn, and I knew he'd be relentless unless I acquiesced. And maybe, I thought, if I forced myself to draw something new, I'd stop seeing that other horrific drawing over and over in my mind.

But as I stared at the models, dragging my pencil across the page, I felt a hopeless rush of ennui. Even my fingers rebelled against holding a tool.

After an hour of fruitless effort, I quit. "I'm going back to my studio," I told Clifford.

He shook his head. "I'll just drag you back here. Do just one more sketch. That's all. Then we'll brave the elements and get some lunch."

Although I didn't want to, the idea of fighting him required even more energy than doing what he asked, so I sat back down and tried again.

As I drew the man's arm around the woman's shoulders, my thoughts wandered to Clara and Monty. Where did the dark impulses that tempted them stem from? What kind of animals were we that our sexual urges put us in such extreme danger? Why did some people find themselves able to resist while others danced right into the abyss, eyes open, lips pressed together?

Clifford called a break after a half hour and came over to see what I'd done.

"Well, that's certainly different from how *I* interpreted the picnic," he said.

I had drawn one of the men with a tiger's head, the other with the head of a jaguar. The three women all had lush female bodies and snake heads. And they weren't enjoying a picnic on the blanket but were engaged in a naked bacchanal. I had turned the scene into an illustration of my thoughts.

After a few more days of Clifford's coddling, I told him that I needed work but couldn't return to my shadow portraits—not yet, probably never. He contacted a Broadway theater manager who'd been after him to do some work and pressured him into hiring me to do a poster for an upcoming play.

My assignment was to create an illustration for a romantic tale, *Dark Angel*, which would be opening at the Longacre that spring. The synopsis contained enough of the story to suggest ideas.

During the war, Captain Alan Trent—on leave in England with his fiancée, Kitty Vane—is suddenly recalled to the front, before having been able to get a marriage license. Alan and Kitty spend a night of love at a country inn "without benefit of clergy," and he sets off.

At the front, things go badly for Alan, who is blinded and captured by the Germans. When Alan is reported dead, his friend, Captain Gerald Shannon, discreetly woos Kitty, seeking to soothe her grief with his gentle love.

After the war, however, Gerald discovers that Alan is still alive, in a remote corner of England, writing children's stories for a living. Loyal to his former comrade in arms, Gerald informs Kitty of Alan's reappearance. She goes to Alan, who conceals his blindness and tells Kitty that he no longer cares for her. She sees through his deception, however, and they are reunited.

The plot had eerie similarities to my own life. A blind hero and a lover willing to sacrifice his happiness for the sake of his beloved. I cried reading it.

The job required that I deliver concepts first. Over the next two days and nights, with great effort and fortified by a few too many glasses of wine, I managed to sketch out some ideas. If I hadn't needed to pay my rent, I would have given up in the first hour. My concentration was off. My imagination was impaired. Even my lines were less assured than usual.

I showed Clifford my work. Inspecting my drawings, he suggested which two ideas were worth submitting.

I knew how lackluster my work was compared with what I usually did, but as it turned out, it was still better than what the theater manager usually got for the price.

In the background, I'd drawn a battlefield. In the foreground, Gerald held a wounded Alan in his arms. Looking down on both of them, like an angel above, was Kitty's lovely face.

In the second sketch, against the same background, Alan holds Kitty in his arms, saying good-bye to her before he goes off to war, and Gerald watches them. That second one was accepted, and I was commissioned to create the final poster.

I'd never struggled harder to accomplish anything. My fingers revolted at holding brushes. I could only stand at the easel for a half hour at a time without feeling fatigued. I didn't have a fever, a cold or cough, or a stomach problem, but I was ill. My soul was sick.

The first day yielded nothing worthwhile. Neither did the second. By the end of the week, I thought about resigning. But that would have meant disappointing Clifford, who'd gotten me the job. And I needed the money. My only alternative was wiring home to borrow some, which would worry my brother and bring up questions I wasn't prepared to answer. No one in my family knew of my broken engagement, and I wasn't ready to discuss that, either. It was all tied to my shame.

"Your visibility is an important part of your success, Delphine," my brother had explained more than once. "There's a cachet to your work. People whisper about it and about you. *Who is she? How does she do it?* We need to always keep them wondering about your mystique. Like Houdini, like Mina Crandon, hold them in awe."

No, I couldn't alert Sebastian. I needed not only to finish the illustration but also to do a good enough job to get more poster work.

Enough, at least, for rent. Even if I couldn't assuage my guilt, I had to function.

After a lost third day, I hired a model. Maybe that would inspire me. Gordon Belling was about my age, with long mahogany hair and high cheekbones. I had him pose first as Alan and then as Gerald, and while I sipped brandy, I filled pages with quick sketches of his form in various postures and attitudes. But when it came to the romantic stance, I was at a loss.

"Do you mind posing without your outer clothes?" I asked.

"No problem at all," Gordon said, as he took off his jacket and then his shirt and stood bare-chested, with just his slacks on. He smiled at me. "Is this all right?"

Was he flirting?

"Yes, better," I said, in what I hoped was a neutral tone.

As I drew him, I thought again about the instincts that drove us, our urges and yearnings and our passions. Where did they stem from? What was the purpose of our coming together? In school, they had taught us that sexual needs were nature's way of ensuring procreation. But was that all there was to men and women sharing one another's bodies? Was the pleasure simply there to tempt us so that we would continue to breed? If the story of La Lune had taught me anything, surely it was that sex wasn't just about procreation. But what *was* it about, exactly?

The following morning, I spread all my sketches out on the floor and chose the ones that best fit the characters. Then I blocked out the scene. I had the poses I needed for both men but not for Kitty. I had two choices: spend more money I couldn't afford on a female model or use myself. It would mean hours of looking into the mirror. But did I really have any choice?

That evening, I removed the chiffon from the entryway mirror, turned on the foyer light, took my sketchbook in hand, and looked.

It was just as I'd dreaded. The room was dimly lit behind me, and in the shadows were frightening shapes, swimming by, caught in a vortex. I felt nauseated but had no other choice than to bear it and work quickly, getting the angles right and then covering up the mirror again as quickly as I could. Within minutes, I was enveloped in freezing-cold air, causing my teeth to chatter and my fingers to tremble.

Once I finished the sketch, I drank more brandy, choking on it in my haste to warm up.

Later that night, I'd painted myself into the poster, in the handsome model's arms. It wasn't up to my usual quality. The painting lacked a certain clarity and crispness. If only I could have called on magick to improve this undistinguished work. But it didn't work that way. It was the same with my mother. Whatever magick we possessed was finite. Like everyone else, we relied on hard work. But this painting looked average. Would it do? It was certainly competent. And better than what most would produce. But that didn't mean I had to be satisfied with it.

I turned the easel to the wall so I wouldn't have to look at the painting. Then I poured myself a glass of wine and settled down with a book. I read only a few pages but was distracted and nervous. Not even a second glass of wine helped.

Sometimes drawing soothed me. I gathered some pencils and a pad and began to sketch a man, similar in form to Gordon but in a very different pose. Lying down, naked, he had a tiger's head instead of his handsome face, and beneath him, crushed by his body, I drew myself with the head of a swan.

Searching for answers in the lines and shading, I drew us over and over. On each page, exploring different positions—most I'd never known myself but could imagine. My hunger to learn more about the impulses I'd drawn in that horrible sketch of Clara and Monty consumed me.

What kind of animals were we that our sexual dances led to such tragedy? What was the point of so much passion? Mathieu was the only person I'd shared my body with. He was all I knew of that kind of fervor. When I was with him, it was silk and fire, wild colors, intensity and tenderness all at the same time. Transcendent and glorious, it felt anything but animalistic. Rather, it seemed as if our souls were meeting and joining. And yet our attraction to each other was dangerous, too, fated to end. The choice of just how tragically was left up to me.

During my explorations, I drew men with powerful bear, jaguar, or leopard heads and women with the faces of wise owls and sly foxes. Turning people into members of the animal kingdom, I searched for the perfect metaphors.

The following week, I received a second theatrical commission and hired Gary again. After I captured the pose I needed for the poster, I positioned him in more suggestive positions, always holding an imaginary woman, his arms embracing air. After he left, I drew myself in, trying, always trying, to understand the ephemeral meaning that lay tantalizingly just beyond reach—the reason for all of this.

Once I completed the drawing, I threw myself onto my bed and touched my body, appalled but curious about how the act of painting these dreams made me so hungry for sex. Tommy and I had been only moderately physical with each other. He'd pushed for more, but I had resisted. Not because I didn't enjoy his kisses and caresses, but something always held me back. So many women didn't resist after the war. Tommy said he admired my strong sense of morals. And I let him think that; it was easier than trying to explain something I couldn't talk about. I'd only been with one man, and he was still very much in my heart.

So it was ironic that February, for me, a twenty-five-year-old artist and self-imposed celibate, to be alone and finally aroused after ending the two-year relationship I'd had with a man I thought I was going to wed.

A wildness I didn't know I possessed took me over during those winter weeks in New York. I cut my hair and enhanced the red with henna. I drew darker lines around my eyes. I didn't eat as much as I drank. When I glimpsed myself in the mirror, I saw the wantonness that I felt. Almost desperately, I tried to stop making the drawings I indulged in. Tried to prevent the debauched fantasies that filled my mind. And when I couldn't, I attempted to convince myself that this was an artistic quest, an aesthetic search for a carnal truth. Wasn't there merit in looking for answers? Wasn't it an artist's job to find a metaphor and use it to explain the human condition? After the war, didn't each of us need to find out what it was that had driven humans to act with such inhumanity? Wasn't I just searching for the fence that kept us on one side of the animal kingdom and the beasts on the other? Or were we really just beasts ourselves?

And every night, before I went to sleep, I tortured myself by reading another entry in my Book of Hours. Wallowing in the magnificent pain of remembering what I'd had and what I'd given up.

Chapter 10

Today began with rain, but by the time I met Mathieu at the florist around the corner from Maison de la Lune, the sun was peeking out of the clouds. He was waiting in a hansom cab and told the driver to proceed to an address in the tenth arrondissement.

"Today," he said, "is the beginning of your secret tour of Paris. Every spot chosen for your enjoyment and delight."

Once we arrived at our destination, after he paid, Mathieu helped me out. A few steps off the boulevard de Strasbourg, we came to an arch leading to a small alley. Taking my arm, Mathieu led me into a passageway lined with shops. We stopped at no. 34 Passage du Désir, a chocolatier. He purchased one small sack of chocolate-covered orange peel. Back outside, he opened it and pulled out a piece.

"Open your mouth, and close your eyes. Don't bite on it at first, just let it start to melt. There's an art to eating fine chocolate."

I did as I was told, and he fed me. My body reacted to the

delectable citrus and cocoa flavor and also to the intimacy of the act. Once the chocolate covering had melted, I chewed the candied peel.

Before I could open my eyes, Mathieu leaned forward and kissed me. My entire being reacted to this small act. Two lips pressing two lips. His tongue explored just a bit. It was shocking. But not unwelcome. Suddenly, I was unsteady. My mind reeled. I tried—but failed—to absorb and understand what was happening. A unique feeling. One kiss, a hundred sensations. I smelled the chocolate and the oranges and his burnt-vanilla, honey, and amber cologne, and the scents mixed and merged and, along with the pressure from his lips, went right to my head.

In the midst of the explosion, a voice inside me whispered, Pay attention to all this, Delphine. Savor this. It is extraordinary. Make the memory of it even as it happens. Delight in it . . . don't squander it.

After a few more moments, Mathieu pulled back. He looked down at me and smiled his secret smile. An invitation to a new world of touch, taste, and smell, so tempting and powerful, sensational and special.

"How did you know?" I asked.

"What?"

"That it would be all right to kiss me?"

He laughed. And then became concerned. "Wasn't it?"

"It felt as if . . ." I struggled for the words.

"It felt, dear heart, as if we had both been moving toward that kiss for lifetimes. Is that what you wanted to say?"

I nodded. Surprised he'd understood exactly what I hadn't even begun to express.

"One of the great mysteries," he said, running his finger down my cheek, "is what makes two people right for each other." He touched his finger to my lips and then outlined them

as if he were drawing them. "Sometimes I think we spend too much time trying to figure out the how of things—the war, man's inhumanity, destiny, genius . . . one simple kiss that the whole world fits into. All that matters is that we try to live the best things and turn our backs on the worst."

And then he held up the bag of chocolates.

"Now, which would you like? Another of these? Or another of these?" And he touched the center of my lips with his fingers, which set off a new avalanche of sensations.

After our second kiss, he steered me out of the passage and down one street and then one more until we reached our next destination. The short street looked fairly ordinary. Apartment houses lined both sides. A Gothic church stood at its end.

Mathieu pointed to the street sign: rue de la Fidélité.

I read it. Thought for a moment. Then smiled. "Rue de la Fidélité. We were just in Passage du Désir," I said.

"You catch on quickly."

"And where are we going now?"

"You'll see."

As we walked toward the Saint-Laurent church, he told me that it had been built in the sixth century as a monastery and then rebuilt in 1180 and rebuilt yet again in the fifteenth century. Mathieu peppered his history lesson with the story of a parishioner, a young widow, who in 1633, with the help of her confessor, Vincent de Paul, created the Daughters of Charity order to help the poor and care for the sick. The community, he told me, spread to all corners of the world and was still active in areas as far afield as Israel, the Americas, and Australia.

"They say her body is incorruptible," Mathieu whispered in a forced dramatic sotto voce. "She's been nominated for sainthood."

"How do you know all these details?"

"My uncle started the bookshop with the idea of specializing in what fascinated him: all things unexplained—magic, the occult, mysteries and miracles, ancient wonders, spells, curses, hidden treasure. Growing up around him and in the shop, I've become just as fascinated with the arcane and esoteric."

He stopped and pointed to the street sign. "Here we are. From desire to fidelity, and now we're on rue de Paradis."

Every store on the street was dedicated to the arts de la table. Every window display of crystal or china tempted. The buildings were a combination of styles from the last fifty years; the passage of time was visible in the tile work, the stained glass, and other architectural details.

Mathieu led me to Baccarat's store. As we walked through the elegant lobby, its giant glittering chandelier cast tiny rainbows on the floor, the walls, even our faces and hands.

Inside a large, high-ceilinged room were cases of historical objects all produced by the glass manufacturer, dating back to the late 1700s.

"These," he said, pointing at a set of goblets, "were made by Count Thierry for his mistress in 1826."

I looked at the wine and water goblets. Five sizes, each a watery shade of pale blue, highly faceted and with ornate silver filigree work on the stem.

"The count had the glass matched to his lover's eyes and ordered more than one thousand of them in the years they were together. Only these six still exist. All the others were smashed."

"Why?"

"The count was so jealous he didn't want anyone to drink from a glass touched by her lips. Each goblet she drank from was destroyed after she used it."

Mathieu took my hand.

"Always love to the point of madness," he said, "or else what is the point of love?"

Chapter 11

The calls requesting my attendance at parties continued. Monty's death had actually increased my notoriety, and the more I stayed away, the greater the demand. But I couldn't return to the circuit. Clifford traveled a lot that late February, and I was lonely by myself. I could have done a party every night, but until the first week of March, I resisted, stayed to myself, and explored the strange series that had seized my imagination, filling page after page with ideas, never satisfied with any of them. Not willing even to try to commit one to canvas. Without putting my blindfold on to sketch, nothing was turning out right. But I couldn't . . . wouldn't ever again. Even if I was alone. Even just to explore my imagination.

"You can't just disappear, Delphine," Muffy Van Buren insisted. Born into one of New York's wealthiest families, she had married into an even wealthier one. Both she and her husband were great patrons of the arts, and while he favored Renaissance masterpieces, she focused on discovering new and fresh talent. Once Clifford had introduced us, she became fascinated with my shadow portraits and was now my biggest supporter and a good friend. "And I want you at this party. Consider it your reentry into society."

Muffy was only six years older than I, but she'd been raised in a more conventional way, befitting women in high society. She hadn't bobbed her hair or raised her hems. Although publicly she professed to be scandalized by my lifestyle, in private she whispered that she envied my freedom. Visiting my studio that afternoon, she'd been both shocked and titillated by my current canvases. After viewing them, she picked two that she wanted to purchase when they were completed and then decided I needed some sustenance.

"So will you come?" she asked.

We were sitting at a marble-topped table in the dimly lit Caffe Reggio on MacDougal Street. Owned by Domenico Parisi, an Italian immigrant, it had an atmosphere that was both exotic and artistic. The walls were filled with paintings, one supposedly from the school of Caravaggio, although I doubted its provenance. I was equally suspicious about the marble bench that Parisi claimed came from a Medici family estate in Florence. But there was nothing dubious about the elaborate chrome-and-bronze espresso machine, topped with an angel, its base surrounded by dragons, that sat in the position of honor and brewed the most heavenly coffee. Since the place had opened in 1902, it had become a favorite gathering spot for so many artists who lived and worked in Greenwich Village. That afternoon, I noticed two other painters, Arthur Davies and John Sloan, both from the Ashcan school and quite well known, seated across from us in the tiny restaurant.

Muffy said she had been worried about me since I'd dropped out of sight and wanted me to come to her birthday party the following week.

"You can't just hide away forever. We all miss you."

"I won't put on my blindfold if I come."

The waiter brought over our steaming cappuccinos, a drink Parisi had introduced to New York.

"That's fine. I don't want to hire you. I want you to have some fun. You look . . ." She hesitated. "You look like you need some. And you need to show off that new do—it's so brazen."

As she sipped her coffee, I thought she'd chosen the perfect word.

I felt broken and brazen. I was a miserable artist, barely making my own way in New York. Maybe it was time for me to get out of the studio and put some distance between me and the Clara and Monty incident.

"Delphine? What did you do to your hair?" Tommy asked.

I'd only been at the party for a half hour and had only had one glass of champagne. I wasn't ready to see my former fiancé quite yet. It had been almost a month since he'd delivered his coup de grace and severed our relationship. But there he stood, examining me with a disturbing scrutiny.

"Are you all right?"

"Of course."

"You look . . ." He trailed off just as Muffy had.

"How do I look?"

"Different."

"Is that so?"

"Wild."

I laughed.

"Your hair . . ."

"Yes, I dyed it."

"But it's almost orange."

"I prefer copper."

"And your dress."

"You sound quite idiotic, Tommy. Are you going to dissect me completely?"

"Well, the dress makes you look practically naked."

"It's no business of yours, but I'm not even close to naked. It's simply a flesh-colored slip with a sheer chemise over it."

He was still staring. Then he leaned down and said, sotto voce, "I miss you terribly."

I shrugged.

"I don't suppose you might let me take you home later tonight?"

I laughed sardonically. "No, I don't suppose I might."

"I've heard you are painting couples mating."

I burst out laughing. So Muffy had been talking about the paintings I'd shown her, and word had already gotten around.

"Yes, that's a nice way of putting it. I call them 'Exploring the Beast.' I'm just following in the surrealist footprints of what's being done in Paris."

"But you are a woman. All of the Surrealists are men."

"I see you've been listening to your parents' dinner conversation. So they are, and so I am," I said, as I drained my glass of champagne. "Be my savior, will you, and get me a refill?" I held out my glass.

"You're acting as if you've had enough."

"One can never have enough champagne."

"*One* might not, but you have. Delphine, you're not yourself."

"No, I suppose not. I looked death in the face and didn't much like what I saw."

Tommy, though not strong enough to stand up to his parents and fight their boycott of him marrying a Jewess, was still fond enough of me to be worried and to do something that in the end had unforeseen and far-reaching ramifications.

For a long time that spring and into the summer, I cursed him and his meddling and hated him for interfering with my life after he'd walked out of it. Looking back from a distance, though, it's clear that in his way, he did, in fact, save my life. My depression, drinking, and dissolute ways had me headed for disaster.

But three weeks after Muffy's party, on an ordinary Wednesday afternoon in late March, when I heard the knock on my door, I didn't know that.

I'd woken up and begun drawing without bothering to dress. I often did that in those days. My animal series kept me in a state of perpetual bewilderment. I'd expected to find understanding of our impulses and impetus to embrace danger, but insight still eluded me.

I kept waiting for that ephemeral spark to come back into my world that had disappeared since I'd put my blindfold away in a glove box. For good, I had thought.

Wearing a silk robe with a green and blue circular pattern on it, and nothing underneath, I sat at my easel and drew a man with a faun's head, lying on a zebra rug in a jungle that was similar to Gauguin's but a bit more realistic. The man on the rug was, of course, nude. The woman sitting astride his midsection looked a bit too much like me, with her short curly hair, extreme cheekbones, pouty lips, and flashing eyes.

I'd stopped drawing twice so far to check my position in the mirror, to figure out first a bend in an arm and then a curve in a leg. I had some charcoal smudges on my cheek and on my breast where my robe gaped open. There were black fingerprints on the label of the bottle of wine sitting beside me. I'd started drinking early that day.

When I heard the knock, I pulled the robe a bit tighter and opened the door, expecting it to be the food I'd arranged to have the restaurant on the corner send up. Clifford was away, and I was a dreadful cook. Making plans took too much energy. After the long days of frustrating drawing, I needed something to eat before working all night or venturing out to another party.

But when I opened the door, the man who stood there wasn't holding a tray of food. In one sweep, his evergreen eyes went from my face to my chest and past me to the canvas of the fawn on a rug, naked and tumescent.

"*Mon Dieu*, Delphine! I was in touch with Clifford, who said he was watching out for you. But then Tommy wrote and said you were in bad shape. He certainly didn't exaggerate," said my twin, as he sauntered past me into my studio, taking in the bleak scene. "Thank goodness he alerted us. And thank goodness you broke off your ridiculous engagement to him. Not only is he totally unsuitable and ordinary, but it would have meant your remaining in New York forever. And that would have been completely unacceptable."

My brother, to whom I was closer than anyone else, whose hand I had been born holding, who managed my career from afar and sold my paintings in his gallery, rearranged my robe on my shoulders and then took me in his arms.

Sebastian towered over me by at least six inches. I tucked my head under his as he rubbed my back in little circles, the way he had done all my life. I wanted to cry, but this time no tears came.

Chapter 12

"You need to come home with me, Delphine."

Sebastian and I were sitting on my velvet-covered couch, drinking the strong coffee he'd insisted on brewing instead of the wine I wanted to pour. Outside, the sun was setting. I hadn't turned on the lamps, and my studio had taken on the gloom of twilight.

"No, I live here now, in New York." I gestured to the window from which one could see the rooftops and water towers that constituted my city view.

"Maman could see with her scrying that things had gone terribly wrong. She was coming to bring you home."

"Why didn't she, then?"

"She contracted some kind of food poisoning, so I took her stateroom."

"Maman never gets sick." It was true. My mother had uncanny health, thanks to the potions and elixirs she made.

"Oysters." He shrugged. "It is possible for even Maman to succumb to a poisonous crustacean." He stood. "I'm getting more coffee. Do you want some?"

"No."

He walked to the kitchenette, still chattering. "We have tickets to return home on the SS *Ile de France* on Tuesday. Enough time to pack you up, pay the bills, and leave."

"But I'm not going with you, Sebastian. I'm happy here."

"Happy?" Sebastian laughed sarcastically. "You are as far from happy as I've ever seen you. It's as if you are somehow getting pleasure from the pain you are in. It's masochistic. It's hard to leave something that's broken and do the work of moving on, but you must."

"I don't understand anything you just said."

"I have a friend studying psychiatry in Zurich, and he's explained to me the theories being expounded at the clinic there. You need to come back home. You need to remember who you were and give yourself a chance to reclaim that, Delphine. You don't have to stay in France forever if you don't want to, just until the end of summer. I've put together a dozen commissions for you."

"I can't do shadow portraits anymore. Ever."

"Why?"

"I just can't. Ever again."

"We'll talk about it, but if you really can't, then fine. You won't have to put on the blindfold. We'll arrange for ordinary commissions. As if"—he winked at me—"any of your work could be ordinary."

When we were children, that wink had been a secret we shared. His acknowledgment that we were twins, connected in ways that our other siblings weren't.

"Come home with me, Delphine. We'll go to the beach and get all brown. Maman will make magick spells to cure you, and Papa will spoil you with presents. You can come back here in the fall if you must, but you can't stay now . . ." He spread his arms out. "It isn't healthy for you anymore."

My brother and I didn't look very much alike. I favored my mother, with my russet hair and honey eyes that flashed almost orange. Sebastian looked like my father, tall, with hair the color of raven's wings and dark forest-green eyes.

"I am fine," I insisted.

"Are you blind? Look around. There are plates and glasses everywhere. Clothes dropped wherever you took them off. Empty bottles of wine gathering dust." His jaw was tight, his hands clenched into fists. His anger was a red aura around him.

But I was angry, too. We never referred to the time I'd lost my eyesight. He knew better than to raise the specter of my nightmare, and yet he had. And so callously. And he knew it.

"I'm sorry, Delphine. But you are being so stubborn. Always stubborn." Picking up his cup, he stomped into the kitchen and made more noise than was necessary, first cleaning out the coffeepot and then starting a new one.

I often felt Sebastian's fury inside my own chest, like a ball of fire, burning me. I also sensed his fear as cold, puckering my skin. His sadness affected me, too. As if the ground under me was giving way.

His pleasures eluded me, though. When passion overwhelmed him, I wasn't aware of it. If he was happy, the only way I could tell was by hearing laughter in his voice.

My mother always said my judgment was clouded when it came to the negative aspects of my brother's character. She loved him, too, of course; he was her son. But she said she saw his faults and I didn't. How could I? He was my savior and protector. Maman said I made him into a star that shone too brightly and that it wasn't good for either of us. Whenever she could, she would point out one of his failings, but instead of listening to her, I'd become defensive and argue with her that she wasn't being fair to him.

Now Sebastian walked over to my easel to inspect the drawing of the faun on the zebra rug. The silence in the studio was broken only by the sound of a bird outside. After a long minute, he turned back to me.

"A debauched life, Delphine, is poison for a talent like yours. You were given an amazing gift of sight and the ability to translate what you see onto a canvas. You create mystery and magic. You can't throw it away over people you barely knew who made mistakes that weren't your fault and a man who didn't have the guts to stand up to his parents for you."

"I know. Tommy was . . ." I sighed. "I'd been wrong to think that we ever had a chance."

"You couldn't have known. Clifford told Maman. Tommy insulted you by throwing you over, and his parents have insulted our entire family. What confuses me is that I know you didn't love him. So why—"

"I don't want to talk about him or his parents."

"You must exact revenge." Sebastian's eyes twinkled. "Come home with me. Come back to Cannes. We'll relaunch your career. Your star will shine. You don't need the Prouts and their money. You don't need to be a part of their collection. One day soon, they'll beg me to buy one of your paintings, and I won't sell it to them. Now, won't that be sweet?"

As a child, I was too sensitive to being teased, and my school years were filled with tears. It's easy for children who don't understand infirmities to make fun of them. For fourteen months, I was blind, and then, until age fourteen, I wore thick glasses while my mother continued working her magick. During that time, I was the recipient of much cruelty. No one ever teased me twice, though, because anyone who made me cry was subjected to Sebastian's retaliation.

From frogs in lunch pails, to homework assignments mysteriously missing, to rumors about cheating on tests, Sebastian was a master at exacting revenge. When the unkindness to me was especially malicious, Sebastian would get me to read the troublemaker's secrets and reveal them in anonymous notes to our classmates.

My parents didn't approve of his efforts at all. They forbade him to retaliate, but he flat-out ignored them, risking and then suffering their ire. Whenever he was caught, they punished him severely, taking away all privileges. More than once, I overheard my parents talking about Sebastian's mean streak and how worried they were for him. I didn't see what he did as cruel. I was never brave enough to retaliate on my own behalf, and I loved my brother all the more for stepping up as my defender.

Sebastian could be devious and vengeful and, in business, ruthless, but I always saw it as proof of his love for me. My mother warned me that I was wrong. And what transpired in the summer of 1925 proved it.

Chapter 13

Almost as soon as we'd left New York Harbor and I started breathing salt air, I began to escape the tight confines of my own thoughts. The stranglehold of the images I'd drawn at the party and those I'd witnessed as Monty fell to his death began to loosen its grip.

The farther we traveled and the more space there was between me and the buzzing metropolis, the less frenetic I became. Walking the deck every morning and afternoon with Sebastian, eating three meals a day, and not disappearing into my complicated canvases settled my soul a bit.

On our third day out, I woke up early and went on deck to watch the sunrise. I was contemplating the vast ocean and its ceaseless swells. Thinking about how little control any of us had. The sea's motion lulled me into a state of calm. Suddenly, I understood that it wasn't Monty's death or my relationship with Tommy that I'd been mourning in New York all those weeks. I hadn't been drinking to drown the sorrow of those losses. But rather, it was because I couldn't accept that my gift, my own precious gift, was evil.

But how could it not be? I'd ruined my own life with it and now the lives of three strangers. And yet I still yearned to put on the blindfold. The magick of seeing was a drug.

I'd been trying to resist its pull by sedating myself with wine, by entering into a series of paintings more provocative than anything I'd ever done, so much so that I was almost embarrassed for anyone to see them. And neither effort had succeeded.

I couldn't imagine my life as an artist without wearing my silken mask. But I knew that doing so would be too great a risk. The bigger problem now was how I was going to convince Sebastian that he couldn't ever ask me to wear it again.

During the crossing, we discussed my professional future often, and while he promised me that the work he was getting me was all on the up-and-up, he made it clear that the shadow portraits were where I would make my mark as an artist and that if I wanted the kind of success our mother enjoyed, I couldn't abandon them for long.

Each time he brought up the shadow portraits, I remained silent. I had never been able to talk my way out of Sebastian's control before, and I was very uncertain about how to do it now.

By the time we docked in Le Havre, I'd gained some much-needed weight and had stopped consuming so much wine. Even if I hadn't figured out what to tell Sebastian about the future, my head was clearer than it had been in a long time. I was not less unhappy, but I was less confused.

We immediately drove north to Cannes. As soon as the car started its climb up our driveway and I got my first glance at the pale-pink Art Nouveau villa my father had designed every inch of, I felt a surge of relief. Things would be better now that I was home. Getting out of the car, I smelled the cypress trees that encircled the house. Fuchsia bougainvillea vines climbed the walls. Forest-green ceramic pots of night-blooming jasmine flanked the door. Yes, things would be better now that I could wake up to the south's golden light flooding in through the extra-large windows my father had installed.

That night, we ate in the dining room at a rosewood table with carved wisteria vines creeping down the legs, sitting in matching chairs. On the walls, my mother's murals of lush gardens brought more of the outside in. She'd arranged for a feast of all my favorite dishes, especially those that weren't plentiful in New York in the winter. A big pot of bouillabaisse, the freshest green salad with olive oil pressed only miles away. Crusty bread, still warm from the oven, and butter churned at the farm our housekeeper's husband owned. For dessert, there were oranges and runny cheese and more of the bread I'd missed so much in America. And with it all, crisp white wine that smelled of summer grass and sunshine. I had two glasses but refused my parents' customary eau-de-vie after dinner.

That first dinner at home was a quiet affair, with just Sebastian and my parents and my favorite cousin, Agathe, who lived nearby. My older sister, Opaline, and my younger sister, Jadine, were both living in Paris and had written warm letters of welcome. They would be coming home to visit but not until later that season.

After my cousin left and my brother had returned to his own villa at the end of Palm Beach, my parents kissed me good night. Upstairs in my childhood bed, I fell asleep almost right away and had my first dreamless slumber since the party on Fifth Avenue almost two months before.

When I woke up, I guessed the reason. After I had breakfast with my parents on the terrace overlooking the sea and my father left for his office, my mother asked me if I'd like a second café au lait.

"Yes, thank you. And speaking of coffee, what did you put in my tea last night?"

"Did you sleep well?" she asked slyly.

"You know the answer as well as I do."

"Wasn't it a relief?"

"Yes, but you should have asked me, Maman. I'm not a child. You can't trick me into taking medicine."

"It wasn't medicine. Just a sleep draft to give you some peace. I can see how much you need it." She smiled at me, as if her interference was completely acceptable, and smoothed my curls down with the flat of her hand.

The sun was shining into the kitchen, and even in the direct light, my mother looked like a young woman, no more than thirty instead of a fifty-five-year-old mother of four grown children. My father and great-grandmother both also looked at least twenty years younger than their actual ages. We all knew that the spells my mother used to reverse an illness or save a life sometimes resulted in slowing down the aging process.

She'd worried that when she restored my eyesight, she might have interfered with my development and that I would be stunted at age nine, but I'd grown up according to schedule after all.

My mother had taught me many of her spells. And as was the custom among daughters of La Lune, she gifted me with my own grimoire when my menses arrived at age fourteen. Unlike my sister Opaline, who was a jeweler and had initially avoided learning the witch's trade, I'd sought out lessons from a young age. I craved the power and ability that my mother had. Much of it was subtle, but she could sway people's minds with a glance. She was a great seductress. Even though she clearly was devoted to my father, she enjoyed melting men's reserves in her presence. Often after a party, I heard her and my father laughing about how so-and-so had left smitten or this one had made a fool of himself trying to impress her.

But nowhere was my mother's talent more visible than in her paintings. She captured magick in every canvas. Her elaborate creations were unique, although you could see the lingering echoes of her symbolist teacher Gustave Moreau in her decorative work. She used Greek and Roman mythology to create illustrative tales that often no one but she understood but that everyone was drawn to. She also did portraits, very personal studies highlighting the obsessions of close family and friends. Opaline's portrait showed her inside the facets of a ruby. Sebastian appeared on a ten-franc note. I was portrayed in pools of paint on an artist's palette. She painted my father in the reflections of all the windows of a building he'd designed.

"We need to speak of some things," she said now, as she walked toward the table with the fresh coffee. "All right?"

"Yes. Of course."

I'd been dreading this postmortem conversation. But given the depth of my mother's insight—a combination of empathy and sorcery—I had expected it.

"I was on my way to New York to get you myself, when I got sick," she said, as she poured hot milk and coffee into my cup at the same time.

"Sebastian told me. He said it was food poisoning."

"Yes. But I don't think it was as simple as that."

"You think it was more than just food poisoning that ailed you?"

"I think I was being a mother, sick with worry over her two grown yet still quite young children," she said.

"Children? What do you mean? Does someone else need rescuing?" I asked.

"Sebastian. He's not the same when you're not around, you know that?"

"No, not really."

"Since childhood you relied on him in many ways, but you functioned fine emotionally without him. Sebastian, on the other hand, is always a bit adrift without you as an anchor."

I took a sip of the coffee, surprised by her revelation.

"The letters we got from New York, first Clifford's and then Tommy's, worried us all," she said.

"I can understand why. I'm sorry they wrote. It wasn't their right. I needed to sort things out on my own."

"But you weren't doing a good job of that, according to them."

I resented her comment. Most mothers have no choice but to watch their children make mistakes and subsequently learn from them or not. But my mother was different. She could influence and even reverse what appeared to be reality. My brother and sisters and I all felt that as a mother, Sandrine was too powerful, that we were often at her mercy, even though she meant well.

"That's your opinion. You weren't there," I countered.

"Either way, you're here now. That's what matters. You're home, where you can heal. And you will. You have the strength to do it. You are like me that way. But Sebastian isn't, and . . ." An odd expression crossed my mother's face.

"What is it?"

She shook her head. "I shouldn't have brought this up on your first morning home. But Sebastian was so clearly back to himself last night with you in his orbit. It was difficult to miss. I can see his aura dim when he's been away from you for too long. You fuel him, *ma belle*. I've always known that his talent feeds off yours. And some of that is all right. He's a showman, a salesman, a dealer. He needs to have artists to present and promote. But he's too dependent on you. And it worries me."

My mother had never been so forthright with me about my twin. I had always thought of myself as the weaker one. I had never considered that he might be dependent on me.

"There's no harm to it, though, is there?" I asked.

She drank some coffee before continuing. "I'm not so sure. I don't often get uneasy, and when I do . . ." She stopped talking. Took another sip. "Sebastian is just too reliant on you. Be aware of it, Delphine. All right? I don't want him to drain your spirit."

"Of course."

"Now, let's unpack your paintings," she said, standing, seeming relieved. "I want to see the work you were doing."

"I'm not sure I'm ready for a critique," I said.

"I'll go easy on you."

"You never have before."

"You never needed me to before." She smiled down at me and smoothed down my unruly curls again, the way she'd been doing since I was a child. She was my beautiful mother, La Belle Lune, the extraordinary artist who had restored my sight, had given me my talent, and yet could be as critical of my work as a stranger.

The crates weren't in the house but just down the path, in my mother's studio. With our arms linked, we walked there together.

Inside, we pried open the wooden containers and pulled out my Petal Mystique series of canvases. My mother didn't examine them until we'd removed them all and leaned them against the walls.

I'd never seen them all in one grouping that way, and I, too, studied them closely. She nodded as she stood before one and then another.

"These are good. Almost groundbreaking. Surrealistic, with a decided *féministe* bent. The boys will be angry when they see them. They haven't accepted a mere female into their midst except as a model."

Then she unrolled the drawings and canvases I'd done since the accident.

The jungle settings and hyperrealistic beastly men and women in various states of passionate embraces were hard for me to look at for long. I hated recalling my state of mind when I'd created them. Despite what they were missing—technical polish and more resolution—I couldn't deny that a part of my soul, dark, angry, and wasted, was exposed in these charcoal strokes. They were nothing like anything else I had ever produced. I couldn't predict if my mother was going to like the work or what it told her about me.

As she looked at them, I didn't see my mother but the artist, Sandrine Duplessi, in her studio, seriously contemplating a young painter's frenzied work of two months.

Finally, she turned to me, her benign expression unreadable. "I'm sorry, *ma petite belle.*"

She turned away from my work and walked to the center of the room, where I'd been standing, and joined me. It wasn't until she got closer that I realized she had tears streaming down her face.

"What a terrible time you've had. I knew it was bad. I felt it when I shut my eyes and focused on you, but I didn't have any idea. How lost you have been. Yes? And still not found."

And then she took me in her arms, and I let my own tears flow freely.

Chapter 14

Book of Hours
June 9, 1920

My secret outings with Mathieu have affected all areas of
my life. When I am not with him, everyday activities such as
studying, painting portraits, and dining with Grand-mère
seem hazy and unfocused. As if I am in limbo, waiting for
when we will be together. Everything only comes into focus,
all of my senses only come alive, when I see Mathieu.

"Here is a place lovers come to hide," Mathieu told me,
as we walked through the Jardin des Plantes. He pointed
out a Lebanese cedar planted in 1734 and led me up a stone
walkway to a shining pergola made of iron, copper, bronze,
and lead. Beneath that, we walked through a tunnel into
a deep green valley with a stream running through it and
masses of delicate flowers.

We sat among them and kissed.

"Victor Hugo once said that life is the flower for which love
is the honey," Mathieu said, when we broke apart, breathless,
both of us wanting more.

I buried my face in his neck and inhaled his scent. "Honey!

There's honey in the fragrance you wear. What is it called?" I asked him.

"A perfumer makes it for me, quite near your great-grandmother's house. Let me take you there. I want to buy you a perfume. And then put it on you here . . ." He touched behind my ear. "And here . . ." He ran his finger down my neck. I arched to expose more skin to him. "And here, too . . ." He touched my collarbone. "And then here . . ." His fingers slipped down my chemise to my décolletage. "Will you allow me?"

I was about to say of course, when he kissed me again, and all words were lost.

The shop was, in fact, on the same street as Grand-mère's house. I knew it well. My great-grandmother bought her perfume there. But I'd never stepped inside until Mathieu took me there this afternoon.

All the walls were paneled in mottled antique mirror. The ceiling, too, was mirrored. The corners were decorated with pink-tinged fat angels and flowers in a mélange of pastels, painted in the style of Fragonard. The four small Louis XIV desks scattered around the room looked like originals, as did the smattering of chairs with avocado-green velvet seats and the glass and rosewood cabinets filled with antique perfume paraphernalia. Oversized bottles of the house's fragrances lined mirrored shelves, with the signature fragrances front and center: Blanc, Verte, Rouge, and Noir.

Mathieu introduced me to an older man whose son he'd served with in the war. Charles L'Etoile invited us to sit down.

"Now, tell me about yourself," Monsieur L'Etoile asked. "What colors do you favor?"

"Very deep burgundy, silver lavender—"

"Turquoise," Mathieu added.

I smiled at him.

Monsieur L'Etoile dipped his pen in a crystal inkwell and wrote down my answers.

"Do you prefer the forest or the beach or the garden?"

"The garden and the beach. We had both growing up."

"Where was that?" he asked.

"Cannes."

"I know the area well." Monsieur made more notes. "We grow our own roses not far from there, in Grasse. Just a few more questions. What is your favorite fabric?"

"Cashmere."

"And do you prefer the sunlight or a night sky of stars?"

"A moonlit sky."

He wrote down my answer with a smile. Then he looked at me and held my glance for a long moment. He turned to Mathieu. "If you'd like to wait, it will be about fifteen minutes to a half hour. It's pleasant in the garden. We'd be happy to bring you some chocolat chaud or coffee?"

"The garden, bien sûr," Mathieu answered. "It's one of my favorite ways to spend the time it takes to make up a scent. Delphine, choose the chocolate; it's as velvety here as at Angelina's," he said, mentioning my great-grandmother's favorite tearoom.

Outside, we sat in wicker chairs with thick cushions in an ornate rose garden. In a few minutes, a young woman came out carrying a silver tray with a plate of madeleines, a pot of chocolate, and fine Limoges cups. She poured the ambrosia and left with a nod.

"Charles planted these rosebushes, importing heirlooms from all over France and England. He cultivates hybrids here before he has them grown in Grasse. His goal is to create scents other houses can't imitate."

I sipped the fine chocolate and munched on a freshly baked cookie, marveling at the exceptional garden, drunk on the tastes and the scents swirling around me.

Mathieu reached out and ran his fingers around my wrist and then up my arm.

"What is this?" he asked, touching the mark near my shoulder.

I was wearing a new rust-colored watered-silk dress and hadn't realized the cap sleeves had little slits in them until that moment.

We never spoke of my birthmark outside the family, but I wanted Mathieu to know about it. I told him about the crescent-moon-shaped mark every daughter of La Lune carried somewhere on her body.

"It's a secret," I warned. Even after a dozen years, the memory of how my schoolmates had taunted me and hurt me for being different still lingered.

"I promise never to tell," he said, and then leaned over and kissed the sliver of my pale moon.

Monsieur's assistant came to get us and escorted us back into the shop. We sat down with the perfumer, and he presented me with a crystal flacon. There was no label. On the silver cap was the engraving of a crescent moon with a star inside it.

I started.

"What is wrong?" Monsieur asked.

"This sign—is it your insignia?"

"Yes, the House of L'Etoile has used it since we opened our first shop in 1780."

"It's a symbol that's part of my family history, too," I said.

"I'm aware of that, Mademoiselle Duplessi. Our families have been acquainted for a long time. My father was a good friend of your great-grandmother. As was my grandfather."

I felt myself blush. A good friend was how Grand-mère

*always referred to the gentlemen who'd availed themselves of
her salon when she was one of Paris's great courtesans.*

"Now, for your scent."

*He opened the bottle, tipped and pressed it to a pale green
swatch of fabric, and then, with ceremony, handed it to me.*

*I inhaled. The fragrance was creamy and well rounded. I
couldn't identify any particular flower or spice, but rather I
was treated to an impression. The perfume smelled like colors:
deep burgundy, pale pink, and midnight blue streaked with
silver. Mysterious like the night, it was secretive.*

*"If you like it, you can try it on," Monsieur said. "It will
smell different once it warms on your skin."*

*I reached for the bottle, but Mathieu took it first. He pressed
his forefinger to the opening and then, with a lover's gentle
touch, stroked the perfume onto the insides of my wrists, the
space behind my right ear and then my left, and after that ran
his finger down my neck.*

*I had forgotten that Monsieur L'Etoile was watching. Was
it shameful of me not to care? I stretched out my neck as the
scent released its full bouquet, which was both an invitation
and a promise.*

"What is it called?" I asked Monsieur L'Etoile.

*"Custom scents don't have names as such. We mark them
with a number that corresponds to the customer. This is
Duplessi number sixteen. Are you pleased with it?"*

*"It's perfect," I said. "I'll never wear anything else." I was
delighted at the idea that I now had my own scent. I turned to
Mathieu. "Thank you for my gift."*

*Mathieu paid for the purchase, and once we were out in the
street, he stopped to bury his face in my neck.*

*"It smells like you, only with roses and lilacs and wind
and salt from the sea added. But that's just on your neck. I
will have to test it and see how it smells on other parts of*

you before I can make an absolute determination. Will you allow that?"

He was asking me if I was ready for us to become lovers. Did I dare say yes? I wanted to. To say yes, yes, please, now, today, before it's too late. There it was again. That terrible feeling that our time was limited. A verse I had learned in school came back to me, Andrew Marvell's cautionary poem:

> *Had we but world enough, and time,*
> *This coyness, lady, were no crime. . . .*
> *But at my back I always hear*
> *Time's winged chariot hurrying near;*
> *And yonder all before us lie*
> *Deserts of vast eternity.*
> *Thy beauty shall no more be found;*
> *Nor, in thy marble vaults, shall sound*
> *My echoing song; then worms shall try*
> *That long-preserved virginity,*
> *And your quaint honour turn to dust,*
> *And into ashes all my lust:*
> *The grave's a fine and private place,*
> *But none, I think, do there embrace.*

Chapter 15

My mother wanted to coddle me, and for the next few weeks I let her. I ate what she cooked, drank what she poured, read the light and frivolous novels she purchased for me, walked on my beloved beach, and inspected all the new shops that had sprung up in Cannes in the years I'd been gone. Most of all, I stayed away from pencils, charcoal, paintbrushes, and canvases. And although I tried to keep my Book of Hours hidden away, I found myself reading a passage every night, wistfully indulging in glorious memories, punishing myself for even thinking I could have lived the rest of my days with someone like Tommy.

The bright sunshine and sweeping sea view were such a contrast to New York City, and I couldn't quite acclimate myself to having left one place and being in another.

April ended. May began, and my mother's gardens came into bloom. I discovered I could waste a whole afternoon sitting under the wisteria arbor, smelling its sweet perfume, reading and dozing.

I had always enjoyed shopping with my mother. Indulging in silks and velvets, perfect pastels, and deep gemstone-colored fabrics was as sensual an experience for me as it was for her. We were artists first and saw fashion through that lens. That season, she took me shopping at all the best boutiques. The long pants and jersey jackets in neutral tones that they were showing suited my mood and my frame. I let my mother dress me like a doll. It was a relief to be pampered. Although dear Clifford had been such a comfort to me throughout my years in Manhattan, nothing beat my mother's attention. It was as healing as the sun.

She bought me a pale cream-colored crepe de chine jacket with my initials embroidered on the breast. A half dozen white silk blouses. A Lanvin evening dress, a column of black edged in jet beads. At the jeweler, she bought me two long strings of pearls that glowed like the moon. She spoiled me at Coco Chanel's shop with two pairs of wide-legged pants, one white, one black. And long silky jersey sweaters to go with them. She took me to the salon, where they reshaped my hair and tinted it back to my original color. With the copper gone and the new cut, I looked less wild and more sophisticated.

At night, I let my parents distract me with evenings at their favorite restaurants and music at the best jazz clubs and cabaret shows up and down the Riviera.

Only when I tried to envision the future did I flounder. Or when I read too many passages in my Book of Hours and remembered too much of what it had been like to be in love. To make love.

My mother found me sitting on the terrace staring out at the sea on May 16. I was especially pensive; it was the anniversary of the day I'd met Mathieu.

She sat beside me and took my hand, looking down at it as if she could read the lines etched there.

"Madame Dujols used to read my palm," she said. "When I lived in Paris at your great-grandmother's house. She told me so many things about you and your brother and your sisters—even though none of you had even been born. Even that you'd have a broken life line. And here it is." She pointed.

I nodded. "She showed it to me, too. I think it must represent the time I almost drowned. When Sebastian saved me."

We were both quiet for a moment.

"Maman, can a curse be reversed?"

"Sometimes."

"How?"

"Each curse would have its own spell. Why?"

I shook my head. "Just something I was thinking about."

"Maybe it's time for you to start drawing a little. You've spent enough time processing what happened. You need to turn your back on the past and take some steps forward."

I knew I looked better than when I'd arrived fresh off the ship. Taking walks in the sea air, sleeping well thanks to my mother's elixirs, eating our cook's food made with all fresh ingredients grown in the hills beyond our house, and drinking sparingly of the rosé wine the region was known for—Cannes was bringing me back to life. But was I ready to pick up my pencils again?

Sebastian, who lived at the Palm Beach end of the Croisette, only fifteen minutes away, visited and dined with us almost daily. He was delighted when I told him I'd begun drawing a little.

"That's marvelous. I'll start talking to clients about some portraits—"

"No." My mother intervened. "Give your sister time. Don't rush her on this, Sebastian."

And I needed time. My thoughts were still in disarray. I wasn't ready to paint, only sketch. And not compositions from my imagination but basic beach scenes or still lifes. I didn't know what I wanted to tackle next. Not the Petal Mystique series. That was from another time and place. Not Exploring the Beast, either. I hadn't learned what I'd hoped to learn from those pieces. I still didn't know why we were driven to self-destruction. Why were we tempted by what was forbidden? Why was it that the path that would bring us peace was always the one we resisted the most?

"All in time," my mother said, whenever I asked her how much longer it would be before I knew what I wanted to do next. Before I could see the steps I needed to take to get to the next plateau.

I knew she was right, but it was hard to wait. Impatience, like stubbornness, was ingrained in my character. Inherited from the woman who insisted that I now subdue both traits.

One afternoon, close to the end of May, Sebastian arrived and pestered me into going to an opening at his gallery that evening. So far, I'd avoided any fetes, but my parents had gone to Paris for the week. The truth was, I was lonely in the villa.

"Put on a pretty frock. I'm showing Marsden Hartley's new canvases, but all eyes are going to be on the prodigal daughter of La Belle Lune returning home."

My brother had wanted to be an artist when we were very young. We both clamored for brushes and paints when we were only toddlers. By the time we were six, my mother was giving us both art lessons. I had exceptional talent for one so young. Who knew whether it was the witchery I'd inherited or my own innate talent that guided my hand and my sense of color? Sebastian's ability, though, was commensurate with his age.

My mother—fair in all things when it came to her children—still had his early work and mine hanging on her studio wall. Sebastian's paintings had a six-year-old's exuberance and delight. Mine were sophisticated, even for a L'École des Beaux-Arts student. Naive in terms of composition but with technique far beyond my years. I don't say this out of pride or to boast. I didn't work for this talent or fight for it. It was as much a gift as my red hair and orange-brown eyes.

Without the magick spark that would have elevated his work from that of an apprentice, Sebastian's interest in learning how to paint quickly waned. The one trait we'd all—both daughters and son—inherited from our mother was her ambition, and so Sebastian moved on, searching for something at which he could excel.

By the time I regained my sight, my brother determined that

one day he would be my dealer, the way Pierre Zakine was Maman's. With my parents' permission, he turned a long hallway in our house into an art gallery. As he continued to be interested in the business of art, my parents did everything they could to encourage him. I think my mother always felt a little bit of guilt that her daughters all had special abilities as part of their La Lune legacy, but Sebastian, because he was male, didn't.

Sebastian's interest grew throughout his adolescence, and he worked in a local gallery after school and during holidays. At twenty-one, he achieved his dream and opened the Duplessi Gallery on the Croisette next door to the Hotel Carlton. There he sold my work, some of my mother's, and the paintings and sculptures of other artists he'd discovered through her and her contemporaries, most of whom had ateliers and took on students.

He had a good eye and an even better business mind. He understood that the best galleries featured a mix: the stylistically avant-garde to get people whispering about how bold he was, classics to soothe the soul, some lower-priced art to inspire impulse purchases, and other pieces that would be considered investments. People were desperate to forget about the horrors of the war and set their eyes on beauty. Dabbling in the local art scene appealed to the tourists, and so the gallery flourished.

That night at the Marsden Hartley opening, I was impressed by the guests who stopped by for a look at the new paintings and to sip a glass of champagne and engage in some witty repartee. Mixed in with the French were quite a few Americans who had left the States for the more libertine and much cheaper lifestyle in France. Sebastian introduced me to Gerald and Sarah Murphy, who arrived with F. Scott Fitzgerald, and to Jean Cocteau.

Aware of the artists and writers Sebastian now included in his circle, I saw my brother in a new light. He'd done a rather good job of finding a place for himself in this world. What a long way he'd come since our Paris days, when I was at L'École studying and making close connections with my fellow classmates and he struggled to work his way in as an outsider. I was the first artist he ever represented, and now I wasn't sure he needed his witch of a sister and her shadow portraits any longer. As pleased for him as I was, I felt a little left out and wondered if I'd ever find my own circle after abandoning Paris and living in New York for so long. Hating that I was indulging in self-pity, I found a waiter who was happy to refill my champagne glass.

I was wandering through the exhibit, thinking that perhaps I should leave, when my brother waved at me from across the room and motioned for me to come over.

Reaching his side, I found him standing with the renowned opera singer Emma Calvé, whom I'd met briefly years before at the Dujols bookshop in Paris. I remembered how everyone flitted around her, in awe of her stardom.

"La Diva." My brother introduced her, using the name by which she was most well-known. "This is my sister. Delphine, Madame is an old friend of Maman's, and she said she thinks you two have been introduced before."

I extended my hand. She took it and held it in both of hers. A critic had once said she had the voice of an angel—an angel of darkness. I'd never heard her sing, but she looked the part, with raven eyes and hair to match.

"We have met, I'm sure. You weren't with your mother, though. I would remember that. I knew Sandrine when she was young. I haven't seen her in years. You look like her, too, but that is not why I think we've met. Who could forget your glorious red hair? Where do I know you from, dear?"

Her musical training was audible in her speaking voice. It poured like molten gold, without impurities. She'd aged a little since I'd seen her last—she was heavier—but her somber beauty was still arresting and her eyes still sparkling.

"It is nice to see you again, Madame," I lied. She exuded nothing but benevolence, and yet all I wanted to do was run from her, get back in the car, and go home. "We did meet once before, in Paris," I said. "At Pierre Dujols's bookstore."

Madame Calvé was one of the greatest divas of her time and had created the major roles of Mascagni and Massenet, but it was her Carmen that had made her famous. She was said to have performed the character as a wanton woman, leaving nothing to the imagination, employing diabolical witchery to seduce Don José. And from what I'd seen of her in Paris, I never doubted it. Madame had been a regular at Librairie du Merveilleux, where Mathieu's bookbinding workshop was also housed. Interested in the esoteric and spiritualist movement, Madame had attended many lectures given by Mathieu's uncle and contemporaries, and I'd often seen her in the audience.

Dujols had some of my artwork on the walls of the shop. When she'd inquired about them, he introduced us. The exchange couldn't have lasted for more than a few minutes. Of course, I'd remember meeting a great star with more clarity than she would remember being introduced to a young painter just starting out.

"Ah, yes. And you were a friend of Mathieu Roubine, weren't you? He was engaged to be married. Did you know? The woman broke his heart. His uncle told me it never healed."

For a moment, I felt as if I couldn't breathe but forced myself to act nonchalant. I couldn't react. After keeping Mathieu a secret for so long from everyone but my older sister, the last thing I wanted was for the truth of our romance to be revealed at this moment with Sebastian at my side.

Was I the fiancée she was referring to, who had hurt him so badly, or had there been someone after me, the idea of which made me feel worse? I was nervous just hearing his name. I longed for him still. I always would. Our connection was forged with unbreakable bonds. But I was Mathieu's poison. In New York, he'd been an ocean away. Now it was just a train ride. Far too close.

"I did know him slightly. I'm sorry to hear about his troubles."

And then, changing the subject, I asked her, "Are you in Cannes for the summer? Do you have a house, or are you visiting friends?"

I was thankful when she didn't notice my abrupt transition, but from the way my brother was looking at me, he did.

"Yes, visiting friends, but I do have a house nearby. An afternoon's ride away, in Millau. I've retired, but I still have soirees there and take in students for the summer."

The aura around Madame Calvé changed from a soft peach to a teal blue, and I knew that for all her greatness and success, she was supremely unhappy and frustrated. My instinct was to put my arm around her and comfort her, but of course, I refrained.

She continued, "My house is the reason I'm here. I bought it in 1894, after I had learned its history. It's said that in the Middle Ages, Nicolas Flamel, the greatest alchemist of all time, was given a rare and magical book called *The Book of Abraham the Jew*, which was rumored to hold the secrets to immortality and transmutation. Flamel spent more than twenty years traveling the world trying to learn its secrets. And once he did, they changed his life. Eventually, the book was stolen by or fell into the hands of Cardinal Richelieu, who, according to legend, was obsessed with learning Flamel's formulas. At some point toward the end of his life in 1642, he hid the book in my chateau."

As befitting any world-class opera singer, Madame Calvé had the skills of both an actress and a storyteller, and she was calling on all her powers to draw me in. I couldn't resist the melodious voice spinning the tale. And at the same time, I sensed danger. Then I thought myself foolish. I'd only had a fleeting impression of something malevolent. It could be nothing. Or a connection to the history of the book she was talking about, not related to her at all.

"Flamel was a great sage and seer," she was still explaining, "and in his lifetime was known for his kindness and generosity. When he was eighty years old, he faked his and his wife Perenelle's deaths and funerals so they could travel to India and live with the mystics for eternity. Some say . . ." Madame paused for effect and lowered her voice theatrically. "Some say they are still alive almost six hundred years later."

Cold pinpricks crept up my arms and down my back.

"My house is holding on to its secret," she said, "which is why I came here tonight. To talk to you. I'm quite desperate."

"I don't understand," I said.

"Madame Calvé has a proposition for you, Delphine," my brother interjected.

I was startled. I'd been listening to her story so intently I'd forgotten his presence.

"I want you to come and paint a portrait of my house," Madame said, leaning in toward me, her eyes pleading. They were the most enchanting eyes, I thought, and along with her voice, she was using them to hypnotize me.

"Please," she whispered. "The *Book of Abraham* is concealed somewhere in the house. It has been since Richelieu secreted it there. I've tried everything to find it, and still the treasure eludes me."

"I'm so sorry, Madame. I'm no longer doing any shadow portraits. And even if I were, they are of people, not châteaus."

I glared at my brother. He'd ambushed me without warning. Set the trap and led me into it.

"Please? I told your brother I'll not only pay for your time but also offer a generous bonus if you can find it."

How could I escape this conversation? My shame, my fear, my frustration, my anxiety and indecision over my future as an artist were all coming to the surface here, with all these people around me. How could Sebastian have been so insensitive?

Looking for an excuse to get away, I scanned the room and noticed Henri Matisse. He caught my glance and smiled. Matisse was one of Maman's oldest friends. They were both the same age and had studied with Gustave Moreau at the same time in Paris in the late 1890s, and they had remained close. Their styles could not have been more different. She created jewel-like fantasies; he painted bold still lifes and interiors that had a sensual looseness and freedom. For most of my life, he'd lived just the next city over, in Nice, and was at our house so often he'd become like an uncle to me. While I'd been away, his beard had started turning gray, and his round glasses appeared to have become thicker.

"I'm sorry. I'm really not taking commissions now. I do hope you'll excuse me," I said. "One of Maman's friends needs to speak with me. I hope you enjoy the show."

I was so grateful for the excuse to get away from her that when Matisse opened his arms to give me a hug, I threw myself into them.

"When will I be seeing your work hanging on these walls again?" he asked, after kissing me hello, his beard scratching my face in that familiar way that made me feel so welcome.

"I just—I just got back," I stammered.

"In March. It's June next week." He held me at arm's length and examined my face. "Too much sadness there." He shook his head. "It's not good to stay away from home for so long. We're glad you're back. Your beautiful *maman* was worried about you. Your brother has not been himself."

"So I've been told," I said, thinking about how angry I was at Sebastian for setting that trap. Why had he done that? Why was he so desperate to get me to paint? Surely he didn't need the money; the gallery was obviously thriving.

Matisse took my arm and walked me outside onto the terrace, where he procured two glasses of champagne, one of which he handed to me. "Now, tell me, *ma petite belle*, why did you stay away so long? What really happened to you in New York?"

Other than my parents, Matisse was the only one who used that endearment. I wanted to answer his question—he'd always been so understanding and kind to me—but I couldn't bear the thought of repeating my sad tale of woe.

"I painted my way into a nightmare," I said.

"Too hard to talk about it?" he asked, with empathy in his eyes.

I nodded, not trusting my voice.

"Well, I'm glad Sebastian went to retrieve you. We all missed you. You'll have to come to the studio. There are some new cats you haven't met. And a litter of kittens, if you'd like a companion."

When I was little, my mother would take me with her when she went to visit him in his studio. A prankster, he always played tricks on me to make me laugh. And then, while he and Maman talked, he'd set me up with watercolors and paper and encouraged me to paint portraits of his cats.

Before the end of every visit, he'd give me a few lessons and an assignment to work on and bring with me the next time I came.

Every cat we ever had at our house over the years had come from a Matisse litter.

"Come see me next week. I would love to sketch you a little and listen to your tales of travails in New York City. I want to visit there one day. I think I would enjoy its energy and certainly its music. Is the jazz as exciting as they say?"

"It is, yes." I smiled, remembering.

"I can't get enough of its rhythm."

"You should go; you'd love it. With all the skyscrapers, it's nothing like Paris. You'll walk around looking up, never at your feet."

"Not seeing where you're going." He shook his head. "That could be dangerous, Delphine. Not to mention messy if a dog preceded you on your path."

We both laughed.

"Well, even if you aren't ready to show, tell me what you are painting."

"I seem to be at an impasse."

"Creativity takes courage, *ma chère*. Don't punish yourself if you run out of bravery for a while. But at the same time, don't forget that work cures everything."

"But it was work that made me leave New York," I said.

"And love as well?"

"More precisely, *not* love."

"You know what I think? In love, the one who runs away is the winner. So you've done the right thing," he said.

We were interrupted by a friend of Matisse who'd just arrived. I kissed the master good-bye and promised to visit soon.

Alone on the terrace, I watched the party going on through the glass doors. It was the perfect time to leave. Sebastian was busy entertaining and wouldn't even notice. I walked back inside and headed toward the door. Just before I reached it, a hand gripped my wrist. I felt the force of the grasp before I could register to whom it belonged.

I turned. Madame Calvé's eyes glittered intently. "Please," she said in a low, pleading tone. "Consider my request. I'm afraid if I don't find the book, someone else will. And in the wrong hands, it could be terribly dangerous. If it—" She broke off and shook her head, as if she was afraid to explain any further.

"I just can't," I said, and, without any other explanation, slipped out the door of the gallery into the cool, breezy night, which was suddenly much warmer than my skin.

I didn't look back. I didn't want to see that beseeching look in her eyes. As I walked along the esplanade, watching the moon's reflection dance on the gentle waves, I focused on its rhythm and considered how similar it was to the jazz that Matisse thought he needed to travel across the Atlantic to hear.

But it was Madam Calvé's words that kept returning. Not those about her château and the alchemist. But what she'd said about Mathieu. My heart seized up thinking about him.

There were certainly others alone that night on the Croisette, but I only noticed couples strolling arm in arm or sitting on benches, stealing kisses. Mathieu had been my one chance at love. No matter where I fled, that truth would forever follow me.

I realized I was even more lonely at home in Cannes than I had been in New York. I missed my routine, my lovely studio, and the Tenth Street crowd. I missed painting. And family dinners with Clifford. Most of all, I missed the distance that separated Mathieu and me. It was the only thing I had to keep him safe.

Chapter 16

Book of Hours
June 16, 1920

As I lie here under the maroon satin covers in Grand-mère's mansion, I'm swooning, both amazed and confused by what transpired during my afternoon with Mathieu. How is it possible to feel such a deep connection with a man I hardly know?

Today we met at the bar of La Rotonde on rue Montparnasse at five o'clock after my last class. Mathieu was waiting for me. I'd never been before, and the restaurant's decor delighted me.

"Just look at all of these paintings and drawings!" I exclaimed, as I examined the walls covered with works by so many of the artists I knew of through my mother—Picasso, Modigliani, Braque.

Although I had never visited before, I had heard of this legendary café. It is said that when an artist doesn't have money to pay for his meal, the owner, Victor Libion, accepts artwork in exchange. He's always letting artists sit for hours nursing a ten-centime cup of coffee and pretends not to see when they take the ends of the baguette from the basket. He claims that one day, he will have one of the best museums in Paris. And I don't doubt it.

Mathieu ordered pastis for both of us and showed me how to add water to it and turn the liqueur cloudy. It tasted of licorice but not as sweet.

He gave me another gift today, the third from this man who seems to know so much about me and how to move me and touch me, even though we've only just recently met. I never before allowed myself to think of anything like this happening to me. It was enough that I had my magick thanks to Maman and my life thanks to Sebastian saving me. But love? I never imagined anything like it—this overpowering exultation, this exaggerated sense of experiencing every moment, every taste, every scent.

I examined his present. Mathieu had salvaged some of my drawings from the ruined sketchbook and carefully pressed them out and bound them together in a simple black leather folio with a silver design on the front.

"You saw all my poor, pathetic attempts and silly notes." I was embarrassed. I wanted him to think of me not as young and inexperienced but as an able partner.

"I saw your talent and sensitivity." He smiled and touched the tip of my nose with his forefinger. "You're far too hard on yourself. Why is that?"

I wasn't sure I liked how he was talking to me. "Even though I'm five years younger than you, you don't have to treat me like a little girl."

"Oh, I know you aren't a little girl."

He leaned forward and kissed me, full on the lips. A long kiss that tasted of the pastis and passion.

"And that should prove it."

I felt the heat flush my cheeks.

"*Do you believe you are a good artist?*"

"*Good, yes. But not great. And I want to be great. I want to try new things, but I don't have the tools. When I look at one of my mother's paintings, I see—*"

"*But your mother has been painting for so much longer than you have. How can you compare?*"

"*I've seen her work from when she was just starting out. She was exceptional from the very beginning. Almost unnaturally so.*"

Mathieu tilted his head. "*Isn't that the answer?*"

"*You know the story?*"

"*My uncle told me he aided your mother in her search for the truth about her ancestor La Lune. And then he helped her accept the spirit of the long-dead witch. Your mother's paintings are the result of three hundred years of talent, aren't they?*"

I nodded.

"*Then why are you so impatient?*" *he asked.*

"*That's what my teachers ask me.*"

"*And what's the answer?*"

"*I want to show in the Salon d'Automne.*"

"*But you're only in your first year at L'École.*"

I shrugged. "*Do you think that's a good enough reason to stop me?*"

He laughed. "*No. Does this mean there is a problem?*"

"*No, not really. It's just that I'm so busy.*" *I told him about Sebastian being my business partner and how he'd encouraged me to use my second sight to create the shadow portraits and the commissions that he was bringing me that were eating away at my time.*

"*Are you sure you want to be doing them?*"

"*Yes, of course. Why?*"

"*Every artist should be free to forge her own path. It sounds as if he's pushing you onto a road that works best for him.*"

"No. It's what's best for both of us," I insisted. "Sebastian has no gifts himself, but, like our father, he supports our mother and sisters in ways even more admirable, because he doesn't have our magick to rely on. He makes things happen through his own natural strength, intelligence, and determination."

"Are you sure he's not taking advantage of you?" Mathieu asked.

I was surprised and hurt that he would think that of my twin.

"Of course not. I want to do this. I help people with my portraits, help them come to terms with loss or find deeper truths that have remained elusive to them. And not all of my portraits are dark or depressing. Not everyone has such secrets—some are mere embarrassments, others memories that are lovely and amazing. My ability gives people the chance to see them in living color and mount them on their walls to enjoy. Some portraits provide hope, some give warnings of danger to come."

"And what happens when they don't? When they are secrets that shouldn't be exposed?"

"That's not happened. Besides, Sebastian has vowed to destroy any that my sitters find too disturbing. That's a strict part of our deal."

The expression on his face still suggested disapproval. We were having our first disagreement, but I wasn't ready to concede. Impatience wasn't my only character flaw. Maman accused me of stubbornness, too.

"You know, if you consider my shadow portraits evidence of Sebastian's exploitation, what do you have to say about virtually everything you and your uncle sell in your shop? Aren't you exploiting your knowledge of the occult for monetary gain? How is what I'm doing any different?"

"We are very selective with our clientele and the items we put on display. As you know, the Librairie is meant to serve as a safe haven and discussion place for those truly interested in the esoteric."

He gently took my hand and held it. His touch was so potent that for a moment I forgot what we were even discussing.

"My point, dear Delphine, is just that you should be the one to decide how and with whom you share your gift, that perhaps your brother might be exerting too much control."

I withdrew my hand and moved my fingers to the folio he'd given me. I fondled a page and focused on the thickness and smoothness that only an artist could admire.

"Thank you," I said, focusing on the book now. "This is so lovely. So is the journal you gave me."

Mathieu gave me a long look, acknowledging that I'd changed the subject.

"I hope you fill that with dreams."

"The quote you inscribed in the journal, what you just said, so many things you say, and the fact that you create books. Are you a writer as well as an artist?" I asked.

Mathieu looked away from me, quickly picked up his glass, and downed what was left in it. Catching the bartender's eye, he ordered another.

"Once I thought I could be a poet," he said.

When he didn't elaborate, I asked him why he'd said once. Perhaps the drink had made me bold.

"The same thing that changed everyone and everything. The war happened. My brother died. Even if I saved other men, my brother died. I lived. How do you make sense of that? Encapsulate it into verse? Everything I saw for all those years was an utter waste. All the pretty words I knew drowned in blood."

Suddenly, I felt a cold, wet darkness surrounding him and

*me, like a mist falling over us. I watched his face change. A
frown marred his smooth forehead. His eyes had gone almost
black.*

*And then, even in the gloom, I saw the beginning of a faint
glow emanating from his chest. Yes, the war had ripped him
open and filled him with terrors and trouble. But some of his
former spirit endured.*

*I leaned forward and did something I had never done
before in my life. I initiated a kiss. And the longer he kissed me
back, the more the light spilled out from inside him, warming
us both.*

*"You make me feel better than I have in a long time," he
said, when our lips finally parted. "As if you're pushing the bad
memories away and making room for new ones." And then he
took my hand and put it up to his cheek and held it there for a
long time.*

Chapter 17

Two days after the gallery exhibit, Sebastian arrived at our parents' house and informed me that we were going to take a drive.

"I'm still angry with you over that incident with Madame Calvé at the gallery," I said. "You should have just come out and told me you wanted me to meet a prospective client."

"And would you have come?"

"No."

"So you see?"

"I don't *see* anything. That's exactly the point. I don't want to see what the blindfold shows me anymore, Sebastian. I don't want to peer into the darkness and pull out secrets that are supposed to remain hidden. It's dangerous."

"Because of one incident?"

"No, because of many incidents that I turned my back on, and so did you, and then one so large I had to accept that what I do is unnatural. It's as complicated as Opaline communicating with the dead or—"

"You are a descendant of a witch, Delphine. So are Maman and Opaline and Jadine. You can't take your ability, stuff it in a bag full of rocks, tie a rope around it, and throw it into the sea to drown it."

I never wanted to talk about my almost drowning, and Sebastian knew that, but he brought it up slyly sometimes when I didn't expect it. As if he needed to remind me that he'd saved me. As if I could ever forget.

"Let's not argue now. It will ruin the surprise I have planned. Get your hat."

"Where are we going?" I asked, as I grabbed the floppy straw hat with the black ribbon that I'd taken to wearing with every daytime outfit. Gone were the cloches in colors that matched the pastel dresses I had worn in Paris and then New York. Gone were the dresses altogether. My style had changed since I'd come home, partly because of Maman's influence and the current fashions and partly because wearing different clothes made me feel less like the woman I was before.

Instead of my old style of narrow, hip-skimming, sleeveless dresses in pinks and greens that set off my hair, skin, and figure, I'd begun wearing only the new wide-bottomed pajama pants and long-sleeved tops in white or black. My outward appearance revealed the absence of color in my life.

"You'll see. Just come with me." Sebastian took me by the arm and walked me outside. In the driveway was a little cerulean-blue road-ster, a Bugatti. My brother opened the door for me, and I climbed into the softest leather seats I'd ever felt.

As he pulled out of the driveway, I asked again where we were going. Ignoring my question, he instead asked me why I'd left the gallery without saying good-bye. "I went looking for you so I could ask you to join me and some of my friends for dinner. The Murphys wanted to get to know you. So did Marsden."

"The crowd was making me feel like I was just one wave from being swept out to sea."

Sebastian didn't respond. He took a right at the next street.

"Are we going to Grasse?" I asked, recognizing the road.

"No."

"Where, then?"

"You'll see."

"And when did you get this car? This isn't what you've been driving."

"A few days ago."

"The opening must have gone very well indeed."

"It did. I sold almost all of Marsden's paintings and one of Maman's. That large one of the bay. Americans love her seascapes."

"Because she puts magick in the water."

"You still believe that?" he asked, laughing.

It was what Maman had always said. That when she was finished with a painting, she blew magick on it to make it especially attractive.

"Of course. I've done it myself," I said. "But not as successfully."

"You amaze me."

"Why is that?"

"Because with all your sophistication, you are so gullible."

"Well, you amaze *me*," I countered.

"And why is that?" he asked.

"Because with all your knowledge, you are so suspicious. Of course she blows magick on them. The very spell is in the grimoire from Grand-mère's house. La Lune's own spell."

My brother took a deep breath, puffed his cheeks out, and exhaled very, very slowly. I used to count. Sometimes it could take him as long as twelve or fifteen seconds to let all the air out. It was his involuntary reaction to discussions that centered around our family secret.

"How can you not believe?" I asked.

"Delphine, of course I believe."

"Then what?"

We'd had this conversation before, but Sebastian would never explain why the topic bothered him so much. I didn't know if he was even aware of the reason. But I thought I was.

Sebastian pursed his lips, his signal that he was shutting down the conversation.

"I think that you should appreciate what we do and not be exasperated by it. Of everyone, you benefit from it the most. Without the gift, I'd be just another artist. Maman, too."

Sebastian inhaled again.

"Oh, I'm sorry, I didn't mean—" I'd insulted him. Said out loud exactly why this subject maddened him. Sebastian didn't appreciate it when I, or anyone else, reminded him that he hadn't inherited the La Lune gift. That he hadn't been enough of an artist on his own to succeed. That the talents he'd been heir to were only adequate. His vision wasn't unique; his ability wasn't special. His canvases didn't sing or move people to feel emotions the way our mother's did. The way many said mine did.

Sebastian was like thousands of others whose desire to create art outweighed their ability. He knew how to use colors and brushes and stretch canvases, but his results were mediocre. And when confronted with what made us, at our core, the most different from each other, he bristled and turned grumpy. And I didn't want to set him off. Sebastian in a bad mood was disagreeable. Especially to me. Because of our odd bond, I felt it doubly.

"Don't apologize. After seeing what you've been going through, I'm almost relieved I didn't inherit what you did."

His voice was light. I wanted to believe him. And I was glad to be talking about him for a change instead of me.

"That's good news. You did look happy at the gallery. It was quite a show. I was impressed, Sebastian," I said, changing the subject.

He smiled. "I didn't expect the gallery to take off the way it has. You saw, we don't just attract the crowd from Cannes and Nice. Duplessi's is becoming a destination for art collectors who take the train down from Paris to see what I'm showing. I'm considering opening one in New York."

"So you didn't just come to America to rescue me?" I teased. "You had business to combine with displeasure?"

"I did take advantage of being there to set up some meetings, but I would have gone anywhere in the world to rescue you. And it would have been reason enough."

His voice, so like my father's, warmed me. My mother had once said she'd fallen in love with my father as soon as she'd heard his voice, that it was like fingers rubbing moss. Or smoke curling. That it sounded like wood worn and smoothed over time. I heard all those things when Sebastian spoke, too. I might have inherited my mother's witching, but my twin had inherited all of my father's handsomeness, polish, taste, and business acumen.

After fifteen minutes of driving, we turned onto the road into Mougins, a small medieval village. Like Cannes and most of the Riviera, Mougins had been untouched by the war. Favored by artists, its tiny streets were lined with ateliers, and seeing them again made me smile. As we were growing up, our mother had often brought us here to visit with some of her friends or to dine in one of the fine restaurants. The town, also a mecca for gourmet chefs, even boasted a hotel with a Michelin-recommended restaurant.

"Who are we visiting today?" I asked. "Why are you being so secretive?"

Sebastian laughed. "The things I always missed the most between visits with you in New York were your impatient questions. You really did stay away for too long, you know?"

"It was for the best."

"You ran away. And still, after all this time, have never really told me why."

"I told you, after getting that letter from the woman whose portrait I'd done, I needed a change."

Sebastian pulled into the parking lot near the hotel. One couldn't drive through the town. The streets were too narrow.

My twin got out of the car, came around to my side, and opened my door.

"The letter might have upset you but not sent you packing. Why did you really run away, Delphine?" In the sunlight, his dark green eyes shone like holly leaves.

"If I had stayed, I would have become embittered and destroyed what I cared about the most."

"How can you be so sure?"

"I saw it, Sebastian. I saw it with my blindfold on."

"You said you never were going to draw yourself or me. You promised me and Maman. She told you there would always be the risk of you misunderstanding what you saw in those shadows and how dangerous it could be if you acted on a false premise."

"I didn't draw myself. I drew someone else, and I saw myself in the sketch."

I didn't want him to ask me any more questions that I'd have to lie in order to answer. I stepped away from him onto the panorama deck and looked out over the vista. From up there in the mountains, the entire valley was visible, all the way past my parents' villa in La Californie, down to town and out to sea. As I watched, an eerily murky rain cloud moved swiftly across the sky, casting much of the land below in sudden shadow. I imagined trying to paint the view, but the scenery was too complex, and the idea exhausted me. I wasn't as good as my mother at landscapes, which was a shame, since there would have been no need for my second sight in order to paint them. My best works were the complex, detailed, surrealistic shadow portraits of people in their homes. The books on a shelf behind a man turning into trees. A woman in her dining room, plates and cutlery and napkin turning into small animals and insects.

"Come, let's go. What I have to show you is this way," Sebastian said.

We walked toward the empty street. No one was out and about. Probably, the impending storm kept them inside. As we passed the hotel, I stopped at the fountain. I reached into my pocketbook, pulled out a centime, and threw it into the stone basin, listening for the *plink* as it hit the surface and then watching it sink and join the other coins.

My mother had always laughed at my insistence that I throw money into any fountain I passed. And now Sebastian repeated her words.

"You don't wish for luck, you create it."

I nodded. "But one shouldn't tempt fate, either."

We continued on, up a little incline and into the heart of the old village. Avenue du Commandant Lamy was lined with picturesque stone houses dating back to the 1400s, each only two rooms across and no more than two stories high. The front doors were either one step down or one step up from street level.

Everywhere you looked were explosions of colors against the muted stones. Window boxes overflowed with deep reds and shocking pinks, lime greens and lavenders. Doors and window frames were painted salmon pink, robin's-egg blue, buttercup yellow, or pale green. Small lantana trees or rosebushes growing in cobalt or emerald glazed pots were gathered on the stoops. Fuchsia bougainvillea vines climbed the facades, some covering windows.

"Will you tell me who you were drawing when you saw yourself, Delphine?"

"You're still thinking about that? I shouldn't have told you."

"I'm glad you did. We needn't have secrets."

"Then tell me about your latest conquest." I prodded my twin, trying to change the subject once again.

He laughed. "That's no secret. An American named Carlotta Simpson. She's a painter studying with Juan Gris. Now will you tell me?"

"I shouldn't be surprised that it's a painter. You can't get away from us, can you?"

"It's all I know," he said, and I detected a forlorn quality in his voice.

"How long has she lasted?"

"Two weeks."

"And how much longer will she last?"

"One week." He laughed again. "She's going back to Paris. At just the right time. She's starting to wear on me. Now, you tell me your secret."

"Mine doesn't matter anymore. It's in the past. I escaped."

"Yes, you went to America, but now you are back. Are you still afraid?"

"Not as long as I'm in the south. But I would be if I went back to Paris. Now, don't ask me anything else, because I won't tell you."

After a few more minutes of traipsing through the twisting streets, we arrived at an intersection.

"This way," Sebastian said, and turned onto rue des Lombards, yet another lane lined with ancient stone buildings and a profusion of flowers, bushes, and vines.

Sebastian finally stopped at number 102. Purple and pink trailing verbena overflowed from window boxes. The front door was painted a pale green, framed with a wisteria vine heavy with perfumed blossoms.

I expected my brother to use the bronze hand-of-fate door knocker that reminded me of the one at my great-grandmother's house in Paris. Instead, he took a key out of his pocket and inserted it into the lock.

"You rented a house here?" I asked, confused.

Ignoring yet another of my questions, he twisted the doorknob and flung open the door. "After you," he said, with a flourish.

I stepped down into a small, cool room with a low wood-beamed ceiling and a stone floor. It was outfitted as an artist's studio; two easels stood by the window, and a stack of canvases leaned against the whitewashed walls. A wicker chair much like the one my mother used in her studio sat before one of the easels. Positioned beside it was a taboret holding two wooden palettes, dozens of silver-foiled tubes of paints from Sennelier in Paris, and a plethora of fine sable brushes.

Fat brass hooks were spaced evenly on one of the bare walls, waiting for paintings to hang from them. The other wall housed floor-to-ceiling shelves filled with supplies and books. Books, I suddenly realized, that I recognized. They were my searching books. Why had Sebastian unpacked the trunk I'd stored at my parents' house and brought all the occult, medieval, and mystical books here to someone else's house?

"Now, come look upstairs."

Sebastian took my hand and led me up a narrow, twisting staircase with a wooden rail worn smooth by hundreds of years of hands holding on to it.

The second floor contained a small but adequate kitchen with a round wooden table and four cane chairs, a bedroom just big enough for a bed and an armoire, and a bathroom with an old porcelain tub. Each room, including the bathroom, had a fireplace. The decor was whitewash with light blue accents, the same color as the Bugatti.

"What is all this?" I asked, turning to Sebastian.

"The color, Delphine, Don't you know from the color?"

I focused on the color. Delphinium blue. My mother had told me the story so often. Usually, the tall bell-shaped flowers bloomed in June, but the year we were born, they'd bloomed early, in mid-May. She'd seen them in the garden that morning. Surprised and delighted, she bent over to cut some stalks and went into labor. And from the moment I'd seen them, I'd been obsessed with them, too. For a long time, I believed they had been named for me, not the other way around.

Understanding dawned. "The car, this studio, this all is for me?"

He held out the key. "To heal. To start anew. As your dealer"—he bowed—"I believe it's time to get you painting again. As your brother, I know you can't do it at home with Maman and Papa underfoot. This seemed perfect. And you'll have the car to motor down to the sea or into town whenever you want."

"Nothing will ever be perfect," I said. I knew that wasn't something I could expect, ever in my life. "But this is awfully close," I told Sebastian, and kissed him on both cheeks.

Chapter 18

Book of Hours
June 27, 1920

With Mathieu's invitation to visit my next secret spot—his workshop—I had visions of a windowless room somewhere in the bowels of the Librairie du Merveilleux. From the outside, the building hardly looked large enough to house a store, much less two apartments.

I couldn't have been more wrong.

"Uncle Pierre's building was erected in the early eighteenth century, incorporating the remains of a small monastery," Mathieu explained, as we climbed up and up the twisting spiral of worn stone steps. "We're in the cloister that was once part of the original larger structure. All that remains was this aerie."

We'd reached the first landing and started up the next twisting staircase.

"The first time I saw this place, I felt as if I'd finally found where I belonged," he said, somewhat wistfully.

"How old were you?"

"Fifteen. I'd grown up in Rennes, where my parents

owned a café," he continued. "When I was twelve, my mother died, and without her, my father struggled. After a year of trying but failing to keep the business going, my father sold it, and we moved to Toulouse, where he had family. But he couldn't find work, so we came here, to Paris, where my mother had family. My father had arranged a position at a restaurant, but he took sick and in less than six weeks died of influenza. That's what the doctors said, but I think it was a broken heart. My father never recovered from my mother's death. Never regained any of his joie de vivre, and without it, he was only half of himself. He was vulnerable to misery. If it hadn't been influenza, it would have been something else. He had no reserves left."

We'd reached the landing, which was almost too small for both of us to stand. In front of us was an imposing oak door, gnarled and stained. Mathieu withdrew a rusty key from his pocket and fit it inside the keyhole. The cylinders clicked, and as he pushed the heavy door inward, a loud creak sounded a kind of greeting.

Mathieu gestured to the room beyond, gave a little bow, and said, "Welcome to my refuge."

I stepped inside. Light streamed in through dozens of leaded-glass windows that reached from the floor to the ceiling. Where there weren't windows, there were shelves of books. Hundreds of volumes, lined up, like guardians protecting treasures.

"This room was once the monks' scriptorium, and my uncle used it for storage until I came along," Mathieu said.

"I can't imagine anyone using a gem like this just for storage."

Beneath my feet, a stunning mosaic sparkled in the sunlight. The design depicted a world map but one that bore little resemblance to our modern-day renditions. I didn't

recognize all the shapes, with some continents swollen,
others shrunk. As I watched, gold, silver, lapis, and jade tiles
glinted, and dust motes danced in the beams of sunlight.
An unusual perfume wafted in the air. I smelled paper,
glue, leather, paint, and what I thought must be myrrh or
frankincense.

Mathieu noticed me sniffing. "It's incense. I found a stash
of it in the rubble and burn it routinely. I like to think of the
monks who toiled here long before me and the continuity of us
all working with books, smelling the same smells, keeping the
same art alive."

He walked over to the windows and opened first one and
then another, letting in fresh air along with the soft cooing of
birds.

"At first," Mathieu continued, "I was just coming up
here to explore and investigate, and then I was studying
what I found and experimenting with all the ancient
papers and inks that had been left behind. My brother
wasn't interested in any of this. He loved discovering the
city and spent all his free time roaming through Paris and
learning its history. So I had the scriptorium all to myself.
And since my uncle both published and sold books and had
no children of his own, he was delighted at my interest and
encouraged me."

As he talked, Mathieu began absentmindedly applying
himself to an unfinished book cover in the middle of his table.
I was mesmerized watching his hands work the leather and
couldn't help thinking of how those same fingers felt stroking
my arm, caressing my neck.

To Mathieu's right were shelves filled with supplies: papers,
boards, leathers, and other fabrics all in a muted rainbow
of blues, reds, browns, and greens. I noticed sheaves of gold
leafing. Jars of silver and bronze and copper paint. Bottles

of gem-colored ink. Sewing supplies. Pots of glue. There were several small printing presses that appeared to date back hundreds of years.

Off to the left, a small collection of finished books and journals sat on a bench. I was drawn to their glowing leathers, their gilt edges and elaborate art décoratif designs all reflecting Mathieu's unique artistry.

"How did you learn to do this? Is there a school?"

"There are some classes now, but I studied bookbinding the old-fashioned way. While I was still at the lycée, Uncle arranged to have me meet Pierre Legrain for an apprenticeship. He's been Paris's master bookbinder for the last fifteen years. Several of his books were shown at the most recent Salon des Artistes Décorateurs."

"How old were you?"

"Fourteen."

"And he accepted you even though you were so young?" I'd pulled up a stool and watched, mesmerized, as Mathieu decorated the leather with gold leaf. Applying it and then brushing it off. Gold dust flying, catching the light, and then landing like tiny shooting stars on the wood table.

"Yes. And I worked with him until the war broke out and we all enlisted. Legrain tried to get me assigned to him—he had a desk job in charge of the secretarial service, which allowed him to draw for publications including L'Assiette au Beurre and Le Journal—but the army needed my brother and me in the trenches."

Mathieu leaned down, noticing something that caused him to frown. I watched his fingers gently flick away a speck of gold on the corner of his work in progress.

The cover boasted intricate geometric circles cut in quarters, some sections filled in gold, others in black, some left as outlines.

"But it's not just a pretty design. Is it?" I asked. I was getting an emotional feeling from the pattern.

Mathieu looked up and into my eyes. He seemed both surprised and delighted by my question. "No, it's not. Like my mentor, I'm considered a modernist. That means eschewing a lot of the more affected and facile ornamentation of traditional bookbinding. I'm really trying to convey the character of the text with the form and color of the design in each book dressing. I search out sumptuousness with unusual materials. Rare skins and woods and leathers that have been tanned with special oils. Unique inks and uncommon metals that can be painted or leafed."

He stopped to show me some of them. "This is yellow China shark, this is galuchat, this is a lacquered skin. This is bronze leafing. And this is pewter paint. I've been learning from the Cubists and the Expressionist school of painters about the arrangement of geometrical shapes in asymmetrical patterns to symbolize a mood or attitude. I'm striving to create objects that enhance the atmosphere of where they are placed. Whose rhythms and designs add harmony."

I was fascinated by his work and his words, by the thought processes behind his designs.

"Legrain once said that a form appropriate to its use equals beauty. I believe that. I'm aware that I'm creating a tool and an object at the same time. Each book dressing has two purposes: to protect the pages within its covers and to give pleasure. Art for function's sake."

I was inhaling his words, breathing them in along with the perfumed and rarefied air, in awe of his dual talents—his design sense and his poetic way of describing his world.

"Do you consider your mother to be your mentor?" he asked me.

"I suppose so, yes."

"Does she do portraits, too? I've only seen her landscapes."

"Yes, but hers are not like mine. I—"

"Do you like it?" He'd finished the section of the cover he'd been working on and held it out to me for inspection.

"It's beautiful!"

"Now, tell me, what type of book do you think it's dressing?" he asked playfully.

I studied the ruby leather, with its black and darkened gold geometric designs. The red made me think of tragedy. The subdued metal suggested high drama. Imposing and inspiring. Striking and remarkable. One author immediately sprang to mind.

"A novel by Victor Hugo?"

"Brava!" he said. "Les Miserables. And once it's finished, I'll give it to you."

"But you've already given me my—" I'd almost said Book of Hours. I hadn't yet told Mathieu that I'd given this turquoise journal a name. "So many beautiful gifts."

He came around to where I was sitting and took my face in both his magical hands, cupping my cheeks and chin. "I plan to never tire of giving you gifts. Especially ones like this," he said, and then leaned down and kissed me.

My arms went around his back as he pressed closer to me. The new scents of glue and ink added to his familiar smell.

While still kissing me, he lifted me and carried me as if I were no heavier than a few of his books. He deposited me on a chaise tucked into a corner of the room.

There, in golden sunlight, Mathieu embraced me again. We might never have stopped kissing and touching if the sun had not set and shadows filled the secret aerie, reminding me that I had to get home to my great-grandmother's house, or they would worry and ask too many questions about why I was late. Pulling myself away was harder than I expected. And not just for me but also for Mathieu.

"I've half a mind to kidnap you and keep you here, like the witch kept Rapunzel in the fairy tale."

"But you can't be the witch. I am. You have to be the prince and save me," I teased.

"Then that's what I'll do. I'll save you." And he bent his head to seal his promise with one more kiss and then one more, until a chill breeze from the open window wafted in and cooled our ardor.

Chapter 19

Mougins was surrounded by forests and fields of lavender and roses and jasmine, all farmed for the perfumes of the fabled French houses of Guerlain, Houbigant, Fragonard, and L'Etoile. Rather than settling down to paint, for the next two weeks I found myself spending more time roaming the countryside than inside my studio. I sat in fields and on rocks, leaned against trees and fences, and sketched the flowers, imagining how I might translate them into surrealistic images. Yet they remained simple studies, showing no creativity or verve. And the paints? The palette? Those lush sable brushes? They sat unused on the pretty rosewood taboret.

"You just need more time to recover," my mother said, one afternoon in mid-June. "Or maybe some help? I could go to work mixing up some soothing teas and inspirational tinctures."

I'd driven down to Cannes to spend the day with her. Anything to distract myself from the empty canvases.

We'd gone shopping on the Croisette to buy a birthday gift for my great-grandmother and afterward stopped for refreshments on the terrace of the Hotel Carlton, overlooking the perfect azure sea. It was the most popular hotel in town, and before I'd gone to New York, when Sebastian had brought clients down from Paris, they'd always stayed here.

My mother ordered champagne, her drink of choice, and the waiter brought it along with a plate of canapés, including radish roses, savory cheese balls, and deviled eggs.

The breeze was blowing, as it often did by the beach, and we were relaxing and watching the sailboats in the distance and the foot traffic on the avenue as men and women strolled by. The fashion parade of chic costumes and fabulous jewels entertained us as we sipped our drinks.

"You know, there have been a couple of times in my career when I needed to open my grimoire and find remedies."

"When?" I asked, curious. She'd never referred to barren periods before.

My mother looked out across the terrace to the sea. "When you and your brother were born, I bled too much. If I'd been a normal woman, I might not have made it, but the spirit of La Lune saw to it that I pulled through. Afterward, once I was healed and you and your brother were thriving, I had no drive to paint. It was as if I'd lost it with all that blood. So eventually, I used the book of spells and cured myself."

"I had no idea. I feel guilty that we were responsible."

"Which is exactly why I never told you. I know you well enough to know it's the kind of thing that would have that effect. But you understand now how ridiculous that way of thinking is?"

I did, yet I was still disturbed. "And the other time?"

My mother shook her head. "You and your sisters all have an insatiable curiosity."

"Why don't you want to tell me?"

"Because you are too sensitive, and I know it's going to upset you."

"I won't be upset."

She looked at me for a moment, then took a breath. "When you lost your sight," she said quietly.

I fought my instincts and tried to keep my voice even. "What happened?"

She sighed. "We've talked so little about this, and there's so much about it that I've never explained. In order to get your sight back, I gave you some of mine. That's how I cured you. I—"

"You mean you see less well because of me?"

"Not now. I regained all the vision I lost within two years."

"But you did lose some of your vision?"

"It was an ancient, complicated spell."

"Maman, it took more than a year to give me back my sight."

She nodded.

"So you couldn't paint all that time?" I couldn't imagine her not standing at her easel every day, one paintbrush in her mouth, another in her hand, creating the complex, colorful paintings that were worlds unto themselves.

"I had a much more important job to do." My mother took my hand. "So I know how you feel now. You want to work, but you can't. It's not quite the same. Your inability to paint isn't physical. Yours springs from fear. I was incapacitated. But the result is identical."

"Do you think the cure is also identical?"

"It might be. My eyes needed time to heal and regenerate. For you, it's your spirit. And I can help. You're already back on the right path. It's just not a straightforward one. I'll make up some tinctures that will help. This is going to be a complicated summer and fall for you."

I laughed sardonically. "My winter and my spring were complicated, Maman. This is going to be easy compared with that."

"You mean Monty's death. Because Tommy didn't break your heart that badly, did he? From your letters and what I saw in the waters, I never sensed that you loved him. Was I wrong?"

She bit her bottom lip, her teeth white against the red lipstick that was part of her signature style. That and the rubies she wore, either in ropes around her neck or in rings on all her fingers. No matter what other jewelry she wore, she was always bedecked in rubies.

The lip biting was her tell that she was nervous about my answer. And I knew why she was. My mother was worried that I had fallen in love with Tommy. That I'd squandered the one chance that daughters of La Lune are given at that game.

"No, you were right. I wasn't in love with him. But I was content with him, Maman. I liked our life and looked forward to our future but for all the wrong reasons. Because he was safe. Because when I sketched him, he had no secrets. But then he threw me over for his parents, and I felt like such a fool. I never could have guessed anyone would reject me because we're Jewish. For being a witch, yes. But our religion? We don't even practice."

"You've been sheltered here and in Paris, where people are much less prejudiced. Or, at least, those you've been exposed to. Goodness knows there are provincial people everywhere." She took a sip of her champagne. "I'm glad you didn't fall in love. Someday you will, though."

I'd never told her about Mathieu, and that moment didn't seem the right time for it. "And fulfill the curse of La Lune's descendants."

"It's not always a curse. It hasn't been for me and your *papa*."

"No. But you came close to losing him. Wouldn't it have been the tragedy of your life?"

She nodded.

We all knew the story of how my father had fought a duel for my mother's honor in 1894 and had almost been killed. My mother had risked her own life to save his and sacrificed her soul in the process.

She drained her glass and caught the waiter's eye. He was there in a moment to refill her crystal flute.

"Has anyone ever been able to break the curse?" I asked.

"Not that I know of, but if you ever need to, I promise to help. I know it seems bleak . . ." She waited until the waiter walked off. "With your work, in your life, with love . . . but if you trust your sight, it will show you the way."

"Why does everything you say sound so cryptic? I'm not used to it anymore. In America, everyone speaks what is on their mind clearly. With you, there are always shadows between the words."

My mother examined my face. What was she looking for? What was she thinking?

Sebastian and I used to go for walks after dinner when we were younger and dissect the things my mother had said to us, trying to understand their meaning.

"I'll attempt to be more specific, if you will. Tell me how you feel when you sit down to paint and can't. What happens when you pick up a brush?"

I took a sip of the champagne and concentrated on the crisp, dry taste and the bubbles bursting on my tongue. What did happen? I wasn't even sure I knew.

"When I sit down, I just stare at the canvas. I don't know what I want to paint anymore. Certainly not what I was doing in New York. Not when I painted the series I showed you. Then I was searching for answers, not so much for me but to understand Clara and Monty and the passions that had destroyed their lives. I wanted to explore that kind of fervor. But my search put me on a circular path. Even though I kept moving, it was always in the same direction, and I kept returning to where I'd started. Now that I'm back in France, I want to step out of that circle. Find a new beginning. I don't know if I can without putting on my blindfold, yet doing so is too great a risk. That last time was such a disaster."

"You haven't put on your blindfold since February? That's almost five months ago."

I nodded.

"Not since the night of the party?"

"That's right."

"And all you painted after that were a half dozen theater posters and the Beast series?"

"Yes. And since I've been back, I've haven't done anything but sketch beach scenes, flowers . . ."

"No exploratories for paintings?"

I shook my head.

"I'd hoped your move to Mougins might improve things."

"It's almost as if I've gone blind for the second time." My eyes filled with tears, but I held them back and choked on a sob. I wasn't going to cry here on the terrace of the Carlton. I forced a joke. "And if you think this is hard on me, Sebastian is going mad."

My mother squeezed my hand and laughed along with me. "I bet he is."

"He keeps begging me to take just one commission for a shadow painting and try . . ." The tears threatened, but again, I held them back. "But I can't. Never again."

"No wonder you are so unhappy." She reached up and stroked my cheek. "*Ma petite belle*, it's what you do. You can stop for a while, but I don't think you'll ever really be happy unless you are creating the work you are destined for."

"Then I won't ever be—"

"La Lune!" a man called out, and my mother looked up.

I turned and followed her gaze as he approached our table. Extremely short, no taller than I, he had mad, dark, piercing black eyes and jet-black hair parted on the side and falling over his forehead. Despite his lack of height, he was muscular and wore typical fisherman clothes—a striped shirt, espadrilles, and pants rolled up at the ankles. Seeing my mother, his somber face had broken into a smile, and he embraced her warmly, kissing her first on one cheek, then the other.

"You look like you are part of the sky," he said.

With her cerulean-blue dress and long ropes of blue-white pearls wound around her neck and hanging down her chest like falling bits of clouds, sitting against the powder-blue sky, he was right.

"I'd like to paint you just like this, right now," he added, as he reached for a sketchbook.

He had his hand on it when my mother laughed that seductive

dark laugh of hers that men always responded to. As this man also did. He inched closer, his eyes narrowed a bit, his lips pursed. But instead of looking amorous, there was something clown-like in his actions. "Let me kiss you, then, instead of drawing you."

"Enough of this, Pablo. Do you know my daughter?"

"I haven't had the pleasure, no. You've been hiding her from me. I wonder why." The man bowed to me, took my hand, and kissed it with a flourish.

"Because she's been living in America. Delphine"—she turned to me—"may I present to you the overly bold Pablo Picasso. Beware, part of his charm is that he encourages women to seduce him."

He was, of course, already famous by 1925. Not with the global, iconoclastic fame that would eventually elevate him above mere mortals. But he was, along with Henri Matisse and Juan Gris, an artist whose work people were collecting in both France and the United States. He, like my mother, had *arrived*, as they said in New York. They were *important*. And his star shone even brighter than hers.

Having grown up in the art world and known Monet, Matisse, Renoir, Morisot, and Cassatt from the time I was a child, I was curious about Picasso. But I wasn't in awe. Nothing those days created a sense of awe in me.

"A pleasure to meet you," I said, as I peered into his dark yet blazing eyes. Did I see magick there? Or was I just imagining it because of his legend?

I had a bad habit of assuming qualities in someone before giving it full consideration. My mother had explained that as a result of my second sight and impulsiveness, I tended to overread people's emotions and abilities. This habit, she told me, could prove dangerous if not controlled.

"I've seen some of your work in your brother's gallery," Picasso said. "I expected you to be good, considering who your mother is, but I didn't expect you to be as original as you are. Your subject matter surprised me, I must admit."

He was gazing at me intently, and I didn't quite understand the nature of the stare. Flirting? Assessing? Searching?

"I'd like to know more about what you're trying to find in your painting," he continued. "Such originality must come at quite a price."

I was flattered that he'd asked me what I was trying to accomplish, and I smiled to myself. Maman was right about him.

"They were dreams . . . nightmares of beasts. I thought if I put them down on the canvas . . . I might be able to control them."

"They were dreams? They've stopped coming?"

"For a time," I said.

"An intriguing response and one that I understand. You must come visit me at my studio. I want to learn more about your strange dreams. They're similar to the direction my own work is going. Unusual for a woman, even a daughter of La Lune, to be traveling the same path as Picasso."

"Don't flirt with her, you old goat. Delphine is recovering from a miserable love affair."

Like Matisse, Picasso was full of advice. "Yes, yes, I can see that in your eyes. But you can't let it stop you from painting. This is the best moment to paint. Take all that misery, and turn it into colors and shapes. Paint it, Delphine. And after you do, come show it to me. I might want to buy it . . . or steal it."

He was peering into my eyes as he spoke. I felt as if he was looking right inside of me, and there was nothing I could do to keep him away.

Chapter 20

I kept thinking about what Picasso had said to me as I drove home to Mougins from Cannes, about confronting my time in New York and discovering what it meant to me by putting it on canvas. Did I even know how to do that anymore?

When I reached my little house, I sat down at the table to sketch it out. But my hand refused. The effort overwhelmed my fingers so badly they started to shake. I couldn't even draw a straight line.

I threw my silver pencil against the wall, where it left a long graphite scratch. Turning my back on my work space, I went upstairs to pour myself a glass of brandy to help dull the pain and lull me to sleep.

That night, I dreamed that *I* was a portrait. An old Renaissance painting missing pigment, full of craquelure, with a rip down the middle. Picasso was working on my restoration. He cleaned and restretched the canvas and then began the inpainting on the sections with the most damage—my right hand and my eyes.

I was then standing beside him, both of us inspecting the portrait. Looking closely, I could see where the repairs had been done. They had become part of the painting.

"One and whole, together, the loss and repair belonging to each other," Picasso said. "Over time, all paintings are damaged one way or another. A painting cannot survive a long time unscathed."

I woke up feeling even more frustrated. Picasso could talk all he wanted about how art exorcises demons, but it was all words. He couldn't fix me. And if I couldn't find someone who could, I feared for my sanity. Without painting, I was becoming less than myself.

Sebastian was patient as long as he could be. But by the end of June, he was frustrated, too. He arrived at the studio one day with lunch—a cold chicken, a baguette, a wedge of Saint-André cheese, and a bottle of rosé wine.

At first, I thought he was just there to spend time with me, and I was grateful for the company. I hadn't lived in the south since I was a teenager, and most of my friends had married and had families or had moved away, some to Paris, where there might be more opportunities and more men. And even though Sebastian continued to invite me to openings and dinners with his friends, I declined. The questions they posed disturbed me. I knew that Matisse and the others meant well, but their advice was of no use. I could draw and paint only the most mundane compositions. My creativity slept on. Only with the blindfold would it awaken. And I was too afraid to put the blindfold on.

"Delphine, you need to work. Not for my sake—though I do miss the income my share of your shadow portraits brought in—but because you are miserable. You can't live up here alone just taking walks in the woods. Maman is going to start blaming me for isolating you."

"No, she agrees that the quiet and the woods are helping to keep me sane."

"I want you to take a commission—"

"But I told you no."

"Yes, for weeks you've been telling me no. But I also know you are unhappy not painting."

"It's none of your concern," I spit out, as the anger rose in me. I took a long sip of the cold, fruity wine, tasting strawberries and apples. I needed to get my temper under control.

Sebastian laughed. "Of anyone, it is most certainly my concern. Together you and I built your reputation and mine. We are tied, not just as twins but as partners. I am your manager and dealer."

"Then you're fired."

"Delphine, don't say things you don't mean. I can't know how you feel, but I can feel the lack of joy in your life. I can see it in your eyes. I can't watch it anymore. It's as if it is happening to me."

I shrugged. "You have other artists to sell."

"You're being selfish. Don't you know how much this is troubling Maman and Papa and your sisters? And me—most of all me? We're part of a whole, and my other half is broken, and I don't know what to do."

"I'm not a piece of china. You can't mend me. Why does everyone keep seeing me as in need of being fixed?"

"Because we can all see that you are not yourself."

"I'm sick of talking about this. To you, to Maman. I'm going to figure out something else to do with my life and move on. You did. Why can't I?"

My brother winced as if I'd struck him, then quickly recovered. "Tell me you are happy and well and satisfied. Look me in the eye, and tell me that, and I'll stop."

"That's not fair," I said.

"Then let me help you."

"How? Not even Maman's spells are helping."

"But she's not your manager. You can start with some regular portraits. Just to get your hands moving again."

"But they will be so ordinary. Worse than that, I can't even draw a straight line these days," I said. "Anyone can do a regular portrait. It will be the theater posters all over again. Every time I completed one, I felt worse, because they were just competent illustrations."

"Do you remember Mrs. Gould?" he asked.

It was one of the first commissions he'd set up for me. I was on my winter holiday, home after my first semester at L'École. Sebastian escorted me to the Hotel Carlton, not far from his gallery, on a bright morning for a sitting with Mrs. Eleanor Gould, a wealthy society doyenne from the United States.

After taking coffee and chatting about her impressions of Cannes and Nice, I set up my supplies. The blindfold, the sketch pad, the pencils, and my watercolors. I would do the preliminary drawings that day and also capture her skin tone and hair color. And then I would create the final portrait in my studio, after which Sebastian would present it to her.

I put on my blindfold.

"So it's true?" she asked.

I lifted the silky coverlet from my eyes. "What is true?"

"That you wear a blindfold."

"It is."

"I thought it was just a story, an exaggeration. That maybe you just soothed your eyes before you started and someone got it wrong. How mad! How can you see?"

"Well, I've been looking at you for a while now. And I will study you again without the blindfold after I do the first sketches. Is that all right?"

She was nervous and fluttery, quite like a little hummingbird. Deceptively feeble in appearance, the bird's wings are actually so strong that they can hover in the air for long periods of time.

With the blindfold on, I sketched Mrs. Gould with a man I assumed to be Mr. Gould in a bed of fine satins and lace and many pillows. The two people in the bed were lying back to back, neither of their faces visible, but obviously lovers and just as obviously satiated. Between them on the pillow was a diaphanous black flower, and above the bed was a burst of light.

When I took off my blindfold, I worked on the images for a little while and then flipped over the page and did swatches of Mrs. Gould's coloring. Last, I did a finer drawing of her face, concentrating on her eyes, nose, and lips.

She was in her early thirties, with dark blue eyes, a thin upper lip and full lower lip, and blond hair twisted up to show off her ears, which boasted huge teardrop pearls. There were more pearls, two ropes of them, around her neck, disappearing under the neckline of the pink satin dressing gown she'd worn for the sitting.

"May I see?" she asked when I put down my paintbrush after a very exhausting two hours.

"I'm sorry, no," I said, with a smile. "It's too rough now. You won't like it at all. I need to refine it and show you a more finished portrait, and then, if you like it, you can buy it."

"And if I don't?"

"Didn't Sebastian explain?"

"Not to me, perhaps to my husband."

"Oh, yes, perhaps. The way I work is that there is a fee for today. But because these aren't typical portraits, my sitters aren't obligated to buy the finished paintings."

"Do most of your sitters buy them?"

"About half." I told a white lie so I wouldn't sound as inexperienced as I actually was.

"And what will you do with the painting if we don't buy it?"

"My brother will destroy it."

"Why wouldn't I want what you're going to paint?"

"Mrs. Gould, did your husband tell you what kind of paintings I do?"

"Not really. Or maybe. I just remember he said you were all the rage."

Sebastian had obviously lied to Mr. Gould—a bit of publicity spin to secure our first commissions.

"Well, I paint people's secrets."

"What do you mean? Are you psychic?"

"Something like that. I'm good at reading people."

She rose gracefully, aware of her every movement, and came over to where I sat. For a moment, she examined what I'd drawn. Suddenly, the flighty, refined woman disappeared. Eleanor Gould stared down at the drawing and erupted into raucous laughter.

"You've captured me perfectly, Mademoiselle Duplessi. I'm sure my husband will find the painting much to his liking . . . I just doubt very much he'll ever show it to anyone."

"Why is that?"

"You've painted our seduction. While he was married. While his first wife was summering in Newport. He found me in a restaurant, slaving away as a waitress, and spent all of June, July, and August turning me into someone presentable. That's the bedroom in the home they owned on Lake Michigan, down to the color of the bedspread. That's us in his marriage bed moments before his wife returned early from her summer sojourn and found us there. Just moments before."

Eleanor Gould smiled. "And not by accident. He'd arranged for her to find us. She'd refused to grant him a divorce, no matter how much he offered and however hard he pleaded. But he knew that the one thing she couldn't stand would be to have her reputation ruined. So he had a photographer there, and the big flash you painted is when the photographer captured my husband's first wife's face upon seeing us in bed. And that was that. He got his divorce, and I got a husband."

"Yes, I remember Mrs. Gould," I said to Sebastian now.

"Well, she is back in Cannes. She has her daughter with her and wants you to paint both of them."

"I told you I can't."

"Will you just try? You've already seen her worst secret. That's why this is perfect. You won't have to be afraid of what you see."

I thought about it for a moment. Swirled it around in my mind like the wine in the glass. What he was saying did make sense, but . . . "No, I'm sorry, Sebastian. I just can't."

He was angry, but he didn't say a word. Standing, he walked out of the kitchen. I followed him downstairs and outside. He still wasn't speaking to me. He was going to leave without even a good-bye. He opened the door and stepped outside.

It had been raining, and there were puddles of water everywhere. An especially large one in front of my house. The sky was filled with gray banks of clouds, but a single ray of sunshine had broken through and was shining down on Sebastian. I thought he was going to keep going, but he stopped just next to the puddle and turned to me. He was saying something, but I couldn't hear it. I couldn't concentrate. In the puddle's reflective surface, as if I were looking into a scrying bowl, I watched a series of images present themselves to me.

A castle in the countryside. Sebastian standing by the entrance-way, his hand reaching out to me. Sebastian's voice a watery whisper inside my head.

Unless you are here to save me, I am going to die.

"Where? I don't understand?" I spoke out loud to the apparition of my brother.

"Delphine?" The flesh-and-blood Sebastian was calling my name but from a great distance. I couldn't focus on him. I waited for my spectral twin to explain. What kind of danger? Where was *here*? How I was supposed to protect him without more information?

Unless you are here to save me . . .

The water rippled. The apparition was gone. I continued staring, willing him back. I didn't have any answers. What was I supposed to do?

Yet again, my second sight was presenting me with a future disaster. Only this time, I could be someone's savior, not his destruction. I couldn't risk what would be another great loss. I didn't know where I needed to go. Not yet. But I was determined to find out.

Chapter 21

The envelope was on my plate. Pale gray, with bold, bright blue letters spelling out my name. Without postage, it was obvious it had been dropped off. If I opened it at the breakfast table with Grand-mère and Sebastian watching, they'd ask me questions I didn't want to answer. So I slipped the envelope into my skirt pocket and murmured something about it being from a friend at school.

I still haven't told anyone about Mathieu. He knows but doesn't agree with my decision to keep him a secret. I am determined not to be distracted by having him in my life. Not to let my work at school or commissions from Sebastian be affected. I don't want to disappoint my twin; I don't want his judgment, either. I also don't want my mother, my great-grandmother, and my sisters to know and start to meddle, no matter how loving their intentions might be.

Up in my bedroom, I opened the note. Written out in Mathieu's hand were an address, 3 avenue Franklin D.

Roosevelt, a time, dix–huit heures, and a line from a poem: With a kiss let us set out for an unknown world.

Who had written it? From which of the famous poets he was always quoting had Mathieu borrowed these words that filled my heart with such excitement and hope?

He was waiting for me when the taxi pulled up to the address. He helped me out and then, still holding my arm, steered me in the direction of the Palais de la Découverte. After we passed a small white sculpture of the Swiss Alps in front of vine-covered columns, he led me to a stone staircase seemingly heading nowhere. We descended the broken steps and walked through an archway and into another world. The sounds of traffic from the Champs-Élysées were gone, magically replaced by bird calls and splashing water.

Maples and bamboo trees dappled shade on the sinuous pathways. Lilacs, roses, and vines heavy with wisteria perfumed the air. We were lost in green. Awash in nature. There in the middle of Paris, we had found an overgrown garden, magnificent in its obsolescence.

When I was a girl, my father took me on expeditions in the Languedoc region. We'd leave behind the safe, familiar world I knew to climb mountains and explore ruins, while he'd tell me fantastic tales about the Cathars and the Knights Templar.

Now Mathieu is the one introducing me to other worlds, right here in the middle of Paris, all unlike anything I've ever known, full of sensations and emotions, ecstasies and delights.

Past the wooden footbridge, we wandered through arches overgrown with ivy. A meandering pathway led to a pond, where we stopped to watch the last rays of sun illuminate orange carp as they slowly circled their home.

The quiet was profound. Rock alcoves offered benches, but

we kept walking past the pond till we reached a large marble sculpture.

"It's titled The Dream of the Poet. An homage to Alfred de Musset," Mathieu told me. "Quite a romantic one, too. Look at how he's daydreaming about all these lovely women. It's said each was one of the loves of his life."

Orange and lemon trees scented the air. A bird whistled. The stream rushed by.

"Did he write the line in the note you sent this morning?" I was hoping Mathieu would say he had written it himself.

"He did."

"Will you write me a poem one day? A poem of your own?"

He shook his head in warning. "That part of my life is over."

"Not if you bring me to places like this. Not if you can see all this beauty and respond to it."

"There's only one way left that I know how to respond to beauty . . . Only one way the war didn't destroy," he said, and then bent down and kissed me.

Even when I anticipate the sensation of his lips on mine, every kiss takes me by surprise. How many kisses have we given each other by now? A hundred? A thousand? Each is still new and shocking. I can't describe them, but I can paint them. Bursts of molten colors, cadmium reds, flowing into ruby pinks.

This afternoon, there in the park, Mathieu was hungry. He pulled me into one of the hidden alcoves, where we sat on a bench and the kissing resumed. He opened the top button on my blouse and put his hand against my neck. I opened the next two buttons myself and pushed his hand down inside. When his fingers sneaked under my silk brassiere and found my breasts, I lost my breath.

It wasn't enough anymore to have him touch me. I wanted to feel his skin. Had to feel it. I worked my hands under his jacket and undid his shirt, to find his warm and smooth chest muscles. I moved my hands around to clasp him tighter and then felt the hard ropes of his scar, bumpy and uneven.

For a second, I was overwhelmed with the horror of the damage, but then his hand cupping my breast, fondling my nipple, made me forget. My fingers continued down his chest. I pulled his shirt open and then my own. I lifted my brassiere and pressed my naked chest to his. The feel of our skin touching awoke a need in me that was more powerful than anything I'd felt so far.

"I want more," I whispered to him.

"What more?"

"I want you inside me. Now."

"Here?"

I nodded.

The park was deserted, and twilight was descending on Paris. Mathieu found a mossy bed hidden behind a copse of evergreens and laid me down in the green and purple shadows. Joining me, he leaned on his elbow and stared down into my eyes.

"You are sure?"

I nodded again.

He cupped my face in his hands and kissed me. As gentle as his words and hands were, as soft as his lips were, there was a fierceness in his eyes that had turned them dark blue-gray.

I reached up under my skirt and pulled down my lace and silk bloomers, inviting cool air onto the warm place. I took Mathieu's hand and boldly put it there, between my legs, so he could feel how ready I was for him.

It was the first time a man ever touched me there, stroked me there, caressed me there . . . All my words disappeared into colors—swirls of orange-hot red bursting into citrine, whorling into canary yellow, whirling into a light so bright it burned white. Then the white opened and bloomed into a million shades of red and purple and pink.

"I want to know all of you," I whispered.

He undid his belt buckle, and I heard the sound of him unfastening his pants.

I reached for him, bold and brazen. Of course, I'd seen statues and nude models at L'École. Studied erotic postcards with friends when I was younger. I knew what to expect, but, like his kisses, like the feel of his naked chest on mine, I had no idea of how the experience would feel.

I ran my fingers down his ready, smooth shaft and around it, grasping it. He thrust just a little with his hips in a forward motion, and I realized I was doing the same dance against his hand between my legs.

A burst of a deeper red-purple flashed behind my eyes and surged to a royal blue as I guided him into me.

How did I know what to do? Why wasn't I scared? How was it possible that there was so little pain? There was only a momentary lime-green splash of resistance that burst through the scarlet when he entered me, and then it was gone. The sounds of his breathing and the stream and the birds turned into indigo and cobalt and pine-green music rushing over rocks. Sparks of cherry red and mandarin sapphire swirled into ruby, swirled into amethyst, swirled into turquoise, into violet.

And then the maelstrom of colors all pulsed and surged at the same time, all scarlet and ultramarine and lapis and vermillion and emerald and carmine and crimson, like a dam bursting out of its confines and flooding me with an entire rainbow of sensation.

"Now," he whispered. "Now . . ." And then another whisper. "Now you know all of me. I know all of you."

Chapter 22

As June moved into July, my mother's tinctures continued to help me improve. I slept better, ate better. But they did little to restore my creativity. The days passed without painting. Without creating a single drawing that depicted any originality. The quality of my roses and leaves, my grapes and peaches, improved but were bland recreations of nature.

The hot summer days stretched out ahead of me as the bees buzzed around my subjects. I didn't know what would become of my life if I never painted again. I read and reread my Book of Hours, losing myself in memories. Even though only a little more than four years had passed, it seemed a lifetime ago. Sometimes I didn't miss Mathieu as much as I yearned for the girl I'd been, so full of wonder and hope and passion.

Late one afternoon, I forced myself at least to look at the object of my depression. Removing my scarlet blindfold from its velvet-lined box, I held it for the first time since February.

It wasn't alive but had always stimulated a life force in me, a low-level humming that I felt deep inside my chest and womb. Oh, I had missed the thrill of that sensation. I hadn't even realized how much until that dusky hour.

Lifting it to my face, I rubbed its satin smoothness against my cheek. Gliding like a lover's finger, it caressed my skin, the sensation a whisper, begging me to put it on. To join with me again. To show me what I couldn't see without it.

I shut my eyes and stroked the fabric over my eyelids, feeling its familiar, cool touch. I longed to slip the elastic over my head, to position the shade just so, then succumb to the deep visions that would overwhelm me, until there was no other feeling but mysterious awareness, clarity of sight, and then release. Like a drug delivering a euphoric vision and a heightened sense of being.

I let the blindfold fall from my fingers onto the stone floor. Staring down at it, I could almost hear it whispering to me, begging me, tempting me. The blindfold was as lost without me as I was without it. But I couldn't. Not ever again. I wouldn't.

I bent to pick it up, smoothed it, and was putting it back in its velvet tomb when I heard a knock on the door. I left the blindfold out and went to see who it was.

Sebastian handed me a package. "I was at the market, and they just got in some of our favorite cheese. Do you have any bread?"

I put the wedge of Saint-André on a plate, sliced off a few pieces of the baguette I'd bought that morning, and put a bottle of rosé and two glasses on the table between us.

He ate every crumb.

"I have something to tell you," he said. "And I just want you to hear me out before you say no."

"Sebastian, you've turned into a nag."

"So I have. Because you've become as obstinate as a mule. Now, listen. La Diva has made us an offer that is simply too large to turn down."

"Is this about painting her house again?"

"Yes."

"Sebastian, we've been through this."

"No, no, just hear me out. It's a house, Delphine. And it's hiding a treasure that is hundreds of years old. No one can get hurt. You can't see a secret that will harm anyone. You'll be looking for a book, not searching inside someone's soul."

He had stood up and was pacing. He noticed my blindfold in its open box. Lifting it out, he dangled it from his forefinger.

"I'm done telling you that you need to do this for yourself. Now I need you to do it for me. When you lost your sight, I couldn't give it back to you. I was helpless. Maman had magick to use, but I had none. It's been the same since you came home. It's as if you are blind all over again. And I'm helpless all over again. Please, Delphine."

He was right. I owed it to him. Ever since I was a little girl, he had been the one to do everything for me, including being my eyes for that terrible year. He'd championed my work and was tireless in promoting me. Every important commission I'd ever had was because of him.

"I want to say yes, to make you happy, to do it for you." I shook my head. "But I won't. I can't."

"I want to show you something." Sebastian reached into the leather satchel he'd put on the floor, pulled out a magazine, and flipped it open to an illustrated article about Madame Calvé.

I ran my eyes over the page of photos, from top to bottom, right to left: La Diva in costume, in her most famous role as Carmen on the stage in Milan at La Scala. Next, in another costume on the stage at the opera house in Paris. And finally in street clothes, standing in front of a stone castle.

Suddenly, I felt as if a window had been thrown open and cold air was rushing in. Compared with the others, the last photograph shimmered. I stared at La Diva standing in front of a large wooden door, which was open to show a glimpse of the castle's stone interior.

Her intense gaze seemed to bore right through me. I knew that a photograph couldn't literally pull me into it. Even so, I gripped the arms of my chair for ballast.

"There are more pictures of the place." Sebastian turned the pages. "Do you see? It's not just some house, Delphine. It's seeped in all the history you have loved reading about since you were little. Now it's a chance to walk inside one of those castles. The Château de Cabrières was built in the eleventh century. They say that in the thirteenth century, the Knights Templar kept a treasury there, and when they wouldn't reveal its whereabouts, they were put to death. It's smack in the middle of the Languedoc that you and Papa used to explore together. You've been telling me for years that the area is the seat of mystical and supernatural occurrences no one can explain. Madame is looking for a book, but while you are there, you can investigate those caves and grottoes you love so much.

"Emma has access to so much history. Listen to the story she told me about an old letter that a local priest she's friends with showed her. In 1300, the last seneschal of Cabrières, a Templar, passed through the region on his way to a monastery in Montserrat. With him were a squire and six pack mules laden with bags of gold. Realizing that he was being pursued by King Philip's men, the Templar buried the treasure somewhere in the area.

"Days later, when he was apprehended, he refused to divulge where he'd hidden the gold and so was executed on the spot. Since then, twice, once in 1820 and once in 1860, Arab gold pieces have been found in the area. Even if you don't divine La Diva's book, you might be able to find some of that buried treasure and who knows what else."

When my father and I explored the area, searching for artifacts from the Templars and the Cathars, we'd never discovered anything as exotic as gold. Over the years, I found broken pottery, a button, and a metal clasp that must have held a cape together. On one trip, my father stumbled on a rough-hewn granite altar that invited hours of rumination, as we imagined who had prayed there and what their lives had been like. As an architect, he was fascinated with the ruins and the stories behind them. I was the only one in our family as interested as he was. Every summer, we'd take a weeklong hike through the area and explore a different ancient village, looking for buried treasure. The Cathars were a heretical Christian sect that had created all kinds of enigmatic work. The paintings and cave art in the region mesmerized me and, I'm sure, influenced my work. We'd do tracings and stone rubbings and take them home with us in an effort to make some sense of their symbolism. No one had ever figured it out. The Cathars' codex had never been found.

I only half listened to Sebastian's story. As much as I was interested in the castle's history, I was too distracted by the sense that I'd seen it before. Why was it so familiar? Even if I'd once seen a photo of it and not paid much attention, it wouldn't explain the particular cluster of feelings welling up in me.

Excitement, mixed with fear, laced with power. Similar to the bouquet of emotions I experienced when I put on the blindfold. Or when I was scrying. Giving in to irresistible temptation was always dangerously thrilling. To be privy to a secret scene, knowing I was lifting a veil that very few people even knew existed, was exhilarating. Despite the potential danger, the craving to feel that painful elation again enticed me.

And that's when I remembered. I'd been scrying unintentionally days before when Sebastian was standing on the street beside a rain puddle. And I'd seen this very facade in the reflection. But in that watery image, my brother had been standing in front of the castle, warning me: *Unless you are here to save me . . .*

I'd thought I could save someone once before. Would it be different with Sebastian?

Chapter 23

Book of Hours
July 18, 1920

*Mathieu took me to the Louxor movie palace today. From
the first step into the lobby, I was transported. A combination
of Art Deco and Egyptian Revival, every inch gleamed. A
replica of an ancient cartouche hung above the box office. The
ochre walls were decorated with lotus-blossom motifs in dark
green, cobalt, and turquoise. Giant terra-cotta sphinxes stared
with black-and-white glass eyes as the guests filed in.*

*We settled down in plush red velvet seats, and La Belle Dame
Sans Merci, directed by Germaine Dulac, began. I'd read about
the movie when it had opened and knew about the romantic
notion of a woman in a failed relationship which ends when her
male lover, who cannot live without her, kills himself.*

*Dulac's movie was set in the present, postwar France. It
opened with a phone call between the main character, Lola,
an actress, and her lover professing his undying adoration and
passion for her.*

*Mercilessly, she replied that she would forget him "in the
time it takes to smoke a cigarette."*

After the film ended, Mathieu took me to a nearby café for wine.

"What did you think of the movie?" he asked.

"It was sad, wasn't it?"

"Victor Hugo once said that melancholy is the pleasure of being sad."

"Yes, that's a perfect way to describe it."

Once again, Mathieu had found the exact words to explain how I felt.

"It was stunning visually. But Lola was such a victim of love," I said. "So twisted by her own pain she had to employ her talents as an actress to get her revenge on the whole male species."

"She'd been disposed of by men, so she used them."

"And whatever delight that gave her, ultimately she was miserable," I added.

"The poem the title was based on was by Keats. Do you know it?"

"I know no poetry. And no poets but you." I smiled at him, but he flinched at my words. Retreated and grew silent. As he had in the bar the first time we'd talked about his aspirations, he drank what was in his glass too fast.

I'd made a mistake. And now I felt terrible. How could I help him? What magick could I call on to close the gash in his soul that kept him from being the artist I knew with all my heart he was meant to be?

He picked up the half-full bottle of wine. "Let's walk," he said, as he took some coins out of his pocket and left them on the table.

Outside, night had fallen, and the sky was filled with clouds. We walked in and out of their shadows toward the river.

He held the bottle in one hand, the other hand in his pocket. I didn't know what to say to defuse my gaffe, so I was silent.

Finally, we reached the Seine, and I followed him down the stone steps to the shore. There we stopped under a leafy chestnut tree, and he pulled me as close to him as he could and kissed me hard on the lips. Surprised but not displeased by his intensity, I kissed him back.

On the river, a tugboat chugged by. Somewhere a dog barked. My world had narrowed to the space within Mathieu's arms.

We broke apart, and he pulled me down onto a bench. He offered me the bottle. I took a drink and handed it back to him. Either the kiss or the wine had emboldened me.

"I'm sorry for what I said in the café," I whispered.

He shook his head angrily. "No. It's me. The movie disturbed me. It made me think about Keats's life. Such a brilliant but short life. He died at twenty-five. That's the same age my brother was when he died. That's what disturbs me about the movie the most. While it's a romantic notion to kill yourself over being jilted, it's too melodramatic. Too wasteful."

"No, I can't imagine you doing anything like that," I said.

"How would I handle it if you treated me as callously as Lola?" He'd become playful again, teasing me.

"But I never could."

"Ah, but never is a long time, Delphine."

I felt a wave of sadness come over me.

"Someone more handsome, more successful, with better prospects, will come along, and you'll—"

"No. It can't be like that for us."

"Us?" he asked. "You and me?"

"No, my sisters and me."

And so, while we drank more of the cold, dry wine, I told him what each daughter of La Lune inherits. Not the bits and pieces of legends and gossip that he'd heard over the years from conversations in the bookshop but the truth.

"My great-grandmother has always said that for the women in our family, love is not a blessing. It leads to heartbreak and tragedy. For generations, we've been cursed when it comes to matters of the heart. We are only allowed one absolute love per lifetime. And that love, once given, never wanes. Even if the man is untrue or dies, we are destined to pine for him and never find another mate."

"I believe in a lot of things, Delphine, but that is simply not possible. It's suggestive thinking. I've read about it—it's all explained in what the psychoanalyst Sigmund Freud has been writing about."

"I know about him. And Carl Jung. My brother is fascinated by their theories. But believe me, this curse is real. Generations have tried without luck to find an antidote to love, going back to the first La Lune, who lost her lover, Cherubino, and did everything in her power, including selling her soul, to try to bring him back from the dead. She failed. And like every other daughter since who has made a similar effort, she never stopped loving him."

By now, I was crying. Unable to stop myself from imagining how I'd feel if I lost Mathieu.

He twisted on the bench so he was facing me, then took both my hands in his, and my heart lurched. The slightest touch, the scent of him, the sight of him moving so purposefully—I reacted to it all.

"I promise you, I will not leave you," he said.

I could see in his eyes that he meant every word, and as he took me in his arms again, I tried to make myself believe him and be soothed by him and at the same time be set on fire by his lips and fingers and sweet whispered endearments.

Chapter 24

One afternoon toward the end of July, Sebastian picked me up in his black-and-maroon Cottin-Desgouttes Torpedo, a bigger car than my little blue boy, as I had come to call my Bugatti. We were driving to Emma Calvé's château, a trip that would take about four hours. We would stay for a week to ten days, or as long as it took me to paint her home using my scrying art and to help her find the lost *Book of Abraham* that the castle was hiding.

This was Sebastian's scheme to liberate me from my self-imposed hiatus. Finding hidden treasure would be so much safer than uncovering people's secrets. Wouldn't it?

My scheme was to protect him.

The route wound west and then north about four hundred kilometers. Sebastian had planned the drive so that we could stop in Aix-en-Provence and have lunch with Marsden Hartley, the American painter I'd met at the Duplessi Gallery. Sebastian told me that Marsden had a house in Venice but was spending the month in Aix painting some of the local landscape that Cezanne had made famous.

Our lunch on the terrace was a much-needed respite from the long drive. Marsden's housekeeper made a delicious lemon sole served with buttered parsley potatoes and a lovely, chilly rosé. Afterward, there were strawberries, good bread, and runny cheese.

The view from the terrace was a painter's dream, and in the hills I saw the geometric patterns that had captured Cezanne's imagination. I told Marsden that I was looking forward to what he'd do with the vista, and he invited us to stop back on our return trip.

"Where did you say you were headed, Duplessi?" he asked my brother.

"Delphine has a commission. We've been invited to Château de Cabrières by Emma Calvé."

"The opera singer who was at my opening."

"The same," my brother said.

"I heard she has a school there for young girls studying opera. You should have quite a musical visit."

"I hope the school's not in session, Sebastian," I said. "That would be far too distracting."

"It's not an official school," my brother explained. "Young girls study with her at the château, but she assured me there are no students there now. You can count on peace and quiet."

"Where exactly is it?" Hartley asked.

"Millau."

"The land of the Cathars. There are legends on every twisting road," he said. "I'm something of a history buff and explored there a bit. The paintings and cave art in the region are worth taking a look at. They say the Cathars were in possession of many relics, including the Holy Grail."

I told him that I, too, loved the history of the region and how my father and I used to spend time there every summer searching through ruins.

"I would imagine it's the perfect kind of place for you to practice your—what did you tell me it was called?" Marsden looked at Sebastian.

"Scrying," Sebastian said.

Marsden nodded, then turned back to me. "What an exceptional gift. Your brother told me that you've had it since you were about ten?"

"Yes," I said. I was shocked that Sebastian had told the painter about me. My brother had always hinted at my intuitive powers to obtain commissions but had never gone so far as to mention my scrying to anyone outside the family who might not understand. Marsden sensed my discomfort and returned to the previous and safer topic of history.

"I have a book that has some unusual Cathar stories in it. Hold on." He left us but returned moments later. Not long enough for me to say anything to my brother about what I considered his indiscretions.

Marsden handed me a book. The green leather binding was worn and had some water spots on it. The title, embossed in gold, read *From Ritual to Romance*, and it was by Jessie L. Weston.

"This is one I actually don't have," I said.

"Take it. It will prove for some interesting reading while you are in Millau. I'd like to hear what you think of it."

"Are you sure? I'm so possessive of my books. I always worry if I lend one, I'll never get it back."

"Like love," Marsden said, "books are meant to be shared."

Finally, it was time to push on. We said our good-byes and walked out to the car.

I'd no sooner shut my door than Sebastian remembered something he'd forgotten to tell the artist. He ran back to the villa and knocked on the door, and Marsden opened it.

In the shadows, the two men stood on the threshold, speaking.

What is it that makes us see something for the first time that we've literally witnessed hundreds of times before? My brother was half of my soul. We'd shared a womb together. Despite his inheriting nothing of the witching power from our mother, what we shared was atypical. And yet there was so much about my twin that I didn't know, made even more evident by us having spent the last four and a half years apart.

His success at the gallery was partly a result of his charm but had more to do with his artistic sensibility. Sebastian had an artist's soul, even if he didn't create paintings or sculpture himself. He'd created an artistic life. His gallery was itself a work of art, a sensory delight, with just the right lighting, velvet settees, and comfortable couches on which patrons could sit and contemplate the paintings. The gallery served tea or coffee in the loveliest Limoges china and champagne in the most delicate Lalique flutes. Chocolates, meringues, and madeleines were always perfectly arranged on silver trays alongside linen napkins embroidered with the gallery's logo—an Art Deco blue-and-green geometric rendition of Sebastian's initials that he'd designed himself.

Unlike me, Sebastian was an extrovert and had plenty of friends of both sexes. Our early days in Paris had been the only time his popularity had been challenged. For the first time, he had to work at developing connections, but he very soon overcame that. Growing up with three sisters had sensitized him to what pleased and upset us, and women seemed to adore him in that wild, liberated way that so many of us, in both France and the United States, had assumed after the war. In the aftermath of so much sorrow, rules were bent. Lovers embraced with abandon, fueled with too much drink and sometimes too much opium or cocaine.

Sebastian reminded me of a bumblebee, buzzing from flower to flower. As predicted, he had just parted ways with Carlotta Simpson. I'd met so many of his women over the years and knew how quickly he tired of them. I'd stopped looking for the one who might snare his heart. And now I knew why.

Seeing him in the doorway with Marsden, something in my mind clicked. I understood that Sebastian wasn't supposed to be with a woman. He was attracted to men, specifically in this instance to Marsden.

I had known quite a few homosexual artists in Paris while at school and then in New York. There was more tolerance in France, our easy lifestyle allowing a subculture to thrive. The third sex, some called it. But being a nonconformist, even in our country, even in the most liberal times, could still be a terrible burden to bear. I had no prejudice, and if my brother preferred the company of men in his bed to women, it was fine with me. But why hadn't he told me?

Watching him say that second good-bye on the veranda, I thought perhaps the two were not yet lovers. Perhaps Sebastian didn't even yet know himself where his attractions pointed, although I doubted that.

Sebastian joined me in the car moments later. Once we were on the road, with the wind whipping through our hair and the lavender-scented air blowing all around us, I brought up his friend.

"Marsden is fascinating. His work is, too. Have you known him long?"

"A few months."

"He is the real thing. I can see it in his work. He's arrived and is only going to get better now."

"I quite agree. You're a good judge, Delphine. Not every artist is an astute reviewer of other artists. Too often, there's some jealousy that gets in the way," he said.

"I envy that he can observe a scene and only see what's in front of him. My life would be simpler if I didn't have the burden of learning such dire and dark things about people."

"But then you wouldn't be as special. You'd be just another painter struggling to make it. You'd have some awful little studio in Montmartre, burning coal and wearing gloves without fingers during the winter so you could still paint without freezing."

I laughed at the image he painted. "Maman and Papa would never let me! You'd never let me."

"Quite right. We'd all save you from such an existence. We'd never put our Delphine in danger."

He turned from the road to look at me and smile. It was true. I could no sooner imagine him or my parents allowing me to suffer than I could imagine myself allowing him to. Yet he had told Marsden my secret, and that was unlike him.

"You told Marsden a lot about us," I said, not quite sure if I was actually as annoyed as I sounded.

"He's spent a good amount of time in Cannes. He's had dinner with Maman and Papa several times. It's not as if I told a stranger."

"Regardless, you know I don't like being discussed. We don't like being discussed."

"I'm sorry."

"I don't want to be different from anyone. I don't want people to think of my peculiarities when they look at my art. It keeps me on the outside of things. The power we have is unnatural to most of the population, even now. I don't want to be misunderstood or seen as a threat to anyone. You can't have forgotten."

My temporary blindness had been no accident, you see. At age eight, I had not yet experienced the consequences of our legacy. I didn't know how dangerous it could be to show off my psychic abilities. I'd learned a spell and wanted to impress my classmates with my trick. During lunch, I lit a crust of bread on fire. Tales of my witchcraft spread. My classmates and I had all grown up on the same fairy tales. Everyone knew about wicked witches, sorcery, and magic potions. I became an oddity. An object of scorn and ridicule and curiosity. One of my classmates, who had become convinced that I was giving her the evil eye and causing her to do badly on tests, took matters into her own hands. Her father owned a laundry service. She pilfered a bottle of lye from his store and threw it in my face one morning in the schoolyard.

I didn't go back to a traditional school for years after that. My mother taught me at home after I regained my sight and enlisted tutors for the subjects that she wasn't capable of teaching. I remained in a kind of social exile until I was thirteen and returned to the lycée.

Sebastian, who had witnessed my assault, was quiet for a moment now and then said, "I am sorry. I'm sorry for failing you. First when that awful girl attacked you. And now."

I exhaled, exhausted by my current anger and memories of my

painful past. But at the same time, I was reminded of the gift I had in Sebastian. My temper settled. "It is what it is."

"I don't like that phrase. You picked it up in New York. It's defeatist."

"Yes, I suppose it is."

"How badly did that fool in New York hurt you?" Sebastian hadn't asked me much about Tommy on the ship coming home or since I'd gotten back.

"In retrospect, I don't think I was ever really in love with him. Mostly, he just insulted my pride."

"But your pride matters to you even more than matters of the heart."

"What a terrible thing to say about me." I could feel my temper rising again.

"Maybe, but it's true, isn't it? Have you ever been in love?"

I still didn't want to tell my brother about Mathieu, especially at a moment like this. I realized I had no right to resent him for hiding his love affair when I had done the same exact thing and was continuing to do so.

"Well, the truth is, given the family curse, it's safer for Duplessi women to have hard hearts," I said.

"But not much of a way to go through life. Having your heart broken can be quite excruciating, but being in love is exhilarating."

"Spoken as someone who has had his heart broken," I said.

"At least a hundred times." He laughed.

"And who broke it the worst?" I was fishing.

"You, dear one. You. When you ran away to New York. When you separated us. I'm not myself when my twin is three thousand miles away across the sea. I opened my gallery to sell your paintings, and then you abandoned me. You forced me to find other artists—none of whom I loved. I was building a reputation as an avant-garde gallery owner, and then my star disappeared on me. Worse, the other half of my soul departed. Without any thought for me at all."

When I didn't answer, he turned and examined my face.

"You're crying?" he asked. "I'm the one who was hurt."

"I'm sorry that I hurt you. I didn't think—"

"No, you didn't, and that's what hurt the worst. But it's water under the bridge now. I survived. Asserting your independence was more important to you. I suppose I understand. You had to prove who you were. On your own without me." He paused. "That's not it?" he asked.

I shook my head.

"Then what was it?"

"I didn't leave to become independent."

"Then why?"

I shook my head again. I was tired of giving Sebastian answers just because he asked questions. "You've been pestering me for weeks to accept this commission, and I'm here, aren't I? You wanted me to scry for Madame Calvé even though I never wanted to put on my blindfold again. But telling Marsden about me broke our covenant, Sebastian."

"What do you want?"

"I want an apology."

He looked at me as if I were a stranger instead of his twin. A moment passed, and then he grudgingly murmured that he was sorry.

If I had the opportunity to save him, I would. My love for him was unconditional, but I was tired of being indebted to him. With startling clarity, I realized that I wasn't a little blind girl anymore who needed him to guide me out of the rough water.

Chapter 25

The weather changed, and the sun disappeared behind heavy storm clouds that chased us the last half of the way to our destination. The Aveyron region was lush, and the green fields and grassland were even more vibrant against the gray skies. In the distance, the mountains created a majestic backdrop.

My father and I hadn't visited Millau, but I'd read about it. Like Cannes, it had been inhabited since the Gallo-Roman era, and its history was as rich as its soil. We drove past architectural ruins that made me want to ask Sebastian to stop so I could explore, but I knew we were expected at the château at a certain time.

We reached an intersection where the ancient Roman road from Languedoc to the north crossed the Tarn river and joined the Dourbie. In a scene that Monet or Cezanne would have loved to paint, remains of a truncated medieval bridge jutted out into the water.

I saw a man strolling out toward the very edge where the stone stopped. He was too far away for me to see his features or even his hair color, but something about him reminded me of Mathieu. Standing at the precipice, he looked down. As we drove past, I turned around to watch. I was afraid for him. His desolation showed in the way he held his head, in how his shoulders sloped, and in the color of the air around him. This man had a wide swath of green-blue coming off him in waves.

"We need to go back," I said.

"What's wrong? Where?"

"To that bridge. There's a man on it who is going to jump."

"There was no one there. And we're expected at the château, and we're already running late."

"There was a man standing there in trouble, and you're concerned with upsetting our hostess?"

He shook his head and turned the car around. There had been many instances like this in his life, and he'd learned that common reason was no match for a Duplessi woman and her hunches.

Sebastian maneuvered the car as close to the jetty as he could get.

"Delphine, there's no one here."

I pointed. "He was right there."

Sebastian shook his head. "It had to be one of your visions. No one is there."

I knew Sebastian could be right; the man might be a leftover apparition, someone who had once stood there and left such a strong impression that I could see it still. But I had to be sure it wasn't a trick of light that revealed him to me but made him invisible to my twin.

I climbed out of the car and ran out onto the truncated bridge. Sebastian was right. There was no one there. What had I seen? A lost fragment of time? My mother had taught us not to refer to the people we saw in visions as ghosts. Such a term had too many implications. For one, that the people we were seeing were dead, when they often weren't. Sometimes what we were witnessing was a spectral projection that wasn't occurring in the present time or at least in that moment.

The way my mother had explained it, there were moments in people's lives so powerful that they remained behind, even after the people had moved on, and sometimes when the light fell a certain way, we could witness those moments.

Could it have been a vision of Mathieu? Had he once visited this place? Stood on this very bridge? Looked at the sea and thought about me as I was thinking about him?

"Are you all right, Mademoiselle?"

The voice came from my right. I looked. There was a man there. But a wholly different one from Mathieu. And he was climbing up over the rocks, back onto the jetty.

He had silver hair brushed back from his forehead that contrasted with a youthful-looking face only faintly lined. If not for his hair, I would have assumed he was about my age. His clothes suggested that he worked outside; his boots had mud on them.

"Whatever it is, it can't be that terrible. Why don't you just step back a bit?" His voice was so gentle I was caught by surprise.

He thought I was going to throw myself over the edge? His earnestness and concern were evident.

"No, no. I'm not. I wasn't . . . I thought I saw . . . It was you. It looked like you had jumped."

He laughed, and the sound made me smile. "Actually, it was Pepin here." The man had climbed all the way up now. I saw that inside his jacket was a little brown-and-white spaniel with lively black eyes. Seeing me, the dog squirmed.

"We were walking when Pepin decided to explore the rocks down there. But he's still a pup and got stuck. I had to climb down to get him."

I put out my hand, and Pepin licked it.

The man smiled, and I noticed how fast the expression reached his eyes and how they crinkled at the corners.

"Delphine?" Sebastian put his hand on my shoulder. "Are you all right, darling?"

"I am. Turns out what I saw was a dog rescue."

"Well, that's wonderful," Sebastian said. "Now we really need to move on."

I turned to the man. "I'm glad you and your puppy are all right."

He smiled at me again, with eyes of an unusual golden brown color, as if rays of the sun were captured within their depths. And for a moment, I even thought I felt the warmth of the sun break through the cloudy day.

Back in the car, Sebastian tried to make sense of the incident.

"You must have seen him just before he started climbing down. He probably was standing there and calling to the dog. What you thought was despair was just frustration."

"I suppose so." I no longer knew what I'd seen. I reached into my pocketbook and ran my fingers over the soft leather cover of my Book of Hours.

The clouds darkened even more as we drove through the valley, and by the time we reached our destination, rain had descended.

My first look at the Château de Cabrières was through a downpour, with lightning streaking the sky and thunder echoing in the valley. Although modest in size, with its moat and drawbridge and tall ramparts, the castle looked imposing and impervious. Whatever secrets it held, it would not give them up easily.

Sebastian parked. "We'll have to make a run for it," he said.

"No, look." I pointed.

A butler was coming out to meet us with two big umbrellas. Reaching my door first, he opened it and held the umbrella over me, shielding me from the storm.

Sebastian had come around and joined me.

"Welcome to the château," the butler said. "I'll send someone out for your bags. Please, follow me."

As we approached the castle, even over the sound of the rain, I heard the most extraordinarily beautiful voice singing.

I didn't recognize the music. I wasn't an opera fan; not understanding the words was so frustrating that I found I couldn't concentrate on the art. But for the first time, I realized how with certain arias, words are irrelevant.

I not only heard the song, but I visualized the sound's aura.

Mother-of-pearl, it shimmered, casting me in an opalescent glow. I heard birdsong, harp glissades, waterfalls, and what I imagined were the fluttering of angels' wings. In the richness was a desultory tone that made it all the more moving and poignant.

I felt the sting of tears in my eyes. Without knowing the aria or the opera it came from, I felt the singer's pathos. And then, as if someone had lifted the needle on a gramophone, it stopped. Could that have been a recording? Until the abrupt end, I'd been certain it had been live singing.

"This way, if you please." The butler gestured.

Sebastian and I walked up three stone steps to an overly large wooden door with an ancient-looking iron keyhole and a complicated latch system.

The butler opened the door for me and gave a little bow, allowing me to enter first.

In my life, I'd had hundreds of experiences with the unknown. I had put on my blindfold and seen sights I could never have imagined. But nothing prepared me for the emotional reaction I had when I walked over the threshold of the Château de Cabrières.

My vision changed. I actually saw the room before me with more clarity than normal. As if I'd put on a pair of spectacles that fine-tuned my ability to see. Having had issues with my eyesight since I was eight, no one was more aware of or sensitive to the nuances of vision than I.

From the doorstep, I took in the grand two-story ancient stone staircase leading up to the next floor. A basil-green, juniper, and powder-blue rug with purple flowers the shade of amethyst—Aubusson, I guessed—covered part of the green marble floor. Ficus trees with trunks twisted like gnarled fingers, sitting in copper pots, stood sentry on both sides of the stairs.

A crème de menthe teardrop crystal chandelier hung overhead, its arms silver tree branches. The light it offered was enough to show the way but not to chase away the shadows in the recesses of the room.

And in their depths, I saw faint movements, as if I were wearing my blindfold or looking into a mirror or a pool of water. Was I suddenly scrying without a reflective surface for focus? I'd never been able to do that before. But, emanating from those dimmed alcoves, I heard footsteps and whispers and saw figures made of smoke.

A wave of cold greeted me, which was then replaced by one of warmth. As if I were being welcomed by parts of the house and warned away by others.

I wanted to step further inside and at the same time wondered if I should leave. It felt as if the house had been waiting for me. And that without knowing it, I had been waiting to visit it for a very long time.

Madame Calvé descended the stairs, making an entrance wearing an emerald frock with several gold necklaces that jangled melodically as she walked.

"Welcome to my farmhouse." She opened her arms expansively.

"Hardly a farmhouse," Sebastian said. "It's magnificent."

"It may have the bones of a castle, but this is the one place that offers me peace and accessibility to nature. Here I'm not a star but a farmer. We employ more than a hundred people, and I often work alongside them, feeding my chickens, raising my donkeys, milking my cows. It's not what you expected?" She laughed.

"Hardly," Sebastian said, and I agreed.

"Don't worry. I promise you won't have to collect your own eggs for breakfast. And I'm sorry I wasn't outside to greet you. I was practicing," Madame said.

So it had been her singing, not a recording.

"We heard you as we got out of the car," I said. "It was a privilege."

"Thank you, dear. After dinner sometimes, I perform a bit. Now that I know you're interested, I'd be happy to do a little entertaining. Come this way, dears, and let's have some refreshments before I show you to your rooms."

She took my hand and drew me deeper into the foyer, past shadowy recesses. My vision remained hyper-sharp. Although we were inside, it seemed we'd stepped into a forest. The walls had been painted by a muralist to suggest that we were gazing into an ancient grove of twisting yews.

We followed her into a drawing room, where a fire was lit and tea had been laid out. There were no shadows there. Nothing out of the ordinary except that it was an incredibly beautiful, delicate, and exotic room.

Gilded tree branches formed frames around mirrors and paintings. Ferns sat on glazed majolica jardinieres in the forms of flowers. The furniture was velvet and silk in various shades of green. Arms and legs were carved animal heads. More majolica—garden seats—sat on either side of the fireplace; these were black with a lotus leaf and flower pattern. Large moss balls sat atop copper pots covered with aqua verdigris.

"Let's all sit. I'm just so delighted you've come to visit," Madame said.

She made it sound as if we were on holiday. Quite the contrary, Madame was paying handsomely for Sebastian and me to spend as long as it took for me to paint shadow portraits of the castle in order to discover the hiding place of Nicolas Flamel's lost book.

"You have the most beautiful home," I said.

"Thank you. Yes . . ." She looked around the room. "My home, my castle, my fortress . . . mostly my enigma. I've spent a long time here, captive to its mysteries. I hope that your visit may finally answer some of the questions echoing through these halls."

And, I thought, while I was here searching for them, I hoped I would be vigilant and alert enough to save my brother from whatever darkness followed him.

Chapter 26

After tea, which we drank out of green china cups in the shape of leaves with handles resembling twisted stems, on saucers in the shape of larger leaves, Madame suggested giving us a tour of the downstairs and then showing us to our bedrooms for a rest before evening.

"My decorating is a bit of a hodgepodge, isn't it?" Madame said, as she led us through a warren of rooms, each one more dramatic than the last. Darks played against lights, mysterious sculptures and framed calligraphy from the Orient mixed with Belle Époque posters advertising her performances.

In every corner, Emma Calvé had created small theater sets, with flowers, ferns, dried moss, shells, silvered orbs, malachite pyramids, lapis lazuli eggs, and quartz plinths. Majolica jardinieres, garden seats, and vases of every configuration added splashes of color and whimsy. Dried Spanish moss hung from branches arranged artfully in vases covered with sea glass or shells. Topiaries in the shapes of orbs and pyramids sat on mantelpieces. Where there were no murals, the walls were covered with paintings. Ivy grew around their ornate gold frames, forming second frames, with no thought to how the plants might be affecting the gilt wood.

And there were Buddhas everywhere. Sitting on mantels, shelves, and side tables, tucked into pots, mixed in with photos on top of the piano. Ivory, jade, quartz, gilt, wood, silver, in every size and shape. Some rustic, others so refined they looked as if Fabergé had carved them.

One room had been turned into a Japanese-style meditation garden, with rice-paper screens, a koi pond edged in rocks, and fragrant bonsai. Its Buddha was the largest of them all, almost as tall as I was, carved out of rosewood, so smooth it invited touch.

There were also very fine oil paintings hanging on the walls. At first, I thought they were scenarios from operas Madame had performed in, but on closer inspection, I saw that each was a staged tableau of magickal events and occult spectacles throughout history. While the styles were different, the subject matter corresponded, and together they created a fantastic narrative telling the history of the arcane and esoteric.

Rich rugs covered the marble floors. The furniture was upholstered in velvets and silks in a riot of wild purples and blues and deep, rich reds and pinks—chairs, couches, and pillows—creating gardens of fabric flowers.

Madame's home was a giant stage with a hundred sets. Shelves and tabletops and corners, each a story waiting to be deciphered. With an air of fantasy and theater, secrets and drama, which Madame moved through like the diva she was. Hidden everywhere were mirrors of all shapes and sizes, and in their reflections I saw moving shadows that surprised and disturbed me.

The more of the house I saw, the more I understood my initial excitement. And my fears.

"I keep bringing in architects and interior designers to work on one section and then another. We rip out walls and floors and renovate them, all the while looking for the book. We've taken apart and rebuilt almost every room, to no avail. Everything would suggest it's not here, yet I'm certain the book *is* hidden here *someplace.*"

I opened my mouth to ask her why she was certain, but Sebastian, anticipating my question—which he did too often—shot me a silencing look. In the car, he'd warned me that I should humor Madame Calvé, since she was paying the largest commission he'd ever been able to secure and the last thing he wanted was for me to plant doubt in her mind that the treasure might not exist.

We'd made it back to the grand staircase.

"Your rooms are up here. My students are usually housed in this wing, but they are in Paris for a week, taking a bit of a break from my hammering away at them. I'm a brute of a teacher, and every few weeks, I send them off to see the sights. This year, they are all from America."

I couldn't help but wonder if that was the only reason they weren't here. Sebastian had warned me that the search for the book was a secret. In order to protect her reputation, Madame had never publicly associated herself with the occult in any way. For more than thirty years, her interest had gone undiscovered by the press, and she was determined to keep it private.

We reached the first landing, which was decorated with a large painting of Madame Calvé as Carmen, the role she was most famous for. In the painting, she was at the height of her career, sensual, powerful, and seductive. The artist had somehow managed to catch the music playing in the swirl of her skirts, and I could hear strains of her aria in my mind.

She looked at it with me for a moment. "Carmen was a wonderful combination of uncontrolled desires and strange powers. An interesting combination, don't you think?"

"I do." Hadn't I been living a life that combined both those things since I'd left Paris almost five years before?

"I first performed it in 1894," Madame continued. "That was the year I met your mother. Carmen was an auspicious role for me. My life had already become enmeshed in the occult, and my knowledge of fortune-telling and supernatural phenomena allowed me to bring something unique to the role."

She continued gazing at the painting for a moment. "It's been a wonderful run. Glorious. And now I teach other young women to be glorious." There was a hint of sadness mixed with delight. "I still sing at my soirees, though. I'm having one this weekend for a few of us to gather and say good-bye to a dear friend who's passed over. You'll know a few of the guests. Some of my friends are also yours."

"Mine?" I asked, worried that she was referring to Mathieu and at the same time wishing she was. There it was again; ever since I'd set foot in this house, I kept feeling a push/pull. Stay/go. Feeling welcomed/repelled. Elated/fearful. And now desperately wanting Mathieu to be one of her guests and praying he wasn't. I wasn't strong enough to renounce him a second time. But what was I even thinking? Renounce him? He wouldn't even look at me long enough to say hello, and that would be worse, wouldn't it? After the way we parted and the betrayal he must have felt, I was certain he'd never speak to me again. Hadn't that been the whole point of my charade?

Madame nodded. "Yours and your brother's. The art world is quite small, isn't it? And so many artists from Paris are at the beach this year. It never used to be like this. The south is flooded with English and Russians during the winter, but in the summer we residents enjoyed it all to ourselves. Now Saint-Tropez, Cannes, Juan-les-Pins, and Nice are full of tourists, and the roads are clogged with cars."

The mellifluous sound of her voice made me want to just go on listening to her. She was rumored to have had—and to still have—many lovers. I didn't doubt it. Despite her body being a bit stout and the lines etched on her face, her every turn of phrase was luscious and rich. Her dark brown eyes drew you in and sparkled with a kind of bronze-colored glee and seductiveness that were ageless and infectious.

"Now, this is your room, dear Sebastian."

She opened the door to a stately suite with pale green walls and dark gray accents, silver knickknacks, and silvery gray curtains hanging on the tall windows. The view looked out over the valley. Lush and green and still clouded over with dark shadows.

Leaving my brother, we proceeded down the hall, passing three more doors, until she stopped.

"I've given you my favorite room. And it has a secret." She smiled at me conspiratorially and opened the door.

I felt as if I were stepping into the inside of a conch shell. The walls were painted an exquisite silvery pink-peach, a color made all the more intense by the sudden shaft of sunlight that broke through the clouds.

"This is your sitting room," she said.

The curtains were the same color as the walls and shimmered in the breeze from the open window. Two velvet couches, upholstered in a slightly darker but still luscious peach, sat opposite each other, a low coffee table covered with books between them. Creamy peach marble faced the fireplace. Above it hung a painting of an elderly man who looked like Merlin, peering into a crystal ball.

"Come," she said. "Let me show you the rest."

We went through one of the two doors on either side of the fire-place and entered a studio. There was no carpet here, rather a floor made of stone pavers. The ceiling had a skylight and north-facing windows—the painter's preferred light.

In the center sat an easel and a taboret, its shelves filled with supplies.

I looked at Madame. "Do you paint?"

She laughed. "No, but a long time ago, I was in love with a painter and had this room turned into a studio for him. I thought it would suit you. Will it suffice? Will you be able to work here?"

I nodded. I did think I'd be able to work there. The space had a peaceful quiet that was unlike the rest of the theatrical house, which sang with excitement.

For the first time since February, I felt calmer about donning the blindfold. After all, as Sebastian kept reminding me, what secrets could a house hold that I needed to be scared of?

"Yes, it's perfect," I said. "The light will be ideal."

"Now, here"—she took me back out through the sitting room and through the other door—"is your bedroom."

The walls were covered with a decadent damask in the same peach tones. A half dozen ancient mirrors hung on either side of the bed and on the facing wall, so it was like being inside an antique kaleidoscope. The reflections were softened by the weathered glass, but as I peered into one, I saw a distant vista.

"What is it, dear?" she asked.

Frozen to the spot, I couldn't take my eyes off the mirror.

"There is so much shadow play inside the glass," I said. I'd learned over the years not to blurt out what I saw and frighten people. It was one thing to tell Sebastian, who was used to it, or my mother, who in a way took credit for it because it was she who'd restored my sight and, with it, this other ability.

"These are the original mirrors of the house. We had them taken from different rooms and hallways so we could use them in this suite like wallpaper. It was the designer's idea. Do you like them?"

"How old are they?" I was afraid my voice belied my wonder. For I was seeing within the depths of the glass fragments of stories that had to be ancient.

"I wouldn't know exactly, but the château was built before 1200."

I was afraid to speak, because I was watching a group of six pilgrims climbing up a mountain, slowly, painfully, carefully. As if a movie were trapped in the glass. As if the mirror were a peephole into a play being enacted on a faraway stage. I couldn't see myself, which was atypical. Was it because these were so old and marred with mercury spots?

As long as I wasn't in the images and they didn't relate to me, I wasn't as concerned as I might have been. If I started to see myself, I could always ask for fabric to cover them or have them removed. Based on what I knew of Madame's extensive forays into the occult, she'd probably be fascinated by my scrying—if that's what this was.

Then, in the mirror, I noticed that around the next bend, four marauders were lying in wait for the pilgrims. If only I could call out to them and stop them—but this scene was from the far distant past. I kept watching, riveted. As the group came around the curve, the robbers rode up and blocked their passage. Two of the thieves jumped off their horses, swords pointed. A sharp edge caught the light.

I could hear faint screams as the women watched the highway-men attack the men, who fell despite putting up a fight. What were mere hands against foils? One woman fainted. Another threw her body over that of her husband—or maybe he was her father.

Laughing, the thieves began attacking the women, pulling rings off their fingers and necklaces from around their necks. Then one grabbed hold of a woman's robe and ripped it off her body.

"No!"

I didn't realize I'd spoken out loud until I felt Madame Calvé's hand on my arm and heard her voice.

"Are you all right, dear? What is it?"

I was going to have to tell her about the mirrors. That she'd have to cover them. Even if it meant explaining more about my talent than I wished. I'd learned one thing very quickly. There *were* secrets in this house. And my instincts told me I was going to find them. I just couldn't be sure they would be the ones Madame wanted me to uncover.

Chapter 27

Book of Hours
July 22, 1920

Mathieu shows me his secret Paris but keeps secret parts of himself locked away. I can't bear to see his suffering. What is it that plagues him so that he won't even allow himself to talk of it? What secrets hide behind the barricade he's erected? I'm tempted to offer to draw his shadow portrait. Maybe I can help save him from the darkness that I can see he battles, even though he thinks he's hiding it from me.

As we walked toward Notre Dame today, Mathieu stopped at various shops. By the time we arrived at our destination, the Square du Vert-Galant at the tip of the Île de la Cité, we had gathered a feast: a bottle of wine, peaches, cheese, and a fresh baguette.

Sensing that Mathieu's emotional block had to do with his brother's death, I decided to try to get him to talk more about Maximilian and asked what he'd been like. At first, he hesitated, and I thought he was going to refuse. But then, with a sigh of resignation, he turned his head, looked out at the flowing river, and began.

"Max was six years older than I. A student of history. I told you he was going to be a professor at the Sorbonne, didn't I? When I was small, he used to take me all over Paris, showing me the important landmarks, telling me stories. He once said that history was soaked into the earth beneath every step we took."

Mathieu picked up my hand and held it. If I could have willed him healed, I would have. I sensed the break in his soul again and wondered if it would ever mend.

Then he let go, pulled the cork out of the wine, and handed me the bottle. I took a sip and handed it back to him.

"Right here, for instance." He gestured to the park around us. "This spot was created by King Henri IV. A most amorous ruler. They called him Le Vert-Galant—the grand spark—and his sexual exploits were notorious. His appetite insatiable. He kept several mistresses at a time and still visited brothels."

"Why was this spot named for him?" I asked.

"He loved the view and thought it very romantic. But as for what went on here? You'd have to get the trees to tell you. Can you call upon your magick to make them give up their secrets?"

I've confided more to Mathieu about my abilities than to anyone outside my family. I have no reason but instinct to trust him, and I hope I'm not making a mistake. Yet each time I see him, each hour we spend together, deepens my conviction.

We ate the bread and cheese and fruit. When we were finished, we drank more of the wine, and Mathieu licked its remains off my lips.

Then, as we sat and looked out at the Seine, clouds rolled across the sky, and a storm blew in. When the rain came, we took shelter and huddled beneath a chestnut tree, the water releasing the leaves' sweet smell.

We watched the swans swim past. They were as untroubled by the rain as we were.

Mathieu reached out, took me in his arms, and kissed me. A kiss that lasted until the rain stopped. Five minutes? A half hour? I didn't know, but the swans had returned by the time we stopped. Mathieu studied them for a moment. Two of them faced each other, their curved necks forming a perfect heart.

"They aren't that different from what you told me about the women in your family, you know?"

"What do you mean?"

"They find one partner and mate for life."

He reached into his jacket and pulled out a midnight-blue velvet ring box.

"I probably should be quoting some magnificent poem now. I usually have verses at the ready, but you, darling Delphine, leave me speechless."

He opened the box and held it out to me. Inside, nestled against a silk cushion, was a crescent-shaped moonstone surrounded by a curve of pale blue sapphires.

"Will you be my swan?" he asked.

I felt the tears sting my eyes and saw my own sudden joy reflected in Mathieu's eyes. For a moment, every trace of sadness was gone, forgotten.

When the rain ceased, we collected our things. As we left, Mathieu took my hand, rubbing his fingers over the ring I now wore.

"Ah," he said. "I just thought of the perfect line of poetry. I can't believe I forgot about it till now. From a verse by Alfred de Musset."

"Tell me."

"'I don't know where my road is going, but I know that I walk better when I hold your hand.'"

Chapter 28

I dreamed every night of the ten days I was trapped in the château. Later I would discover that I was dreaming not only my dreams but also those of other people, some long dead and buried, but I didn't realize that at first. The castle housed more than Madame's eclectic collections of art, esoteric objects, and antiques. There was magick in the cracks of the stone walls, in the crevices in the foundation, in the very air that circulated through the drafty hallways and endless rooms.

That first night, I dreamed I was traveling in a foreign land, unrecognizable to me. A snake charmer sat, bare-chested and cross-legged, in front of a hand-woven basket. Playing a plaintive melody on his reed, he swayed slightly. I began to move to the rhythm of the song. Slithering and sliding, uncurling, pushing my way up through a murky and dank hole toward the light. Then, with utter disgust, I realized I was the snake the charmer was calling. I was that monstrous forked-tongued creature, and as I pushed off the top of the basket and emerged, screams greeted me. Women shrank back in the crowd. Men struggled to hold their ground. Children ran away. Even the snake charmer himself seemed disgusted by me, as if he had been anticipating a much more lithe and lovely creature and I'd disappointed him.

I awoke exhausted. Downstairs I found Sebastian and Madame Calvé at the piano. She was singing for him, and he was charming her. The maid brought me some coffee, and I sat and listened and tried to shake the nightmare.

When she stopped playing, Madame asked me how I had slept. There wasn't any reason to beleaguer her with my dream.

"Very well, thank you."

"I'm so glad. The castle can be drafty and sometimes damp, even with all the wall hangings and carpets." She shook her head, disturbed. "Nothing ever seems to solve it completely. But I didn't notice it last night. I had the best sleep I've had in a long time," she said. "And the mirrors?"

I smiled. "They behaved."

Sebastian looked over at me inquisitively. "Mirrors?"

"There are a dozen antique mirrors in my bedroom. But Madame covered the larger ones with scarves, and they're not bothering me at all."

"Now, are you sure?" Madame asked. "I can remove them. I want you to be completely comfortable."

"I'm sure."

"Will you join us for some breakfast? There's always a buffet in the dining room in the morning."

I declined her offer, saying the coffee was enough, and excused myself, telling them I wanted to take a walk so I could get my bearings and understand the placement of the house and its surroundings in preparation for the portrait.

A cloudy sky threatened more rain, but I took my chances. I walked out past the courtyard, through a wooden door, and into an extensive, exotic garden in full colorful bloom. Like in Monet's gardens in Giverny, the flowers here were arranged so the colors either contrasted or flowed into each other. Nothing appeared accidental, and yet it looked natural. In one bed, royal purple and ultramarine delphiniums grew next to violet and deep fuchsia foxgloves, while orange daylilies brightened the bouquet. Bushes of fat, fragrant roses in shades of pink surrounded a fountain where several beautiful black-and-white jaybirds splashed. On either side of a stone path, red-orange and salmon-pink poppies grew in profusion, their paper-like petals blowing in the breeze.

To the right was a knotted garden bordered with privet and to the left an old-fashioned herb garden. All the various shades of green—from yellow to blue and purple—had been planned out with a painter's eye.

My mother had created elaborate gardens in Cannes. She claimed not to sprinkle any spells on her flowers, but I never quite believed her. These gardens put hers to shame. The gardener here had to be not only an artist but some kind of magician.

Beyond the gardens, I followed a stone path through a field of wildflowers until I reached a rusted iron gate. The latch stuck at first, but after a few tries, it swung open. Beyond was a wooded glen without any discernible path. I stood for a few moments, wondering if I should continue or go back. Then I heard the invitation of trickling water just beyond.

After a few minutes, I found a little stream and followed it to a pool being fed by a small waterfall. I sat down on a wide, flat boulder, mesmerized by the sounds of the splashing water, the loamy scent of the earth, the deep, rich black and green colors of the ferns and other foliage that grew between the rocks.

I pulled out my sketchbook and spent a half hour drawing aspects of the scene. Trying but failing to capture any of the magic, until I began to put faces on the stones that circled me, as if a master sculptor had carved them. Each one an ancient, wise-looking man with a tale to tell.

I was lost in capturing their different visages for quite a while. I'm not sure how long I'd been feeling the earth beneath me pulsing without realizing it. But once I did, I couldn't ignore the subtle but real sensation of a heartbeat matching mine. Not frightening. More companionable. Once again, I felt as if I had been called to this place. That it had been waiting for me. And I for it.

I put away the sketchbook and continued to follow the stream deeper into the woods, not aware until it was too late that I'd entered a labyrinth made of yews at least seven feet high.

A wave of panic hit me. I hadn't told anyone where I was going. These woods, which had been suffused with enchantment, now seemed to be saturated with diabolical spirits. Could they be trapping me here? Was that even possible? My fear began to overwhelm me. I felt dizzy from the solid walls of never-ending green. If I had to, could I break branches and create a tunnel through a hedge to escape?

I turned a corner and found myself at a dead end. I doubled back. But then I faced a choice of two ways to turn. The one I took led to yet another dead end. My panic grew. Stopping mid-step, I shut my eyes. I had to find a way out, rely on something other than sight. Listening hard, I heard birds. I saw a wren fly overhead and land on top of the maze wall, which was about twice my height. Listening harder, I heard insects. But neither the bird nor the bugs could help me crawl or fly out of these evergreen confines.

But perhaps I could do it on my own. My mother had taught me an exercise during my sightless year that allowed me to project my astral self and see through my third eye. Very dangerous if not done correctly and a little frightening to experience. She'd allowed me to do it only under supervision with her voice leading the way. I hadn't tried it in years, but I needed it now.

I extended my arms until my fingertips brushed the leaves so that I'd stay tethered—a key aspect of the exercise, my mother had warned, because an astral self can have a very hard time, if not an impossible one, reconnecting to a corporeal body if it doesn't have a bond.

Feeling the glossy leaves, I relaxed my breathing the same way I did when I put on the blindfold. Once I calmed, I focused on the sound of the wren whistling and threw my energy up toward her. Seeing, in my mind, my opalescent aura rising from inside the labyrinth toward the wren sitting on a hedge top. Reaching her, I sat beside her on her perch. And then I peered down. I saw myself standing, arms reaching out. I looked at the configuration of the tunnels, followed the pathways, and saw the way out. And then, still with my eyes shut, I commanded my feet to step in that direction, making sure my fingers were touching the foliage the entire way.

I thought of my mother as I kept moving, hearing her instructions in my mind. When I'd reached the exit, I connected back with my corporeal self and opened my eyes. I'd come out on the opposite end. In front of me was a stone cottage. Relieved that I'd escaped, I stood and caught my breath, aware for the first time that for the last several minutes, I'd been running.

"How did you find your way here?" I heard the man's astonished question before I saw him. Searching in the direction of his voice, I saw a shadowy figure inside the house, looking out through an open window.

I started to answer, but he was gone. A moment later, the front door opened. A dog ran out and came right up to me, tail wagging. I recognized Pepin, the brown-and-white puppy from the pier the day before. His owner, the silver-haired man, was close behind.

"I didn't mean to startle you," he said.

As he came toward me, I felt that same warmth I'd felt on the pier. It had been a long time since I'd responded in any way to a man, but seeing him again, I felt a flutter of anticipation.

"I think I startled you just as much."

"Not many people wind up here. I was surprised to see you."

"I got lost."

"I know," he said, nodding as if he understood that I didn't just mean today, didn't just mean here.

The dog was jumping around my feet. I petted him.

"Where did you start from?" he asked.

"I'm staying at the castle."

"You walked from the castle?"

"Yes. Through the gardens into the forest and got turned around somewhere."

"The gate into the forest was unlocked?" He frowned, concern in his topaz eyes.

"It was." I'd stopped petting the dog. Pepin barked for more. I leaned over and gave him more pats.

"But it's never unlocked." He studied me, taking me in, considering me intently. It reminded me of how my mother looked at people, searching inside them, testing them, seeing if she could trust them. Maybe he was an adept?

I caught myself. It was too soon for me to assign qualities before I had any reason to.

As if he realized what he was doing and how I was reacting, he reached down and pulled the dog back.

"Pepin, don't be a pest," he said. Then, rising, he smiled at me. "I hope you weren't lost for long. The forest is a mean one. She can do that."

He'd said *she can do that*, but what I heard was *she's meant to do that*.

I was getting the distinct impression that he was disturbed that I'd gotten this far into the forest, as if it was his fault.

"Where are my manners? My name is Gaspard Le'Malf." He held out his hand.

I took it and felt a slight, almost unpleasant electrical vibration. A warning. My mother had schooled me to recognize the slight and subtle signs that identified people who were like us and in touch with realms beyond our own. Had he felt the shudder, too? Was he aware of his ability? Of mine? His face remained impassive. Alerted,

I needed to be on guard. Not everyone uses his or her power for positive outcomes. He could be the best friend I would find at the castle or a true foe.

"Do you live here?" I pointed to the cottage.

"I do. I'm the groundskeeper for the château."

"Then I need to compliment you. I've been walking about, and the gardens and fields are beautiful. It's all enchanting."

He nodded in thanks. "You could say it's been my life's work."

"I followed the stream . . . Did you plant all those mosses and ferns, or are they indigenous to the area?"

"About half and half. You know, very few people notice the stream. Fewer still ever make it to the waterfall."

"Really? The sound was so inviting, how could anyone resist?"

"Not everyone notices the sound. And you made it through the labyrinth . . ."

"You say it as if it's hard to believe."

"Actually, it is. It's quite complex. How long were you inside?"

"Not long. Ten minutes?"

He was staring at me now. "I see."

"Why?"

"I'm only aware of one other person who has made it through without any missteps."

"Who was that?"

"It was a long time ago, before my time. Just a story. The labyrinth was designed more than two hundred years ago." He shrugged. "Are you thirsty? Would you like some water or cider before I take you back?"

I realized I was parched and, even more, wanted to see the inside of his cottage.

"Cider would be wonderful."

He pointed to a group of wicker chairs and a wrought-iron table. "Have a seat, and I'll be right out."

I was disappointed but couldn't very well follow him uninvited. Especially when I sensed he'd known why I had accepted his offer of refreshment. It appeared he didn't want me in the house. But why? Someone who kept the grounds so well-groomed wouldn't keep a messy house. Was there someone inside he preferred I not meet? Something he didn't want me to see?

Gaspard came out with two glasses and a blue enamel jug. Sitting opposite me, he poured out the cider and handed me a glass.

"So are you visiting from Paris?"

"No, from Cannes."

"Not a bad drive up, then."

I took a long sip of the dry, crisp drink. "Just an afternoon."

"She loves her grand parties." I must have made a face, because Gaspard said, "You don't like parties much, do you?" He'd guessed correctly.

"No, not at all, in fact."

"But you came anyway?"

The curious conversation flowed easily, as if we'd been friends for a long time. Unusual for me. Was it for him, too?

I shook my head. "No, I'm a painter. I'm here to paint the castle."

"A portrait of the castle?" he asked.

"Of a sort." I explained about being a bit physic and then said, "Madame Calvé wants me to help her find a book."

I caught the same frown I'd seen earlier.

"Did I speak out of turn? Please tell me you know about the book?" Worried that I'd said more than I should have, I held my breath until he answered.

"Oh, yes, I know all about her treasure hunt."

A flicker of anger flashed in his bright eyes—or at least I perceived it as such. The expression appeared and then disappeared so quickly I couldn't be positive, but he did seem disturbed by what I'd told him.

"You work for Madame Calvé. Perhaps I shouldn't be discussing this," I said.

"I don't actually work for her." His inflection alerted me.

Had I stumbled onto an area of conflict between Gaspard and his employer?

"I work for the castle, no matter who the owners are. I'm part of the deed."

"I don't understand."

"It's a bit complicated, but suffice it to say that my family has been the castle's caretakers for generations. We own the bit of land my cottage is on, plus a few other parcels within the castle's grounds. Our duties include tending Cabrières's gardens and keeping the forest. It's written into the contract each time the castle is sold."

"That's extremely unusual, isn't it?"

He nodded. "But necessary."

"Why?"

"Continuity. With the passage of time and turnover in ownership, there has to be a link from the past to the present to ensure that all continues into the future. Taking care of this land requires a fair amount of specific knowledge."

There was something beyond what he was saying. I studied his face, and our eyes met. I sensed that by *specific* he meant *magickal*. But before I could glean any more, he lowered a curtain. On purpose? Accidentally? I wasn't sure, but I knew he was hiding something.

My mother said certain people were old souls. They'd lived many lives, had returned to our plane often, and were more highly evolved than the rest of us, since over all those lifetimes, they'd accumulated great wisdom.

She taught me how to spot it in their eyes. And sometimes in their smiles. She also showed me the look of someone who didn't have many more earth journeys left before he was finally—and blessedly—relieved of the burden of more incarnations.

Gaspard Le'Malf, I had no doubt, was an old soul. And I was equally sure he had more information about this castle and what I was here to find than he wanted me to know.

Before I could ask him, a high-pitched shriek rent the air.

"Papa, Papa! Look what we found!"

An excited little boy, about six or seven, came running over, holding something tightly in his cupped hands. Behind him, at a distance, was a young woman, smiling as the boy reached his father.

"Wait, wait. Nicky, where are your manners? We have a guest."

· Nicky looked over at me. He had tousled blond hair, a round cherubic face, and perfect pink cheeks. He also had his father's eyes, wiser than his years suggested.

"Hello," he said, very formally. "I am Nicky Le'Malf. I would shake your hand, but I have a surprise for Papa."

"I'm Delphine Duplessi," I said to him, with the same formal tone. "And I'd love to see your surprise."

The boy looked at his father, who nodded.

"All right, both of you, watch now. See what Mademoiselle Gris and I found."

So the woman was not the boy's mother. A nursemaid, then?

"Ready?" Nicky asked.

"Ready," I said.

Gaspard nodded. "Me, too."

Nicky opened his hands. A butterfly, white with bright orange tips, fluttered its wings and flew out. The beautiful creature hovered in the air, at eye level with Nicky, as if communicating with him.

"Thank you," the boy said to the butterfly, bowing slightly.

As the insect flew off, Nicky turned to Gaspard. "Papa, was that an orange-tip *Anthocharis cardamines*?"

Gaspard nodded.

"I have to get my book and write it down." Nicky turned to me. "Would you like to see my book of butterflies?"

"No, Mademoiselle Duplessi has to get back to the castle."

The boy looked crestfallen.

"If you don't mind," I said to Gaspard, then turned to Nicky. "I love butterflies. I'd be honored to see your book."

Nicky ran off into the house, followed by Mademoiselle Gris.

"He's charming. Do you and your wife have others?"

"No. We were expecting another. But my wife was in an accident. Two years ago. The car she was in . . ." He took a deep breath, as if saying the words took enormous effort.

Before he could finish, Nicky was back, shoving a book into my hands. It was a journal. And I trembled as I took it from him, because I recognized the binding style. It was Mathieu's work. For a moment, I felt dizzy. Confused. How did this child have one of Mathieu's books?

"What a beautiful butterfly diary," I said.

"Last year for Christmas, Madame Calvé got it for me in Paris."

That made sense. Madame Calvé was a regular at Pierre Dujols's bookshop.

"Madame is very good to Nicky," Gaspard said. "She treats him like her grandson. It's sad she never had children of her own."

"Not always sad," I said. "Sometimes a child is just competition for an artist's other creations."

Gaspard was about to say something when Nicky interrupted.

"There are more than one hundred and fifty different butterflies in this part of where we live." He started turning the pages in the book. On each one was another drawing, carefully outlined, not as carefully colored in. As he continued flipping through the books, I noticed a photograph of a woman with Nicky's coloring, but he didn't stop to show it to me.

"Whenever I see a new kind—I mean species—I bring it home to show Papa. We study it, and after I draw it, we let it go." His face became very solemn. "Some people kill them and collect them. We always let them go. I ask them all to fly up to heaven and visit Maman. And they always say they will. She loves them, too."

My heart seized up. There was something about this little boy that touched me profoundly.

Gaspard stood. "I think we should get you back to the château,

Mademoiselle Duplessi. It's almost time for lunch, and Madame doesn't like having to send out search parties for her guests."

"Please, call me Delphine."

Gaspard nodded.

I said good-bye to Nicky and thanked him for showing me his book of butterflies.

"If you'd like, you can come hunting with me tomorrow?"

"That sounds wonderful. I have to work tomorrow, but as soon as I'm free, I'd love to join you."

"Mademoiselle is an artist. She might be able to show you how to color inside the lines," Gaspard said.

Nicky pouted.

"I think coloring outside the lines is much more fun." I winked at him, and he winked back.

With the dog at his heels, Gaspard led me around to the other side of the cottage, through a gate, and back into the woods.

We talked about his son for most of the way. And then about the woods and the fact that, like Nicky, he had been studying butterflies since he was a boy.

"How many have you seen?"

"I think by now I've seen them all."

Something about how he said it made it sound as if he'd lived longer than what I guessed was thirty or so years. He spoke like an old, old man.

After about ten minutes, we came to a second gate, which he unlocked. On the other side, we walked down a small hill and from there took a path that led to a cobblestone road. I couldn't believe I'd walked so far that morning.

"Is the route through the forest much shorter?" I asked him.

"No, it's actually longer." Gaspard pointed to the left. There, not far off—possibly another ten-minute walk—was the castle. "I'll leave you here. It'll be easy now. In the forest, it's almost impossible to see through the ceiling of trees and find the château's towers. But anywhere else you go, just look up and search for them. That's how to orient yourself."

"Thank you. I really had no idea where I was. I'm not sure I could ever find my way here again, even if I wanted to."

Gaspard's expression surprised me. I thought he'd enjoyed my visit, that he'd been happy I'd met Nicky, but the look in his eyes suggested that it would be better if I didn't try.

Chapter 29

Back at the château, I was just in time for the abundant midday meal that had been prepared for us—country bread, pâté, and a robust niçoise salad made the same way we served it at home, with a variety of crisp vegetables including raw red peppers and artichoke hearts, along with tuna, olives, and tart vinaigrette.

I had questions about the book I'd be searching for, and Madame was only too happy to talk about her obsession.

"Flamel was a scrivener and manuscript dealer. Not well off. Not very successful. And then, around 1365 or so, he purchased a mysterious book written in what appeared to be Hebrew. He made it his life's work to learn more about it. Finally, he traveled to Spain in 1378, where there were more Jews than in France, in the hopes that he'd find someone to translate it."

She stopped to pour more of the local rosé into her glass and then Sebastian's. I had barely touched mine.

"Flamel's mission failed. But on the road back from Santiago de Compostela, he met a sage, a *converso* who recognized the book as a copy of the *Book of Abraham* and aided him in the translation. Everything changed for Flamel after that." She took another sip of wine. "Do either of you know very much about alchemy?"

Sebastian and I both said we did not.

"I have been a student most of my adult life. The principles come from ancient Egyptians, who learned it from Arabs. It's an art that involves sacred geometry, magick, chemistry, philosophy, hermeticism, and cosmology. The true goal of alchemy is not to create gold—that's just a by-product of the methodology. The real goal is to create the Elixir of Life in order to delay the aging process and even perhaps lead to immortality. Alchemists, you see, were simply scientists and seekers of knowledge. But in the Middle Ages, the church forbade their experiments and labeled them heretics, forcing the alchemists underground. And so their research became known as the black art."

"Why would experiments with metals for the purpose of a longer life be heretical?" I asked.

"Because the secret to immortality is bound up in the Great Work. Through the ages, we've come to believe that turning base metal into gold was the formula for the elixir." She flipped her hand as if making that look easy. "Flamel accomplished that in the early 1380s, when he first created silver and then gold."

"That's astonishing," I said.

She picked up the basket of bread, took a second slice, and passed it to me. I had been listening so intently to her story that I hadn't touched my food. I'd read about Flamel but had no in-depth knowledge of him. What she was recounting was tickling my memory, but I wasn't sure why.

"Yes, but more astonishing was the portal his achievement opened. The threshold one crossed into spiritual enlightenment, where slowing down or stopping the aging process is merely one aspect . . ." Madame's eyes glittered. Her voice lowered to a seductive whisper. She wet her lips. "The Great Work is a state of being. A life force. An act of secret initiation and physical revitalization. Its symbol is a hermaphrodite. You know it?"

Sebastian and I both said we did.

"Then you know it is a male who is a female, a female who is a male. The perfect symbol for sexual union and the moment of orgasm."

She looked at us to see if she had gone too far, if either of us was shocked or uncomfortable. Sebastian didn't seem to be, and I wasn't. Although it certainly wasn't the norm to talk of orgasms at the lunch table in 1925, how could we, descendants of France's most famous courtesans, have possibly been shocked?

"It is in that moment of coming together that real magick occurs. That the Great Work is achieved. When male and female become part of each other and can reach a mystical awareness of both themselves and the universe and in that moment know the secrets to achieve immortality. Very few can reach that pinnacle, but with the help of the book, on January 17, 1382, Nicolas Flamel and his wife, Perenelle, did."

She paused for dramatic effect.

"Having become wealthy, thanks to the ability to change metals to gold, Flamel then turned to philanthropy and was well known for his good deeds. Sometime during 1410, when he was in his eighties, he designed his own tombstone, decorated with carvings of esoteric symbols and signs, a code that's never been cracked. Eight years later, in 1418, he staged his and his wife's deaths, even going so far as to have elaborate ceremonies performed in order to convince everyone they had passed on. But it was only a ruse set up to allow them to escape their notoriety, take their secrets with them, and live in peace."

Her stagecraft was superb, and it made her a riveting storyteller. When she spoke, I could see all the scenes playing out, like in a film. But a familiar one. Where had I heard this story? And then I realized. The scene in the bedroom, in the mirror, of the pilgrims on the road—Flamel had been one of them. He'd been on his journey to Spain to find someone to help him translate the book.

"When Cardinal Richelieu first became obsessed with discovering all of Flamel's secrets, he hired a grave robber to dig up Flamel's coffin and discovered it was empty. Without a trace of the mystic. His wife's coffin was equally barren. Some say Flamel and his wife survived another hundred years after their supposed deaths, some say three hundred. Others claim they are still alive. No one knows."

Madame finished her tale with a flourish. I was surprised not to hear an orchestra add a few telling notes.

"You haven't eaten a bite," she said to me.

"I was so caught up in your story I forgot." I laughed and obediently picked up my fork. The salad was fresh and delicious in the simplest way. Like so much of the food from the south. But as good as it was, eating was an odd accompaniment to the discussion of sexual magick. My older sister and I had scoured my mother's library for books about it so we could read the "dirty" parts. My friends had their mothers' risqué novels by Colette and her contemporaries, but we giggled over the orgiastic rituals described in books written by Aleister Crowley, who created the Golden Dawn society, or Maria de Naglowska. And then we gagged reading about the disturbing black masses that used human waste, sperm, and menstrual blood as sacraments.

"And the formula for the Great Work is contained in the book we're searching for?" Sebastian asked.

Madame nodded. "I believe so."

My twin turned to me. "Hasn't Maman talked about an elixir like that? Something that La Lune handed down?"

Once again, Sebastian was breaking our family's unspoken rules. Yes, my mother had told us about the potion. From La Lune's grimoire, the formula had been passed down through the centuries. My mother used it for the first and last time in 1894 to save my father's life shortly before they married.

"Your mother told me and Pierre Dujols about her elixir," Madame said, surprising both of us. "Years ago, during her transition. We think there are similarities, but your family's version is weak and unstable and can only be used by a daughter of La Lune."

"Do you have a physical description of the *Book of Abraham*?" I asked Madame, wanting to change the subject.

"Varying descriptions. Some say it was made of gold or vellum or parchment. Some sources have it at seven pages, others at twenty-one. But everyone agrees that on every page there are secrets." Madame's eyes shone.

A lemon mousse, light and tart, was served for dessert, along with espresso. Once I'd drained my cup, I announced that I was going to my studio to set to work and earn my keep. I'd wanted to start sketching. The sooner I could solve Madame's mystery for her, the sooner Sebastian and I could leave. I wanted to be gone before the party Madame had mentioned. Especially after seeing Gaspard's son's journal and being reminded of the relationship between La Diva and the bookshop. I didn't want to take any chances that she'd invited Mathieu.

In the studio, I arranged my tools on the table by the easel. A drawing pad, my silver pencil, an assortment of softer leaded pencils, and my blindfold. Just touching it, my fingers tingled. For a moment, I sat, holding it, a portal to so many secrets. My gateway to hidden mysteries of the soul. A light illuminating shadows. For good and for ill.

But not this time. I was using it to see hidden corners of the castle. To look behind its walls and passageways. Under its floors.

I let out a long breath. After five months of trepidation, I put it on quickly. Like diving into the cold sea on a chilly morning. I adjusted the elastic behind my head.

I could no longer see what was in front of me. Everything inside my eyes was dark. I waited for what was hiding to be revealed.

I began sketching the rooms I'd walked through. Drawing scenes frozen in time, rapidly capturing them on paper. Vaguely aware that there were people in the rooms and that their clothes suggested I was getting images from different time periods.

A scullery maid in a kitchen, stirring a cauldron over an open fire. Behind the bricks was a hidden room. I could smell the dust. A storage area of some kind, abandoned. But footprints through the dust suggested someone had been there recently.

The library with its book-filled shelves. A gentleman in a cutaway taking leather volumes off one particular shelf. He reached behind it and pulled a lever. The shelves opened like a door. Inside, I could see the corner of a couch.

A bedroom, dark rose and lavender. A lady's boudoir. Perfume bottles on the vanity. Their scent overwhelming. Her back was to me, and I could see her in the mirror as she lifted a gold necklace over her head, an old key dangling from it, and tucked it inside her corset.

For room after room, I sketched scenes that revealed secrets about the inhabitants of the château over the years. None obviously about an ancient book. But all of them revealed or suggested hiding places.

The last drawing I did was the most strange. I sketched a dungeon. Stone walls and floor. Moisture dripping into a pool. The stones were uneven, pitted with dark recesses. And in one, I saw something glitter. Was it gold? A gemstone? I tried to step closer, but I couldn't walk any deeper into the grotto. An invisible force held me back. I pushed against it, but it didn't give. I heard music, far off. I knew the music was playing expressly for me, trying to tell me something that the stones couldn't. I struggled to listen and catch more of it, but it remained elusive. I was certain there was a clue in that music, if I could just hear it more clearly.

I stopped drawing. I took off my blindfold. Around me were more than a dozen sketches. Surprised by the time on the clock, I sat where I was and tried to make sense of what had happened. Usually, I worked for a few minutes. Ten at the most. But according to the Limoges timepiece, I had been working for almost two hours.

I extended and flexed my fingers. They were smudged with graphite and ached. I stood. Bent over, I let my back muscles stretch. When I returned to a standing position, I was a little dizzy.

From the sideboard, I poured water out of a crystal pitcher into a matching glass, which I took to the open window. I looked out into the gardens below. Gaspard was there, Pepin at his heels. The gardener was clipping deep blood-red roses.

Tipping the glass to my lips, I sipped the water. As I watched, the silver-haired man with the golden eyes looked up at the castle, toward me. Even though I doubted he could see me in the shadows, it appeared that he could. First a look of pleasure played around his lips, followed by a frown creasing his forehead.

I'd seen the same reaction from him at the cottage. As welcoming as he'd been, and despite the *simpatico* I'd felt from him, I had the distinct impression he wished I had never come.

A chilly wind blew in. I put the glass down and lowered the window. Halfway, it slammed shut, catching my forefinger. The pain was intense. My finger throbbed. Luckily, it was my left hand. In the bathroom, I ran the cold water and held my finger under the tap. Once it was numb, I shut off the water, dried my hand, and returned to the drawings, to inspect them again and see if any tiny details struck me as clues. I was always vaguely aware of what I was drawing as I worked, but upon scrutinizing the sketches after they were completed, I often discovered new elements that in the moment hadn't reached my consciousness.

Searching through my afternoon's work, I found what looked like Arabic writing on the stones in the dungeon. What appeared to be a skull in the dust in the room behind the oven. And odd markings I couldn't decipher at all on the spines of the books in the library. But it wasn't until I showed the sketches to Madame Calvé later that I noted the most curious thing of all.

We were huddled over a card table in the coziest room in the castle. A sitting room decorated in cabbage roses and green-leaf chintz. The walls, painted a faint blush color, were covered with botanical prints. Topiaries in the shapes of robins sat in bronze planters. Birdcages hung from each window, inside them parakeets of exotic purples and greens.

"I recognize some of these rooms," Madame Calvé said as she pored over my sketches. "But not these." She'd pulled out three sketches and separated them from the rest. "And not this hiding place in the library." She shook her head. "I thought by now I'd been over every inch of the château and feared the *Book of Abraham* was missing. When I saw you, I had a hunch and am so glad I paid it heed. Because it wasn't really a hunch, was it? The spirit world works in wonderfully original ways. It wasn't a coincidence that I read about the gallery opening. I'm supposed to find the book. I was urged to go down to Cannes. The spirits put you in my path, and now you are going to lead me to the most important esoteric artifact discovery in the last three hundred years."

She reached out and patted my hand, and I thought I saw tears glisten in her eyes.

"Let me arrange for some help, and we'll go find these spaces. I need you with me, in case you recognize something you saw but didn't sketch."

I was going to argue that we'd come so I could draw the castle's secrets, not actually help her hunt for the book. But before the words came out, Madame Calvé pointed to one of the drawings. The cavern with the odd-shaped stones.

"Look at this wall."

"I don't see anything unusual. It's just rocks, Madame."

La Diva turned to me. Her eyebrows rose in amazement. "You don't see it?"

I shook my head.

"There's a shadow of a figure here."

I stared at the area she'd indicated. When I'd been seeing it from behind the blindfold, there had been nothing there but uneven, unremarkable stones. I was certain of it. But now, studying from a distance, it appeared I had shaded in a woman's shadow. And she looked very much like me.

Chapter 30

The next morning, Wednesday, I came down to breakfast to learn that Madame Calvé had enlisted help and we'd spend the day searching for the places I'd drawn. That gave us two days and nights left to find the treasure and leave before Madame's party guests descended on her.

Over croissants and café crème, she discussed her plans for the day, saying we should start in the library because that would require the least amount of destruction.

"Gaspard Le'Malf is on his way over. He's our groundskeeper. His family has been taking care of the castle for centuries, and he's more knowledgeable about this building and the land it sits on than anyone," she explained. "And he's strong. Between him and you, Sebastian, we'll be able to move anything in our way."

"I met Gaspard yesterday," I said, and told La Diva about my getting lost in the forest, finding his house, and meeting his son.

Madame shook her head. "Sophie was wonderful. She was a historian. They'd met when she was doing research on the area."

"How did she die?" I asked.

"Her car skidded in a rainstorm. They didn't find her for two days. It was so tragic for Gaspard and his little boy. He's hired a wonderful nursemaid, but she can't replace the child's mother."

Gaspard arrived just as we were finishing breakfast. Madame introduced him to Sebastian.

"And Delphine tells me you met yesterday," La Diva said.

"Yes," Gaspard said, and turned to me. "It's nice to see you again. So your drawings proved fruitful?"

Did I detect sarcasm? I wasn't certain, but I sensed that same tug-of-war of emotions from him that I'd felt the day before. He wanted to talk to me, draw me in, discuss something with me, and yet at the same time, he wished that I wasn't there, that I wasn't doing this.

"Gaspard, do you want a café before we go to work?"

"No, but thank you, Madame." He was respectful but not deferential like an employee would have been.

"All right, then." She took a deep breath, as if she were preparing for a performance. "Time to begin," Madame said, "with the library."

We followed her into the beautifully appointed room with its floor-to-ceiling carved wooden shelves. Somewhere among them, I'd seen a mysterious segment that opened like a door. There were more than a dozen partitions in the paneled room, and we each took a section.

"Of all the rooms in the house, this one was in the best shape when I moved in," Madame told us. "Many of these books were here, left behind. We searched through them, of course, but never took the room apart. A secret door in a library is such an obvious plot device. I should have guessed, what with all the opera I've performed."

"Sometimes the most obvious solutions are the right ones," Gaspard said.

"Nonetheless, I never thought of it. If the book is here, I'll feel quite ridiculous."

"When do they say the book was hidden in the castle?" I asked.

"In 1655, Pierre Borel wrote about Flamel and his great discovery," Madame began. Her voice had become deeper and more melodramatic. She turned away from the shelves and toward us. She was onstage again. The books were the backdrop. We were her audience, poised to listen to her every word.

"It was that book that I found in Dujols's shop in Paris and that led me to purchase this château. I know the passage by heart. Borel wrote, 'Now the book by which Flamel said he came to achieve the Great Work is that of Abraham the Jew. Many have worked to recover it . . . but these searches have been useless. I have nevertheless been assured by a gentleman of Rouergue called M. de Cabrières, tenant of his château of Cabrières near Millau, where I went specially to see this Monsieur, that he had the original of this book, which M. le Cardinal de Richelieu recovered a short time before his death.'"

Sebastian and I were riveted by the recitation. Gaspard, however, didn't seem to be affected and continued searching the shelves. Madame had owned the château for thirty years; he doubtless had become inured to her dramatics. Just as Madame finished, he called out, "I've found the movable section. It's right here."

We all turned to watch him open and pull out an entire unit of shelving, just like a door.

The three of us crowded around him. Beyond the shelves was a room cast in darkness.

"No one set a foot inside yet. We don't want to disturb anything. First, we need a light," Madame said in an excited voice.

"I'll go get a lantern," Gaspard offered.

I was a bit surprised that given the years Madame had been looking and the potential monumental importance of the book, Gaspard was so blasé about the discovery. It was almost as if he knew that the famed book wouldn't be there.

He returned with a lantern, which he handed to Madame, and let her do the honors. As she held it out in front of her, a warm glow illuminated the room. Holding her breath, she took a first step into the hidden enclave. We crowded in behind her.

Two comfortable-looking chairs with ottomans flanked a fireplace faced with dark green marble. On the opposite wall, a luxurious chaise longue was covered with maroon and purple pillows and a fur throw. A thick Persian carpet lay atop the wide wood-planked floor. Two side tables, one between the chairs and another beside the chaise, were crowded with all kinds of paraphernalia. And everywhere layers of dust suggested that no one had entered in quite some time.

Madame shone her light directly at the objects on the table, on the long pipes, bronze lamps, small china bowls stained with a black tarlike substance, and an exotic Middle Eastern tea set complete with an elaborate silver pot and glass and silver cups.

"It's an opium den!" she exclaimed.

Gaspard picked up a newspaper near my feet. "This is dated 1872."

"I'd imagine no one has been in here since that very day," Madame said.

I was in awe of the perfectly preserved time capsule, but La Diva was all business. "Now, carefully, we must go over every inch of this room. What a perfect place to hide an ancient book! In a room almost no one knew existed."

She assigned us to different areas, and for the next hour we explored. I had the fireplace and worked each carved scroll and decoration, looking in vain for one that might be hinged to open a secret compartment. Next, I moved on to the mantel. Above it hung an oil painting of an Arabian harem. Like everything else in the room, it was covered with dust. I peered at it . . . Something was familiar. Then I remembered. When I was at L'École, I'd studied a very similar painting by Ingres in the Louvre. I took a handkerchief from my trouser pocket and swiped the canvas. I was no expert, but it looked very much like a slightly different view of the same Turkish bath Ingres had painted around 1860. I wiped the bottom right corner, looking for a signature. Nothing. But it was there in the left corner.

"Madame!" I called out, excited by my find.

She was by my side in an instant, and I realized my mistake. She'd thought I'd found the book.

"Do you have it?" she asked.

"Not the book, no, but this painting is a masterpiece by Ingres. Its sister is in the Louvre."

"An Ingres?" Sebastian asked, coming over and looking at the painting with us. "This is a historic discovery."

"But not the discovery we are searching for," Madame Calvé said, with a sigh of despair. "Gaspard, I hope you are going to have better luck?"

He was taking apart a shelving unit in the far corner. "Not so far. But I do believe I found a good bit of opium here."

After an hour, Madame called off the search. "Let's all go have some coffee and figure out what room to tackle next."

The four of us returned to the dining room and regrouped over freshly made madeleines and steaming cups of espresso.

"I have all of the castle's floor plans here," Madame said, as she unrolled them.

Some were recent, drawn up as part of her renovations, others were old, and still others were ancient, and she was careful with the fragile yellowed paper.

Sebastian studied them. With an architect for a father, we were both well versed in reading blueprints. "Maybe we should try the kitchen next," he said, as he pointed. "This section looks promising."

"Yes, and tomorrow the room in the servants' quarters," Madame agreed. "And then the only room we'll have left to find is this . . ." She picked up my strange drawing of the dungeon with my shadow on the rocks. "I just don't recognize anything about it. Gaspard, does it look familiar to you?"

I watched as he examined the drawing, his face remaining impassive. "No," he said. "I don't recognize it either."

I wasn't convinced that he'd told her the truth. But what made me suspicious? Had his fingers clenched? Had he handed it back to her perhaps too quickly?

"Do you think it could be a subbasement?" she persisted.

"I suppose it is a possibility," Gaspard answered. "But it's hard to imagine that I wouldn't know about it and that you would never have stumbled upon it when you did the repairs to the foundation."

"Well, no one knew about the opium room," she said.

"True," Gaspard said. "But you didn't renovate the library."

"Is it possible there had been such an area a long time ago but it was filled in to build on?" Sebastian asked. "I remember one commission my father had. In the process of tearing down a house, they found an ancient Roman cistern underneath. Someone at some point had just wanted a house there, and they built over it."

"Yes, anything is possible," Madame said hopefully. "We'll leave the basement for tomorrow. This afternoon, let's find our fireplace and cauldron. Inside an iron pot would be a clever place to put an alchemical treatise. Now, look here . . ." Madame Calvé pointed to the most current floor plan, dated 1893. "When I bought the castle, I'd hoped to find the book while in the process of renovating. Some rooms were pristine and only required minor repairs. Others were in dire need of a total overhaul. The kitchen, which is here now, was a sitting room at that time. And . . ." She unrolled another floor plan, which was slightly aged and from 1824. "The original kitchen was here." She indicated a rectangle on the lower elevation. "One story below the front of the château but flush with the back of it."

"Before we start searching, we should make sure the kitchen was always there. It might have been relocated more than once. What about before 1824?" Sebastian asked.

"I don't know. But let's look. Some of these older plans should tell us."

We all began inspecting other blueprints. We found the kitchen in that same place going all the way to the earliest drawings done in 1658.

"What did you do with the old kitchen?" Sebastian asked.

"Nothing. It's just empty. Other than the wine cellar, we don't use any of the rooms on that level."

"Then I guess we have our work cut out for us," Sebastian said, standing.

As we walked out of the room, Gaspard caught up to me. "I didn't realize when you described what you were doing here what you meant about painting the house's portrait. It's very impressive. How do you do these drawings?"

I briefly described the process.

"How long have you had this gift?"

"Since I was almost ten."

"Did it come upon you suddenly or develop over time?"

Any mixed messages from before were gone now. He seemed genuinely interested in my ability.

Now I, not my brother, was more forthcoming than usual. But there was something about Gaspard that told me I could trust him. That he would understand.

"I was blinded in an accident. During my recovery, the scrying began." I looked at him. "Do you know the word?"

"I do, yes."

"After I regained my sight, I retained the ability to see from behind the blindfold, but I don't use it very much anymore."

"Well, I'm very glad your sight was restored. And it's good to know that if I ever lose anything, I'll know where to turn." He smiled.

"Don't give me any credit yet. So far, we haven't found what we're looking for."

"True. But we have discovered a painting that belongs in the Louvre. And a small fortune in opium. Maybe in the old kitchen, we'll find some pirated gold bars from Spain."

For the second time, I had the distinct impression that Gaspard was certain that no matter what we might find, it wasn't going to be the *Book of Abraham*.

Chapter 31

It only took a few minutes of inspecting and examining the old kitchen to find enough carbon residue on one wall suggesting where the cauldron had once hung. Luckily, the mortar between the stones was old and easy enough to remove. Within an hour, Sebastian and Gaspard and I had cleared away enough of the wall for Madame—who had been watching us work—to step inside.

Like the room off the library, this one offered a surprise. But instead of an opium den, we found a medieval torture chamber.

No one spoke for several minutes as we examined the horrible scene, taking in the gruesome-looking utensils and mechanisms.

"These are the instruments they used, aren't they?" I asked.

Madame was silent.

"Yes," Gaspard said, his voice almost a whisper.

I knew why he was keeping his voice low. I felt it, too. The pain of the victims still vibrated in the air. It was a cruel and holy place.

"Did they make people sit in this?" Madame asked, pointing to a wooden chair covered with spikes on every surface—the back, the seat, and the armrests. Old worn leather straps that showed use hung down from each side.

Gaspard nodded. "That's a Judas chair. People bled to death on those spikes."

"And this?" I pointed to a clawlike handheld device.

"An iron spider. They used it on women who had given themselves abortions or were adulterous."

"What did it do?" Sebastian asked.

I wasn't sure I wanted to hear.

"They used the claws to rip off their breasts."

The implement was covered with rust . . . or dried blood.

"I'm not sure I really want to know this, either, but what are these horrible things?" Madame pointed to a pair of scissors.

"A tongue tearer," Gaspard answered.

"And this?" Madame asked, as she reached out and opened a cabinet. Inside, the walls and door were lined with long, sharp spikes.

"The iron maiden," Gaspard said.

"How do you know about all this?" Sebastian asked suspiciously.

"From stories passed down from generation to generation in my family."

"So you haven't seen it all before?" I asked. He'd been so knowledgeable, with answers to all our questions at the ready.

He didn't answer me but instead said, "You're shivering. I think the atmosphere here is too disturbing?"

"I'm fine," I said, but I wasn't. How had he known?

"We should go, Madame," Gaspard said. "There's nothing here."

"How can you be sure?" she asked.

"I can't, but . . ."

"Gaspard's right," I said. "I don't know how I know, but I can feel it. There's nothing here but screams soaked into the dirt on the floor and the stones."

"Go upstairs, dear," Madame said to me. "We need to be thorough, but you don't have to stay. We'll meet for lunch."

I hesitated. I wanted to stop them from disturbing this horrific place. The people who had lost their lives here had left something of their pain and sorrow behind. It needed to be respected and not agitated.

"Go ahead," Sebastian urged. "You did your part helping us find this place. We'll meet you upstairs."

I looked at Gaspard, for some reason waiting for him to give me permission.

"Your brother is right," he said. "And maybe put on a sweater." He smiled.

An hour later, Sebastian knocked on my door. "It's time for lunch," he said, as I opened it.

"Did you find anything in that awful room?"

"Not the book, no."

"What, then?"

"I don't think you want to know." He looked shaken.

"That bad?"

He nodded. "All that matters is that we are done with that section of the house."

I needed to know what they'd found. To understand my reaction to being in the room. "No details, but what did you find?"

"Remains of someone who'd been tortured there."

"Oh, how horrible. How is Madame? Shaken?"

"Not as badly as I was."

"And Gaspard?"

"He's a curious one, isn't he? Very quiet, keeps to himself, but he has a look in his eye as if he knows all."

"So you noticed it, too?" I asked.

Sebastian nodded. "And that he seems to have taken a liking to you. But not to me."

"What makes you think so?"

"A different look in his eye. I said something after we determined that the book wasn't down there . . . about how I was sure you'd find it. And he asked me if you'd wanted to come here or if it was my idea. As if that was any of his business."

"What did you tell him?"

Sebastian's eyes searched my face. "You care?"

"We're having a conversation. I'd like to know what you told him."

"I said that I was your manager and that you are always happy to take the commissions that I get for you."

"In other words, you lied."

I didn't know why it bothered me that Sebastian hadn't told Gaspard the truth. After all, it wasn't any of Gaspard's business.

"You always have been happy to take the commissions that I get for you."

"I used to be. But you know that's not true anymore."

"Madame is waiting, Delphine. Let's go to lunch."

No one was better than I was at deflecting questions and changing the subject, except for my brother.

I followed him out of the room, leaving my sweater behind. I wouldn't need it anymore. The crisis had passed, and I never had to go down into that chamber of horrors again. And I could hope we'd find the blasted book soon and leave this medieval alcazar.

Gaspard had gone back home to eat with his son, so it was just my brother and me and La Diva at the table. Over a quiche and salad with a crusty baguette and more of the delicious fruity rosé from the region, the talk returned to the missing book.

"What admirable perseverance you have, Madame." Sebastian was charming her. "To have searched for this book for more than thirty years and still have the energy to carry on."

She smiled. "It's been a labor of love, and I believe it is my mission to find the Great Work and discover Flamel's secrets."

"But you've never lost faith," he said.

"No, I never have had any doubt."

"How is that?" I asked.

"I have proof that the book is here."

She hadn't mentioned proof before.

"Really? What kind?" I asked, hoping she was going to say she had a letter written by Flamel himself, which I could look at and touch. I sensed there was a connection between his elixir and my ancestors' and wondered if I could pull any information from something he'd held. I'd had a little experience with that. Maman had taught me. My sister Opaline could hold stones and learn from them, actually hear them speak. If the stones were combined with a personal item, such as a lock of hair, Opaline could actually receive messages from the dead.

"Nicolas Flamel told me," La Diva said, as normally as if she were reporting back on what the cook had told her had been sold at the market that morning. "We've had several séances with Flamel over the years," she added.

Sebastian raised his eyebrows. "And he spoke to you about the book?"

"He did."

"Did he tell you where it was?" I asked.

"Yes, but we've never been able to find the area he said to search. That's why it's so important that you're here."

"What exactly did he tell you? What did he describe?" I asked.

"You *do* believe in the power of séances, don't you?" Madame asked, looking first at Sebastian and then at me.

"Do we need to remind you who our mother is?" Sebastian smiled.

"No, of course not. In fact, your mother was present at several séances I attended in Paris. None, though, when Flamel visited."

"Maman has always said that séances can be very revealing but they can also be confusing," I explained. "There are too many powerful influences that can alter and affect what occurs."

"Of course. That's why we've conducted quite a few with the great alchemist. And except for Jules and Pierre and me, we always mixed up the attendees, to prevent just such a situation."

"Jules? Pierre?" Sebastian asked.

"Jules Bois. You'll meet him this weekend; he's coming to my party," Madame explained. "Jules is a novelist and my oldest and closest friend. We were going to marry at one point . . ." A smile lifted the corners of her mouth, and for a flash, I saw the young girl she once was. "And Pierre." She looked at me. "You knew Pierre Dujols, didn't you? He owns the Librairie du Merveilleux. He's quite ill now and bedridden. His nephew has taken over running the shop."

After her reference to Mathieu, I changed the subject. "Where did Nicolas Flamel tell you the book was?"

"He said the book is in the library of light and shadow, but . . ." She paused as if remembering.

"But?" I prompted.

"He told us that only someone who could see in the shadows would be able to find the book."

The room was suddenly chillier than it had been. I looked at Madame and Sebastian to see if either of them had noticed, but it didn't appear so.

The cold washed over me along with a wave of dizziness. I had a memory flash of fighting churning water. The current spinning me in its vortex, trying to pull me down.

I stood up. "I . . . I need to get my sweater," I said, and left the table.

I could feel Sebastian's eyes boring into my back, but I didn't turn around. I had to get away from whatever I'd sensed in that room. It wasn't unusual for me to feel a temperature change during a psychic episode. But it was extremely rare for me to have a flashback to my childhood drowning incident. What had triggered it now?

In the studio, sitting among all the discarded sketches, I hugged myself and intoned the chant my mother had taught me when I was a child, to center myself whenever I was overwhelmed by my fears. I hadn't had to use it in a long time, but I had never forgotten it:

> *Make of the blood, a sight.*
> *Make of the sight, a symbol.*
> *Make of the symbol, life everlasting.*

I repeated it again and felt the warmth return.

Each of the daughters of La Lune had a mantra that was hers

alone and that encapsulated her powers. Some were more enigmatic than others. It had taken my mother months to understand hers, just in time to save my father:

> *Make of the blood, a stone.*
> *Make of a stone, a powder.*
> *Make of a powder, life everlasting.*

My sister Opaline had also learned hers only weeks before she found herself in need of it:

> *Make of the blood, heat.*
> *Make of the heat, fire.*
> *Make of the fire, life everlasting.*

I had known mine since I was ten years old and had understood its meaning as soon as I'd heard it. My mother said that was because out of all of our powers, mine was the most accessible to me, and I recognized the mantra as having to do with my second sight right away. She and my sisters had had to struggle to find theirs.

> *Make of the blood, a sight.*
> *Make of the sight, a symbol.*
> *Make of the symbol, life everlasting.*

I repeated it to myself three more times until I was completely calm.

There was a knock on the door, followed by my brother's voice. "Delphine? Can I come in?"

"Yes."

"Are you all right?"

I nodded. "I am now."

"What happened?"

"I'm not quite sure. Suddenly, I didn't feel very well."

He sat down beside me. "Do you have a fever?"

"No, quite the opposite. I was freezing cold." I shook my head, trying to get rid of the residual feeling, the way a dog shakes off water.

"Can you come back downstairs?"

"Sebastian, I think we should leave the château," I said.

"There's too much at stake."

"What's at stake?"

"Well, there's the money she's promised if you find the treasure. We need it."

"Why do we need it? You keep saying that. But the gallery is doing so well. You have a stable of such good artists."

Sebastian was holding something back.

When he didn't answer, I said, "If I could put on my blindfold and draw you, I would."

Usually, the threat made him smile. But now Sebastian remained as silent as one of the Buddha statues on display downstairs in Madame's living room.

"Sebastian? If you don't tell me, I won't stay."

When he didn't say anything, I went to the closet, pulled out my suitcase, and started packing.

He came over to me and took my hands. "Don't do this."

"Then tell me."

"You are being overly dramatic. La Diva must be wearing off on you." He grinned. "Your reputation can use the infusion of attention. People have stopped talking about you. We can't let that happen. You need to think about your career."

My brother's endless charm, the ease with which he navigated his way out of any unpleasantness, was impressive. But I wasn't convinced. I wrested my hands away and continued packing.

"Delphine, please."

"Tell me the truth."

Sebastian exhaled a deep sigh. Sitting down in the armchair, he turned his head toward the window and looked out at the mountain vista.

"You won't like this." His voice was so low I could barely hear him.

"What?"

"Bad debt."

That was all? I was surprised. "A lot of people have bad debt. Tell Papa, and he'll get you out of it."

"He did last time and vowed he won't again."

"Last time?"

"I've developed a nasty habit of frequenting the casino." He tried to smile again. This time, the expression failed and turned into a grimace.

The gallery was making enough of a profit for him to cover any normal debts. From the extent of his discomfort and his admission that our father had bailed him out in the past, I surmised that the situation must be dire. I'd known several artists who had suffered addictions. With some, it was opium. With others alcohol. And still others, gambling. I remembered one of our parents' friends who had been so ruined by the lure of the beautiful Belle Époque casino in Monte Carlo that he shot himself.

"It's quite bad. It could ruin me, Delphine. Or worse."

"Worse?"

"I borrowed money from some unsavory types who are threatening me."

"Threatening to kill you?"

I suddenly knew what I'd seen in the puddle outside my little house in Mougins. Why I had to come here to save my brother. I had to find the book and get Madame's bonus so he could pay off his debt.

"All right. If I stay, if I do this for you, will you get help when we get back to Cannes?"

"What do you mean by help?"

"From Maman. She will know what to do."

"No, I can't tell her."

"But you told Papa."

Sebastian shook his head. "Not quite. I told him that I'd invested in a group of paintings that didn't sell."

"You lied to him?"

My father and Sebastian were the two outliers in our family, the only two without supernatural powers. They had a special father-son bond. The idea of Sebastian breaking that bond and lying to my father disturbed me almost as much as his gambling problem did.

My brother was entangled in a complicated web of duplicity. And I was caught by surprise. I was his twin. I thought I knew him. And yet in just days, I'd discovered the truth about his sexuality and an addiction I couldn't have even guessed at. He'd grown up while I'd been in New York. And I suppose I had, too. We'd both struggled with love and gotten ourselves into trouble. At least Sebastian had only lost money. Someone had lost his life because of me.

"So what will it be, Delphine?"

"I'll stay and help if you promise that when we get home, you'll confess to Maman and ask her to help. Will you?" I asked.

I was holding a folded sweater above the suitcase. About to lay it down.

Sebastian couldn't meet my gaze. Instead, he took the green sweater out of my hands. I took the garment back and returned it to the closet. Then, leaving the suitcase half-packed, I went to the door.

"Come on, Sebastian, let's find the book and then get out of here."

Chapter 32

Book of Hours
August 14, 1920

There are secrets waiting on the Paris streets but none as compelling as those Mathieu and I are discovering about each other's bodies. For the last week, I've stolen as much time as possible from family obligations to spend it with him, making love in his little one-room flat in Montmartre.

Leaving the maison, from under my dress collar I fish out my ring, which is hanging off a gold chain. Not quite ready to share Mathieu yet, I am, of course, keeping our engagement a secret.

Opaline knows something. Once I got over the surprise of his gift, I realized Mathieu had gone to the jewelry shop in the Palais Royal where my sister works and that she'd designed the ring for me.

I would have preferred he'd visited any other jeweler, but then the ring wouldn't be as perfect. So far, Opaline hasn't questioned me about it. Probably since she hasn't seen me wear it, she doesn't know he's given it to me yet and hasn't wanted to ruin his surprise. A few times when we've been alone, she's asked me about him, but I've held my enthusiasm in check and told her that while I do like him, I don't want anything or anyone interfering with my studies just now. I'm not sure she believes me, but she's not one to pressure or pry, and for that I'm so thankful.

During the carriage ride from our house to Mathieu's lair—which takes the better part of a half hour—I am in a heightened state of anticipation. The journey has become a ritual for me. I sit straight up in the cab, my gloved hands in my lap, thinking of him waiting for me. Trying to keep the fluttering deep inside me from overwhelming me. I don't speak to the driver. I try not to breathe in any smells. I try not to touch the seat any more than I have to. I don't want anything to sully my sensations. I don't want to feel anything until I can feel Mathieu's skin under my fingers. I don't think about school or my paintings. Instead, I imagine what we will do to each other. How it will feel and taste, and just thinking of it makes me breathless.

I, who have never taken a lover before, who have never read romantic novels or had crushes on stage stars, have become as lovesick as any heroine in any melodrama.

Today there was construction going on in the avenue de l'Opéra in the first arrondissement, and the ride took twice as long. When the cab finally pulled up in front of Mathieu's building, I practically threw my money at the driver and raced up the steps.

I knocked on the door. Mathieu opened it and, before I could utter a word, pulled me toward him.

I've never swooned. Never felt unbalanced. But the kiss he gave me took away my breath and made me unsteady. I grabbed hold of his arms.

"I think I might faint," I whispered.

"Then I need to put you right to bed." He laughed.

As Mathieu led me away, I realized that he was wearing only trousers. His chest was bare, and his golden skin glinted in the afternoon sunlight.

The apartment was just two rooms. The front parlor was small but decorated with the most modern furnishings, all simple geometric-shaped pieces in blacks and rusts. More evidence of his highly evolved sense of style. And beyond it his bedroom, with one tiny circular window that framed the snow-white basilica of Sacre Coeur almost perfectly.

Mathieu sat me down on his bed and kneeled at my feet.

"If you feel faint, we should take off your hat," he said playfully. With nimble fingers, he pulled the cloche off my head and then continued his game. "And this dress. Mon Dieu! It's positively constricting."

I sat obedient and still, reveling in his delight, as he undid the pearl buttons at my neck and wrists. "You'll have to stand for a minute. Do you think you can?" he asked, as if I really were infirm.

Nodding, I rose and was surprised to find I actually was still unsteady on my feet. His every touch and glance took me to the next level of arousal. Mathieu pulled my peach-colored pleated chiffon dress over my head. I stood before him in my matching pale peach silk charmeuse brassiere and slip. His eyes roamed over the lingerie, and his gaze pierced my very insides. As if he were making love to me with just that look.

He pulled down my slip, and I stepped out of the pool of silk. I began to shiver.

"Now you are cold?" he teased. "We need to take off your brassiere and stockings and shoes and get you under the covers."

First he undid the brassiere's hooks and then gently slipped the straps off my shoulders and dropped the lacy garment. He leaned down and mouthed first my right nipple and then my left. My skin puckered under his ministrations.

"*Now for these . . .*" *he said, as he ran his hands up my legs, fiddling with the garters that held my hose in place. He deftly undid each one. Then, more slowly, he rolled the stockings down. As he did, he embraced my thighs, my knees, calves, and ankles.*

By now, my breath was coming in short puffs. I reached out and buried my fingers in his hair, feeling the silken curls. He threw back his head and looked up at me again. His mouth was open, his eyes glazed.

"*One more little thing, and then we'll get you under the covers,*" *he said huskily, as he pulled down the lace garter belt, which he left lying on the floor as he indulged in the place between my legs with curious but very gentle fingers.*

I heard a moan escape from between my lips.

"*Oh, you're in pain. No, no, that won't do.*" *He laughed as he yanked down the coverlet and helped me into his bed.*

Standing in front of me while I watched, he undid his trousers and stepped out of them and then his shorts. He was boldly and beautifully naked, and I felt my breath catch in my throat. I was torn between wanting him to join me in the bed or having him stay right where he was so I might continue gazing at him.

"*Can I get you anything?*" *he asked.*

I nodded, not quite trusting my voice, and held out my arms.

How do I describe what it is like when Mathieu and I are together? I am not the poet. Not the bard. Every word seems so pedestrian when I put it down. I want to write about how it feels as if the sky is raining stars on me. As if I am floating, then flying, then soaring. As if we are no longer earthbound. As if I am not flesh and blood anymore but pure sensation, and Mathieu is light—pure, burning, searing white light— entering me, gracing me, ennobling me, setting me on fire until I am burning and burning and then have no choice, want nothing but to explode. And I do.

After we played at love, I took a nap. While I slept, he slipped downstairs to the patisserie on the corner, and so I awoke to the smell of delicious, creamy coffee.

"Did you have a nice nap?"

"I did."

"Take your pick." He offered me the plate. On it was one Paris-Brest—a wheel of choux pastry filled with a delicious praline cream—and a lemon tart. I chose the Paris-Brest.

I took a bit of the delectable treat. The pastry was light, the flavored cream even lighter.

"I can't believe how deeply I slept," I said, with my mouth full of dessert.

"Life is a deep sleep of which love is the dream."

"Yours?" I asked, hoping.

"No, Musset."

"One day, you will recite your own poetry to me."

He took a bite of his tart, first chewing too hard and then swallowing too quickly. "Why can't you let that go?" he asked.

"Because I know how painful it would be for me to stop painting. Like losing part of myself."

"But I'm not you. And it's not painful."

Except I could see in his eyes that it was.

"Can't you tell me what happened to make you quit?"

He put the plate down on the floor with such force the fork jumped off.

"No!" he shouted. "I can't. That's the problem. I don't know what happened past a certain point. I can't remember anything after the attack started. The day I was wounded. The day Max was killed."

I took his hand and held it. For a while, we just sat on his bed, amid the rumpled sheets redolent of our sex.

"Why don't I draw you?" I said, the idea suddenly occurring to me. "I can look into the shadows and see what happened. Fill in the blanks for you."

"I don't need you to do that. Your presence is already a source of healing. I don't think it's a wise use of your power. Your supernatural gifts should remain sacred, only to be used when absolutely necessary. Otherwise, they can be made vulnerable by others' greed, lust, and selfishness."

"You don't have to worry about that. I don't have a limited amount of insight."

"You don't understand, Delphine. Your power is as sacred as our love . . ." He hesitated. "You shouldn't be using your gift to do portraits on commission."

I told Mathieu I couldn't give them up, that the portraits were how I helped people.

"But taking money cheapens your gift. I wish you wouldn't let your brother talk you into doing it."

I bristled. "No one is talking me into doing anything I don't want to do. And until you let me draw you with my blindfold on, you won't understand."

"And any secrets the universe is keeping from me I can leave well enough alone. Some things are meant to remain hidden."

I shook my head. Saddened for him. For his stubborn refusal. "Please, let me help you heal," I said.

"But you do. You make me feel lighter than I have in so long. As if you're pushing the bad memories away and making room for new ones."

Chapter 33

The morning after we'd found the instruments of torture, Madame Calvé, Gaspard, Sebastian, and I descended into the castle's basement one level below the old kitchen. We were looking for an entry to the strange stone room I'd drawn. It was the only sketch that didn't offer a clue to where it was. But judging from the amount of rock, the consensus was it had to be subterranean.

The cool air smelled of earth and age, dust and dirt. The ceilings were low and the spiderwebs profuse. Using lanterns, we proceeded to examine the deepest level of the castle.

There was nothing there. Just an emptied-out, hollow space that ran the length of the castle and led to an underground exit. An escape route created by the castle's builders, we surmised.

Slowly, we made our way through the tunnel, tapping on walls and shining our lights on the ground, looking for trapdoors, thinking that perhaps there was yet another level that no one had ever discovered.

Shortly after noon, Madame called a halt to our efforts so we could break for lunch.

As he had the day before, Gaspard went home to eat with his son, and my brother and I and Madame dined together.

Gaspard joined us two hours later.

"I have something for you," he said to me, before we descended into the depths of the castle. He held out a sheet of paper.

I looked down at a very well-articulated drawing of a butterfly, wings spread, filled in with delphinium-blue and black designs—some color inside the lines, some extending beyond.

In handwriting that was not as sophisticated as the sketch were the words *For Mademoiselle Delphine. A friend for you to fly with.—Nicky.*

"This is beautiful," I said to Gaspard. "I'm moved that he thought to do this for me."

"He was quite taken with you. He's been talking incessantly about coming here to visit you for an art lesson. The only way I could leave the house just now was to promise that I would ask you."

"Of course, tomorrow. I'd be delighted. He's a very special little boy."

Gaspard gave me an enigmatic look, as if he were trying to decide if my words held a deeper meaning.

"You can talk about your plans later, both of you," Madame interrupted. "We need to get downstairs. I have guests coming this weekend and need to make preparations."

For the next two hours, we continued our exploration of the damp, dingy lower level.

"There could be any number of false walls down here," Madame said, as five o'clock approached. "We just can't tell for sure by all this tapping and prodding."

I knew she was disappointed. But I hoped she was going to accept defeat and Sebastian and I would be able to leave. I wasn't ignoring my brother's financial crisis, but I had thought up another solution. I owned a spectacular string of fire opals my great-grandmother had given me. When we got home, I would pawn it so Sebastian could start to pay down his debt, and in the meantime, I'd go to my parents and ask for help. I was satisfied that I'd come up with a way out that would allow me to leave the castle without feeling I'd failed my twin.

"But I'm convinced that the book is here, Delphine," Madame said emphatically. "I have no doubt of it. Monsieur Flamel would not have told me to look if he didn't think I could find it." She turned around slowly, her lamp like a lighthouse searchlight, dust motes dancing in its beams. "Let's go upstairs and have a cocktail. I have an idea. Gaspard, I want you to stay, please."

I still hadn't quite grasped the relationship between him and Madame. They didn't treat each other like employee and employer. Nor like friends or equals. I sensed she tried his patience but that he found her entertaining—as we all did. And she seemed to rely on him and certainly trusted him.

Despite our dirty clothes, she led us to the sitting room, called for champagne and canapés, and then proceeded to mix us aperitifs by adding a layer of crème de cassis to each flute before pouring the sparkling wine.

"Delphine, I would like you to return to drawing and try to see something else about the room with the strange stones. I have a feeling that if you just look deeper, you may find a clue."

I took a sip of the champagne laced with citrusy-sweet black currant liqueur. It was delicious but didn't quell my mounting anxiety about staying, especially if it meant into the weekend.

I wanted to ask Madame about Mathieu. It would ease my mind to know that she hadn't invited him. But even to say his name out loud was too tempting.

I felt Gaspard's eyes on me and looked over at him. He offered me a caring, thoughtful smile that took the edge off my anxiety almost instantly. A sense of peace came over me, confusing me even as it soothed.

"You can try to look deeper into the room, past the stone walls, can't you?" Madame pressed further.

Reluctantly, I nodded. "Yes, I can try."

"Tonight?"

I looked at my half-empty glass of champagne.

"I'll try, but I'm afraid it might not work. Sometimes alcohol interferes. If I can't do it tonight, I'll try again tomorrow morning."

Sebastian was looking at me from across the table, his perfect smile beaming. I felt the sudden urge to stick my tongue out at him.

Instead, I looked back at Gaspard. "And please tell Nicky I'd be happy to come over tomorrow during lunchtime, if that is convenient, and give him a lesson."

"We'd both be delighted." He gave me another smile, the light catching his eyes, the fire in them softening into an amber glow. "But if it's a nice day, why don't you meet us at the little folly just past the garden by the pond? I'll bring a picnic."

It was such a pleasant invitation that it didn't strike me until later that evening that it was the second time Gaspard had kept me away from his house.

Chapter 34

As I'd promised, I spent the early part of that evening, Thursday, by myself in the studio, wearing the blindfold and sketching. Despite the champagne, I did six more drawings of the mysterious grotto with its cold, wet stone walls etched with curious letter forms. No matter how hard I tried, I couldn't find anything in the room to suggest where it was. There were no windows. And the only door remained shut, even as I pushed and pulled at it in my mind.

When it was time for dinner, I called for the maid and asked her to have a tray brought up to the room. I needed more time. I knew a trip downstairs, having to make conversation with Madame and my brother, would just interrupt my concentration. Nervously, I went over my plan. Madame would pay us handsomely whether or not I was able to locate the book. That and the money made from pawning my opals would surely get my brother out of trouble. Then I would force him to confess to my mother. Even Madame's party stopped preying on my mind. All that mattered was saving Sebastian. And all I felt was the danger coming closer.

I stopped drawing to eat the meal the kitchen sent up—roasted chicken with an artichoke soufflé and a lovely slice of apple tart served with crème fraîche. I didn't drink the burgundy that arrived with the food, because I needed to keep working.

After I ate, I picked up the blindfold once more. It was cold when I lowered it over my eyes. I welcomed the satin touch. I heard faint noises outside my window and wondered if Madame and Sebastian were taking a stroll. Concentrating, I shut out the sounds and focused my attention on the pencil I held, running a finger down its smooth wood. My other hand rested on the paper, its rough grain centering me. In my mind, I searched the black abyss. Sightless, I peered into that empty stage and waited for the riddles to resolve, the shadows to settle.

I saw the stone room once again. The gray, wet, cold rock walls. The ancient carvings. I saw a shadow cast on the wall. If there was a shadow, didn't there have to be a light source? Of course. Why hadn't I looked for it before? In my mind, I turned around to find it. There was a man holding a lantern. It was Gaspard! On his face was a look of both surprise and resignation. He couldn't understand how I'd found the place. And yet he'd known I'd find it eventually.

"Where are we?" I asked.

He began to tell me, his mouth moving, forming words, but there was no sound. I couldn't hear his answer.

"One clue," I asked him. "Just one hint, so I can give it to Madame and leave."

The way he was looking at me, I sensed he was torn. That he wanted me to go and also to stay.

He held out a sheet of paper. I assumed it was a map and was grateful that he was sharing it. But when I looked at it, I saw it was his son's butterfly drawing. Not a map at all.

I took off the blindfold, opened my eyes, and looked down at what I had sketched. Not the room, not the stones, not Gaspard. I'd drawn the butterfly.

I snapped my pencil in frustration. It split in half and cut my finger in the process. In the bathroom, I rinsed my hand off, my blood turning the running water pink. The sight of it made me gag. I was never good with blood. Neither was my sister Opaline. Her squeamishness had kept her from volunteering as a nurse during the war. I felt weak and grabbed hold of the sink. I closed my eyes and concentrated on relaxing, on breathing.

Finally stable, I let go, grabbed a linen, and wrapped it around the fleshy part of my thumb to stop the bleeding. Back in my room, I rang for the maid, this time asking for a bandage.

While I was waiting, Madame knocked on my door. "Are you all right, dear? I heard the maid was asking for a bandage."

"My pencil broke. It's just a scratch," I said as I let her inside.

In a very maternal voice, she said, "Let me see," and took my hand. "Not just a scratch at all. That's a nasty gash, and it has a splinter in it. We'll have to remove the wood and put some salve on the wound. Come with me."

I followed her down the hall and into her suite. If the common rooms downstairs were forests, her suite was the inside of a flower. Everything was pale pink and delicate. The walls were covered in blush-colored moire silk, the Aubusson was leaf-green and the pink of a ballet slipper. There was a white piano in the sitting room, smaller than the grand black one downstairs, and the seat beneath it was a luscious shade of salmon. Her bathroom was done in the same pinks but in tile and marble with gold accents. And in the triple-winged mirror, I watched the world-class opera singer pour alcohol over my wound.

The gash was the shape of a perfect crescent moon. The symbol of the daughters of La Lune. I flinched.

"Am I hurting you, dear?"

"No, it's fine."

"Is it the shape?" she asked.

"You know about that?"

"You forget that we were close, your mother and I, when she was young and confused about her ancestry. Pierre and I knew all about the symbol of La Lune."

Madame spread an ointment on the wound and wrapped it with gauze that she tied expertly in a neat little knot.

"Thank you," I said, examining the bandage.

"When I was a young girl, I made a promise to my patron saint that if I ever became a singer, I would repay her by helping God's poor. I fund an orphanage nearby where I take young girls from the slums in Paris. And I try to visit them often. Not just to stand and stare at them but to give them singing lessons. Eat with them. Nurse them when they're sick. I've learned how to tend to a wound or two. Now, just one more thing?"

"Yes?"

"Will you show me the drawings that caused this mishap?"

"I'm afraid you'll be disappointed. I was going to try again in the morning."

She couldn't be deterred.

Back in the studio, Madame examined one after the other of my most recent sketches. She scrutinized each for so long I got bored watching her and poured myself a glass of the wine that had come with my dinner.

I'd finished one glass and poured a second when she finally put down the last sheet.

She shook her head. "There really is nothing here to tell us where the subterranean cavern is. Damn you, Nicolas!" She balled her hand into a fist and banged it down on the side table where I'd put a jar of pencils. She hit the wood so hard that the jar bounced and then fell, spilling its contents all over the floor. I immediately got down to pick them up.

"I'm sorry," Madame said, as she stood, preparing to help.

"No, I've got them." I finished gathering them. "And I'm sorry about the drawings. I keep trying to leave the room in my mind and get beyond it so I can see where it is. I can usually move around like that while I'm wearing the blindfold. Go past a first scene into another. But not when I'm in the stone room. I feel trapped there. As if there is no way out."

"I wonder if that's a clue to where it is? That you can't find an exit or an entrance."

She picked up the drawings again and went through them carefully. "Where could there be a space like this? How can you hide an entrance?" She paused. "In Egypt, we toured the pyramids. Once the kings were entombed, the entrances to their resting places were hidden. Do you think this might be a tomb?"

"I suppose it could be."

"And you will try again in the morning?"

"Yes, I promise. I'll see if I can get on the other side of the walls and try to get in. So far, I've put myself inside and tried to find a way out."

Madame seemed like a good person with a pure heart, someone I might even be able to trust, and I realized I cared about helping her achieve her goal.

"My guests will be arriving tomorrow in the late afternoon. After dinner, we're going to have a séance. You will attend, won't you? First we need to communicate with a deceased friend, but if that goes smoothly, we can call on Nicolas Flamel and ask him, you and I together, where he's hidden the book. He'll tell you, I'm sure of it. Remember I told you he said that only someone who could see in the shadows would be able to find it? I have no doubt that's you, Delphine."

"I'm not sure I should attend. I don't want to expend energy on anything but your drawings," I said as an excuse. I had no idea if a séance would have any effect on me. But I would say anything to avoid it. Clearly, her party guests included friends from her occult circle. That meant people who frequented Pierre Dujols's shop, the bookstore and meeting place that Mathieu now ran. The idea of interacting with so many of his acquaintances made me shiver.

"Are you cold?" Madame asked. "I've noticed you're quite sensitive to temperature. Do you want me to have a fire lit in here for you?"

I shook my head. "I'm fine."

"I'm excited to have my friends meet you. They'll be so interested in your talent. Don't worry, dear. None of them will judge you. It's just a small group of sympathetic artists and writers and musicians.

We gather frequently. The creativity feeds us all. And makes me feel young."

Despite my anxiety, I smiled. There was so much vitality about her that the idea of her needing to feel young seemed impossible. I'd heard her singing earlier that day and had again been mesmerized. Certainly, her voice was ageless. And I knew the most powerful moments I'd experience at her house would not be those I spent drawing but when I was listening to her sing.

Some artists had magick. A power beyond them, often beyond their knowledge, that pulled energy from the cosmos. Moon-fed and star-polished, their artistic talent shone.

My sister Opaline said that she could hear that energy when she was around me or my mother when we were painting. Throughout history, there were great artists whose work transcended the material world, and what fueled them was itself a puzzle. I believed that's what the occult was, at its most simplistic—a willingness to accept the impossible and try to understand the meaning behind it.

My mother spent hours teaching me how to harness my power during the time she helped bring my eyesight back. Yes, there were spells and potions and strange ceremonies of bathing in moonlight in the sea and chanting while standing in the middle of a pentagram made of shells. But it was when she taught me how to connect to the cosmos through my third eye—by pressing her forefinger to the space between my eyebrows—that I felt the energy change my world and sharpen the murky blurriness a little more each day. This essence or spirit had been with me all along. It was powered through my cells and my blood. It was a surge I felt inside me that she and our ancestors, and now I, knew how to call forth.

"So it's settled, then. Did you bring an evening frock? We're all dressing for our send-off for Erik Satie to wish him a safe journey."

"Where is he going?"

"To the next plane. He's the friend I mentioned who passed over."

"Satie died?"

"Yes. It's very sad. He was a great composer and friend. But a difficult man, and he didn't make it easy for us to take care of him at the end. Did you know him? Your mother certainly did."

"Yes, of course. He visited us in Cannes several times. I wonder if my mother knows he died. I can't recall when she last spoke of him, but I'm sure she would be upset. Maman told me she first met him in Paris when she was at L'École. The same time you met her, from what you've said."

"Yes. She was unsteady on her feet those first few times she came to Dujols's library." Madame smiled, remembering. "But how she changed once she found her passion! She became so brave. It was astonishing."

"It must have been quite a metamorphosis. My great-grandmother has told me stories of how lost my mother was when she first arrived on her doorstep."

"A true metamorphosis."

I liked listening to Madame describe my mother's transformation from a scared New York City socialite escaping a bad marriage into a bold artist who practiced the dark arts and accepted her heritage.

Madame continued, "Satie wrote some music for her once—celebrating her finding her wings, I think was how he described it."

I nodded. "I've heard it. He played it when he visited."

"Satie and Debussy astonished us all with their compositions back then . . ." She shook her head, drifting into a memory of Paris almost thirty years before. "We were all so sure of ourselves and our mission. Certain we could learn the greatest secrets of the universe and use them to change the world. But the secrets we searched for proved more elusive with every passing year." She extended her arms. "When I met your mother, in 1894, I had just bought this château and naively believed it would reveal its mysteries willingly. For three decades, it's held tight to its treasure, like an oyster refusing to offer up its pearl." She shook her head, as if confounded that the house would still disappoint her this way. "Your being here is the first real hope I've had in years."

"But I haven't helped."

"Of course you have. First you discovered a masterpiece. A painting that must be worth hundreds of thousands of francs. And you've uncovered a bit of history, in all its gruesomeness, about the castle's past. And you've seen this . . ." She picked up one of the drawings of the stone room. "We don't know where it is, but I'm certain I know *what* it is, and it's where the book is hidden. How does it feel to you, how does it look to you, this world that is invisible to everyone else? I wonder if it is like what happens to me when I step onstage dressed as someone who I am not and take on her persona."

"No, I don't become the people I draw. Or in this case, the house. Everyone has a shadow life where his or her secrets live. When I put on the blindfold, I see through people into those shadows."

"Are the shadows always in the past?"

"No, I can look forward, but it's more difficult."

"And with the castle, are you looking through the walls?"

I nodded.

"What a gift," she said.

I shook my head. "It doesn't always feel like a gift. It's not pleasant to look into someone's darkness. We tell people—Sebastian does and I do—that I might see moments from their past that they don't want exposed. Usually, they aren't terrible secrets. But some have been truly embarrassing, perverse, unethical, criminal, and frightening. When I did shadow drawings at parties in New York, I always asked people if they wanted me to draw negative secrets if I saw them, or if they wanted me to render only more innocent ones. A childhood game of stealing candy. A first kiss at a dance. Taking out a book from a library and never returning it. Trying to hurt a little brother or sister out of jealousy. Even when they were warned, I was continually surprised at how many people told me to draw whatever I saw—good or bad—because they didn't believe I was for real and never expected me to expose anything dreadful. And then I'd have to deal with the consequences."

"We humans are odd creatures, aren't we?" Madame said. "Craving the unknown, flirting with disaster instead of enjoying what we have. Years ago, I traveled to India and Egypt with a wise Hindu monk. We visited ancient shrines and temples and places of holiness. He taught me more than anyone to accept what I don't understand with equanimity and find solace and joy in the moment."

"What was Egypt like? I've always wanted to visit, especially since seeing photos of Howard Carter's expeditions."

"I'm not sure that in the long run Carter will be happy that he's disturbing so many burial places. There are ancient curses protecting those sacred spaces that shouldn't be tampered with."

We spent another half hour together, sipping wine as Madame regaled me with tales about her adventures in the Valley of the Kings. As she recounted stories and described the ancient rites and cults, I wondered about her own secrets.

Before I took this trip, my mother had reminisced about Madame Calvé and how despite being in the public eye, she had kept her occult life a closely guarded secret. She was not only a member of the most extreme occult circles in Paris—a clandestine cult rumored to practice black masses—but she was one of its priestesses. She was also sexually linked to several well-known mystics—the occult master Papus, the novelist Jules Bois, the illustrator of the tarot Oswald Wirth, and the master Péladan.

As kind as many members of the group had been to my mother during her first exploratory year, she said they had sometimes frightened her. Their single-minded commitment to finding the secret to transmuting matter and expanding their minds to reach heretofore unknown levels of consciousness led to dangerous practices that she eventually decided she wanted no part of.

Now, after Madame left my room, even though I'd drunk two glasses of wine, I decided to try once more to conquer the impenetrable castle's secrets. But this time with paint, not pencil.

After I set out a canvas and put a curl of black paint on my palette,

I placed a brush in my lap, where I'd have no trouble finding it, and then I put on the blindfold.

I began, dipping the soft bristles into the mound of silky pigment and dabbing. How many times does an artist pick up a brush in her lifetime? How many times does she dip it in paint? Sweep or dot or smooth it onto the canvas? Millions, I would imagine. It was an action as natural to me as breathing. With just a pat of my left hand to orient me to the edge of the canvas, I touched the brush to the stretched fabric. And so the dance began.

With the silk over my eyes, I once again saw what I had seen an hour before: the inside of the grotto. As I'd told Madame I would, I forced myself out of the stone chamber, through the thick rock wall. I looked around. I was in the forest. But where, exactly? I turned around and around, looking for a landmark. Tall pine trees surrounded me, their sharp resinous smell so intense I felt almost dizzy.

Find a spot where you can see through the trees, and look for the spires, Gaspard had told me. So I walked forward in as straight a line and as far as I could until I came to a clearing and looked out toward the horizon.

I saw the château with its sandy-colored stone walls built as a fortress against eleventh-century invaders. And there on the watchtower someone stood, peering out. Looking right at me. Who was it?

After almost thirty minutes, I took off the blindfold and studied the canvas. The château perched on its hill. A perfectly fine painting. With no magick about it at all. No subtle pointers to where the secret chamber might be. None at all.

Perhaps the château had a veil around it. Maybe it was protected from eyes just like mine. Tomorrow I would have to try to pierce it another way. There was still enough time to do that and leave before guests began arriving for Madame's evening event.

Chapter 35

I can barely hold my pencil. Am hardly able to string my thoughts together. But I promised to keep all my days with Mathieu recorded here, even the very last of them.

Tonight feels endless. The pain unrelenting. What began as a perfect day will forever be etched in my memory as the worst. I know what I must do, even though it seems impossible that I will be able to.

To love someone so wholly and completely. To be in harmony with another soul. To have him give himself to me. To have given myself to him, withholding nothing. And now to have to walk away in order to protect him? And why? I did this to myself because I was impatient, stubborn, and full of pride. Sure that I could help Mathieu when no one else had been able to. And yet I have to remember that what I will do next will save his life. Would it have been better not to have looked into the shadows? To selfishly stay with him and then be the very cause of his destruction?

Today began in the Bois de Boulogne, where Mathieu brought me for lunch.

"This is one of my favorite secrets," Mathieu said, as he helped me into a boat.

He gave me another of his history lessons, describing the park as quite large. "Almost nine hundred hectares, it's what's left over from an ancient oak forest. In the seventh century, royalty hunted boar and deer and other game here. There was a monastery built on some of the land and an abbey. It's been a sanctuary for monks, nuns, and robbers and several times the site of battles. In 1852, Napoleon III gave the land to the city of Paris, and Baron Haussmann supervised its creation into what you see now."

He rowed our boat across the lake toward an island in the distance. I watched as he dipped the oars into the water and they emerged dripping. The droplets catching the sun and shining like diamonds.

Reaching the shore, Mathieu docked the boat in front of a rustic pink-and-green building outfitted with terraces. Across the front were wooden letters spelling out Le Chalet des Îles.

"Proust and Zola came here often during the Belle Époque. And it hasn't lost any of its charm. At least, I don't think it has. You'll have to decide for yourself."

Over a luncheon of delicious lobster bisque followed by a delicate roasted capon with a chestnut sauce, Mathieu told me stories about the park and the days he'd spent there with his brother.

"My aunt and uncle used to bring us every weekend, and we'd explore another section. There's a waterfall I must take you to see. We used to run under the rushing sheet of water. Behind it is a hidden grotto. If you could get past your fear of water, I could show it to you. It's a marvelous, gloomy, secret

place that stirred our imagination when we were boys. We used to hide in there and look for buried treasure, sure we'd find it. And one day, we did. A bag of gold coins. We whooped and hollered. It was the very best of days." He smiled. "Years later, my uncle told me he'd buried the coins there the day before and hoped no one would come across them but us."

After lunch, I invited him to our house. I wanted to show him my studio and so rarely had a chance, but my great-grandmother was spending a few days in Fontainebleau with friends. Sebastian was in Cannes. And Opaline always stayed at the shop during the week. We would have the maison to ourselves.

"I feel as if I'm walking through a museum," Mathieu said, as I showed him through the downstairs rooms. He stopped to study a nude painting of Diana done by Corot in the front parlor.

"I thought I saw this painting in the Louvre," he said.

"A very similar version."

He stopped in front of an almost full-size marble sculpture of another Diana wearing her crescent-moon headpiece. Someone had once draped a double string of gray pearls around her neck, and they hung there still.

"This place is both appalling and appealing," he said. "I've only read about the homes of the Grand Horizontals," he said, using one of the more eloquent terms for Paris's great courtesans. "Every inch is designed to please her gentlemen callers, isn't it?"

"Just wait." I took him upstairs and showed him the many fantasy bedrooms. "Whatever a man's desire, there is a room to match," I said, as I opened the door to one that recalled the mirrored palace of Marie Antoinette and then another that resembled a monk's chamber with a single bed, a straw rug, and religious frescoes on the wall. I showed Mathieu the Egyptian

room, a Chinese pagoda, and a Persian garden, its walls
painted with trees and flowering bushes against a midnight-
blue sky complete with stars, a perfect crescent moon, and the
onion-shaped minarets of Persepolis in the distance.

"Would you like to try one out?" I asked, half-teasing, half-
serious. I'd fantasized about being with him in these rooms in
the last weeks since we'd become lovers.

"No, I think I'd rather see yours."

"Down this way," I said, and led him to the cream and
blue bedroom that had none of the fanciful decorations of
the chambers where my great-grandmother and her ladies
entertained.

Mathieu laughed when he saw it. "Quite subdued compared
with the rest of the maison. And a relief," he said, as he looked
around. He walked to my dresser and touched my silver
repoussé mirror and the bottle of perfume that he'd bought me.
He studied a picture frame that held a photograph of Sebastian
and me at the beach when we were both about ten.

"Is this after your sight was restored?" he asked.

"Yes."

Mathieu peered at the photo as if he were gleaning some
critical information from it. "What a terrible time you must
have had."

I sat down on the edge of my bed. I didn't want to talk
about it and was about to change the subject. But then I
thought that if I did open up, perhaps it would encourage
Mathieu to talk more about his brother. It was like an itch
that demands to be scratched, and I was obsessed with helping
him discover the secret buried so deep in him that he couldn't
cast any light on it.

"Everything was dark. I kept waiting for morning. But it
never came. And I became so clumsy. Always bumping into
things and hurting myself. I don't know how I would have

endured it if it hadn't been for Sebastian. He attached himself to me as if we'd become Siamese twins overnight. He was my eyes. I became so dependent on him and my art. Because I could still draw. I couldn't see what I drew, but I could feel the paper under my hands and the weight of the pencils in my fingers, and I had control of the sweep of the lines. My sisters and I became more discreet about our gifts after the accident. Psychics and séances and fortune-telling may be popular and acceptable to discuss even in polite society. But we are all wary of using stronger words to describe our abilities."

"Now that you mention it, you hardly ever use the words witch or witchcraft."

I nodded.

"But you can, you know, with me. In private. I'm not scared of it." He smiled. "In fact," he said, touching his finger to my lips, "you can say anything you want to me."

He put his arm around my shoulders before leaning in to kiss me. I leaned forward and kissed him back.

"I've imagined you here in my room," I whispered. "Does that shock you?"

He laughed. "No, it delights me. Tell me what you imagined."

And I did. I told him that sometimes after we'd spent too many days apart, I would wake up having dreamed of being with him and stay in my bed, conjuring his image, the feel and the scent of his skin, and how I'd use my hand between my legs, mimicking what he did to me, until I managed an explosion on my own.

"Show me," he whispered.

Suddenly, I felt shy. He sensed it and urged me on. "I want to see what you do when you are by yourself. I can't imagine how beautiful you must look lying in your bed, touching yourself, thinking of me."

*With seductive words of encouragement, he persuaded me
to get undressed and into my bed. I lay down on my stomach,
my head buried in my pillow, my hand between my legs, and I
began to stroke myself.*

*He only lasted a few minutes before he replaced my fingers
with his own, and I felt his body join mine. Our lovemaking
was slow and languorous. Both of us enjoyed the surprise of the
new position we'd discovered.*

*Afterward, he fell asleep, and I watched him for a while.
His body was so beautiful. Like one of the graceful marbles in
the Louvre. Without disturbing him, I reached for this Book of
Hours and my silver pencil and began to sketch his long lines
and lean form, wincing as I used the side of the graphite to
shadow his skin, capturing the brutal battle scars that marred
it. What had happened to him in the attack? Why was he still
living half a life because of it?*

*I moved on, and when I reached his thighs, I didn't shy
away from drawing his still slightly tumescent penis.*

*This was so unlike drawing live nude models in class.
Their nakedness was impersonal and removed. Mathieu's was
redolent with our lovemaking and passion.*

"I hope that's going to be flattering," he said.

"I didn't realize you were awake."

"I haven't been for long."

*I showed him the drawing and saw his eyes take in the
delineated scars.*

*"Mathieu, please, let me put on the blindfold and draw you
again. Maybe I can see—"*

"No," he interrupted.

"Don't you trust me?"

*"Of course, I do, but I don't think you should use your power
that way."*

"But it's who I am. It's what I do. If you want to be

with me, you have to let me try to help you remember what happened."

Despite himself, maybe because of how I'd couched it, Mathieu reluctantly acquiesced.

I gathered up a proper sketch pad and pencil. I knew his face so well that I didn't have to study him first. I simply put the blindfold on, placed my hand on the edge of the sketch pad, and allowed my fingers to take flight.

I saw a scene at the battlefront. The same one I'd seen in the reflective surface of the pond in the Luxembourg Gardens. Mathieu was about to be attacked by the Hun. I saw the German soldier slash Mathieu's arm with his bayonet. Blood soaked through Mathieu's sleeve and then dripped down his hand and onto the ground. I could smell its sweet metallic scent. And the stench of the German soldier's uniform. And the loamy fragrance of the earth and pine needles as the man's boots crushed them. The Hun pulled out the blade. Pointed the gun at the back of Mathieu's head.

Suddenly, a third man leaped out from between the trees and jumped on the German, grabbing him around the neck. Pulling him off of Mathieu. The German fought back, trying to push his thumbs into the Frenchman's eyes and disarm him.

"Max, no!" Mathieu cried.

What? Was the other French soldier Mathieu's brother?

The German and the Frenchman had each other in death grips. Then the German got the upper hand. Then Max. Mathieu lay there, his eyes filled with terror. Unable to move, all he could do was watch his brother fight the enemy on the blood-soaked ground. And then there was an extraordinary sound, louder than any scream, as the air all around us exploded in a piercing, metallic shriek.

The blast was massive, dislodging rocks and earth, blowing leaves off trees, felling branches. In the smoke, I lost sight of the three men. *The earth reverberated under my feet. What was happening? Pushing through the vapors and debris, I moved ahead in time, until the smoke had cleared. All three men lay on the ground. None of them moving. Three corpses. Or so it appeared, until one of them groaned. Which one?*

I walked among them. Mathieu was still alive. His groans turning into cries. And then the cries turned into shouts.

I pushed ahead further in time. Two soldiers bent over Mathieu, lifted him, and moved him onto a stretcher.

Another soldier hovered above Max, prodding him, then treating his body with less grace and care once he realized there was no hope left for him.

I knew how hard this would be to tell Mathieu. How painful these pictures would be for him to see. But I'd discovered the secret he'd pushed so far down that it was paralyzing him.

Max had died saving Mathieu's life. Died doing what he'd been trained to do. Surely Mathieu would come to realize that he would have done the same for his brother had he been the one under attack. Once he accepted that and stopped blaming himself for Max's death, even if he wasn't conscious of doing it, he'd be able to let go of the crippling guilt that was blocking his ability to write.

I thought I was done. I wanted to be finished. Because the blindfold was wet, I knew I'd been crying. But there was one more image in the shadows. Just up ahead, at the end of a trail of blood leading away from Mathieu's body through the trees. Tentatively, I peered into the gray fog there. Dim, gloomy light barely illuminated the scene. Mathieu lay on the ground again. But not in uniform. He looked a few years older. He was lying on a stone floor. Faceup.

I stopped drawing. I couldn't bear what I was seeing. There was a knife in Mathieu's arm. A hunting knife this time. And around it a hand. A woman's hand, pushing the blade down, down into his flesh. I recognized the ring on the hand. My ring. Mathieu's blood and my murdering hand.

I dropped the pencil. Heard it hit the floor.

"Delphine?" Mathieu said.

I didn't answer, couldn't. Now I was the one who was paralyzed. Still wearing the blindfold, I ripped the paper off the sketch pad and tore it. Once, twice, three times. A hundred times. Shredded the drawing. Thinking foolishly in that moment that I still hadn't seen it. Not really. I was still blinded by the silk mask. Maybe I'd been wrong. And if I destroyed the drawing, it would only exist in my mind's eye. I could deny it. Pretend I'd never seen it.

"Delphine? What is it?"

Mathieu removed the blindfold. He looked at me and saw my tears. He wiped them away with his fingers, as he asked me again and again what was wrong. Why was I crying?

How could I tell him what I'd seen? How could I explain? And then I knew. I wouldn't tell him. Not all of it. I'd show him the first set of drawings. Of him and his brother. Help him understand what had occurred at the front. How Max had saved his life. How he, Mathieu, would have done the same thing if their positions were reversed. I would try to ease his guilt and give him absolution. And then I would do the only thing left to me. Let him live his life. Even if it meant leaving him.

Chapter 36

The next day's highlight was giving Nicky an art lesson. Gaspard brought him over as promised, and we had a picnic in the gazebo amid the wildflower field, feasting on ham and cheese baguettes with cold cider. I showed Nicky some tricks, and Gaspard watched, proud of how quickly his son picked up on what I taught him.

I told Gaspard that I was surprised by how much I enjoyed being with his son, as I'd never spent any time with children.

"Nicky feels connected to you, I can tell. He senses the same thing in you that I do."

"And what is that?"

"You've lost someone, haven't you?"

I nodded.

"And for a time, it broke you."

"It did." I felt my voice crack as my eyes filled with tears.

"We have, too . . . we've been broken as well."

"But we healed up," Nicky interjected. Of course, he'd been listening. I just wouldn't have guessed a six-year-old would understand. "We still have scars, though. Invisible ones, but Papa can see mine, and I can see his. They have Maman's name on them. And at night when I'm asleep, she flies into my room and kisses them so every day they hurt a little less."

Over his head, I looked at Gaspard. I'd never really healed, had I? And until that moment, I hadn't realized it. That's why I read and re-read my journal. As if by going over and over every moment I'd spent with Mathieu, I'd wear down the memories, until they disappeared.

"Love isn't like that," Nicky said.

"Isn't like what?" I asked the little boy. I hadn't spoken out loud.

"It won't go away."

"How did you know what I was thinking?" I asked him, trying to keep my voice light, when, in fact, I was afraid he'd read my mind. No one, not even my mother, had ever done that.

"Sometimes what people are thinking just flies into my head."

"Thought butterflies?" I tried to keep him engaged and not pressure him.

"Thought butterflies," he repeated with delight, and turned to his father. "Thought butterflies. Can we call them that from now on?"

Gaspard nodded and tousled Nicky's hair. "Of course, and we will always remember the afternoon we spent with Mademoiselle Duplessi whenever we talk about them."

Tears sprang to my eyes again. The idea that I wouldn't see him or Nicky again saddened me.

"I don't live far from here. We can see each other again, can't we?" I asked, surprised at my own boldness.

"We very well might," Gaspard said. "I'd like for that to happen."

There it was again, the sense that he knew something he wasn't telling me. I was about to ask about it when we were interrupted by Sebastian, who'd come out to fetch me. Madame was hoping I could try one more set of drawings before the guests began arriving.

I spent the afternoon in an exhausting effort to draw my way out of the castle. Finally, at five o'clock, I gave up and gave in to the inevitability that I was going to have to attend Madame Calvé's soiree.

I hadn't brought a dress with me, but Madame lent me one of hers from when she was younger and slimmer. It was a simple black sheath made of a fine diaphanous material. In the right light, it shone with a purple-blue sheen, and the sleeves fluttered like butterfly wings. The shoulders were cut out, and my bare skin peeked through.

I slipped on a pair of my own sandals with tiny straps across the instep and a little crescent-moon-shaped button holding them closed. They were daytime shoes but delicate enough to work with the dress.

I only had one piece of jewelry with me, the ring Mathieu had given me. Although I never wore it on my finger, I always kept it on a chain around my neck. Perhaps I'd put it on my finger, since I didn't have anything else in the slightest bit festive.

I wished I'd packed the bangle my sister Opaline had made for me. It was a wide rose-gold bracelet studded with rubies, amethysts, and garnets set in star shapes. I wore it high up on my arm, above my elbow, to hide my birthmark whenever I bared my arms in a sleeveless frock.

I had always been moved by La Lune's story, about a woman so desperate to feel love again that she searched for almost three hundred years to find a strong enough descendant to host her. All that suffering so she could experience passion. And pain. For there is never one without the other, I thought. All that so she could feel again what she had felt for the man she'd lost. And she finally succeeded on the day my mother saved my father's life and in doing so incorporated La Lune into her soul.

The mark on my upper arm was so clear and precise that I preferred to hide it rather than entertain questions about it. When I was a child, my mother made sure my dresses had sleeves. When I was older, Opaline created the disguising bracelet in solidarity, for she understood as well as anyone what a burden and a curse our gift was. A lithomancer who could hold gems and learn through them, hear the dead through them, she'd also had her share of pain because of her ability.

I looked at my paints, tempted to use them to cover up the crescent. But they were oils and wouldn't dry, and if I got flesh-toned paint on Madame Calvé's dress, I'd be mortified.

Music was drifting up the stairs, inviting me down. I felt a jolt of anticipation. I reminded myself that I could relax. Madame had reassured me that I wasn't going to be a party favor this time. I wondered, however, if Sebastian had other plans. My strong need to save him seemed to match my growing distrust of him.

It wasn't the time to think about that. I was due downstairs. As I walked to the door, the heel of my sandal caught in the rug, and I went sprawling. Only when I sat up, rubbing the spot above my right eyebrow, did I realized how much damage I might have done to my sight if I'd hit one of the table's clawed feet from a different angle.

I wet a towel in the bathroom and sat for a few moments while pressing the cold cloth to my forehead. Once the pain subsided and I felt more composed, I left my suite and, on slightly wobbly legs, walked down the stairs to the main floor, prepared to meet Madame's guests.

I felt the quickening that sometimes accompanied a revelation, not sure why I was experiencing it. It was the fall, I supposed.

Below me in the foyer, I saw Sebastian, looking up at me, waiting for me, smiling. Then the front door opened. A crush of people hurried in, escaping the rain that had started. With the rest of them hidden under umbrellas, I could only see three sets of trousered legs.

The men had their backs to me as the butler moved among them, divesting them of their raincoats and umbrellas. Just as one turned, Madame bustled past and blocked my view. Her voice rose over the wind that blew her words away.

"Eugène, welcome. I'm sorry about the storm. It must have been madness driving here in all that rain. And Yves, it's so wonderful to see you," Madame greeted them.

I was holding my breath, waiting to hear her address the last man in the group.

"And Mathieu. Be still, my heart, to have so many handsome men arrive at once," Madame said, with a lovely, flirty laugh in her voice.

My hand tightened on the banister. I stopped moving. It wasn't possible. Except, like a train rushing toward a certain destination, I'd known this would happen since I'd first arrived. And then it occurred to me that there must be thousands of men with that name. This Mathieu wasn't necessarily the one I'd known and loved. How embarrassing that I'd just assumed it was. How pathetic a creature I was.

In New York, at a party, I'd once overheard a conversation between two women. One was talking about a man she'd just met, whom she might be falling in love with. The other, an older woman, asked her why she'd do that. "Love is the very worst way to punish yourself."

I'd never forgotten what she'd said. It certainly was true for me. The worst pain I'd ever endured was a result of the greatest love I'd ever felt.

I shook myself out of my reverie and resumed descending the stairs. Almost relaxed, thinking myself foolish to have believed that the one man I had run away from, had left France to avoid, would be here in the château and I'd have to see him.

Sebastian called out to me.

Hearing him, Madame turned and looked up. "Delphine, you look lovely. And to think I once fit in that dress. What age does . . . what age does . . . Come, you're just in time to meet my guests."

One of the men stepped forward, blocking one of the others. Madame was blocking the third.

"Eugène Leverau, this is Delphine Duplessi."

He took my hand and kissed it.

"Eugène has been in Egypt on an archaeological dig since his fiancée's death," Madame said to me, and then turned to him. "Delphine is a fine young painter."

A frown creased his brow for a fraction of a moment and then disappeared. "A pleasure," he said, a bit stiffly, and moved away.

My view of the second man was now clear.

"And this is Yves Villant, the director of the Paris Opera," Madame introduced us.

As Villant bent to kiss my hand, Madame stepped aside. With a mixture of horror and deep visceral pleasure, I saw the man I'd run away from almost five years before, standing just inside the door, his beautiful blue-gray-violet eyes staring up at me, and I felt as if I were seeing stars in the night sky, sparkling for the very first time.

Chapter 37

I must have stood there paralyzed, speechless, for a full minute. A flush rose from my chest, warming my cheeks. My heart beat so audibly in my own ears that I worried everyone else might hear it, too. I felt pain I didn't understand, until I realized that the shank of my ring—the ring he'd given me—was digging into my flesh because I was gripping the stair rail too tightly.

What I'd both feared and longed for had materialized. Mathieu Roubine was here. A horrible and wonderful accident of fate had brought him to Emma Calvé's house during the week I was staying there.

I saw and heard Madame Calvé introduce Sebastian to Mathieu and tried to make sense of what I was watching. My brother and my lover, shaking hands. Exchanging pleasantries while I looked on.

Ever since I'd arrived and stepped over Madame's threshold, I'd been at war. Wanting to stay and wanting to go. Feeling welcomed and unwanted. Enjoying Gaspard and made uncomfortable by his distance. My instincts on the staircase were also opposites. I wanted to turn and run and lock myself inside my bedroom and at the same time rush down the stairs and throw myself at Mathieu, feel his arms encircle me, smell his familiar, sensuous burnt-vanilla, honey, and amber scent.

I did neither. I remained frozen on the stairs, holding on to the railing, while Mathieu walked up to me. He took each step slowly, smiling that sly half smile of his that I knew so well. As if he had a secret to share but wanted to hold back just a little longer. He had been that way as a lover, too, slow and teasing, making each and every moment something to savor. No. This was highly inappropriate. Thinking of him that way was the very last thing I should have been doing.

"Mathieu . . . I didn't expect to see you here. How lovely," I said, in a voice that embarrassed me for all its false bravado. I sounded like some idiotic girl running into a school friend at a restaurant, not a woman confronting the man who'd burrowed so deeply into her soul that she'd sailed across an ocean to escape his pull and still felt it every day of her life.

Mathieu Roubine was my elixir, and I was his poison. He was my savior and I his executioner. I had drawn him to try to help him discover his past and in the process had seen his future—destroyed because of me. Unwilling to take any chance that I'd follow in my mother's footsteps and put my lover's life in danger, I'd fled. Yes, my mother had saved my father but only by moments and only at a great price. I was willing to pay the price but not to risk failing at the task. I was not nearly the force my mother was.

To imagine a world without Mathieu in it was a far worse fate than not being with him. At least I would know he was living and breathing somewhere on earth.

He'd reached me. Without saying a word, he took my right hand in his. I felt his fingers find the ring and outline its shape. I saw a moment of confusion in his eyes. Was he wondering why I still wore his ring if I'd thrown him over for someone else? He continued running his finger around the stones. He cocked his head a little to the left, raised his right eyebrow in that mischievous way he had, and I felt my heart, which was still pounding, skip a beat.

Nothing was different. Despite all the space I'd put between us.

All the time I'd spent without him. Nothing had changed. I loved him still.

As if he knew exactly what I was thinking, he grinned a little and then bent over and pressed his lips to my palm. The gesture was at once so formal and yet so intimate that it brought a second blush to my cheeks. And then he returned his eyes to my face.

I might have been able to break free and escape but not after his deep, searching gaze met mine. Not while I saw so many things in his beautiful eyes: sadness, pain, betrayal, blame, anger. And yes, still love. Love and passion.

I felt as if I were drowning, but instead of swirling in the water, flailing and confused about which direction was safe and which disastrous, it was emotions that tossed me, crashed over my head, and pulled me under. More feelings than I knew how to cope with.

There was always something otherworldly about Mathieu's appearance and behavior. As if he'd been born in the age of chivalry, gone to sleep one night, and awoken four hundred years later. And sometimes I even wondered if that wasn't exactly what had happened. If he'd been sent from the past. A knight who had failed to save a damsel in distress being given another chance lifetimes later. With destiny intervening and turning the tables on both of them.

Could it be possible? A bond like ours had to traverse more than our present. And if anyone would, a daughter of La Lune would know that there are more things under the stars and the moon than we can explain or make sense of.

He was two steps below me, still holding my hand in his and my eyes with his. I looked at his shining golden curls, and my fingertips remembered how soft his hair was. I looked at his strong arms, and my torso remembered how it felt to have him hold me. I wanted to bury my face in his neck, inhale his scent. I wanted to lift my lips to his and feel their delicious pressure.

But I held back, because I had rigorously taught myself to resist him. Of all the temptation that the earth had to offer, hadn't I made a deal with myself that I could indulge in anything and anyone else as long as I kept away from Mathieu?

"Everyone is watching," I whispered, as I looked around and saw my brother's eyes fixed on us.

"I don't care." He laughed. "After all this time, I don't care."

"You're embarrassing me."

"I am not. You never get embarrassed. You don't care what anyone thinks."

"You're wrong. I care what our hostess thinks."

He took a step up and leaned even closer to me. I smelled his scent. "I wish I could tell you that I didn't miss you," he whispered.

He was still holding my hand. And still holding me in place with his eyes. I was tethered to him and couldn't have moved if I wanted to.

"I wish I could tell you that we will grow old and forget about each other," he continued. "But you know, as I do, that won't ever happen."

"I don't want to—"

He put his forefinger up against my lips. I felt his flesh on mine, and my skin burst into flames.

"A night out of time, Delphine. One night here in this old château, with Emma's fine wine and her food and music. Let's just take it. Steal it. I'll forgive your trespass against me, and you forget your act of transgression. Gamble with fate that we can survive it. Surely you've gambled before? From what I've heard, your life in New York involved quite a few gambles. You lost some of them and still survived, didn't you? You can survive me."

But could he survive *me*?

"What do you say?" he asked.

"You still have a velvet tongue, but no, I can't indulge in a night out of time." My voice was deliberately cold.

I could see the faint dusting of freckles on his impossibly high cheekbones. The twinkle in his twilight eyes. I couldn't stand looking at him anymore and focused just beyond him. As much as I wanted him, giving in would be self-immolation. I'd burn up with passion and put the one man I truly loved in danger.

I pulled away, taking back my hand. "Madame Calvé is waiting. I don't want to be rude. Let me be, Mathieu. It's a mistake that you're here. Let's not compound it. You only want me because I rejected you."

"Rejected me for no good reason, while you were in love with me and I with you."

I didn't answer but somehow put one foot in front of the other and forced my feet to take me past him and down the steps. I'm not sure how long he stood there, but I felt his eyes boring into my back, willing me to turn around. I didn't.

I found Madame Calvé inside the large living room, giving last-minute instructions to her butler.

She glanced over at me, then frowned. "Are you all right? You look flushed."

"Yes, I'm fine."

"Come, darling girl, I want to introduce you to the rest of my guests." Taking my arm, she escorted me over to the first grouping, which included Sebastian, who was looking at me curiously, and then I noticed another familiar face. Picasso's intense eyes appraised me seductively as I approached. Or was I just overly sensitive after the way Mathieu had been looking at me?

"You know Pablo, I'm sure?" Madame said.

"Yes. It's a pleasure to see you again, Monsieur Picasso." I had enough wits to address him formally, hoping it would signal to him that I saw him less intimately than the way he was looking at me.

"The charming Mademoiselle Duplessi," he said, his eyes sparkling, his expression telling me he wasn't taking the hint.

"And Jean Cocteau? The prince of French poetry," Madame said, indicating the man beside Picasso. He was as long and lanky as Picasso was short and thick. With his foxlike eyes, thick eyebrows, delicate lips, and impeccable suit, Cocteau exuded style.

He reached for my hand with his elongated fingers, and I almost pulled it back, not wanting anyone to take away the residue of Mathieu's kiss. Then I made myself shake his hand. I needed to get rid of Mathieu's touch, not hold on to it.

There were twelve of us that evening. In addition to Madame, me, and my brother were Mathieu, Cocteau, a dancer named Liselle Veronique, Paris Opera director Yves Villant, the poet and spiritualist Anna Poulent, the novelist Jules Bois, the archeologist Eugène Leverau, and Picasso.

After we'd seen Picasso that day on the Carlton terrace, my mother had told me she'd never met a man who had more magnetism, except for my father. And I understood what she meant. There was an intensity to his eyes, a fire that burned in him, that warmed the air around him.

At dinner, I hoped I would be sitting comfortably close to Sebastian, but he was at the far end of the table. I was a bit intimidated to find that I was seated with Jules Bois on my left and Picasso on my right.

Monsieur Bois was a gentleman, but Picasso wasn't, and his sexual energy was as palpable as his verbena cologne. As a topic of conversation, I asked him the least suggestive question I could think of: when his interest in the occult movement had begun.

"When I was young and poor and living in Paris, I shared a flat with Juan Gris and learned the tarot from him. I've studied myths and magic in many cultures, from Spanish and French to African. I'm fascinated by exorcisms, both spiritual and literal. I believe everything is unknown. Everything is the enemy. I'm anxious about it all and inspired by it all. That's why I paint. To give spirits form. If we do that, we become independent of them. Our paintings and sculpture are weapons against their influence. We Spaniards are very superstitious. And believe all these subjects are connected. Those superstitions are responsible for my first meeting your *maman* at one of the occult bookshops in Paris before you were even born. Cocteau"—he nodded toward the poet at the other end of the table—"took me with him once."

"And that's where you met Satie?" I asked.

He nodded. "Paris was a small city before the war. We all went to the same bars and cafés. Studied one another's paintings, read one another's poetry, and listened to one another's music. Eventually, we worked with one another. Satie, Cocteau, and I collaborated on a ballet in 1916. Cocteau wrote the scenario, Satie composed the music, and I designed the sets—" Picasso broke off, as if suddenly remembering. "It was only nine years ago but seems a lifetime. Things were so different then. You are too young to remember. Now, with everyone having a telephone and an automobile, as convenient as it all is . . . the modern age is separating us."

Monsieur Bois, who'd joined in the conversation, laughed. "Such a pessimistic way to approach modern marvels, Pablo."

"I'm trying to charm Delphine. Don't point out that I'm really just a curmudgeon."

Mathieu was seated across from me, and I felt his stare. Unwilling to meet his gaze, I searched out Sebastian at the end of the table, but he was engaged in conversation with Yves Villant.

I focused on Picasso again.

"Is mysticism part of the Spanish culture?" I asked. "I haven't been to Spain, and I'm afraid I don't know very much about it."

"Spain is a very Catholic country, and Catholicism is a very mystical religion. I can actually pin a date on my first experience with the mystical. It didn't turn out well. In fact . . . it's a sad story. The saddest of my life. Do you want to hear it?" He was experiencing a painful memory and at the same time flirting shamelessly.

I was a bit uncomfortable, but anything was preferable to turning and seeing Mathieu. I nodded. "Of course."

"When I was thirteen years old," Picasso said, "my seven-year-old sister, Conchita, contracted diphtheria. My parents did everything. So did the doctors. But she got worse and worse. So I made a pact with

God, because that's what we Catholics did. We *prayed*." He practically spit out the word. "I had been painting since I was very young and was already distinguished by that point. Everyone spoke in reverential tones about my 'gift.' And so I offered up that gift in exchange for my sister's life. I promised God that if he let her live, I would never paint again. When she died, I had to examine my faith, and I concluded that this God was evil. He was my enemy. In my mind, he changed places with Satan. I learned then to question everything. The faith of my parents held no answers for me. But that didn't mean I could exist without some kind of faith. I began a quest, which I am still on today, to understand different ideas and philosophies."

I was deeply moved by the story. My brother and I were so close that I'd imagined myself in Picasso's place. "I'm sorry about your sister."

He took my hand. Across the table, I felt Mathieu's stare intensify.

"It was a long time ago," Picasso said. "We learn to live with sadness, don't we? I had a long run until I lost anyone again. And then it was my first love."

I extracted my hand. Love wasn't a subject I wanted to discuss with a man they said was sexually insatiable. Especially not while Mathieu sat opposite us, listening, I was certain, to our every word.

I leaned back a bit in my chair so I could include Bois in my next question. I was exhausted. Trying to keep the flow of conversation going while avoiding Mathieu was draining every ounce of energy I had.

"And Satie? You knew him well also, Monsieur Bois?"

"Yes, for years. Although lately he'd isolated himself. Satie was a genius," he said simply. "He didn't let us say good-bye to him while he was alive. So we are going to do it in another way. In our own way. After dinner. I suppose Emma told you about the séance. But if it frightens you, you don't need to participate."

"No, it doesn't frighten me."

"Given her *maman*, how could it, Jules?" Picasso asked.

I knew a little about Jules Bois, from bits and pieces I had picked up over the years. One doesn't grow up a daughter of La Lune without hearing about others involved in the same study. The novelist had been a member of several secret societies, including the one that had saved my mother's life when she first came to Paris.

Bois was about to ask me something else when Anna Poulent, who was on his left, asked him a question I couldn't quite hear.

"Oh, good, you're all mine again." Picasso smiled as he leaned closer to me and asked me how my own work was going.

"I haven't been painting."

"Still?"

"I guess I've become frightened by my work."

"Spoken as a true Surrealist," he said.

The conversation had veered too close to the personal again. "But it seems you haven't accepted any women as part of the Surrealist movement. As your muses, yes. I read a lengthy interview just last week in which you talked about the other artists involved, and not one woman was included."

He looked wounded. "If you suffer with your brushstrokes and explore your dreams on canvas and if the process makes you come alive like nothing else, you are an artist. No matter what your sex. But there hasn't been a woman who's been doing what we've been doing. I hadn't heard of any when I was interviewed for *Le Figaro*. Do you have some of your work with you?"

"I don't have any finished paintings. Just some sketches I've done since I've been here." I was purposely cryptic. I didn't know if Madame had told anyone about my reason for being at the château. After all, I was searching for secrets; perhaps she didn't want my mission revealed.

Picasso stood, grabbed my hand, pulled me up. "Let's go look at them now. If they meet the criteria of our new movement, then I'll declare you on the spot."

"Pablo, do sit down. We are in the middle of dinner," Madame called out from across the table. "Is he bothering you, Delphine, dear? I can make him trade places with someone else."

"You will not. I would refuse," Picasso said, as he took his seat again. Then he leaned into me and whispered, hot breath against my ear, "After dinner and the séance, you will show me the sketches, won't you?"

"So you'll also be participating in the séance?" I asked.

"I've been to quite a few over the years and find them fascinating. Especially when Anna Poulent is officiating. She seems to be a magnet for spirits. And these days, I have more in common with those who practice black masses than their counterparts. The monstrous and uncontrolled and unknown—isn't that what we are trying to discover when we stand in front of a canvas? If you aren't, then you aren't a real artist. Anyone can learn to paint pretty roses like Renoir."

"You don't believe that," I said.

"Which part?"

"The part about anybody painting like Renoir."

He laughed, and his intelligent black eyes sparkled. "Well, maybe not quite, no. But I do think we have an obligation as artists to push the boundaries and search for the truth. Art," he said, "is the lie that tells the truth."

I couldn't hold back a shudder. Of course, he noticed.

"What is it?" he asked.

"That's what I do. What I try to do. What I do despite myself. But people don't all want the truth."

"That may be, but you must never stop giving it to them. You have to promise me. Because that's the only way to be real. To create something that has meaning."

He looked at me intently, waiting. When I didn't respond, he put his hand on my arm. "You're at the beginning of your career. If you are serious about this, you have to declare it. I've been at it twenty, twenty-five years longer than you; I can steer you in the right direction. Promise."

"I promise, I do."

"No matter how difficult it is, yes? Because in the long run, only that which is difficult, only the art you pull from deep inside you, is really worth anything."

"Yes."

The maid arrived with our second course and put lovely plates of sole meunière and boiled parsley potatoes in front of us, and we started to eat.

The conversation turned to Paris at the turn of the century, when most of the people at the table had met each other and the absent guest, Erik Satie. Several times, Sebastian caught my eye when the stories were familiar, because our mother had told us about the very same incidents. That she had known most of these people made an uncomfortable night a bit more bearable. But Mathieu's presence was impossible to ignore. It was painful, like a splinter, no matter how I moved or whom I spoke to or how interesting the conversation.

A few times, when his head was bent in conversation with Veronique or Madame, I sneaked a glance at him. He had changed. Of course he had. It had been almost five years since I'd seen him. He'd been twenty-five then, fresh home from the front. There were more lines on his forehead that I could just glimpse under the golden curls and also around his mouth.

Like every young man his age, he had gone to fight for France in the most horrific and devastating war anyone had ever seen. Over one million Frenchmen had died. More had been wounded. Mathieu had been one of those. After three years in battle under the worst of circumstances, he had been shipped home. The doctors thought he would never regain any use of his right arm, but he had confounded them all. He spent a year in a rehabilitation center and recovered almost full use of the limb. A miracle, he had said, and one that you never forgot for long because of the slightly awkward way he had of reaching for something or putting on a jacket. Yes, there were wounds on his arm and his back. Marks—some deep and menacing, some thin and barely visible. But it was the damage to his psyche that affected him more than anything else.

So many men suffered the ravages of war. I'd always been thankful that Sebastian had been too young to go. The toll it took was incalculable. Many never recovered. Some returned home only to enter institutions and never leave. Some saw ghosts. Or heard bombs for the rest of their lives. Many couldn't cope, no matter how much help they got, and killed themselves.

During the time I'd spent in Paris in love with Mathieu, I'd seen how he endured nightmares and memory loss. At first, he thought it was his duty to suffer, but in time, I persuaded him to try and let me help. It was how I knew he finally trusted me. When I truly understood that he loved me. He took the drafts I made and slept better and longer, and as time passed, he needed less and less of the tisane I'd concocted from my grimoire.

I wondered how he was sleeping now and if the nightmares had returned. How was he coping with the guilt of knowing his brother had died saving his life? I remembered the awful night I put on my blindfold and drew the past.

"We were engaged to be married," Jules Bois was saying, to my right. And the words were oddly resonant, considering that Mathieu had proposed marriage to me. I touched the ring on my finger. The ring Mathieu had touched only an hour earlier.

"What happened?" I asked.

"Emma was too curious about life to settle down with one person. And I was too jealous of her need to experience everything. She has an open mind. So do I but not about her. I wanted her to myself. I could share her with the audience but not with other men." He smiled. "But as it's turned out, we've wound up married to each other in our own way. Devoted companions. Caring friends. Ready lovers. I would die for her if I had to. That kind of love never alters, never fades. Does it?"

"I wouldn't know," I said.

"Really? I sensed you'd know about that sort of thing."

"Why?"

"I'm not quite sure. But isn't that what makes for the most exciting conversations? Intuition and curiosity?" Bois asked.

"I'm not quite sure of that, either." I smiled at him. "Certainly the most unusual."

"Does the unusual disturb you?"

"Sometimes yes. There are a lot of things about this world you all inhabit, that my mother inhabits—"

He interrupted. "That you inhabit, too, yes?"

"Yes, that I inhabit, too. There are a lot of things about it that disturb me, because the occult is the search for hidden knowledge, and hidden knowledge is in the shadows."

"And shadows frighten you."

"No."

"But I can see that they do," he argued.

"You're mistaken, Monsieur Bois." I didn't want to encourage any more prying.

"I think not. Let's find out what the others see. Picasso? Cocteau?" Bois got their attention.

"Let's play a little game to help Delphine understand the aura she projects."

My discomfort increased. "No, I don't want to—"

He interrupted me again and said with a smile, "It's just a game. And it will help you."

"What are the rules?" Picasso asked. "I need to be forewarned so I can break them."

Everyone laughed.

"Name me five adjectives to describe Delphine," Bois said. "There are no rules. You first, Picasso."

Picasso studied me the way I study my subjects—as if he were going to paint me.

"Sensual . . ." He cocked his head, searching my face. "Frightened, secretive, intelligent, and angry."

"Cocteau?"

"I see intelligent as well. And curious. Rebellious. And yes, frightened. Some sadness. Definitely, sad."

"What are you doing, Jules?" Madame asked.

"Helping Delphine see what she would prefer not to see. Describe her in five adjectives, Emma."

I was becoming more and more embarrassed and uneasy, as everyone at the table turned his or her attention to me, including Mathieu. I watched his face but couldn't read his expression.

"I only need one. She's upset," Madame Calvé said. "With you, Jules. Do apologize to Delphine. She's not one of your characters."

"Mathieu?" Bois asked, ignoring Madame.

He was about to answer, but before he could say a word, I interrupted and stopped both him and the game. "I think I understand, Monsieur Bois. There's no need for anyone else to play. You've made your point."

Sebastian sensed my distress. "Are you all right, Delphine?"

I nodded. "I'm fine."

My brother asked Cocteau what he was working on, Madame said something to the opera director, and conversations around us resumed. I still felt Mathieu's eyes on me but kept from glancing his way.

"I bow to your ability to see through me, Monsieur," I said to Bois.

"So the shadows have you in their grip?"

I wasn't sure what he knew or which shadows he meant, but it didn't matter; it was true, they did. I nodded again.

"You need to embrace them, you know. The only way to cope with them is to invite them in, to sit down with them at your table and look them right in the eye and confront them."

The idea was horrific to me. It was terrible enough to look at other people's shadows. But my own? I'd never tried to purposely paint my own shadow portrait. The one time I'd done it by accident had been destructive enough.

Amid the comments about how delicious the chocolate mousse was, rain started to pelt the windows and grew in intensity. Not a gentle, comforting drizzle but an erratic, disturbing downpour. And as I listened to it, I thought of Satie in the heavens, writing this composition for an orchestra of rain and thunder and wind, the symphony of storm.

Chapter 38

Anna was a well-known medium, famous for her séances. One of her biggest supporters, Arthur Conan Doyle, had attended several and written about how astonishing he believed her to be. There had been numerous articles about her talent, and of course, I'd read a few of them. One couldn't be interested in the occult—and it seemed everyone was in the 1920s—without stumbling upon her name. She wasn't popular just in France but also in England and in New York. Like an opera singer or a theatrical star, she'd gone on several world tours. For as many people who believed in her and flocked to see her, there were even more who tried to debunk her. But so far, no one had been able to prove she was a charlatan. She appeared to have a true gift.

Séances could be very disturbing when taken seriously. I'd never been drawn to them. There was enough tumult in my own mind and no need to invite more.

Yet I was curious now to watch Anna in action. Her reputation wasn't the only reason. When we had been introduced that evening, I was surprised not to sense any mystery about her at all. She was pretty in the most ordinary way. Blond curls, peach-colored skin, lovely hands with perfectly shaped oval nails. She'd looked at me with clear gray eyes that showed no hint of guile. She reminded me of a doll in one of the more fashionable shops on rue Saint-Honoré in Paris. Her frilly silver frock and silver slippers matched her eyes. Her mouth, a delightful bow, was lipsticked in a sassy magenta. Her words practically bubbled over when she spoke in a girlish voice that I imagined could become most grating.

Despite my initial hesitation, I felt no apprehension by the time I sat down at her séance table after dinner. Because of her fame, I assumed she had a keen ability to read people's thoughts. That wasn't witchery at all but more connected to science, similar to the way a radio picks up signals. And with an actor's ability to mimic other people's voices, one could put on a very powerful performance.

There were ten of us at the table. My brother and Yves Villant had begged off and were in the library smoking cigars. I sat next to Cocteau, and before anyone could take the seat on my other side, Mathieu slid in.

This made me nervous, since I feared we would have to hold hands when Anna called the spirits to gather, and I didn't know if I would be able to bear the feel of his skin on mine again.

While Madame and Anna prepared the room, Mathieu chatted to me as if I were just another guest. No one listening could have guessed how loaded his questions were.

"Did you enjoy your escape to New York?" he asked.

"I did."

"What brought you back? Friends? Family? A lover?"

I tried to keep my voice light and teasing. "Monsieur, you embarrass me. That's quite a personal question, isn't it?"

"Are there any other kinds of questions that matter? There's too much small talk at parties. Too much surface chatter. If it's even possible to truly know someone, to begin to know someone, you must ask questions that are sometimes embarrassing."

"And accept that the person being questioned won't answer truthfully."

"Which would be a shame, for how else can someone get to the heart of the matter?"

"What about you? Are you enjoying your shop now that you run the Librairie du Merveilleux?"

"It's quite an honor for Uncle Pierre to have turned it over to me."

"And you continue to get quite a lot of acclaim for your bookbinding, too. You must be working long hours."

"So you keep track of me?" he asked.

I ignored the question. "Are you quite happy with your work?"

"I'm satisfied. I don't know if I can be happy."

"I saw one of your books just yesterday. Madame gave one to the groundskeeper's son."

"You'll see another later. I brought one for you. You know about Emma's plan for us, don't you?"

"Her plan? For us?"

I had no idea what he was talking about. No idea of what *us* might mean in any context. There was no *us* and hadn't been for nearly five years. Only my sister Opaline knew Mathieu existed. We'd run into her by accident one afternoon near L'École. She thought he was one of my classmates, and I didn't dissuade her from that notion. But then, later that summer, Mathieu visited her jewelry shop to commission my ring. Even though he told me he'd described it to her as a gift of appreciation and friendship, as opposed to an engagement ring, my sister knew we were not just friends but were involved in a serious love affair.

After Mathieu gave the ring to me, I went to Opaline and begged her to keep my secret. Lying, I said that I wasn't sure how I felt about him and that until I was certain, I didn't want the family to know. Why had I been so intent on keeping him a secret? Rereading my Book of Hours, it seemed I was afraid that if I talked about him and shared him with my family, he might disappear like quicksilver, which vaporized when mixed with water even at the lowest temperatures.

"Don't worry, *mon chat*," Mathieu said.

He'd often told me I reminded him of a cat because of the lazy way I stretched after I'd been painting for too long and because of the way I stared at him—just the way his cat did—unblinking for so long, inscrutable, telling nothing of what I was thinking.

I winced at the endearment and the flood of memories it brought back. As if I weren't already bombarded with enough of them.

"Emma's plan," Mathieu said, "is for me to take your sketches of her house and put them into a book. To keep all the drawings in one place."

"So you know everything about why I am here?"

"I do, yes. Emma and my uncle have been friends since the early days of Péladan and his secret society. She was a member of the original inner circle and has attended the salons and ceremonies for years. I've known her since I was a boy working at the bookshop after school. Once she bought this castle, she enlisted Uncle Pierre to help her find the lost *Book of Abraham*. He's tracked down dozens of rare books for her, anything with even a single mention of the treasure. When she heard about what happened to you in America and your return, she came to the shop to discuss her plan with my uncle right away."

"And you were there, of course."

"Of course."

"And you told her you knew me?"

"No. She had a recollection of having met you before and remembered that we'd known each other."

"And you confirmed that you knew me?"

"Yes, Delphine. Why would I have denied it?"

"And is that all?"

"That I told her? Yes."

"What are you not saying?" I asked.

"Nothing. It's all very innocent."

"Is your being here also innocent?"

"Yes. I knew that she'd hired you when she asked me to make the journal for the drawings. But I didn't know this was the weekend you'd be in residence."

"If you didn't know I'd be here, why did you have the book with you? Why are you here?"

"I was Satie's friend. All of us here were. We are also all friends of Emma. We all meet often for dinner and to enjoy one another's company and explore our shared interests. Emma commissioned the book and asked me to bring it along. She didn't divulge her guest list."

He was annoyed, and I felt the chill coming off him. I'd accomplished my goal. He shifted in his seat and turned to the Ballets Russes dancer on his right.

As much as it pained me to be aloof with Mathieu, to annoy him, to have him turn his back on me, I was also relieved. I had no intention of reopening my wounds. They'd finally scarred over, if not entirely healed. I'd convinced myself that it was for the best that I'd left. To save him. To keep him safe. Nothing had changed.

Or had it?

My mother said she believed in the fluidity of time. That everything was in flux in every dimension and that we could not know for sure that the things we perceived in one moment would still be true in the next. One butterfly wing flapping in India, she always said, could have an effect continents away.

I thought of Nicky and his butterfly book. All those wings. All those marvelous colors and patterns. What changes did he conjure when he captured those creatures for those minutes, before he set them free again?

Maybe what I'd seen when I painted Mathieu had changed. Perhaps by leaving Paris when I did, I'd altered the trajectory of his future. And mine.

Could I dare believe such a thing? Should I put on the blindfold and sketch him again? What if the scene were different this time? Or what if it were the same? Then I would have to endure all the feelings of loss again. The truth did not change. And the truth was that I was Mathieu's destruction.

"And so we begin." Madame Calvé's voice interrupted my thoughts.

"We are here to say good-bye to our brilliant friend Satie. A sad night for us but not for him. Our poet is finally at peace. He's been released to enjoy the next phase of his journey." Her voice was luscious and rich, like syrup set to music. Her dramatic sense so powerful she had everyone at the table in her thrall.

"Now, Anna, dear, I turn it over to you."

Throughout dinner, whenever I'd heard a snippet of Anna's conversation, I'd thought her flighty and inconsequential. Perfectly in keeping with her blond marcel curls and bright pink bow-shaped lips. But now, commanding the table, she took on an entirely different persona. For one, the flounces were gone. She'd slipped on a navy velvet robe, embroidered with silver stars and moons. Its hood hid her curls, so instead of looking like a young jazz singer, she now appeared as a timeless sage. My fingers itched. I couldn't help but imagine what secrets I'd see if I put the blindfold on and tried to draw her.

She poured a few drops of a golden oil into a brass dish. On top of that, she laid a tightly wound bundle of sage leaves. Then she lit a match and set fire to the dried plant. Immediately, I smelled the aromatic odor of the herb and frankincense. The oil was a sacred scent that, as I knew from studying my grimoire, helped the mind travel out of the earthly realm and reach beyond. The incense opened our sensors, enabling us to be more receptive.

While I hadn't seen the proof of Anna's gift when I first met her, I saw it now surrounding her in a silvery aura. My mother had a similar aura around her when she was engaged with other realms. So did my sisters. The air waved in a subtle but visible pattern, comparable to the way heat escaping from an oven caused a visible disturbance if the light was just right. And the color of the air took on the moon's shimmer.

"I'd like to request that you lower the lights, Madame. And everyone, please close your eyes," Anna said, in a voice that was quite deeper and more serious than the one she'd used to chatter during dinner.

There was a difference in the sound and tenor and timbre in the intonation of someone who believed in the dark arts and the beyond. I'd heard it all my life. I heard it now from Anna.

"Everyone take the hand of the person beside you," she instructed.

On my left, Jules offered me his hand, which was cool to the touch. Not yet old but no longer young, the skin was firm but not smooth. On my right, Mathieu's hand reached for and took mine. My breath caught in my throat. His grip tightened. I tried to focus on the objective differences between his hand and Jules's. Mathieu's hand was much more muscled and the skin rougher because of his binding work. And his touch communicated so much more.

My true gift was drawing what was beneath the surface, in the present or the past mostly, sometimes in the future. But if I made a great effort, I could sometimes learn about someone by touching him or her. A talent that usually lay dormant. Especially because I'd never learned how to easily access it or fine-tune it.

When Gaspard had first shaken my hand, I'd been surprised by how easily I was able to gather information about him, or at least a sense of his inner being. Now surprise came yet again. A hot energy from Mathieu surged through me. Heating me inside, deep down in my womb. A part of me that had been asleep for so long fluttered, stretched, and flickered. Reminding me of what I'd once known, what I'd once had . . . and what I'd lost.

Anna was speaking again, but I was hardly listening. Mathieu's hand in mine was all I could think about.

"Madame Calvé, you've invited us all here tonight, so perhaps you'll begin?"

"We've come together to say good night to you, Erik," Madame said, in her powerfully rich voice.

"Erik? Are you here?" Anna called.

Madame must have turned on a gramophone, because one of Satie's most haunting melodies filled the eerie silence.

I realized suddenly how astonishing it was that I, a daughter of

La Lune, had actually managed to get to the age of twenty-six without ever having attended a séance. I didn't know what to expect and became anxious. Other than my mother and my sisters, I'd managed to avoid others who had gifts. Spiritualists of every kind had become wildly popular after the war. But I'd been in art school, and Sebastian had encouraged me to concentrate on my painting. He had plans for us and didn't want my gift corrupted in any way.

Even though Anna had asked us all to close our eyes, I opened mine. Unless I was wearing the blindfold, I couldn't bear being awake and having my eyes shut. The sensation was too much like being blind, and it scared me.

"Erik? Are you here?" Anna asked again.

The music grew a little louder. I smelled tobacco. Other than that, there were no effects. No flickering lights or objects moving across the room. Anna's body didn't collapse; her face did not contort. None of the silly dramatics the newspapers were always reporting.

"Tell us something so we may know it is you," Anna cajoled the sprit.

The voice that came from the medium when next she spoke was no longer hers. We heard a man's muffled voice, as if he were speaking from behind his hand, and he spoke quickly, as if he were in a great rush.

"Thank you all for being here."

"Erik?" Madame whispered. "Is that you?"

"You require more proof than me raising the volume on my music, Emma?" He laughed. "Let me remind you that I prefer only to eat white food: eggs, sugar, veal, salt, rice, pasta, white cheese, certain fish, chicken cooked in water. And that you served none of that tonight to honor me. Or that I boil my wine and drink it mixed with juice, which you didn't have on hand, either. Or that I was so afraid of strangling myself I never spoke while eating, but you were all quite querulous tonight with food in your mouths, weren't you?"

"Of course it's Erik," Jules said. "Who else could that be?"

"Dear, darling Erik. We were so sorry not to have said good-bye while your body was still on this plane," Madame said.

"I'm not sorry that I've left. It was time. I'm only sorry that you are all still grieving."

While the words continued pouring out of Anna's mouth, her eyes remained shut. Her face showed no animation or consciousness.

"We want you to feel our love, Erik. And take it with you on your journey." Madame's eyes were wet, and she dabbed them with her handkerchief.

There was a sudden shift in the temperature in the room then. It had been cool, the rain outside having taken away the summer's heat. But now the air turned freezing. In my thin chiffon dress and bare shoulders, I felt it instantly and shivered. Looking around, I noticed everyone else had felt it, too. And strangest of all, the window panes appeared frosted over with ice crystals. But it was the middle of the summer. How was that possible?

The music came to an abrupt halt, and the needle skidded across the disk with a shriek.

"Eugène, I'm here." Anna's voice had changed again. No longer was she speaking for Satie, but now a woman's voice came through her, a woman older than Anna, a voice ragged and out of breath. As if this woman had been running, rushing to get to us.

Eugène Leverau's head jerked up. "Thérèse?"

"I'm here."

"Thérèse? Oh, God!" The archaeologist let out an animal's wild cry of anguish.

The name Thérèse held unpleasant memories for me. I couldn't help but think of Thérèse Bruis and her devastating letter. My shame and Sebastian's reassurance. The reason I'd given him for leaving Paris and the shadow portraits, if only temporarily. Almost five years had passed since then, since Sebastian had told me he'd cleared up that unfortunate misunderstanding and removed her portrait from his gallery.

Across from me, Eugène's face had lost all color. He'd opened his eyes and was staring at Anna as if what he was hearing was impossible.

"Please close your eyes." It was Anna's voice now.

Eugène did as requested.

Once his eyes were closed, Anna resumed speaking in the older, out-of-breath voice. "Eugène, you can't do what you're thinking."

"Why did you leave me? Why didn't you come to me and tell me?" Eugène pleaded. "We could have worked it out."

"Everyone believed what they saw. You believed it."

"You didn't give me a chance." His voice broke.

"I was wrong. I am sorry. But you have to accept what's happened. Your wife and I . . . Eugène . . . we're both worried for you now. We're here to warn you. We know what you're thinking. No good will come of it."

"You should have told me." He was weeping. His agony was difficult to listen to.

"Don't do this, Eugène . . ."

I began trembling. Of course, I didn't know what the woman talking through Anna was referring to, but the disjointed conversation still made me afraid. The air around me began to grow even cooler and to swirl like a vortex, as if I were caught in an unrelenting current, the way it sometimes did when I was drawing the shadows and uncovering a secret that was buried deep for a reason . . . a secret that shouldn't be excavated.

"I have to," Eugène whispered. "I waited so long . . . and now . . . don't you see it's fate?"

"I can't help you from the void."

"Help me?" Eugène had gone from bereft to angry. "No one can help me anymore. Sophie abandoned me, then you. What's left for me?"

"You still have a future—"

Eugène cut her off. "No!" he shouted, and stood, disturbing the circle of hands, breaking the psychic's fragile tether to the other world.

The cold that swirled around me disappeared quite suddenly. The room was flooded with the scent of orange blossoms. And then that, too, was gone.

Confusion reigned. In standing so quickly, Eugène had upended the table. The dish of burning leaves slid toward Jules, who moved so abruptly his chair fell backward, landing on my foot. I let out a little yelp. Mathieu turned and stepped forward to help me. Carmen, Madame's terrier, came running at the sound of my cry and started barking.

Eugène ran from the room, straight into Sebastian and Yves, who had come to see what the melee was about.

Madame ran after Eugène.

"Is your foot all right?" Jules asked me. "I am so sorry."

"It was hardly your fault. And yes, it's fine."

"What happened?" Sebastian asked me.

"We had an unexpected visitor. Erik Satie was interrupted by a woman from beyond, who arrived to warn Eugène about something he is planning. He was more than surprised. He was acutely disturbed, and it was awful to witness. The poor man."

"Don't let it bother you, Delphine. Emma will console him. She's wonderful at that," Sebastian reassured me.

"I think it's time for some brandy," Picasso said, as he walked toward the bar. He poured out glasses and then distributed them. We all retired to the living room and sat around discussing the séance and the spirit who'd visited Eugène.

Finally, Madame came back. Alone. "I've put Eugène to bed with a glass of port." She looked at our glasses. "But brandy is a better idea."

"Let me get it for you, Emma," Jules said. "You need to sit down."

"What was that all about?" Picasso asked. "What terrible thing happened to Eugène?"

I noticed my brother was still staring at the door, as if he were watching Eugène running past him again.

Cocteau, who'd been quite silent until now, explained. "Thérèse was Eugène's fiancée. A few of us knew her. She came with him to the Librairie du Merveilleux several times. Poor man—first his wife died and then, a year later, Thérèse. I know how devastated he was, but it's been four years. I didn't think he was still so cut up about it."

"That's terrible," I blurted out. "To lose two people so close together. How did it happen?"

"His wife died of a long illness. As grief-stricken as he was, we all felt it was a relief for her. Suffering like that is no life. Thérèse had been her nurse. That's how Eugène met her. And after Sophie died, Thérèse was there to comfort him. Eventually, they became engaged. I don't know much about how Thérèse died, although I tried to get him to open up about it. But I thought he was better. Since he's returned from Egypt, he's come to a few soirees, seems more engaged. You know better than me, Mathieu—he's been a regular at the library."

"I know his fiancée died of a combination of absinthe and laudanum," Mathieu said.

"Accidental?" Picasso asked.

Mathieu shrugged. "He never shared any of the details with me, and I never pried, so I don't know the circumstances, but I always got the impression that it was a suicide. He's never been the same since. And as Cocteau said, it's been a while. Except . . ." Mathieu's gaze drifted over to me for half a second. "Some love affairs never fade." He looked back at Picasso.

Had anyone else seen Mathieu's glance rest on me? Had Sebastian? I looked over, but couldn't tell.

"Time does little to dim their luster. Altogether, Eugène has had tragic luck with the women in his life."

Mathieu's words about love affairs that never dim echoed in my mind. I was having trouble focusing on what everyone else was saying.

"I'm exhausted," Madame Calvé said. "I'm going to bed, but you're all free to cavort to your heart's content."

"I'll go up with you," I said, and stood. I was getting a headache, one of the maladies my sister Opaline and I both suffered from as a result of "events," as she called them. I could never tell when one was about to descend on me, and they could be brutal unless I caught them early. I had some headache powder in my room. If I took it quickly, I might escape this attack.

Together Madame and I climbed the stairs in silence. At the top, we said good night to each other. Before she turned to go toward her room, she pulled me close and hugged me. "There is so little in life that is worthwhile and without risk or pain. Loving someone is very hard," she said.

And before I could ask her if she was referring to Eugène or someone else, she walked away.

Chapter 39

In my suite, I grabbed my toiletries case, found the powder, and spilled it into a glass, which I filled with water from the tap. I mixed it with my finger and then sat on the edge of the bathtub and drank it down. I was anxious to get ahead of the pain and not allow it to burst open.

After I finished the draft, I rinsed out the glass and went back into the bedroom, where I noticed a package on my pillow. A silver ribbon encircled green watery silk wrapping.

Taking it in my hands, I judged its heft. It had the feel of a book. The size was also right. I untied the satin ribbon, which fell onto the floor, curling like a snake into a perfect coil. Then, because the paper was so beautiful, I unwrapped it carefully.

Inside was indeed a book. The front and back covers appeared to have been made of peacock feathers. I ran my finger over one of them. The iridescent colors twinkled in the light. Emerald, amethyst, sapphire, and turquoise with flecks of gold. The silky feathers against my skin mesmerized me and distracted me from the nascent headache.

The eye of the center feather had been cut out to reveal a deep purple shagreen circle decorated with a crescent moon and out-

lined in silver. Inside were my initials: *DLD*. Mathieu had said he'd
brought a book for Madame, but surely this wasn't that. He'd said he
didn't know I'd be here. But this book had my initials on it.

I ran my fingers over the feathers again. I traced the initials.
I knew Mathieu's work almost as well as my own. During the
four months I had been with him, I'd spent many evenings in his
workshop, painting while he created his marvelous book dressings.
People brought him favorite novels or historical tomes, memoirs or
family records, so that he could elevate their exteriors into works of
art. He also created journals, like this one, that he sold in his uncle's
shop. They were ideal as personal diaries or sketchbooks. Some
people used them to record dreams, an ancient art that had recently
gained popularity, partly because of the writings of Carl Jung. And
for a few rare shoppers who were habitués of the Librairie du Merveilleux, Mathieu also made covers for grimoires holding collections
of spells.

Bookbinding was an art like any other, but it didn't gain much
recognition until the turn of the century. Around the time I met him,
Mathieu's books were being shown alongside other great craftsmen's
wares: Rene Lalique's glass, the ceramics of Charles Catteau, the
House of Cartier's jewelry, Edgar Brandt's wrought-iron lamps and
furniture, and the lacquer screens and furniture of Jean Dunand.

Holding the journal to my chest, I tried to imagine Mathieu
walking into my room and looking around. Had he stood by the
vanity? Touched my brushes? Had he sniffed my perfume and remembered the day he'd taken me to L'Etoile's shop? Had he come
over to the bed and smoothed out the pillow before placing the gift
there? Now I had another entry to add to my Book of Hours. Another artifact to worship.

I placed the book in a drawer of the armoire. I didn't want its
beautiful colors to speak to me, to whisper and tempt me. My
mother had taught me that the most powerful force of a daughter
of La Lune was not the gift bestowed on her. It wasn't my mother's

ability to cast spells, or Opaline's ability to speak the language of stones, or my younger sister Jadine's talent for reading tears, or my own ability to draw secrets. Our greatest strength and most dangerous power was our determination. With our iron wills, we could do anything once we decided. No one could bend a daughter of La Lune once she made up her mind. And I had made up my mind about Mathieu. I'd left Paris and stayed away. I had orchestrated a good-bye scene so cruel I knew he wouldn't try to contact me. And he hadn't tried.

My decision had been the right thing for both of us. My only mistake had been not returning the ring he'd given me. I looked down at the crescent moonstone surrounded by a curve of pale blue sapphires. All the secrets of the orb intensified by the surrounding gems. I hadn't been able to give it back to him. I'd known how hard my sister had worked on the piece so that it reflected me, choosing sapphires the exact color of Mathieu's eyes and finding a moonstone with magical qualities. Nothing I could have told her would have justified my returning it.

After I left Paris and had been in New York for a few months, I received a package from Opaline that included six letters from Mathieu. She wrote that he had come to see her at the jewelry store. Distraught that he couldn't reach me, he begged her for my address, but she refused. Finally, he asked her to at least send me his letters.

Without reading a single one, I burned them all in the fireplace in the studio. And then I wrote my sister and asked her never to forward anything from him to me again. I could never be with him. I knew that. So to read his letters would only be continuing the torture of missing him.

I lay in my bed, my head nestled in the pillow. I breathed in deeply, trying to locate the faintest whiff of the burnt-vanilla scent that Mathieu wore—and succeeding. I grew warm.

Was he still downstairs? All the guests were staying overnight. Had Mathieu gone to his room? Was it near mine? Was it possible that tonight, somewhere in this castle, Mathieu would be sleeping in a room down the hall from mine?

Mathieu. On whom I'd squandered my one and only wild chance at love—and then had to walk—no, run—away from it.

He was my splendid torture. I shut my eyes, and scenes from our time together came unbidden. His face hovering above me, his hair falling in my face, his penetrating eyes, staring into mine, saying so many things all at once. His long, tapered fingers, rough from the work he did with leather tooling, running up my arms, down my breasts, my stomach, teasing me between my legs. His lips on my lips. Breathing into me and taking my breath into his own lungs. His caramel voice, whispering my name so beautifully that it sounded the way the suede he used on his books felt under my fingers.

Oh, Mathieu. Why are you here?

My hand drifted to all the places his had explored. Now between my legs. My hand was his, stroking me awake and alive and electrified. My hand was his, dipping into the slick and teasing lightning-bolt feelings. My hand was his, sending shudders up and into me.

Oh, Mathieu. Why are you here?

I couldn't imagine how any man would ever come close to making me feel what even the diluted memory of Mathieu did. Tommy certainly hadn't. I knew I'd accepted him because he was so clearly different in every way from Mathieu that he'd never remind me of him.

Being with Mathieu was like living inside a secret, magical cave. Being with Tommy was like gliding across a marble dance floor, far from the soul-searing pleasure I had found with Mathieu, the kind that sends you out into the sky past the sun into the deep inky blueness, past the stars and up toward the glow of the moon. I never had to move Mathieu's hand or squirm away from him. His kisses were never too wet or too dry or too rough or too gentle. From the first time Mathieu touched me—that day in the Luxembourg Gardens when he took my arm—I knew that we were the fit that some people only dream of ever finding. Even trying to explain it to myself, I was confounded. Spontaneous combustion was impossible, wasn't it?

My mother talked of souls and spirits and alchemy and the power of the unknowable. All of it was in our coupling. All of it was how we were, Mathieu and I. And lying on the bed in Madame's château, knowing that the man I had offered my heart to, who had taken it and given his own back for me to break, knowing that the man who with one look could cause powerful tremors deep inside me, who seemed to match me passion for passion, who understood all of my thoughts and dreams . . . knowing that he was just a few steps away made me breathless and afraid.

My hand moved faster and faster between my legs. Just once more, I would let myself remember the full force of what I had been trying to forget for these long years. What I'd tried to forbid myself to think of when I was looking for someone to make me forget. My heart breaking each time I realized that I was never going to find someone else. That there was only Mathieu. He was my curse. My mother had said not one woman in generations had broken it. Almost five years, and I had yet to push the thoughts of my golden-haired lover out of my mind.

So there in Madame's château, I succumbed to remembering all of the glorious wonder of what it had been like to be with Mathieu, but this time, it was worse, because he was close by. And that made all the difference. The memory brought both an explosion of deep pleasure and the sting of tears, because as close as he was, he might as well have been sitting on the crest of the moon. I could not go to him. I could not allow him to come to me. Because the only thing worse than living without him would be knowing that his life was in danger because of me.

At least if he was alive somewhere on the earth, I could breathe the same air he was breathing. Loving him from a far distance, the only way I could.

But would one night matter? Just one night? My determination to do the right thing, dissipating, dissolving.

Twice I started to walk to the door and then retreated. I couldn't give in. I had to. Couldn't. Finally, I opened the door. Crossed the threshold. Stood out in the hallway. Did I dare go to him? How could I not? This might be the only chance I'd ever have. I was strong but not strong enough to sleep under the same roof as Mathieu and keep away from him. If it was only for a few hours, what harm could come? The night offered a blanket of protection around us.

As I stood, barefoot and trembling in the hallway, I realized there were more than ten guests sleeping in this house, on this floor and the one above, and I only knew where my brother was. Even if I wanted to go to Mathieu, I couldn't.

I willed him to sense me. The minutes ticked on.

What kind of an occultist was I to not have the power to awaken him? How could he sleep through my need, my willingness to break my vow to myself? How could I not make Mathieu sense me? How could I sense him in the house but not be able to pinpoint which door kept him from me?

And then I wondered if us even being under the same roof now was fraught with danger. Was I a threat to him that night? Would I be the next day? My vision hadn't been stamped with a date. I had to leave the château. I'd borrow Sebastian's car. For one last moment, I stood there in the silence, memories sliding from my eyes and dripping onto my nightgown, soaking into the silk.

Chapter 40

Book of Hours
September 6, 1920

My trunks are all packed. I've cleaned up my studio and put everything away. I'm taking my art supplies, of course, but leaving behind all my drawings and canvases. I'll start afresh in New York.

And now, while I wait for the appointed hour when the cab will come to take me to the train, there is time for one last entry, one last secret to inscribe in my book that holds all the other secret, stolen hours.

I don't imagine I will ever be able to open this journal and read through these entries again. But when I began this chronicle in May, I resolved to record every hour I spent with Mathieu. And so our last few minutes must be included, despite their excruciating melancholy.

After the blindfolded drawing session when I saw into the future, I avoided Mathieu for more than a week, claiming a sudden illness. And I was ill—sick over what I had seen and my understanding of what I must do about it. I stayed in bed, eyes red from crying, uninterested in any of the food Grand-

mère sent up to my room. While I hid away, I made plans to leave Paris. That part was easy compared with figuring out how to tell Mathieu. What could I say that wouldn't invite questions? That would kill the relationship without leaving any possibility for reconciliation? I was determined it had to be a clean, decisive break. I wasn't sure I'd be capable of remaining steadfast in my decision to go if he begged me to stay.

In the end, I took the coward's way out. I arranged for him to see me in a compromising position with another man. I paid Claude Cherchez, one of my fellow students who was always short of funds, to act the part of my lover. The plan was for us to be seen together, heads close, holding hands, and then kissing passionately in the café a few blocks from the bookshop where Mathieu and his uncle ate lunch every day. I'd told my friend only enough to get his sympathy. That Mathieu had become a bore but wouldn't leave me alone, and I was hoping if he saw me with a new lover, he'd understand it was time to move on.

It was a scene worthy of Alexandre Dumas. Claude and I were already seated and had finished half a bottle of wine, when Mathieu and Pierre Dujols entered Café de Flore.

Neither of them noticed me at first, and those minutes of waiting while they walked to their table were agony. Claude held my shaking hands and whispered what looked like words of love but were really gossip about our fellow classmates. I prayed I'd get through the encounter without breaking down and concentrated on Claude's banter rather than turning my head.

In the window's reflection, I watched Mathieu and his uncle sit down at a table where they couldn't avoid seeing me once they got settled. And indeed, after only a few moments, I saw Mathieu look our way, then stand and head toward us.

I whispered to Claude to kiss me right away. He played his part well, if not with a bit too much enthusiasm. But it was all for the best, because the kiss stopped Mathieu in mid-step, and he didn't approach our table. Not then. Not at all.

When I next checked in the window's reflection, the table Mathieu and his uncle had occupied was empty.

That was a week ago. Every day since then, a letter from Mathieu has arrived at the house. I've burned them all. What good will it do me to read Mathieu's words? Whether he is hurt or confused or furious, I cannot be swayed. I have to go.

The dawn has broken. Outside my window, the pink-orange sky will soon be turning pale blue and then a more intense cerulean blue, and it will be time for me to go.

I feel lost. I am lonesome. All the dreams I've dreamed for the last four months have died, and along with them, some of my soul has died, too.

I don't know if I'll ever be able to return to Paris. Wouldn't the memories haunt me and drive me mad? Even now, here in my bedroom, I turn my head to the window and for a moment see Mathieu standing there, naked, after our last lovemaking, backlit by the late-afternoon sun.

I go to sleep, and even though I know the sheets have been laundered a dozen times since he lay on them, I still inhale them, searching for a hint of his cologne.

What would I do if I walked down a street and saw Mathieu walking toward me or spotted him in a café? Or simply heard his name spoken in passing?

Every scenario is untenable.

I know I can't completely escape. No matter where I go, there will be moments when I will think of him. For the rest of my life, every time I see two lovers embrace, I will miss him.

I can't remember which kiss was our last. How is that possible? I don't have an exact count of how many times we kissed. According to my Book of Hours entries, we saw each other more than sixty-four times and spent more than three hundred hours together. If Mathieu kissed me a dozen times during some hours and only one or two times during others, that would be at least a thousand kisses. And yet, as I sit here, as much as I try, I can't recreate the sensation of his lips on mine. I can remember that it happened and that it made me feel sublime, but experience it anew? No. How cruel is love? How mercurial? To be all bright, strong, bold, and powerful splashes of colors while you are in its midst—and then, once you're out of its immediate presence, all you have left are thinned-out, pale hints as memories.

If only I could kiss him once more and could write down every nuance and keep it safe on these pages, so whenever I am needy, I can open my book and feel one of his kisses again in all its red, purple, deep-magenta intensity.

I hope that one day I will find solace in believing I have done the right thing by leaving him to keep him safe. That one day the pain of missing him will be attenuated by knowing he is alive and well.

But now I can only think of how I always believed I would be with Mathieu forever. Of how the world changed color when he came into my life. Of how lonely I was until I met him. And how that loneliness has returned and will stay with me forever. I always thought I'd see Mathieu again. And again. And now, I know, I never will.

Chapter 41

My younger sister, Jadine, collects people's tears and uses them to help her clients find their happiness through the salty water. As I dressed to leave the château, I thought that if she were there that night, I would have let her collect my tears so she could offer me advice. But she was in Paris.

My mother might have been able to hold my hands and feel my energy and give me insight into how to exorcise Mathieu's pull. But she was in Cannes.

My father, with no magickal thinking, would have put his arms around me and told me he loved me and understood. That might have been what I needed the most at that moment. But he was in England, building a country house for an eccentric art collector.

And Sebastian? My twin, my other half, who knew me in many ways better than anyone else, who had been my eyes when I couldn't see, who shared my determination and my passion for art—he would want to fight my battle for me. He would see Mathieu as the villain in this story. Would somehow blame him. But none of my despair was Mathieu's doing. Like so many times before, the doing was all mine.

The house was quiet as I crept down the stairs, not wanting to disturb anyone. I'd drive into town. There was an inn there. A place to spend the night away from temptation. And then, in the morning, I'd telephone Sebastian and explain, and he'd understand and pack up my things and join me, and we'd go home.

While I'd been in my room, the storm had intensified. Rain pelted the castle. I didn't have an umbrella. I hadn't thought I'd need one, so I ran from the front door to the garage, getting soaked in the process.

Sebastian's car started without any problem, and I pulled out of the sheltered area and onto the open road. The night was dark, the moon only a blurry crescent peeking through the clouds. I strained to see through the rain. Fighting the road, slick with water, I drove on, away from the castle and my temptation. Driving farther away from Mathieu. I was proud of myself for making such a wise decision. I went around a first curve. A second. The more distance I put between myself and the castle, the more I relaxed.

And then the car skidded. I could barely see ahead of me. What was I supposed to do? Brake? Turn the wheel into the slide? Away from it? Even though I couldn't see them, I knew there were gorges and ravines on either side of the narrow road. The momentum was taking me where it wanted to. The car kept sliding. How wide was the road here? I gripped the wheel and turned away from the edge. Was I doing the right thing? What if another car was coming? Was I in the wrong lane? And then I heard a crack and felt a sudden impact throw me back and forward.

And then nothing, until I felt strong arms lifting me and heard the sound of rushing water. Never-ending rain. A man's voice saying my name over and over, soothing me as if I were a child. A sense of well-being suffused me. I was safe. I heard words but wasn't sure if they were inside my mind.

The voice was kind, loving: "You little fool. Not even a witch can escape her destiny."

And then nothing.

I awoke in a bed. Soft pillows behind me, a comforter cushioning me. The sound of rain pelted the windows. Opening my eyes, I saw light and turned toward it. A lamp was beside the bed, lit. And then I saw Madame Calvé, sitting in a chair, asleep at my bedside.

As I stirred, she woke quickly and began examining my face with anxious eyes. "Oh, Delphine, you gave us such a scare."

"What happened?"

"You had an accident on the road."

"I thought I was dreaming that. It was real?"

"All too real."

"Not a dream?" I was truly confused.

"No. For some reason that I'm hoping you'll explain, you left the castle in the rain in your brother's car and were heading toward town when you crashed."

"The rain . . . the car skidded in the rain." I was remembering.

"On a very dangerous stretch. If you had gone right instead of left, you would have gone over the side and into a ravine. We've had too many accidents there . . ." Her voice drifted off.

I knew without having to be told. "Gaspard's wife? That's where?"

Madame nodded. "So tragic." She took my hand. "The idea that you could have been another victim of that treacherous passage . . . it's too much."

"Someone found me. Who?" Even as I asked, I knew.

"Gaspard," Madame said.

"How did he know I was there?"

She shook her head. "You'll have to ask him. He didn't explain, except to tell me he pulled you out of the wreck. He walked all the way here carrying you. He was worried you were chilled. That you'd hurt your head. How do you feel?"

I flexed my right hand before I did anything else. No pain at all. Then I stretched and flexed my feet. "Surprisingly all right."

"Gaspard brewed you some broth. He's always making up natural remedies. He woke you up. Well, you didn't seem to come to, exactly, but you sat up and drank what he gave you from the cup. Do you remember that?"

I shook my head. I didn't.

"He said when you fully awoke to give you the rest. It's right here. I think you should drink it."

I took the cup from her and sipped. I tasted honey, brandy, and herbs, although I couldn't identify any of them.

"I'm in my nightgown. Did I undress? I don't remember getting into bed at all."

"I'm not surprised. You were not very receptive when Gaspard brought you back. Not unconscious but woozy, sleepy. I undressed you with my maid's help."

"Thank you," I said. But I felt embarrassed that they'd had to do that. "And how long have I been sleeping?" The curtains were drawn. I couldn't glean any information from the sky.

"About fifteen hours. It's Sunday afternoon now. We still have a full house. The storm hasn't let up at all, and the roads are flooding. You must be starving."

"I am, actually. I can dress and come down."

"No. Not yet. Gaspard and I both agreed you should stay in bed for the rest of today. I'll have a tray sent up. I have to go and tell them you're all right. Everyone has been in a panic. Your brother, for one, as you'd expect. Is it all right for him to come up?"

I nodded.

"And not just your brother. Picasso has been terribly worried. And Gaspard, of course, who has stopped in twice to check on you and asked me to send word immediately when you woke up. And then Mathieu." Madame gave me a sidelong glance. "From the way Mathieu reacted, one might assume he had sent you out in that storm."

In a way, he had, I thought. But of course, I didn't say it out loud.

"I wasn't aware the two of you knew each other that well." Madame pushed me to explain.

"Until last night, I hadn't seen him for almost five years."

"Should I not have invited him?"

"To your own home?" I asked.

She was smart enough to know I wasn't going to share any information.

"Let me go order you some food. Just rest, dear. You've gone through quite an ordeal."

After eating a fluffy cheese omelet, croissants with raspberry jam, and a pot of wonderfully strong coffee, I lay in bed and dozed again.

When I woke for the second time that day, I looked at my watch and saw it was seven at night. There was a note beside my bed from Madame saying that she hoped I slept well and to ring when I was ready for dinner. Which I did.

Other than my neck and shoulders aching a bit, considering what had happened, I felt surprisingly fit as I got out of bed. What had been in Gaspard's brew?

Having slept for so long, I found myself restless and in want of diversion. I picked up a novel I'd brought with me, *Chéri* by Colette. But a melancholy story about separated lovers wasn't the smartest choice of reading material given my circumstances. I always traveled with two books for just such instances. *The Shadow on the Glass* by Agatha Christie was a far better choice, and I read contentedly for a half hour until Sebastian came up with my dinner. He sat and talked to me while I ate, waiting until I had finished to ask me why I'd gotten in the car and driven off during the night.

I didn't want to tell him the whole truth. So I told him the part that I assumed would make sense to him.

"The more we stay, the more disturbed I am by this place. It finally seemed like too much. I couldn't sleep. I felt as if I was going to lose my mind if I didn't get away."

"Maybe that means you are close to a breakthrough."

"Sebastian, we can get the money another way. I can pawn some of my jewelry. Please, can we just leave?"

Despite my newfound friendship with Madame Calvé, whom I did wish I could help, I couldn't deny my increasingly urgent need to leave. Besides, I hadn't been able to find the book. I felt certain the house didn't want me to find it.

He took my hand. "If we could, I'd say yes. But it's still raining, and there have been mudslides, and all the roads are blocked. No one can leave."

I sighed.

"I'm sorry," he said.

"Well, the flooding certainly isn't your fault."

"No, but bringing you here was. You told me you didn't want to do any more blindfold drawings. I shouldn't have insisted."

"But you did." My sympathy for Sebastian was waning. As much as I wanted to protect him, there was no denying I was trapped in this castle because of his greed and bad judgment.

"I think I want to go back to sleep," I told him.

He kissed me good night on the top of my head, took the tray, and went out.

I tried to pick up with my Agatha Christie novel where I'd left off, but I could no longer concentrate. My neck ached. And I was still under the same roof as Mathieu. My attempted escape had failed. Gaspard was a mystery I hadn't even begun to solve. And the unrelenting rain on the window panes had a foreboding tenor.

I pulled on my robe and wandered into the studio. Inspecting the drawing table, I made sure everything was where I needed it to be and then sat down. After removing my blindfold from its velvet-lined leather box, I placed it over my eyes. Feeling for the pencil, I picked it up. I waited for the images to appear, and when they did, I began to sketch the castle once more.

From the very beginning, my ability to draw a scene without consciously knowing what it was going to turn out to be frightened me. I sensed it had frightened my mother, too. Several times, at my request, she had tried to reverse the gift she'd unintentionally given me but never found a spell to expunge my ability to see secrets. Despite my protests, after a few tries, she curtailed her efforts, fearful that if she meddled too much, I might once again go blind.

She'd also warned me not to try to draw my own shadow portrait, especially once I'd turned fourteen and my menses arrived. For that was when daughters of La Lune came into their full power. The flow of blood somehow opened a door to the arcane and preternatural universe.

After drawing for more than an hour, I grew tired and put my head down on my arms for a moment to rest.

When I raised my head, I took off the blindfold and looked at the clock. Several hours had passed, and it was the middle of the night. I crawled into bed and slept until morning.

When I woke, I first looked out the window, hoping the rain had stopped so the roads might clear, but it was still teeming. I rang for coffee and, while waiting, walked into the studio, sat down at the desk, and looked at the pile of drawings.

I had never fallen asleep with the silken mask on before. I had never drawn in my sleep. But I'd done exactly that the night before. And it was those illustrations, the sleep-induced sketches, that I was staring at.

One by one, I examined the graphite vignettes. Each a secret of the château. Some were connected to the drawings I'd done during the last few days, others brand-new. There was a bedroom scene of a couple copulating. An addict smoking in the opium room. A maid pocketing silverware in the kitchen at least a hundred years before, judging by her clothes. A roguish-looking man shoving another man out of the turret window. A nursemaid mixing a poisoned draft in the kitchen. A chest full of iridescent pearls hidden in a rusty trunk in an attic.

There were more. More than a dozen drawings of secrets. Some criminal, others illicit or just sad. But nothing connected to Madame Calvé's thirty-year search for Flamel's alchemical masterpiece.

I finally reached the last of the sleep sketches in the pile. At first, I couldn't understand it at all. And then I realized it was drawn from the perspective of someone standing at the top of a spiral staircase, looking down into a room. It was the same room I'd drawn before. Stone walls. Shelves carved from rock. But in this drawing, I saw beakers, alembics, jars, and bottles of elixirs on some of the shelves. The particulars surprised me. Usually, these sketches were rougher. Well enough rendered to understand, certainly well enough for me to use as blueprints to create the finished portraits. But this was different. The details were completely clear. Even the smallest articles were readable.

In the corner, a compass showed the east-west orientation. A series of vignettes in the upper corner illustrated particular vistas. As if looking through windows outside. Clues to where this area of the castle was in relation to the landscape. I'd drawn an actual map. There were also numbers in the margins, as if I had been working out mathematical equations. And symbols, too—the same ones I'd included before and some new ones—all unintelligible to me. And then I noticed the most peculiar aspect of my sleep sketch.

Neither the drawing style nor the hand that had written the notes and numbers was mine.

All artists had a signature—not the way they signed their names but the way they drew a line. It had to do with the pressure they put on the pencil or crayon or brush, how steady their hands were, how careful their eyes were, how well they were able to render what they saw or imagined and the sensitivity of their fingers to translate them into action.

I knew my own signature. And I knew I hadn't done this drawing. If I thought it was possible, I would have claimed someone else had come into the studio while I slept and planted this sketch in front of me. But my windows and door were locked from the inside. I'd locked them myself. And if someone had broken in, I would have heard it.

I continued to study the picture. Madame would be happy that I'd found more clues about her treasure. I'd given her a staircase, a detailed tunnel, a compass. She had the egress to the treasure. Now, as soon as the rain abated, Sebastian and I really could leave.

Chapter 42

Dressing quickly, I grabbed the illustration and went downstairs to find my hostess and deliver her treasure map.

The scent of coffee and freshly baked bread wafted in the air. I rushed into the breakfast room, calling out, "Madame, Madame," before I realized how many people were seated around the table. As soon as I saw them, I quickly folded the drawing and shoved it into my trouser pocket.

Picasso, Cocteau, and Anna all said how relieved they were to see me and asked how I was. Mathieu wasn't there, which actually relieved me.

"Sit down, and have something to eat," Madame Calvé said, as she fussed over me.

Once breakfast was over and everyone but Sebastian had gone off to play cards or to read and the three of us were alone, I told Madame I had something to show her.

"I mapped the room," I said.

Madame moved plates and cups well out of the way, then took the sketch from me, laid it out on the table, and began studying it.

For a few moments, the only sound was the rain beating on the windows. I glanced over at Sebastian, noting the gleam in his eyes.

"I've never seen this area, Delphine," she said. "You've drawn something that just isn't here. I've examined every corner of the basement. Architects have charted all the tunnels underneath the structure. There are no spiral stone staircases like this. And the only area of the castle that faces that direction is the drawbridge and tower. And we've taken that apart already. I'm afraid this isn't going to help."

I turned to my brother. He'd assured me that as soon as the rain ceased and the roads were passable, we could go. I expected him to tell Madame now that we were done. My twin smiled at me.

Then, to Madame, he said, "Delphine will find it, Emma. She's a perfectionist. We're stuck here anyway. She'll stay at it until she does." He turned back to me. "Won't you, Delphine?"

I was amazed. He'd promised me I could stop. I shook my head. "No, I'm not sure I can."

I was disappointed in my brother, whom I'd trusted to help me. He'd betrayed me. He couldn't give up. I'd told him I'd pawn my jewelry. Didn't he believe me? Was Madame paying more than I knew? Did Sebastian owe more than he'd let on? My anger built, this time not mitigated by the memory of the watery image of my brother standing in front of the castle, warning me: *Unless you are here to save me . . .*

What was the truth? What had brought us here? What was keeping us here?

After breakfast, I donned a rain slicker and Wellingtons brought by the maid so I could take a walk. I'd spent too long up in my room sleeping the day and night before. I needed some fresh air, even if it was wet. Maybe looking at the castle from the outside would give me a different perspective.

Walking the château's perimeter didn't reveal anything new. The only thing I noticed was that in the rain, it loomed even larger, grayer, more melancholy. Occasionally, I stopped to peer out at the distant landscape. None of the images I'd drawn matched up.

I had worked my way around three-quarters of the stone fortress when I tripped on a loose cobblestone. I fell and landed ungracefully on my right foot, which I'd hurt slightly in the car accident. When I stood and tested it, I was relieved to find I hadn't injured it even more. I brushed myself off and walked on, hoping none of the guests had been looking out the window and seen my ignominious fall.

I worked my way around to the castle's north side. As the daughter of an architect, I understood buildings and how they were constructed. But even with my father talking about his designs all my life, I'd never thought about buildings as living things. I'd never searched in their shadows for the stories they held.

He'd be interested to hear about the château, I thought. He loved this region and its history. Maybe I'd bring him some of the sketches I'd done. Or perhaps do a painting for him. What if I did a series of the château's rooms as sections of the human mind? Took thoughts and turned them into different chambers? My father had told me once about an ancient Greek device called a memory palace. Maybe I could explore that concept surrealistically using the castle.

I didn't see the tree root. Just as I hadn't seen the loose stone. This time, I went sprawling.

Two falls in less than an hour. And there had been the rug in my bedroom, the broken pencil, and the window that closed too quickly on my hand. Not to mention the disaster with the car.

That was too many accidents in too short a time, wasn't it? I wondered if the house wanted me to go. If it was determined to keep its secrets buried. I meddled, I knew, with the natural order of things when I put on the blindfold. We were not meant to see inside one another's souls with such ease. I'd thought a lot about that since coming home from New York. All my commissioned portraits might have fulfilled the sitters' curiosity at first, but what havoc I'd created. My art was, in fact, a trick. A circus act with an expensive price of admission.

"Are you all right?"

I looked up into Gaspard's face, his silver hair wet with rain, his eyes full of questions.

"I think so."

With his help, I stood and tested my foot. It was no worse.

"The castle isn't always welcoming to guests," he said, startling me.

"I was just thinking that and then how silly I was to anthropomorphize the château. Stone and wood and glass can't have thoughts."

"Not the way we do, but they're from the earth and are living things and have their own form of consciousness."

When I'd tripped, my sketchbook had fallen and lay on the ground, splayed open. Gaspard bent to pick it up and was about to hand it over to me when he stopped. The page the sketchbook had opened to captured his attention.

I looked to see which one it was and saw my rough version of the stairs and the tunnel leading to the stone room. I'd included some of the key information so I could refer to it without having to carry the large drawing in the rain.

"This drawing is different from the one you showed us all the other day, isn't it? It's more recent," he said.

"Yes. When I tried again yesterday, I found more markers. That's why I was out here." I pointed to my drawing. "There aren't any windows in the chamber, but there are in whatever is above it. And this is the view from that section. If I can find that, I'll know where the vault is situated."

"The vault?" His voice was strained. And a vein on his temple throbbed once.

"I don't see it as a dungeon anymore but as a vault protecting riches. You don't think it could be cursed, do you?"

"Do you believe in curses?" he asked.

"I'm not sure. I've read about all the disasters that have befallen the Carter team and other archaeologists in Egypt, haven't you? It certainly seems as if those tombs are cursed."

"Well, if there's even a chance this one is cursed, why keep searching?" he asked.

"Yesterday I would have said because it's a well-paying job and my brother and I need to make a living. And then there's Madame. I also have an obligation to her."

"Now?" His gaze was so intense I felt almost violated and wanted to turn away, but before I could, he apologized. "I'm prying. I'm sorry."

I waited for an explanation of why he was so curious. I sensed it was coming; when it didn't, I was a bit surprised.

He handed me the sketchbook.

"Well, thank you for rescuing me a second time," I said.

"I hope there won't be a third."

"So do I." I laughed.

"Let me walk you back, just to be sure."

Hugging the building, both of us sharing his large umbrella, we circumnavigated the château. As we came around a bend, I looked up and saw a lone figure, a man, standing in a window, seeming to look right down at me. Was it Sebastian? Mathieu? I didn't think it was either. I shivered.

"It is windy and wet. Let's hurry before you get even more chilled," Gaspard said.

But I didn't move. I couldn't take my eyes off the figure. His malevolence reached out to me through the glass, the rain, and the distance. Which one of the several men who'd come to the château for the séance was it? And why would any of them be so angry with me? He was too tall for Picasso. But it could have been any of the others.

Gaspard followed my gaze. "Do you know who that is?"

I shook my head. "No, he's too far in the shadows."

"Shadows again. They haunt us here." He opened a doorway that I hadn't noticed. "Come this way; it's a shortcut to the kitchen. We can get some coffee. You need to be warmed up."

I followed him. In a few minutes, we were sitting in the kitchen with big cups of café crème and a plate of the cook's freshly baked madeleines.

"What did you mean about the shadows? I call my paintings shadow portraits. Did I tell you that?"

He nodded and began to tell me about the different people who had lived in this land and the secrets they had left behind.

"Many believe that in these hills, the ghosts of the Knights Templar still guard their Grail from beyond the grave. For more than a hundred years, they performed valiant acts and were repaid with gifts: money, gold, silver, land.

"At their zenith, their wealth was second only to that of the papacy. With their riches, they became what some say were the first international bankers. Instead of travelers carrying their gold and silver with them and having it so easily stolen by highwaymen, the Templars accepted deposits and gave the travelers intricately coded notes. When the traveler reached his next destination, he could visit the local Templar house or castle, present the note, and withdraw what he needed. These codes were the secret to their system. Masters of encryption, they were said to have used them to safeguard other secrets.

"Some of the legends about them are fabrications, but there is one I can attest to. A man named Bernard Sermon I joined the Poor Knights of Christ in 1151. He was a benefactor of the order, which allowed him to take part in the Knights' spiritual life.

"In 1156, he learned of a group of marauders searching the countryside for treasure. Concerned for the Templars' considerable store of silver and gold, Bernard had a massive bell cast from the precious metals and hid it underground. As if the earth had opened and devoured it, the bell was never seen again.

"Every year on the night of October 13, pale shadows rise from the graveyard. All together, the ghosts of the Templars move slowly in a solemn procession to a castle not far from here. There they hold vigil while the invisible bell tolls, and they mourn their losses."

"Have you heard the bell? Have you seen the ghosts?"

He nodded. "Many of us have. We're a strange breed. Living in the Languedoc, we're more susceptible than most to the arcane and mystical. We have Cathar blood in our veins."

"My father is fascinated with their history. When I was younger, we used to take trips searching for their ruins."

"They're holy sites. You can feel it when you find them. Almost as if the earth that soaked up their blood hums."

"My father calls it the choir of the dead."

Gaspard shook his head in remorse. "And all they did was try to live peacefully. Innocent farmers who believed our souls were reborn each time with more knowledge and goodness. Doomed because they believed in two Gods, an evil one and a good one. It was just their way to explain everything malignant and terrible in the world. How, they asked, could a benevolent God allow for the sickness and strife, the war and misery that man was subjected to? Logical, wasn't it?"

"But dangerous. Isn't that what got them branded as heretics?"

"Exactly. In 1209, with the help of the nobility, the church organized an army to attack them. By 1244, more than thirty thousand men, women, and children were massacred in the name of the Catholic Church.

"The ghosts of those good souls and the promise of their hidden treasures cast great shadows over the land. You're sensing them. You're a shadow seer even without your blindfold."

I had finished my coffee but lifted my cup to my lips to see if I could eke out one last drop, and then I put down the cup. Always hesitant to discuss my gift, I just nodded.

"That day on the bridge, you saw my shadow, didn't you?" he asked.

"I saw someone else's shadow, not yours."

"And you saw him in danger?"

"Yes."

Gaspard leaned close to me. "Listen to your instincts."

"You mean stop looking for Madame Calvé's treasure?" I asked.

"Some mysteries are destroyed if solved. Some confidences, once buried, shouldn't be disturbed. If a secret is hidden, revealing it could prove dangerous. There are reasons we can't always know."

He was speaking in riddles that could have been applied to any one of a dozen things. My feelings for Mathieu. The secrets I exhumed for pay. My being here working for Madame.

"Tell that to Madame Calvé. She's determined," I said.

"She's always been determined. But she never succeeds. You might be the one to change that after all these years."

"And you don't think I should? You don't think the past should be disturbed?" And then I realized something and was certain of it. I blurted out my next question. "Are you protecting whatever it is?"

"With all the people Madame has brought here to try to divine the secrets, there have been so many talentless fakes. It's amazing how easy it is to believe when you are desperate. And she has been desperate. But with you, she finally stumbled on the real thing."

"I'm afraid I'm the one who's been stumbling. Both literally and figuratively. You are protecting the secret. Who are you?"

"If I asked you to stop trying to suss out the location of that cave you keep drawing, just enjoy the company in the château until the roads clear, and then let your brother drive you away, would you?"

"If you could give me a good reason, I might."

"The best reason. To protect you. To keep you safe. Stop looking, Delphine. Don't meddle in thousands of years of history."

"But what if I'm the one who is supposed to be meddling?"

Chapter 43

I slowly climbed the stairs, trying to decipher the puzzle Gaspard had left me with. I felt as though I were facing a blank canvas, with only a glimmer of an idea of what I wanted to paint.

When I opened the door to my studio, I found Sebastian looking through my sketches. "I was hoping I might assist in decoding your drawing," he explained.

"How? Even Madame doesn't recognize the markers. I went outside to try to find something but still have absolutely no idea of where it might be."

My brother held up one of the sketches. "Why is the background so dark in these drawings?"

"No one has turned on the lights? It's not electrified? There are no windows? It was built five or six centuries ago? I have no idea."

Sebastian looked at me. "Something's changed. What's wrong?"

"I'm not sure. I saw Gaspard just now when I was out walking, and he got me thinking. All along, we've assumed we're aiding in an innocent search for an ancient book, but we really don't know what the book contains. Only what Madame Calvé believes it contains."

Now it was my turn to read my brother's face. His light expression turned dark and concerned. "What do you mean?"

"Madame said the book contains Nicolas Flamel's secret to immortality."

He nodded.

"Which you and I and our sisters and mother and father know is at least partly possible. Our mother and great-grandmother may not be immortal, but there's no doubt their chemistry has been altered. Grand-mère is almost ninety, and everyone thinks she's sixty. And Maman? She's past fifty. Do you ever think about that when you look at her? She and I look like sisters. Papa, too. Once people become adults, no one in our family ages in real time."

"We all know about the spell she found in the ancient grimoire that belonged to the original La Lune. Maman can slow down time. It's amazing, but what does it have to do with Flamel's book?" Sebastian asked.

"Maman's spell only performs for her. None of us, not one of the La Lune family of daughters, can activate it. We can only activate our own spells."

"Your point?"

"The spell to slow aging has a limited value. Only Maman can use it. But what if the formula in the Nicolas Flamel book could be mobilized by anyone?"

Sebastian's eyes flashed with a reaction I couldn't read.

"What are you thinking?" I asked him.

"Nothing. Why?"

"When I was talking just now, about the Flamel formula, you looked—I don't know . . ."

He cocked his head and changed his voice, affecting a deep, accented baritone. "Did I turn into the creature from the hills?"

When we were children, Sebastian and I often had the same nightmares. A curiosity that both delighted and scared us at different times. To chase them away, our mother had us imagine a monster made of tree bark, worms, bats, ants, spiders, dead leaves, and mushrooms. Together we invented a story that he came from a cave we'd visited in the Fontainebleau forest and made up rules for when and how he traveled to us. Sometimes Sebastian would even pretend to be the creature, squinting his eyes into slits, disguising his voice. Almost scaring me but not quite.

There was a clap of thunder right over our heads and a flash of lightning. The lights flickered and went out.

"Don't worry," Sebastian said, his voice soothing me. He had, of course, anticipated and understood my reaction to the dark.

After a few moments, I heard the scrape of a match and smelled sulfur, and Sebastian's face emerged in candlelight.

"The storm must have blown out the electricity," he said, holding the silver candlestick out to me. I took it, and he lit the second one for himself.

Given my fear of the dark, I was grateful that Madame had candles at the ready. Thunderstorms were frequent in the summer in this part of the country and were no friends to modern conveniences.

"There's a candelabra here on the mantel," I said, as I walked toward it.

I struck a match and lit the first candle, and then, as I'd seen my great-grandmother do during the Jewish holidays, lit each of the other candles using that first one. I'd never performed the ritual, and as the flames illuminated the room, I wondered what the ceremony meant to her.

The wicks burned brightly, casting odd shadows on the wall. Sebastian's was long and thin and strangely ominous.

For the second time that afternoon, I looked at my brother with concern. What did I know about my twin? Was I really sure of his heart's desire? We had spent almost five years apart, and we acted as if nothing had changed. But it had. He was twenty-six years old now, far too handsome and wealthy to want for much, but he was heavily in debt and desperate to keep that from my parents. Since childhood, he'd always burned to be a success, but now that ambition seemed to be exaggerated and colored by frustration. And anger. I'd noticed it before but not really focused on it. Sebastian was as unhappy as I was, wasn't he? The gambling was just an outward manifestation of an internal crisis. I knew what had happened to me in the last five years to make me cynical and lovelorn. But what had happened to him?

I wasn't sure what to ask. Where to start. But it seemed imperative that I do something. A long time ago, he'd saved me from a turbulent sea. He'd come to New York to pull me out of that morass, too. Now it was my turn. My brother was going to drown unless I figured out how to help him.

Chapter 44

Sheets of water continued to fall from the heavens at a steady, frightening pace. We had a lunch of thinly pounded veal with a vegetable terrine and drank more rosé than usual. At the table, we all tried our best to entertain one another, but we were nervous and distracted. The rain was too heavy. The storm was continuing for too long. Other than Sebastian and me, no one had planned on staying over Sunday night, and everyone was restless to get home. Only Mathieu seemed unperturbed at being marooned. Did I dare think it was because of me? More likely, it was because he'd been spending his time in Madame's library sorting through her collection of arcane books about the dark arts. I'd overheard her ask him to make an inventory of what important works he thought she was missing so he could look for them when he returned to Paris.

Around two o'clock, I went up to my room to try, for what I hoped was the last time, to solve the puzzle that eluded me.

I had settled myself in the studio and spread the drawings out all around me when there was a knock on the door, and I called out, *"Entrée."*

It was Mathieu.

"Oh," I said, startled. "I wasn't expecting you."

"I don't imagine you were. I'm sorry for surprising you."

"No, I meant that I expected one of the servants. Madame always sends up a pot of tea when I come up here to work."

"Yes, she sent me up with libations. Right here." He went back out into the hall and returned holding a fully loaded tray. "I put the tray down to knock."

As he settled it on a low coffee table by the couch, I saw it held two glasses and a bottle of wine, deep red, the same color as my blindfold.

"Now, that's not tea."

"No, I switched it. I thought wine would be a better idea."

"Why is that?"

"I don't like tea. And if I remember, you also prefer wine to tea."

"Not when I'm working, which is what I was doing." I didn't like the idea of being alone with him in my suite.

"That's convenient. I'm actually here to talk to you about work." I must have let my surprise show on my face, because he said, "Really, I am. We do have work to discuss."

"What work could that be?"

"I mentioned that Emma's commissioned me to make a book of your drawings when you are done?"

I nodded.

"I'd like to see the size of the paper you are using so I can prepare the leathers."

It seemed a fairly harmless request, and I opened my arms to indicate the spread of paper around me. "Take your pick."

Mathieu picked up one of my drawings and then another. "This is a very detailed chamber."

"Yes, I saw it very clearly."

"Your style has evolved so much. Your lines are even surer than they were before, and this is just a sketch. I'd love to see your paintings."

I lowered my head and looked down at my hands to escape his eyes. My insides were roiling. Being alone with Mathieu wasn't a good idea. I needed to get up and run, out of the room, out of the house, away from Millau. Away from Mathieu. Away from what I wanted. What I'd always wanted. What I couldn't have. I couldn't be the artist my mother was. Or have the man I loved by my side. I couldn't find peace with my gift. I couldn't save people from the secrets that gave them so much pain. I couldn't stop being a victim of my own making.

Mathieu pulled the cork out of the wine and poured it. He handed me a crystal goblet. Taking it from him, I was careful not to let our hands touch. He held his glass up to make a toast. But he didn't say anything, only clinked his glass with mine, and then he drank. As did I. The wine tasted of blackberries and coffee. A sensual, dark flavor that surprised me with its intensity.

"That's delicious," I said. Discussing the wine seemed a safe enough topic.

"I chose it from Emma's extensive cellar. It's quite amazing."

"Have you ever been here before?"

"Not for a long time."

"What a coincidence that you are here now." I sipped the wine. "I wish you weren't."

He ignored my comment. "Delphine, I know that the little scene you set up in Paris was a fake. That you weren't having an affair with that man I supposedly caught you with in the restaurant."

I was stunned at the turn in the conversation. "I was seeing him. He was a fellow student. We fell in love. I was meeting him behind your back."

Mathieu laughed. "You're really a terrible liar. At first, I was so stunned and hurt. I believed you were cheating on me and that you'd betrayed me. But once you left Paris, something didn't seem right. It was one thing for you to be with another man, but why leave Paris? School? Your family? I did some sleuthing, and I found the gentleman, who was happy to answer my questions for a bit more money than you had paid him. He confessed."

"He did?"

"I wrote to you about it."

He was looking at me, waiting for a response.

"I didn't read your letters," I whispered.

"I wrote so many. I even tried to write you a poem."

"Did you? Have you started writing poetry again?"

"Only three lines, over and over. I can't move past them. And I don't even completely understand them."

"Will you tell me?"

"Being with me, you kept me alive. Leaving, you killed me. Let me die with you rather than live without you."

I understood the lines. Every word. "It's beautiful."

"No. It's awkward and unfinished. But I . . ." He shook his head. "I need to know. Why did you create such an elaborate ruse? If you wanted to end things with me, why didn't you just tell me to my face? And if you did want to end things, why are you still wearing my ring?"

What to tell him? I didn't know. I hadn't expected this confrontation.

Mathieu put his glass down, got up, and came to sit down beside me on the couch. He took my glass out of my hand, put it on the coffee table, and then leaned forward and kissed me.

I thought I had remembered what it felt like to be in Mathieu's arms. But I'd forgotten so much. How his kisses lit little fires wherever they touched. Those flames now licking my lips, my forehead, my neck, each of my fingertips, the space where my collarbones joined, behind my ear, where my shoulder met my neck. I lost any ability to think clearly. All I knew was that I was with Mathieu, was smelling Mathieu, was tasting wine on his lips and inhaling his scent, was slipping and sliding into a place of velvet smoothness and honey thickness, as long, languorous waves of sensation took me and rocked me and stroked me. One by one, he removed pieces of my clothing, as I removed his, so that more and more of our bodies could touch, and more and more of our naked skin could press together, and my consciousness warned me less and less that this was dangerous, because danger didn't matter anymore, only the delicious wantonness of being in his arms and having him in mine. Of feeling him all around me. Of taking him in. Of giving in. Of living out this dream that I had dreamed for the last six thousand days. This was my nighttime secret that I shared with no one. Mathieu reaching my innermost core. This was Mathieu, and as he touched me and I touched him, I remembered something else I'd forced myself to forget. He was more than the man I loved; he was the man for whom my body had been made, the man whose body had been made for mine. As if once there had been . . .

And then he began to whisper the story he'd told me the first time we'd been together like this.

"Once there was a single being, a complete whole, a man and a woman as one entity in paradise. As a punishment, they were cleaved apart. And for eternity forced to spend their lives trying to find their perfect puzzle other half. When you find your perfect puzzle other half, Delphine, it is blasphemy to walk way, to deny the pleasure that is due you. You can't leave me again. It will kill me if you do. And I don't want to die. I want to live. I want to live with you."

And with that, with that one passionate whisper in the dark, with the rain beating on the windows and the wine on our lips and our bodies wet with our lust pressed together and the sheets dank beneath us . . . with that one plea, Mathieu ruined everything. He made me focus on the danger. Made me remember fully and with clarity that I was his poison. He couldn't be with me. To do so was to invite his own demise. I could love him, but I could not be with him. To do so was to put the period at the end of his death sentence. I knew what had happened to the other men whom other daughters of La Lune had loved. It was too risky. My father had almost died for my mother. La Lune's own lover had been killed. There was always a slim chance that we could fight the curse. But a greater chance that we could not.

"Don't cry," Mathieu said, wiping away tears I had not realized I'd begun to shed. "We're finally together now."

I shook my head. I had to tell him that we weren't and couldn't ever be. But not right away. Surely I could steal just one afternoon. One more day to write about in my Book of Hours. One new set of memories to survive on for all the empty years ahead of me.

Chapter 45

At six that evening, everyone convened in the living room for cocktails, accompanied by puff pastry hors d'oeuvres filled with either salmon pâté or cheese. Anna and Jules retired to the card table for a game of chess. Eugène sat at the piano but didn't play. He turned his body from us and stared out the darkened window into the rain.

"This could turn out to be a surrealistic nightmare," Picasso mused, as he sipped his gin, "if this storm never ends and we are all trapped here forever."

"What a fabulous idea for a play," Cocteau said. "*The Endless Weekend*. Ten very different people trapped in a castle. Ten small acts. The séance. The mudslide. The flooding. The hidden treasure. Picasso, imagine the sets."

"I'll get paper and pencils." Madame shot up. "How exciting to create our very own drama out of our unfortunate circumstance."

The idea of a play occupied everyone for the next forty-five minutes. All but Eugène got involved in plotting out the action, which mimicked what had occurred so far in the château.

When it came time to recreate the séance, Eugène finally stood up and joined the party.

"I don't want you to include what Thérèse said."

For the first time, I noticed his eyes were bloodshot and the glass he held in his hand shook a bit.

"It's just a game, Eugène," Madame said.

He laughed sardonically. "With Cocteau and Jules writing? It's not a game. This thing will be performed on a stage six months from now, with Picasso turning the spirit of my fiancée into a hideous beast. I won't have it."

Picasso raised an eyebrow. "Don't hold back on how you feel about my paintings."

Eugène waved his hand. "You know exactly what I mean. Don't pretend you are insulted, Pablo. You've discussed this yourself. You're proud that you walked away from the kind of easy beauty that others still hold on to."

Madame, ever the hostess, quieted Eugène down. "We won't write about that part of the séance. We'll make up another spirit who belonged to one of the other guests." She looked around, her eyes alighting on me. "Delphine, do you have a spirit we can borrow?"

As I shook my head, Anna said, "Delphine's spirit hasn't moved on. She's haunted by one who is alive." Her voice was distant, her eyes unfocused. She looked as if she were in a trance again.

"How extraordinary," Madame said. "Cocteau, we have to use that moment exactly. Anna coming in on the middle of all this commotion." Then Madame turned to me. "Are you haunted, Delphine?"

"Not that I know of," I said, as lightly as I could.

"No, she's the one who does the haunting," Mathieu said softly. I wasn't sure anyone heard him but me.

It was one thing for all of them to come for a party and stay overnight but quite another not to have the choice about leaving. The entrapment was weighing on the group. While I should have been excited at the thought that Mathieu was trapped with me here, instead I was filled with a sense of dread. The more time we spent together, the more difficult it would be for me to let him go again.

Sebastian was only pretending to enjoy working on the play. He glanced over my way too many times and studied Mathieu's face with too much scrutiny. I was waiting for my twin to question me, still not sure how I would answer his queries about what this man he'd never before heard of meant to me. I think he was secretly glad for the company staying longer. He and I had been here alone with Madame for almost a week now, and the hours passed more pleasantly for him with a houseful of guests.

By dinnertime, most everyone except Anna and me had imbibed too many cocktails. The meal was a complicated affair. Eugène was even moodier than he'd been earlier. Cocteau and Picasso were more ribald. Madame's personality was exaggerated, her actions and speech a bit more theatrical. She seemed almost desperate for excitement.

The roast chicken was a bit overcooked and the potatoes a bit underdone, and I thought the wine was too dry. The air crackled with anxiety, although I couldn't quite locate its fountainhead.

At some point, Madame asked Eugène—who was still sullen— about his next project. He was headed back to Egypt, he said. Madame regaled us with stories of her own time there, about how she had visited the pyramids and slept inside one of the tombs for two evenings.

"Talk about Surrealism," she said, and nodded at Picasso. "Nothing about that experience comes close to anything in our reality. There were so many spirits residing in those stone walls we felt we were at a party."

"Surely they weren't all glad to see you," Cocteau quipped.

"Surprisingly, none of them tried to frighten us away."

Ever the gracious hostess, Madame asked Cocteau and then Picasso what they were up to next. And then she moved on to me. I was hesitant. I didn't know who at the table other than Mathieu and my brother knew exactly what I was doing there. They'd all acted as if I were just another guest.

"I'm still in the midst of my current commission," I said.

"Don't be so coy," Picasso teased. "A commission for whom?"

I looked across the table at Madame.

"For me. She does portraits that reveal the sitters' innermost secrets."

"Really?" Jules asked her. "You've decided to allow the world to see your secrets?"

"No, no. I brought Delphine here to help me find the château's secret so I could discover its hidden treasure."

"What a perfect sojourn for a treasure hunt. Storm and all," said Jules. He turned to me. "How exactly do you suss out someone's secret?"

I explained a bit, using the stock answer I'd worked out when my brother first began getting me commissions in Paris six years ago.

All but Anna and Eugène were fascinated and asked me quite a few questions. I was uncomfortable being the center of attention, especially when Picasso said, "I think I'd like to commission you to paint my portrait. I'd be curious what you might discover."

I felt blood flood my cheeks. Picasso was famous for not sitting for any of his friends the way most artists in his circle did.

"And I'd also like to do that," Jules said. "Maybe you could discover the enigma that disturbs me. A series of events in my childhood that I can't quite remember."

"Sounds like Sigmund Freud would be more likely to help you than Delphine," said Yves Villant.

The conversation was lively, but I wasn't enjoying it.

"I think I'd like to hire you, too. My secrets are not buried deep, but I think they'd make for an interesting portrait," Cocteau said.

"A scandalous portrait," Picasso added.

"My sister can be hired, of course," said Sebastian.

"I know! Why don't we have an auction, now, here?" Picasso suggested. "Delphine will paint the secret portrait of the highest bidder."

"No, no, that would be . . . I'd be very uncomfortable," I said.

"Please, Delphine, do agree. We're all so bored," Madame pleaded. "You'll make the money, of course, and I'll match it and donate the same amount to my orphanage in town."

"I couldn't," I demurred.

Madame implored, "Not even for the poor little girls?"

My brother was looking at me, exhilaration in his eyes. The more I did, the more famous I became, the better it was for his reputation. And now there was the added benefit of even more money.

"I'll start," Picasso said, without waiting for me to acquiesce. "Fifteen thousand francs."

I knew that at the time, Ambroise Vollard was getting close to one hundred thousand francs for one of Picasso's paintings. My mother's were selling for twenty-five thousand. At parties in New York, I got twenty-five dollars for the evening, which had seemed like a fortune, since my rent for the whole month at the studio was only sixty dollars.

One American dollar was worth twenty-five francs in 1925. Picasso's offer of fifteen thousand francs was six hundred dollars. A fortune. I was stunned by the amount.

"Sixteen thousand francs," said Jules.

"Seventeen thousand," offered Yves Villant.

"Eighteen thousand," said Mathieu.

I shuddered. It hadn't occurred to me that he might bid. What would I do if he won? I couldn't draw him again.

"Twenty thousand," said Picasso, with a devilish laugh.

"Twenty thousand two hundred," said Jules.

"Twenty one thousand," offered Picasso, jumping again, hoping, it seemed, to end it.

But, to my surprise, Mathieu bid five hundred francs more. There was a lull in the back-and-forth, and then Picasso stunned us all by bidding five thousand more.

I didn't think he wanted the portrait as much as he wanted to win.

I was just relieved that Mathieu hadn't continued bidding. The idea of putting the blindfold on again for him frightened me.

"Once we're done with our dinner, let's begin," Picasso said.

"Oh, good, a show!" Madame said, clapping. "Anna, let's add to the excitement. You're clairvoyant. Can you see what Delphine will see? Write it down, and we'll seal it in an envelope and take bets on whether you guessed correctly."

"I don't think any of Monsieur Picasso's secrets will be revealed," she said.

"And why is that, Anna?" Madame asked.

"I can't be certain of the reason, only the outcome."

"And what outcome do you see?" I asked.

She shook her head and continued staring at me. "I'm not quite sure. Only that there won't be a portrait of Picasso."

"She's right. There won't be. Because I'm outbidding him," Eugène said. "Thirty-five thousand francs!"

No one said a word. The room was utterly silent.

Finally, Madame broke the silence. "The orphans will be most appreciative, Eugène." Then, as an afterthought, she looked at Picasso. "Will you best him, Pablo?"

He shook his head. "As much as I'd love to see Delphine's portrait of me, I bow to Eugène's generosity."

I was frightened. The idea of painting Picasso's portrait had intrigued me and challenged me as an artist. Even titillated me a little as a woman. It was impossible not to be curious about his reputation. But there was nothing about Picasso that scared me. I hadn't sensed that his secrets would have disturbed me. But with Eugène, I wasn't as sure. The aura around him was turning brown-black. The shadows were as dense as the ones I'd glimpsed when Gaspard had been talking about thousands of Cathars who had been slaughtered for believing in a different version of heaven and hell.

As we finished our main course, my anxiety increased. I didn't want to do the portrait of Eugène but couldn't think of how to get out of it. On top of the money Madame was paying us, this windfall would help Sebastian.

Dessert was served—a delicious *tarte au citron*—but I only pushed it around on my plate. Mathieu noticed and with one glance told me he was worried for me. But what could I do? All that money would solve my brother's problem.

"I think you should do the drawing downstairs, here, where we all can watch," Madame said.

I looked over at Sebastian to save me.

"I'm not sure that's a good idea," he said. "Delphine doesn't do her best work in a large crowd."

"But you worked that way at the parties in New York," Madame countered.

"Since then, she's changed how she works," he answered solemnly. "She prefers to work alone."

"I think it would be best in the studio," I said.

Eugène stood up. "That's fine with me."

As we left the dining room after dessert, Sebastian caught up with me. "Are you all right?"

"No, I'm worried. The atmosphere in the house is darkening."

He put his arm around my shoulder. "It's too much pressure, isn't it?"

"It is, but what can we do now? You should have stopped it when it started."

We reached the staircase, where Eugène was on the steps watching us, waiting for us.

"Sebastian, why don't you come, too? It will be more comfortable for your sister if you are there."

Chapter 46

The drawing session commenced fifteen minutes after I'd left both men on the steps, requesting a bit of time to prepare my sketch pad and pencils.

"Eugène, why don't you have a seat here?" I motioned to a chair. "And Sebastian, over there." I pointed to another.

Eugène sat down and fidgeted for a moment while I explained what I'd be doing and asked if he had any questions. He said he didn't. He continued to be restless, which bothered me. His aura was darkening to an even deeper muddy hue, and I didn't spend as long as usual learning his face. I wanted to get the session over with as quickly as I could.

I put on my blindfold and immediately began to draw. As usual, not knowing what I was sketching, unclear of the images that emerged from the shadows in the darkness of the silk.

From across the room, I could still sense Eugène's discomfort. "Are you all right?" I asked.

"Yes, fine."

After a few more minutes, I felt Sebastian shift in his chair behind me. It was subtle, but the air around him moved. His cologne wafted toward me. It was unusual for him to become disturbed during a session. Trying to ignore his tension, I kept at my work, starting a second drawing and then a third.

After ten minutes more, I laid down my pencil, took off my blindfold, and studied my work.

"These images are all so familiar," I mused out loud.

I'd drawn similar sketches once. I was sure of it. But when? And then I remembered. These were almost identical to the drawings I'd done of Thérèse Bruis almost five years ago.

Before I could stop him, Eugène was up off his chair, and looking at what I'd drawn.

"So it is you!"

"What do you mean?"

"I've been looking for you for years."

"What are you talking about?" I was becoming more and more frightened.

"I'd heard about you but never knew your name," Eugène said with disgust. He turned to Sebastian. "And you, have you always been your sister's manager?"

"I have."

"Always?"

"Yes, since she was in L'École. Why?"

"And normally"—he turned to me—"next you would paint this? Do a full oil painting?"

"Yes, usually I do."

"I don't want that. I'll pay you, of course. But I don't want a painting of this."

Sebastian was standing behind me, looking at the drawings.

The first was of two women in a sickroom. One in a bed, the other standing, adjusting her pillow. It was harmless. Kind, even. In the second drawing, the woman who had been adjusting the pillow was holding it aloft. And in the third drawing, she was smothering the woman in the bed with it.

I looked at Sebastian. "What is going on?"

Sebastian didn't answer, but Eugène did. "Yes, you drew these before. You drew the last moments of a desperately ill woman's life, as she secretly begged her nurse to help her die so she wouldn't have to endure any more pain. The last moments of my wife's life, with her nurse, Thérèse Bruis. But you drew it as a murder, not a mercy killing. And your brother blackmailed Thérèse with what you painted. He told her he was going to hang the painting in his gallery unless she bought it from him. Thérèse sold everything she had, but it wasn't enough. And so he did it. He hung the painting. One of our friends saw it and told Thérèse. She went to see it, realized how recognizable she was, and begged your brother to take the painting down. But he refused. And then she wrote you and begged you, too. But you just ignored her. I would have given you the money. I would have bought the damn painting. I would have done anything to save her. But she didn't think she could explain it to me. Thérèse thought I'd always see her with blood on her hands. That I wouldn't understand that my wife had wanted her nurse to help her die. That I wouldn't believe that Thérèse hadn't set out to fall in love with me. That I would never accept that our love was not tainted. And because neither of you would help her keep her secret, she wrote me a letter, posted it, and then overdosed on laudanum. Thérèse took her own life because of what you drew and then committed to canvas."

I looked at Sebastian, shocked. "You blackmailed her?"

He didn't answer. Out of the corner of my eye, I saw a flash. Eugène had pulled out a knife. The blade shone in the candlelight.

"Watch out, Sebastian!" I screamed.

Sebastian rushed him. Pushed him. Eugène fought back. The two men overturned a chair. Crashed into a table. Porcelain figurines fell and shattered on the floor.

The studio door was flung open. Madame rushed into the room, followed by Mathieu, who grabbed me, pulled me back toward the doorway, and told Madame to hold on to me.

Their entrance had distracted Sebastian. Eugène had taken advantage of that to grab my brother in a choke hold. The knife was up against his neck, the point almost piercing the skin.

"Eugène, this isn't a good idea," Mathieu said calmly, as if he were talking about choosing a cigar. "Whatever Sebastian said or did . . . there are other ways to work out your differences." He took another step closer to the two men. "Whatever is wrong, you can't resolve it like this. Not like this."

By taking slow, small steps, Mathieu had finally reached Eugène's side. Suddenly, in one quick move that stunned us all, Mathieu pushed Sebastian out of the way and grabbed Eugène's arm—the one holding the knife—and pulled it backward.

The push had been too rough. My brother fell backward against the fireplace, and there was a *crack* as his head hit the marble mantel.

I screamed.

Mathieu let go of Eugène to kneel down and see if my brother was all right.

Eugène lunged. He was blind with the fury of the fight, with the desire to get his revenge. I didn't even know if he realized that Sebastian was the one lying on the floor and that the man he was about to stab was Mathieu.

I could see that the blade was headed for the middle of Mathieu's back. Eugène was going to drive the knife into the flesh between his shoulders.

I tried to break free, but Madame held me back. I pushed her away and ran forward, throwing myself on Eugène, trying but failing to stop him from stabbing Mathieu.

Suddenly, there was blood everywhere. Eugène stumbled, as if stunned that he'd actually used his weapon. I knelt down beside Mathieu. I hadn't stopped Eugène, but the impact of my jumping on him had ruined his aim. The knife had gone into Mathieu's arm. The same arm that had been so damaged in the war.

There was so much blood. Had the knife severed a vein? The wound had to be stanched quickly. But first, I had to pull out the knife. I grabbed it and yanked, but it wouldn't budge. I tried again, gritting my teeth, gripping the handle, I tugged as hard as I could. It gave. For a moment, I just stood there holding the knife, blood dripping on my legs, my stockings, my shoes. Seeing the scene in my mind. Recognizing it from a drawing I had done so long ago.

Then I sprang into action. "We have to stop the blood!" I heard myself scream.

Madame grabbed a linen cloth off a table and wrapped it around Mathieu's arm, pressing it as tightly as she could around his wound.

His eyes were closed. He wasn't moving.

All the guests had come running. I saw Picasso and Anna and some of the household staff crowding in the doorway.

As I watched Madame doing what she had learned how to do in the orphanage, all I could think about was the image I had drawn years before of me standing above a felled Mathieu. Knife in my hand. The exact same scenario, down to the blood spatter pattern on the floor.

"I was wrong," I whispered to Mathieu's inert body. "I didn't hurt you. I didn't hurt you. It wasn't me."

Chapter 47

Madame and I sat beside Mathieu's bed all that night. Watching over him and waiting for him to regain consciousness. Hoping he would. Praying to some God I'd never engaged with before. Desperate to see a sign that the worst was over. That infection wouldn't set in. That Madame had done all the right things. That Mathieu would recover.

I didn't know where my brother was. For the time being, I didn't care. Madame told me he hadn't been hurt badly at all. Not even suffering a headache. Meanwhile, Picasso and Cocteau and the others had locked Eugène in one of the bedrooms, and the butler was standing guard. The atmosphere in the house had taken on a metallic gray sheen and a sour smell.

"This, too, shall pass," Madame said, trying to reassure me. "All will be well again, you'll see. Order will be restored."

Tears came to my eyes. I tried to speak but failed. I wanted to believe her, but could I? She put her hand on mine.

"All will be well again, you will see. I promise."

After a moment, I found my voice. "I'm sorry. I've failed in finding your treasure. And I'm sorry my brother and I brought this tragedy to your house."

Madame shrugged. "Where there is tragedy, joy will follow. And where there is joy, tragedy will follow. There's always passion and pain and death and birth. That's what opera has taught me more than anything. One can't control the fates or change destiny, nor can one escape tragedy or court comedy. All you can do, Delphine, is sing."

She took my hand. Between us, Mathieu slept on.

"And your painting is my singing. Do you understand? The book . . ." She shrugged her shoulders. "It's an old woman's folly. My diversion. I think I should take up love again instead. Jules has suggested we take a voyage to Egypt. He knows of a sage there who might have a copy of the same book."

"And there you are, back to the book," I said.

She laughed. It was infectious. I joined her. The sound was so strange after the long, sad hours we'd just endured.

"Delphine," she said, and nodded toward Mathieu.

I looked at him. His eyes were open, and he was staring right at me.

"Mathieu?" I whispered.

He gave me one of his half smiles, mouthed something I couldn't understand, and then closed his eyes again. In seconds, he was asleep once more. Madame touched his forehead with her hand.

"No fever. All will be well again, you see? As I promised."

My relief was almost overwhelming. I felt tears fill my eyes.

Madame got up, stretched, and went to the window. "And the rain has stopped," she said, and twisted open the handle, letting in the fresh, damp air. "At last."

Even though the wound appeared stanched, there was no fever, and Mathieu had regained consciousness, Madame and I took turns sleeping for a couple of hours and then sitting by Mathieu's side. The rest of the night was uneventful. Dawn broke, and we kept up our vigil until Mathieu awoke at seven in the morning. Madame called down for strong coffee and helped Mathieu sit up so she could check his wound.

"A very clean cut. And not showing any signs of infection. I put a salve on it," she told him. "But when you get back to Paris, you might want a physician to make sure it's all right."

Mathieu nodded, thanked her, and then looked at me. "Last night is a bit foggy. I remember Eugène attacking Sebastian. Then the rest of it is a blur. Except for you. You got in his way, didn't you? You took a chance and tried to stop him."

"She certainly did," Madame said. "And thank God she did. That knife was aimed right at your spine. I can't even imagine what—" She shook her head and closed her eyes for a moment.

Mathieu was staring at me. "And there's a particular thing that keeps going around in my head. It doesn't make any sense. 'I didn't hurt you. I didn't hurt you. It wasn't me.' Did you say that?"

"I did."

"Why?"

There was so much to explain. And he was still groggy from the draft Madame had given him to help with his pain.

"Years ago, I saw us in a drawing I did before I left Paris. I thought from what I saw that I was going to kill you. It was this very scene . . . but I misunderstood what I'd drawn."

He reached out and took my hand, wincing as he did. "You saved me, *mon chat*. You've been trying to save me all along, haven't you?"

Tears filled my eyes.

I'd fallen victim to my own ability. Maman had warned me so often over the years to treat my ability with respect but never to worship at its altar. I was only human, with a soupçon of extra ability, she'd said. A human capable of making serious mistakes.

"And you'll go on doing it, won't you?" he asked, as his fingers worried the ring on my right hand, feeling its crescent.

My tears spilled over. I couldn't say anything, but I could nod. And I did. Vigorously.

By later that afternoon, the roads were passable. The police had been called to deal with Eugène. Jules was staying on. Picasso, Cocteau, and Anna were leaving.

After we all said our good-byes, Madame told us she was going to see to dinner and insisted that I go for a walk. She said I needed to stretch after the night spent sitting vigil. She was right. It would also give me a chance to try to find my way back to Gaspard's cottage and say good-bye to him.

I left the château and had just set off when I heard my brother call out.

"Delphine, wait!"

I turned around to see him running toward me.

"We need to talk," Sebastian said, reaching out, taking my hand, trying to hold me there.

I pulled free. Looking into his eyes, I realized how fully my unconditional love for him had kept me from seeing his true colors. Had my brother done what Eugène accused him of? Was Sebastian really that cold? That manipulative?

Sebastian was my beloved twin. He had been my savior. But if what Eugène had said was true, Sebastian had betrayed me in the most egregious way. And I had let him.

"Why did you lie to me, Sebastian? To me? I showed you the letter from Thérèse Bruis, and I told you I was so devastated that I was leaving Paris, and you promised to take care of it. I believed you would do the right thing—"

The air around him was colored the pale, icy blue of panic. Sebastian began to protest, but I didn't want to hear any of his sly excuses. I had to finish, or I'd never say it all, and it had to be said. My twin had to be confronted with his transgressions. And acknowledge them. To me and then our parents. It was the only possible path to his real salvation.

"I never dreamed you were scheming behind my back. The irony is that the letter wasn't even the real reason I left. I used that as my excuse because I couldn't tell you the truth. It was Mathieu. I was in love with him. Wonderfully, desperately in love. But then I drew his portrait. What I saw made me think I would be responsible for his death if I stayed with him. That's why I left Paris. To protect Mathieu."

"But Delphine, I can explain why—"

I walked away from him, not willing to hear his rationalization in that moment. There were things to say and straighten out. He'd abused my talent. Bled at least one poor woman dry trying to extort money from her and in effect been responsible for her death. What else had he done?

I kept going. The ground was soggy beneath my boots. I was glad I'd put them on. It would take days for the earth to dry out.

I made it through the gate and into the forest. The rain had swollen the stream and turned it into a rushing river. The sound of the waterfall, which had been lovely and lilting the first time I'd passed by almost a week ago, was now a rampage.

What else had Sebastian done? Why had I been so blind to his faults?

I stopped for a moment. Water rushing from above churned into the rocky pool. A second waterfall flooded a lower pool. Peering over its side, I looked down into the ravine. All I could see was more water surging toward the lower ridge. Mist filled my view. I smelled the crisp, wet air and the forest's muddy soil. The landscape was overripe compared with how it had looked only days before.

Staying to the path, I moved on. I'd only gone a few feet when I thought I heard my name being called. I paused. The cascading water was so loud I couldn't be sure. But then I heard it again. It was definitely my name being called, in a panicked voice. My brother's voice. Not sure, not certain, not apologetic or worried—but desperate. The voice of someone in terrible trouble.

I doubled back to the waterfall and saw a figure bobbing in the water. I ran closer. Sebastian was fighting the pull of the current, trying to keep from being dragged over the side.

I raced toward the rocky pool. My brother was only feet away from the edge of the rapids, the rushing water ready to carry him away. Gripping what looked like a tree root, his knuckles were white with the effort of holding on. Even as I watched, he weakened.

"It's pulling me . . ."

I hadn't gone into the water since I was eight years old, when the rope tethering me to Sebastian had ripped. I couldn't go in now. I was petrified by the surging water. The only thing that terrified me more was what was going to happen to Sebastian if I didn't do something quickly.

I crawled out onto the rocks, traveling the length of escarpment as quickly as I could, always aware of the churning water on either side of me. The cruel current waiting to claim another victim. I got as close to Sebastian as possible. I stretched out my fingers, trying to grab the root he was clinging to. I got it! Now, if my brother could just hold on . . . and if I could just pull the root toward me . . . I tugged at it, yanking as hard as I could. But my strength was no match for my brother's weight and the pull of the falls.

Inching out onto the rocky promontory, I moved closer to the water, closer to my twin.

"You're going to have to let go of the root with one hand, Sebastian, and reach for me."

I held out my arms.

Sebastian let go with his left hand and pushed against the vortex. But without both hands, he was no match for the water's force. Our fingertips touched for a moment before the rapids grabbed him away from me and carried him toward the second falls.

I was completely helpless, watching in horror—and then, before he reached the very edge, some object or another root or rocks stopped his progress. A reprieve. But for how long? I scurried over more rocks, slipping on the moss, trying to stay balanced. I had to get to him. And then his head went down. I lost sight of him. Held my breath. Sebastian couldn't drown. I couldn't let him drown!

His head popped up again. He was coughing. Sputtering. He was no match for the water. He needed my help. I had no time to weigh my options. I searched the foliage behind me and found a ropy vine. Tested it. I had no idea if it was strong enough, but what choice did I have? Holding on to it with one hand, I lowered myself into the water. Immediately, the current swirled around me, but the vine held. I was close enough to grab my brother. My fingers found his shoulder. I struggled but managed to twist him around, get his head out of the water. With a giant effort, I pulled him toward me. I had him. Held him. He sputtered, spit out water. His eyes, staring into mine, were terrified.

"I've got you. I've got you." The same words he'd said over and over to me, many years before.

Hand in hand, we pushed against the water. Working to get back to the rocks. And we were getting there. We were going to be all right. Then the vine broke. Both of us were at the mercy of the churning current.

My head went under. In the shadowy water, I saw my brother's hand in mine. Just like so long ago. And then I saw a ghostly image from that day, the end of the piece of rope. Not frayed. The rope tethering me to Sebastian hadn't torn apart. It had been sliced. Cut clean through.

I broke water. Sputtering. Spitting. Gasping for breath. Moments later, Sebastian did, too.

"You cut the rope!" I said, gasping, despite the danger around us. "When we were children. When you took me swimming."

Sebastian looked at me without understanding, as he continued fighting the current. We were holding our own, but neither of us was making any progress against the falls.

"What?"

"Tell me, or I'll let go. Did you cut the rope?"

His expression was incredulous. We were fighting to stay connected. To reach safety.

"Tell me!"

"Yes."

"Why?"

"To make sure you knew how much . . . how much you needed me."

My feet found bottom. With a giant surge, I pushed ahead. Sebastian followed and then, gaining on me, reached the rock, and now he pulled me toward him. I was almost there. We were both going to be safe. Then I slipped backward. My hand jerked out of his. And I lost hold. Lost hold of all that was keeping me safe.

The water took me then, quickly, pushing me toward the edge of the falls, and I stopped thinking as I fell into the unknown abyss below.

Chapter 48

Water everywhere. Trying to get my head above the water. Taking in gulps of water. Then gulps of air.

Panic, a voice intoned, *will doom you.*

Gaspard's voice? I listened. Yes, under the sound of the rushing falls, I was hearing his voice.

Let the water take you. Give yourself over to the current. Stop fighting. It's all right. It's all right.

I forced myself to relax, felt the water around me, rocking me. The pull had abated. I opened my eyes. I was tucked under and behind the falls in a calm pool. In front of me, the rushing water came down in a steady sheet and crashed into a green-blue pool. I could hear the roar of the cascade, but I was safe.

I was treading water, catching my breath, stunned that I had survived when my foot touched what felt like a rock flat enough for me to stand on. The water wasn't as deep as I'd thought. I stood up, and my shoulders were out of the water.

I turned around and took a step and then another. There was a narrow tunnel in front of me. Rough stone walls on either side. And at the far end, I saw a light. The rocky floor was rough, and I'd lost my shoes in the tumult, so I swam into the grotto.

The scent of minerals and pine reached my nostrils. And something sweet. The closer I swam to the light, the stronger the fragrance became.

Then the tunnel opened up into a cavern. The light was a fire on the shore. There were even rocky steps leading up and out of the water. I climbed them, sniffing, recognizing the smell as frankincense.

Gaspard stepped out of the shadows and held out a large towel, which he wrapped around me.

"You saved me again," I said. "But how did you know?"

He smiled. "That's my ability," he said, acknowledging for the first time that he was, in fact, one of us.

"What's happened to my brother?"

"I don't know. Once we've dried you off, we'll find out." He offered me a silver flask. "In the meantime, drink some of this. It will warm you up."

I took it and put it up to my lips. The brandy burned my throat but did begin to warm me almost immediately. As I tipped my head back to take a second sip, I noticed the cavern's ceiling. Then looked at its walls. I recognized this place. I knew the carvings that covered every surface. The cavern was far bigger than I'd understood when I'd drawn it. I turned around. Beyond the fire were shelves of alembics, jars, and strange-looking utensils.

I handed him back the flask. "This is the library where the book is located, isn't it?" I asked.

He shook his head. "No." He raised his arms like a winged bird about to take flight. "No. All of this *is* the book."

I walked over to one of the walls and ran my fingers over the carved notations and symbols. Section after section of them. Each numbered with roman numerals. I counted sixteen.

"And we aren't in the castle," I said, as another piece of the puzzle fit into place. "We're not even on the castle grounds, are we?"

"No. We're sitting right under my cottage. I'm the caretaker of the *Book of Abraham*, as my father was before me and his father before him, going all the way back to Nicolas Flamel."

I sat down on a stone bench and felt its smooth surface beneath my fingertips. "You mean Nicolas Flamel was here?"

"After he staged his death, yes. This is where he and his wife came. He wanted to find a safe place to live out his days, work on his formulas, and complete his studies."

"How long did he live?"

Gaspard laughed. "Not as long as they say but to a hundred and twenty-eight."

"His wife, too?"

"A few years longer. And his son and his son after him. We all have long lives. Not immortal, but the Great Work adds years to our life span."

"Your last name, Le'Malf . . . his name backward. How could I not have realized? And Nicky?"

"Yes, named after my ancestor. Like yours, my heritage is full of secrets and surprises."

He sat down next to me and offered me the flask again. I swallowed a long draft, then gave it back to him. He took my hand. It felt natural for him to hold it.

"All around us, this is the secret," I said. "It's astonishing. He did all this work?"

"Yes. He engraved every one of these alchemical secrets. The formula for the Great Work surrounds you. You're looking at the key to opening portals to other realms and claiming wisdom."

"Hidden so the power could never be abused," I said.

"Exactly."

I was still absorbing the information. "And the prophecy about it being found by someone who sees shadows . . . that's me?"

"Yes, you're one of the very few people enlightened enough to be able to grasp what's written here and learn from it."

"Are there many others?"

"A few. Enough." He smiled wistfully.

"Your wife?"

He nodded.

"Not Madame Calvé?"

"Sadly, no." He laughed. "Even though she wants it so very badly."

"You said you've been studying it. Can't you just read it?"

"No. It's a lifelong effort. The lessons can't just be read, they have to be experienced. Each generation must live them. It would be too easy to just be given the secrets. You understand that, don't you? You've seen the danger of just giving people information?"

I nodded. I hadn't known before now, though. All these years, I hadn't realized the real danger of what I did when I sketched those secrets.

"You've always been scared of the dark, haven't you?" Gaspard asked.

I nodded. Of course I was. I had been my whole life.

"Why?"

I started to give him an answer about my blindness, and then I realized that he was asking me a much more complicated question. Gaspard was asking me why I was scared of my own secrets. Why I wouldn't look at them. Why I ran from them.

I was beginning to understand. I hadn't run away from Paris only because of Mathieu and my fear of hurting him. I'd run away because I was scared of Mathieu hurting me. I hadn't understood love at all. I'd thought it was some kind of magick. And I was scared that my magick wasn't as powerful as my mother's. I was scared of being in her shadow. Of never measuring up. I was scared of the curse and that I would fail and be one of the doomed daughters of La Lune. But I'd been wrong about it all. My only failing was living in fear.

"Delphine, I'd like you to stay here. Study the book with me." He paused. "I know about your family curse. I know you don't think you can love anyone else. But I believe the curse can be broken. At least, we could try. Imagine all this knowledge . . . at your fingertips."

I gazed around me. Took in the wonder of the chamber. Candle-light flickered on the deeply etched walls, cast shadows, hid some of the secrets and illuminated others. My drawings hadn't done it justice. The cavern vibrated with energy and magick, and Gaspard was offering it all to me.

"It's tempting." I looked into his honeyed eyes, trying to feel just one spark. "Not just to learn all this but to be with you and Nicky . . . but my destiny isn't to be the daughter who breaks the curse. Mine is to learn not to be afraid of it."

"As sorry as I am that you won't entertain my offer, I'm very happy for you that you know that now, finally."

I smiled at him. "I do. Finally. Because of you. I'll never forget that."

Chapter 49

Gaspard took me back to the forest. To the path just beyond the waterfall.

"I'll leave you here," he said. "You know the way back, don't you?"

I nodded.

"Then we'll say good-bye."

My eyes filled with tears. "You've saved me three times," I said. "I'm not sure how to thank you."

"You don't need to." He reached up and brushed my hair out of my eyes. Then he kissed me chastely on the forehead.

"Take care of Nicky," I said. "Tell him to remember to color outside the lines."

Gaspard nodded. He started to walk away. Then stopped. "There's actually something I would like as a thank-you."

"Anything."

"A painting from you. When you get home."

"Of course. A painting of butterflies, will that be all right?"

"Better than all right. Perfect." He held up his hand in parting.

I mimicked the gesture.

He turned away.

For a moment, I wanted to run after him. To stay with him and Nicky. It would be so much easier than facing what was ahead of me.

Facing what my brother had done. Moving forward with Mathieu without fear. Taking on the risks that being with Mathieu would bring. He still had a crack in his soul through which darkness entered. He might never mend. He might never find peace or poetry again. But he was my fate, wasn't he?

I was suffused by a sense of warmth as a breeze blew golden rays of the sun over me.

I watched Gaspard continue to walk away into the forest, the gray-green shadows enveloping him. The air around him misted. And suddenly, on his right, I saw Nicky, holding his father's hand. And on his left a winsome woman with blond hair. She linked her arm in his as she leaned into him just enough so the lengths of their bodies touched.

When I saw the past, the air around me always chilled. This air was warm. Like the day I'd seen what I thought was my trespass against Mathieu. I knew I wasn't seeing Gaspard's past. His wife had been dark-haired. I'd seen her photo in Nicky's butterfly book. This was his future. The secret he was walking toward. The woman who was waiting for him right around the bend. I was about to call out. I wanted to tell him, but I heard my own name.

"Delphine!"

I turned in the other direction. Mathieu was half walking, half running toward me. Reaching me, he stopped. There was a leaf caught in his hair. A smudge of dirt on his cheek.

"What are you doing here? You're supposed to be recuperating," I said.

"Sebastian . . ." Mathieu was out of breath.

"Easy," I said. "Come, sit here."

I led him to a flat rock, where we sat. The sun, peeking through the trees, had started to warm the stone. The heat was welcoming.

Mathieu took my hand. His touch was nothing like Gaspard's. Not soothing, not safe. Where Mathieu's flesh touched mine, sparks flew and burst.

"Sebastian came back to the castle, soaking wet, a bad gash on his forehead. He said he didn't know what happened to you. That you'd saved him but he couldn't find you. He was in a panic. Madame immediately organized a search party. We've been at it for at least an hour. Combing these woods. Didn't you hear any of us calling?"

I wasn't sure what to tell him. The library was a secret that was not mine to share. I thought of my time inside that stone fortress. Gaspard had asked me a question that I had never asked myself. One I'd need to answer if I was ever going to paint again . . . or ever going to love again.

A long time ago, I'd become afraid, and that fear had blinded me with a darkness more debilitating than what I'd endured as a child. But now I understood.

The real secret that Gaspard's ancestors learned, the secret of Flamel's Great Work, of alchemy, was that love itself is the light. It offers us immortality . . . It is the true portal to enlightenment.

"Delphine, where were you all this time?" Mathieu asked.

"I was lost."

"Well, you aren't anymore," he said, as he buried his face in my hand. I felt a drop of water wet my palm. Then he looked up at me, and I saw more tears. "You're not lost now," he whispered. "Not anymore. I've found you."

Author's Note

As with the most of my work there is a lot of fact mixed in with this fictional tale.

The postwar atmosphere in New York City, Paris, and Cannes are as close to the truth as possible. As is the art world I depicted in these pages. All of the artists whose names you recognize and who interact with my fictional heroine did exist and were in fact interested in the occult or mystical world. When possible—and it was often possible—I used some of their own words and thoughts as well as true anecdotes about their lives.

You can still visit many of the sights I wrote about in both New York, Mougins, and Cannes, including having a drink on the Carlton terrace. In Millau you can drive by the château, which was indeed owned by the very real, very famous opera singer, Emma Calvé. Madame did buy and restore the small castle because of the reports that Nicolas Flamel's treasure, *The Book of Abraham the Jew*, rumored to hold the secrets to immortality and transmutation, was hidden there. The interior of the castle and the library are fiction since the building is now privately owned and, alas, I didn't get to see it or walk its grounds.

All the stories about Flamel included in this novel are part of his legend. La Diva never did find the book but she kept the château until she died.

Acknowledgments

To Sarah Branham and Rakesh Satyal, amazing editors both, who I was so lucky to have work on this book.

To my wonderful publisher and friend Judith Curr and the amazing Carolyn Reidy, CEO of Simon & Schuster—you both make me proud to be an Atria author.

To Lisa Sciambra, Hilary Tisman, Suzanne Donahue, Loan Le, Tory Lowy, and everyone who works behind the scenes at Atria Books—your hard work and creative thinking is greatly appreciated.

To Alan Dingman for covers that get better with each book and are all I could ever ask for and more.

To Dan Conaway, who makes such a difference in my life as a friend and agent and always has my back.

To Taylor Templeton for her hard work and kindness and everyone at Writers House whose help is invaluable.

I also want to thank readers everywhere who make all the work worthwhile (please visit MJEmail.me for a signed bookplate). And to the booksellers and librarians without whom the world would be a sadder place.

And as always, I'm very grateful to my dear friends and family and most of all, to Doug.

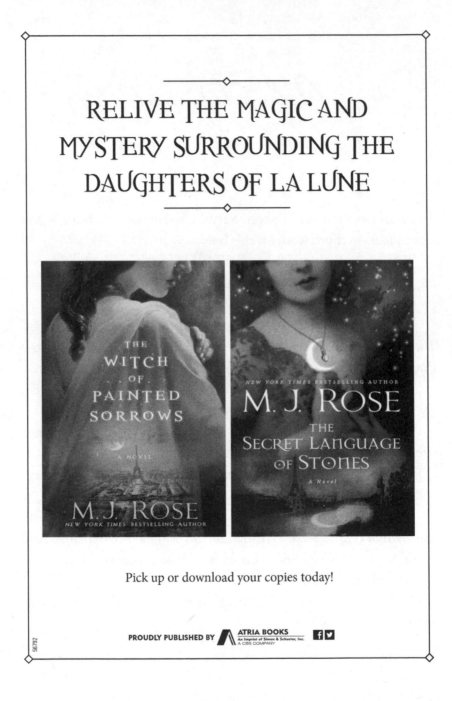